CELIA HARWOOD
lives in Buxton,
the town which has inspired this series.

THE BUXTON SPA MYSTERY SERIES

Widow's Peak
Autumn's Peak

WATERS SPEAK

THE THIRD BUXTON SPA MYSTERY

CELIA HARWOOD

NEUF NEZNOIRS LIMITED

Published by Neuf Neznoirs Limited
Unit 20, 91-93 Liverpool Road, Castlefield, Manchester, M3 4JN.
e-mail: gemggirg@gmail.com

ISBN 978-0-9933261-2-7

British Library Cataloguing in Publication Data.
A catalogue record for this book is available from the British Library.

Printed and bound in England by 4edge Ltd. Hockley, Essex
Tel: 01702 200243

For
Alan Doig
Gentleman and golfer

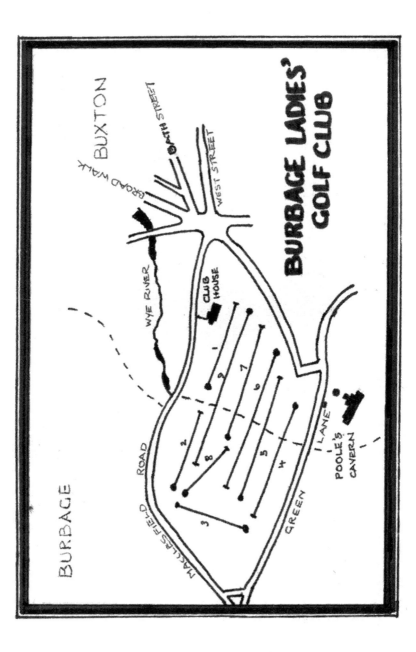

CHAPTER ONE

Gentle sunshine, a breeze so slight it was barely able to stir the leaves of the lime trees, dew still on the grass, and clear air giving definition to the greens. It was May, 1922 in Buxton Spa and a perfect morning for golf. Miss Millicent Lee, captain of the Burbage Ladies' Golf Club, teed-off confidently and, satisfied with the trajectory of the ball, handed her club back to her caddie and moved aside to accommodate her partner, Miss Maureen Fuller, the Club's Honorary Secretary. Then the second pair, Miss Dorothy Shipton and Mrs Hilda Tristram, teed off in turn. All four were keen and accomplished golfers and this was a practice round in readiness for the forthcoming competition against members of the Manchester Ladies' Golf Club.

It was still early in the morning and the ladies had the course to themselves. With nothing to distract them, they were playing well and by the fourth hole Millicent Lee was confident that her team would be in winning form. They had all successfully avoided the notorious greenside hollow on the fourth which was the downfall of many approach shots. Until now, Millicent had been totally focussed on play but, as she stood beside the green waiting for the other players to hole, she looked up towards Grin Low Wood, admiring the glorious weather. As she did so, she noticed off to her right a group of four men standing in Green Lane, which formed the southern boundary of the course. Then, she turned her attention back to the game.

The four players and their caddies walked the short distance to the fifth hole, known as The Valley, which was one hundred and sixty-five yards. Millicent took the wood from her caddie and addressed the ball. She was about to begin the back swing when she heard men's voices behind her, shouting and calling to each other, but she steeled herself not to be distracted. She hit the ball cleanly and watched as it followed straight along the target line towards the green. Only then did she turn and look behind her. The four men, whom she had seen standing in Green Lane, were now walking towards the entrance to the public footpath which crossed the golf course from Green Lane down to its northern boundary on Macclesfield Road. This footpath crossed the fairway of the fifth hole at right angles; however, the men continued walking, seemingly ignorant of the fact that they were proceeding directly into the path of the golf ball about to be driven down that fairway by Maureen Fuller. 'Oh, I say!' said Maureen indignantly, as she paused mid-swing. The men were now blocking her line of sight and she had to wait until they had passed. Her annoyance gave her power and, to her great satisfaction, when she did hit the ball it went much further than usual. The foursome ignored the intruders and played on. When the men reached the end of the footpath, they stood in a group on Macclesfield Road, as if waiting for something or someone. As the players progressed through the next three holes, they could see the group of men in the distance, moving about backwards and forwards between the road and the second tee.

When the players reached the ninth tee, they were close to Macclesfield Road and Millicent Lee noticed that a horse and waggon had now arrived there and was pulled up in the road. She drew the attention of the other players to it.

'Who are those people, do you know? I'm sure it's not anything to do with the Club or the groundsmen,' she said.

'There appears to be some sort of discussion going on, judging by all that arm waving and pointing in various directions,' observed Dorothy Shipman.

Millicent turned to her caddie: 'Percy, you always seem to know what's going on. Do you know who these people are?'

Percy shook his head. 'No, Miss Lee. They was 'ere yesterday as well. Never seen 'em afore that, though.'

Percy was twelve years old and the leader of the group of young boys employed as caddies at the Club. He was dressed in a brown woollen suit of jacket and knee breeches, in a size clearly chosen by his mother to allow for growth. The jacket hung loosely around his thin frame and each leg of the too-long knee breeches drooped over the knee band, hiding the tops of his thick socks. He wore a tweed cap set at a jaunty angle and sturdy boots which laced up to the ankles and were scuffed with wear. At first, he had been employed only at weekends and during the school holidays but, at the beginning of the previous summer, he had been old enough to leave school, narrowly missing the coming into force of the new legislation raising the school-leaving age to fourteen. He was now employed full-time, a fact for which his war-widow mother was grateful because his earnings helped supplement the meagre family budget. He was intelligent and full of energy and initiative. With three and a half years of experience behind him, he generally knew everything concerning the organisation of the golf course and its maintenance. Now, however, he was troubled by the fact that he did not know who these men were and he resolved to find out. He turned to the other caddies for help but they merely shook their heads.

'They seem to be unloading equipment of some kind from that waggon,' said Hilda Tristram.

'Yes,' agreed Dorothy, 'those two men are coming back up the footpath and carrying something onto the course.'

Millicent was finding this activity distracting and particularly annoying in view of the team's reason for being on the course. 'Let's get on and finish this last hole, shall we?' she said. 'Try to ignore them.'

That proved impossible because Millicent's first stroke took her level with the footpath and from there she could see that, in obedience to the directions of one of the men in the group, the other men were depositing equipment on the course. Handing her club to Percy, she walked over to the group of men and, on the assumption that the man giving directions was in charge, confronted him.

'Good morning,' said Millicent. 'I'm Miss Lee, captain of this Golf Club. Would you mind telling me what you are doing? I am not aware that any work has been authorised here.'

The man to whom these words were addressed turned towards Millicent, pushed back his cap with the heel of his hand, and said, gruffly: 'Well, missus, that's as maybe but I'm authorised to do what I'm doing and that's good enough for me.'

'Now, look here,' said Millicent. 'If any work had been authorised by the committee, I would know about it, so kindly answer my question. What are you doing?'

'Diggin',' said the man, sullenly.

'Digging what? Or is it, for what?'

The man pushed out his bottom lip but did not reply.

'You do realise that this is not public land. It belongs to the Golf Club.'

'That's not my concern. I just do as I'm told.'

'And who told you to do whatever it is you are doing?'

'If you want to know more you'll have to speak to Mr Steen.' The man shrugged and turned away.

'And where would I find this Mr Steen?' said Millicent, speaking to the man's back.

The man did not reply. He started to walk off.

'Well, you had better stop what you are doing until I can speak to this Mr Steen.'

'Sorry, missus,' said the man, half turning back towards Millicent. 'I 'as me orders and I've work to do.' He nodded decisively and turned away again, leaving Millicent glaring at the back of his head.

Millicent returned to where Maureen was standing. 'Have you heard of any digging work being authorised?' she asked.

Maureen shook her head. 'Not a thing. As Club secretary, I certainly would have been informed if anything had been authorised and likewise if the groundsmen had been asked to carry out any work. And you too would have been informed, Millicent. I am certain that nothing has been approved or even discussed, but I am pretty sure that one of those men is holding a dowsing rod.'

'What, searching for water?' asked Millicent, frowning. 'On the golf course?' She paused and then added: 'Steen. That's an unusual name. The captain of Manchester Ladies is called Audrey Steen. Do you suppose they are related?'

Maureen shrugged. Millicent was cross beyond words, cross that there were trespassers on the course, cross that the round had been disrupted, and cross that her concentration had gone.

'Let's get on and finish, shall we?' said Maureen.

Disheartened, they played the last shots carelessly, paid the caddies their fees, and went into the Club House for a cup of tea.

Meanwhile, on the High Street, during the hour before opening time, Mr Thomas Brunt, newsagent and stationer, was supervising the renovations to his shop. His business was doing very well and he had optimistic plans for the future, but the existing floor area was not large enough to accommodate them. Generations of the Brunt family had lived on this plot since the mid-seventeenth century. Originally, there was a croft, built at right angles to the street, which had been extended over the years and then, in 1790,

Mr Brunt's great-great-grandfather had built a three-storeyed lodging house in front of the old croft and parallel with the street. Here he offered accommodation to visitors who came to Buxton Spa during the Season to take the waters. The front part of the ground floor had always been a shop, leased to various tradesmen over the decades. The back section of the ground floor was the family parlour where five generations of Brunts had spent candle-lit evenings resting after their labours. In the 1870s, the bootmaker who occupied the shop at the front had retired and Mr Brunt's father, also called Thomas, had taken over the shop and commenced business selling newspapers and stationery. He had dispensed with the lodgers, installed the several members of his extended family on the floors upstairs, and appropriated the old family parlour at the back of the shop for his own use. Here he did his accounts or, when the shop was not busy, sat and read his newspaper and smoked his pipe. His son, the present Mr Thomas Brunt, had continued this habit when he inherited the property from his father.

Mr Thomas Brunt had noticed that there was an increasing market for books and magazines and that, on birthdays and special occasions, it was becoming fashionable to send manufactured greeting cards to friends and relatives instead of the usual hand-made ones or commercial postcards. His four children had now left home and there was more than enough space on the two upper floors to accommodate him and his wife, so he had taken the decision to expand his business and remodel the ground floor. He had decided that the existing shop would be devoted to a wider range of newspapers, magazines, and books and the old parlour at the rear of the shop would be turned into a showroom where he could display a tempting selection of this new style of greeting card. His ultimate ambition was to devote the front room on the first floor into a showroom for toys and fancy goods but that was a project for the future. Today, Mr Brunt was concerned with converting the old parlour.

Joseph Potts, Mr Brunt's brother-in-law and a joiner by trade, was standing in the parlour looking at a triangular shaped cupboard which, many decades ago, had been built into one corner at the back of the room. It was at shoulder height, made of timber now stained dark with age and smoke, and it had just two shelves closed off by a door.

'It's not much cop, Thomas. I reckon as how that's been there a goodish while,' said Joseph.

'Aye,' said Thomas. 'It's been there as long as I can remember. Grandfather used to keep the tinderbox there and a candlestick.'

'Shall I get rid of it for you?' asked Joseph.

'Aye, do. I want to put new shelves on that wall.'

'Any road,' said Joseph, examining the cupboard, 'I doubt it would have lasted much longer; it's already coming away from the wall on this side. It shouldn't damage the plaster too much if I take it down.'

Joseph unscrewed the hinges on the cupboard door, lifted the door off, and propped it against the wall. The cupboard had been screwed onto two battens on the wall and, while Joseph removed all the screws, Thomas took the weight of the cupboard. As they lifted the cupboard away from the wall something which had been wedged between it and the wall fell to the floor. The two men carried the cupboard out of the way and then Joseph picked up a long, oblong document made of very stiff paper. It had been folded in half and then into three like a map. Joseph unfolded in carefully. It was covered in copperplate handwriting with a great many flourishes and curlicues. At the bottom right-hand side was a seal.

'This looks like sommat to do with the law,' said Joseph. 'Aye, look here, it says "This Indenture" and look there "aforesaid" and porsussance or sommat. That's legal talk, that is.'

Thomas stood beside Joseph and looked at the document. He read the first line: 'This Indenture made the twenty-fifth day of March...'

'Lady Day,' interrupted Joseph.

'...in the year of our Lord one thousand seven hundred and eighty-five,' continued Thomas.

'Seventeen eighty-five. That's a powerful long time ago. I don't suppose this is of any use now.'

'Somebody must have put it behind the cupboard for a reason. Why would they do that?' said Thomas, puzzled. He took the document from Joseph and looked at it. 'It says something about an inquisition in the fifth Year of the Reign of His Majesty King George the Third...'

'King George didn't have no inquisition. That were in Spain 'undreds of years ago,' objected Joseph. 'I learnt that in school.'

'Well, that's what it says here. I can't understand much of it but here, look, it says "Between the Duchy of Lancaster, on the one part" and...' He peered at the document, frowning.

'Duchy of Lancaster. That's something to do with the King. He owns some of the land round about here,' interrupted Joseph.

'..."and Charles Brunt, farmer, of the second part." That's what it says. So, it must have something to do with our family.'

'Which Brunt would that be, do you suppose?' asked Joseph.

'I don't rightly know. There's been a few of us over the years,' said Thomas, laughing.

'Ah, well, if it mentions the Duchy of Lancaster then it must be something important,' said Joseph.

'But if it's important why not keep it somewhere safe, not just stuff it in behind a cupboard?' objected Thomas.

'We may as well chuck it out,' said Joseph. 'It's too old to be of any use.'

'No,' said Thomas, 'we'll ask great-uncle William first. He knows all the family history and his memory goes back a long way. He's sure to know what it's about.'

~O~

Messrs. Harriman & Talbot, solicitors, notaries, and commissioners for oaths, occupied premises on Hall Bank. At a quarter to ten that morning, Mr Harriman, the senior partner, was in his office on the ground floor chatting to his daughter, Eleanor, when the other partner, Mr Edwin Talbot, arrived.

'Morning, James,' Edwin called cheerfully to James Wildgoose, the confidential clerk, as he took off his hat and hung it on a peg in the hallway. Napoleon, Eleanor's Boxer dog, came out into the hall to greet Edwin. He looked with interest at the parcel Edwin was carrying. It was a large bunch of rhubarb wrapped in newspaper and tied with string. Edwin made a fuss of Napoleon and then went to the doorway of Mr Harriman's office.

'Good morning, both,' he said, as he held up the parcel. 'Rhubarb. Fresh picked by the gardener this morning. Helen thought you might like some.'

'Oh, yes, please,' said Eleanor. 'We do miss not having our own vegetable garden.'

'Thank you, Edwin,' said Mr Harriman. 'That's very thoughtful of Helen.'

'I'll give it to Mrs Clayton,' said Edwin, as he disappeared upstairs to his own office.

Edwin Talbot lived with his wife, Helen, and their two children at Wingfield, a large house on Spencer Road surrounded by its own garden. The Harrimans no longer had a garden, having moved from their large family home in The Park at the end of the War. Two of Mr Harriman's daughters had already married and left Buxton before the War. Then the Harriman's only son, Edgar, was killed in France in 1915. Shortly afterwards, Mrs Harriman died and then Wilfred, the husband of Mr Harriman's youngest daughter, Cecily, was killed in France, soon to be followed by Eleanor's fiancé, Alistair Danebridge. At the end of the War, the remaining members of the Harriman family had decided to leave The Park and its memories and make a fresh start. Cecily and her young son Richard had moved to Oxford House, a property on Broad Walk owned by Mr Harriman, where Cecily supported the two of them by offering accommodation to visitors during the season. Mr Harriman and Eleanor, in defiance of convention and to the consternation of their friends, had moved to the upper floors above the office at Hall Bank, where they were looked after by a housekeeper, Mrs Clayton. She, too, had been badly affected by the War. Her husband had been killed at Gallipoli in 1915, leaving her with two small boys to support. She and her boys lived with her brother, Alf, and his family. She came to Hall Bank during the day and went home to them each evening. The arrangement suited everyone and the atmosphere at Hall Bank was always friendly and supportive. Eleanor had replaced her brother, Edgar, who had been articled to Edwin Talbot. She had now finished her training and worked with Edwin and Mr Harriman as part of the firm. The two partners were very proud of her achievements and were hoping that she would be able to be admitted as a solicitor as soon as the rules changed and women were allowed to join the profession formally.

James Wildgoose had been Harriman & Talbot's confidential clerk since Eleanor was a little girl and still addressed her as Miss Eleanor. He came into Mr Harriman's office.

'Excuse me, Mr Harriman. Miss Millicent Lee telephoned for Miss Eleanor. Miss Lee explained that you had arranged to meet her and Miss Fuller tomorrow afternoon but she wonders if you would mind meeting them today instead. Miss Lee asked me to tell you that she and Miss Fuller will be at a meeting at the Palace Hotel until five thirty and will meet you there if that is convenient. What would you like me to tell her, Miss Eleanor?'

'Thank you, James. That will be perfectly all right. Please tell her that I shall be at the hotel at five thirty.'

'Very good, Miss Eleanor,' said James and he returned to his office.

Eleanor said to her father: 'The audited accounts for the golf club need to be signed off. And Millicent's wedding has to be discussed, of course.'

'Ah, yes, of course,' said Mr Harriman, with a knowing look and very wisely refrained from asking for details.

James reappeared at the door. 'Miss Lee asked if you would bring the lease for the golf club with you, Miss Eleanor.'

'Oh, did she say why?'

'She gave no reason.'

'I don't recall that there was a formal lease, James,' said Mr Harriman.

'Neither do I,' said James. 'Would you like me to have the file brought up?'

'Yes, please, James,' said Eleanor. 'How curious? I wonder what Millicent is asking about the lease for.'

~O~

Just before five thirty that afternoon, Eleanor walked the short distance from Hall Bank to the Palace Hotel. This was a large and very grand building designed by the architect, Henry Currey, and completed in 1868, the impetus being the arrival into Buxton of the railway, five years previously. The promoters of the hotel reasoned that passengers who could afford to travel first class on the railways would expect to find a first-class hotel in which to stay when they reached their destination. The railway was operated by two rival companies who had built separate lines into Buxton Spa, one from the south and one from the north. There were two separate but matching stations, located side by side and a short walk from the Palace Hotel. The hotel was on high ground, overlooking the town and formed a landmark visible from various vantage points. In its own way, it was just as imposing as The Crescent which had preceded it by some seventy years.

The long front façade of the hotel had all the accepted features of the ornate Second Empire architectural style then fashionable in Paris: three stories plus Mansard roof, topped with a peaked central tower, lavishly decorated with iron finials and cresting; large square pavilions anchoring either end of the long façade, a projecting central pavilion with three-arched entrance portico echoed on the top floor by a three-arched Venetian window; a row of tall, elegant Italianate arched windows all the way along the ground floor between the pavilions; and, on the floors above, pedimented windows with cast iron balconies and decoration. The interior of the hotel was just as grand as the façade. The three arches of the portico were repeated inside at the far end of the entrance hall, behind which a wide staircase with iron balustrade led graciously up to the first floor. The many dining rooms and reception rooms located behind the large arched windows of the façade were high-ceilinged and lavishly decorated with plasterwork, gold-leaf, and mirrors. In front of the hotel was a large garden which sloped down towards the front boundary and a central footpath led through this garden from street level up several flights of low steps to the front portico, allowing the approaching visitor to view the façade in all its splendour.

Eleanor made her way up this flight of steps, duly

admiring the façade as she went. At the front entrance, she was greeted by the linkman, a smiling, rather portly young man in cap and braided uniform, decorated with war service medals. The uniform was becoming a little too tight as a result of his keen appetite and his friendship with one of the hotel's kitchen maids. In the entrance hall, Eleanor said to the concierge at the reception desk: 'I have an appointment with Miss Millicent Lee.'

'Ah, yes. Miss Harriman, is it? Miss Lee asked me to tell you that she and Miss Fuller are in the lounge. Shall you be wanting tea?'

'Yes, thank you. Would you arrange that? For three, please.'

Millicent and Maureen had been attending a meeting of a newly formed committee intended to help unemployed young women find work, a significant problem due to the return of soldiers to the work-force. Their fellow committee members had now left and, while they waited for Eleanor they were chatting about the items discussed at the meeting. Millicent and Maureen came from wealthy families and had been brought up in gracious houses in The Park, where girls were sheltered from the realities of life until the age of eighteen and then expected to marry and occupy themselves with a husband and a family. Millicent and Maureen had both seen too much of the real world serving as VADs during the War to be satisfied with the sheltered world of The Park. They had taken up golf as a distraction from the horrors of the War and were actively engaged in social work trying to improve the lives of those affected by it.

The hotel lounge was light and elegant. One wall was made up of four of the twenty-feet high, floor-to-ceiling arched windows that formed part of the front façade. On the inside of those windows and framing them, was a wall of four corresponding round arches supported by Corinthian columns. The high ceiling, from which hung four large chandeliers, was heavily corniced and lavishly decorated with plasterwork. The centrepiece of the wall opposite the windows was a very large fireplace with an ornate plaster-work chimney piece above it. As the fire was not needed during the Season, there was a large floral decoration in front of the grate. There were armchairs grouped in front of the fireplace and tables and chairs scattered about the rest of the room for the use of guests. As Eleanor entered the lounge, she spotted Millicent and Maureen sitting at a table in the far corner near the windows.

'Eleanor,' said Millicent, standing up to greet her. 'Thank you for coming today instead of tomorrow. It is rather urgent, I'm afraid.'

'Millicent, how are you?' said Eleanor. Turning to Maureen she said: 'Maureen, good afternoon. I've got the accounts. They're all ready for signing.'

Eleanor put down a folder of documents onto the table between them and the three ladies sat down.

'Efficient as ever, Eleanor,' said Maureen. 'Thank you, but actually we wanted to talk to you about something else first, if you don't mind.'

'Yes,' said Millicent, 'did you bring the deed?'

'Well...' said Eleanor, 'is there a problem?'

'We don't know. That's what we need the deed for. We saw some chaps up at the course early this morning, workmen chaps, messing about near the northern boundary and when I accosted one of them I was told they were there on the authority of a Mr Steen. I made some enquiries during the morning and found that the Club had not given any authority to anyone and no-one has ever heard of this Mr Steen.'

'Do you have any idea what they were doing there?' asked Eleanor.

'No. There was a group of workmen milling about and a horse and waggon with some sort of equipment and

Maureen said she was pretty sure that one of them had a dowsing rod, didn't you, Maureen?'

'Yes,' said Maureen. 'My grandfather used to have one. He insisted that it was effective although I don't recall him ever having any great success.'

'We've been wondering if the activity on the course is something to do with water,' said Millicent.

'The course is not far from the head spring of the river,' added Maureen. 'In fact, I remember someone telling me that the location of one of the greens had to be changed when the course was planned so as to avoid a spring.'

'The reason we asked you to bring the lease,' said Millicent, 'is that we wanted to know if there is anything in it about the water. Who owns it? Who controls it? That sort of thing.'

'I don't recall there being any reservation of rights, if that's what you mean. Or any specific reservations at all. You see there is no lease, as such. It was just a general permission to use the land for the purposes of the Club. I've brought that document with me. Let me just check.'

A maid arrived and set the tea service out on the table in front of them. As Eleanor studied the document, Maureen poured their tea. She and Millicent chatted quietly and sipped their tea until Eleanor finished reading. After a minute, Eleanor put the document down and picked up her tea-cup and saucer.

'No,' she said, 'there is no reservation of rights. No mention of water at all.'

'I know our position at the Club has never been very secure and we did have all that trouble during the War with the allotments along Macclesfield Road. We've been asking the Estate to give us a long lease but there has been no response. And, we've got a match next week against the Manchester Ladies' Golf Club. I certainly don't want those men tramping about and making a nuisance of themselves on the course while we are trying to concentrate on the match. And that's another thing. The captain of Manchester Ladies is called Steen. That can't be a co-incidence can it? Not a common name. That's why I want to get on top of this as soon as possible.'

'Quite,' agreed Eleanor. 'However, as it is the Duke's land, perhaps the first thing to do is visit the Estate Office. Talk to the Duke's agent, Mr Sweeting, and see if these men have been given authority by him.'

'Right oh!' said Millicent. 'Excellent idea. Should have thought of that myself. I'll go there first thing tomorrow.'

'In the meantime, I shall make what enquiries I can about this Mr Steen,' said Eleanor.

That settled, they moved on to discuss, first of all, the Club's prospects in the golf match against the Manchester club and then the Club's accounts. Finally, they chatted about the arrangements for Millicent's forthcoming wedding. In a little under four weeks' time, Millicent was due to marry Julian St John, a graduate of Cambridge and an industrial chemist employed in his uncle's factory in Manchester. All three ladies were involved in the wedding, so there were many items for discussion. Eventually, Eleanor looked at her watch and they realised that it was time to leave. The trio left the lounge and walked across the front hall of the hotel, past the reception desk. A gentleman was standing at the desk having just completed registration as a guest. As he left the reception desk and walked through the archway towards the staircase, the concierge called: 'Porter!' and, when a hall-porter appeared, said: 'Carruthers, fetch Mr Steen's luggage from his motor-car and take it up to his room immediately, room one twenty. And then show his valet and chauffeur to the servants' quarters.'

At the sound of the name Steen, Millicent and Maureen immediately turned to look at the disappearing guest but Eleanor's attention was drawn momentarily to the hall-porter. He had literally stopped in his tracks and, for a second, stood frozen. The incident lasted no more than a couple of seconds and then Eleanor turned to look at the now vanishing back of Mr Steen. The three ladies watched Mr Steen as he ascended the lower flight of stairs and then caught a brief glimpse of his face as he turned the corner and started up the second flight before moving out of sight.

As they turned away, Millicent said: 'So that is the mysterious Mr Steen. The man in charge of operations.'

'He was dressed for golf but, given the activity on the course this morning, it doesn't seem likely that he has come to play, does it?' said Maureen.

'No,' said Millicent, 'and I hope he's not planning to take over the golf course for some other purpose. Do you think we should confront him?'

'No,' said Eleanor, 'better to remain incognito for the moment, I think. Let's find out a bit more about him first before we show our hand.'

'It looked as though he was only just registering and the hall-porter's been sent to collect his luggage,' said Maureen, 'so there's every chance he will still be here at the hotel tomorrow or even longer.'

'Yes,' agreed Eleanor. 'Maureen's right. You go to the Estate Office tomorrow morning and let me know how you get on. Then we'll decide what to do next.'

'Right you are,' said Millicent.

Mr Steen also thought it wise to remain incognito for the moment. He considered himself a gentleman, although others did not because he spent his days engaged in manufacturing. He prided himself on being a model of un-failing sartorial correctness and he often drew envious glances from those he encountered in business. However, on this occasion, he did not want to attract attention. He had plans for Buxton Spa and he anticipated opposition to them once the nature of his business was revealed. He wanted to remain unnoticed until his project was well advanced and he was ready to reveal his scheme. He feared that his usual town business suit would betray him and he had decided, therefore, to give the impression that his visit to the town was purely for pleasure. Although it pained him to dress less formally than usual, he accepted that country wear would be more appropriate. He had no intention of actually playing golf – he left that strictly to his wife – or taking part in any other sporting activity but he saw no harm in letting people think that he was intending to do so. He had visited his tailor and was now wearing a bespoke Norfolk jacket in brown Harris Tweed, matching Tweed knee breeches, and long socks. To emphasise the look of a sportsman, he carried a haversack slung over one shoulder.

~O~

Later that evening, as the train from Manchester passed the signal box and the railway sidings at Hogshaw on its approach to Buxton station, Mr Stephen Ashworth of the University of Liverpool closed the notebook in which he had been writing. He tucked it into one of the pockets of his jacket and made sure that he had buttoned down the pocket flap. He stood up and lifted his suitcase down from the overhead luggage rack and moved towards the carriage door. He alighted from the train, handed his ticket to the ticket collector, and made his way across town to Cramond House on West Street where he had reserved a room. A colleague had recommended this accommodation and it was convenient to the area of the town in which he intended to carry out research.

Stephen Ashworth was an archaeologist whose particular interest was the Bronze Age. He had read accounts of investigations carried out in Buxton during the previous century, mainly by amateurs, at Poole's Cavern and at the burial mound on top of nearby Grin Low and he had studied the lists of items found there. He had also read reports of digs carried out in the nineteenth century at various other locations in the surrounding countryside. From the lofty heights of his twentieth century laboratory and the very modern archaeology department of his University, Stephen Ashworth found these nineteenth century Victorian amateurs rather quaint and somewhat of a nuisance. Nevertheless, because of their work and the records they had kept, he was convinced that there had been a Bronze Age settlement in the Buxton area and he wanted to be the first to locate evidence of its existence. This research was to be the subject of his doctoral thesis and he hoped it would gain him an appointment as a lecturer at the University. He was eager to begin looking for evidence and, as he planned to be on site at first light the following morning, he went to bed almost as soon as he had unpacked his things.

Stephen Ashworth's family was not wealthy and he had been able to go to University only because he had a scholarship. He was very intelligent, ambitious, already an expert in his field, and extremely well-read. His father, a successful Liverpool business man, was suspicious of "book learning" and was a firm believer in the adage that it is not what you know but who you know that counts. Although Stephen would have preferred to rely on his own ability, he had reluctantly come to accept his father's view of the world. He had consistently found that if he called on the person in charge of an organisation with a letter of introduction in his hand, doors would be opened much wider for him, and he would be given far greater access to the items he needed for his research, than if he had relied on his own merits. Consequently, when he was planning his trip, he had considered whether or not he knew anyone who could provide him with suitable introductions. During the War, when he had been in hospital recovering from shrapnel wounds, he had met a fellow patient who came from Buxton Spa. Stephen had recalled that the patient's surname was Danebridge, not a very common name, and as he had found only one person of that name listed in the Kelly's directory, he had sent a letter to the address listed there. He had received a very prompt and polite reply. Philip Danebridge would be delighted to be of service and looked forward to meeting him again.

CHAPTER TWO

The following morning, Eleanor was working at her desk drafting a complicated claim for one of Edwin's matters when Maureen Fuller telephoned.

'Eleanor,' she said. 'Millicent and I have just been to the Estate Office. Mr Sweeting wasn't there but his assistant says he is not aware of any plans for the golf club's land. He suggested I speak to the Estate's surveyor but he is not in the office today. So, we've drawn a blank, I'm afraid. We need a spy. Someone up at the hotel who can find out what this Steen fellow is up to. Millicent suggested a lounge lizard.'

'A lounge lizard!'

'Yes, Millicent wonders if you know any.'

'What on earth for?'

'Well, all those middle-aged, partner-less females who stay in places like the Palace make it their business to assess the status and financial prospects of every male who comes through the front door. They are bound to have assayed Mr Steen already: wealth, age, eligibility for matrimony, that sort of thing. They probably also know exactly why he has come here. They always go to the tea dances and dance with the lounge lizard so Millicent thinks he could easily wheedle out of them any information they have about Mr Steen.'

'What a ridiculous idea!' said Eleanor, laughing. 'Please tell Millicent that I do not know any lounge lizards nor am I old enough to be that desperate for a dancing partner. Not yet anyway.'

Eleanor went back to her drafting and several minutes

later was interrupted again, this time by a telephone call from Philip Danebridge. He was the cousin of Eleanor's fiancé, Alistair Danebridge. After Alistair was killed in France, Eleanor and Philip had become close friends because of their mutual loss. Philip was employed by Messrs Willis, Wise and Campbell, a firm which specialised in high quality antique furniture and decorative items. Two years ago, they had opened a showroom in Buxton and they had appointed Philip as manager, which had enabled him to realise his life-long ambition of earning a living surrounded by beautiful objects. When he was appointed to the position, he already had an extensive knowledge of his subject and he had shown such aptitude that the firm soon employed an assistant for the showroom leaving Philip free to attend auctions, acquiring pieces for the business or bidding on behalf of clients. The price of these items was far beyond Philip's own means so now, as well as being able to handle many splendid pieces, he had the added enjoyment of spending other people's money on them. He combined knowledge with instinct and he had many wealthy clients who relied entirely on his judgment and advice.

'Eleanor, I'm so sorry to do this,' said Philip, 'but I'm in a bit of a bind and I wondered if you could help me out?'

'Possibly,' said Eleanor, distractedly, her mind still on her drafting. 'It depends. What and when?'

'You may remember that I told you I had a letter from someone I met in hospital, Stephen Ashworth, an archae-ologist from the University of Liverpool.'

'Ye-e-es,' said Eleanor cautiously.

'I arranged to meet him this coming Monday morning at Poole's Cavern and introduce him to Mr Redfern there but a client has just telephoned to ask me to go to an auction in Manchester on his behalf. It's on Monday morning and there is a very rare piece of Chinese porcelain that he particularly wants for his collection. This is all very late notice, I know, but he is an important client and I should very much like to oblige him, if at all possible, but I am already committed to meeting Mr Ashworth.'

'And…' said Eleanor, teasing him, '…you want me to go to the auction for you.'

'Very amusing, Lella. You don't know a Ming from a Minton. No, I was wondering if you would take Mr Ashworth to Poole's Cavern for me.'

'Yes, of course,' said Eleanor, laughing. 'What time did you arrange to meet him?'

'You're very generous, Eleanor. Thank you. I'll return the favour. The meeting is at half past nine. Mr Redfern stipulated that it had to be before the visitors started arriving. Would it be convenient for me to bring Mr Ashworth to your office later today so that I can introduce him to you?'

'Certainly.'

'Would twelve-thirty suit you?'

'Yes. I shall tell James to expect you.' Eleanor went back to drafting her document.

~O~

Philip arrived at Hall Bank at half past twelve accompanied by Mr Stephen Ashworth. As it was Saturday, James Wildgoose was closing up the office. He would normally have allowed Philip to go straight up to Eleanor's office but, as Philip was not alone, James went upstairs ahead of them and announced them formally.

'Mr Danebridge and Mr Ashworth, Miss Eleanor.'

'Thank you, James. Would you ask Mrs Clayton to bring tea, please, and would you also take Napoleon upstairs?'

Napoleon greeted Philip, they were old friends, but he showed no interest in Stephen Ashworth. He meekly followed James out of Eleanor's office and James closed the door. Philip performed the introductions and, while Mrs

Clayton supplied them all with tea, Eleanor made polite conversation, asking Mr Ashworth about his visit to the town and he explained briefly his interest in Bronze Age archaeology.

'As you probably know,' said Mr Ashworth, 'a gentleman called Mr Thomas Bateman explored a great many sites in Derbyshire early last century, including Poole's Cavern, and many of the items he collected are in Sheffield in the museum at Weston Park. He was only an amateur, of course. I believe another local amateur, Mr Micah Salt, was also very active and I have read various contemporary reports of his "finds" which I believe are still here in Buxton. Mr Salt was a tradesman, of course, and had no special training in archaeology and his work was only reported piecemeal in various archaeological journals.'

Eleanor was beginning to bridle at Mr Ashworth's patronising tone and his condescending attitude towards Mr Salt. She was getting ready to defend the reputation of this local identity whose hobby and discoveries were familiar to the townspeople, but she waited politely for Mr Ashworth to finish.

'However,' he continued, 'I discovered that about twenty years ago, a gentleman who knew Mr Salt and had watched him work collected the reports of his excavations and published them. With that summary, it is much easier to assess the value of Mr Salt's work. Obviously, Mr Salt was a keen investigator but, naturally, his work did not conform to our modern methods of archaeology, the sort of methods that are being pioneered at my university.'

'Well, to be fair, it was fifty or so years ago when he started investigating,' interrupted Philip.

'Precisely,' said Mr Ashworth, 'but the discipline is now a science and much more demanding of resources than those which would have been at Mr Salt's disposal. He would not have had the necessary funds to employ sufficient men to follow our modern scientific principles. Unfortunately, these amateurs have left a mixed legacy. There is often a lack of precision as to where exactly an item was found and, worse, who has custody of the item.'

'A great many of the artefacts found locally are on display at the museum here,' said Philip, defensively.

'Yes, I plan to visit the museum, but I believe some items are still in the hands of private collectors. There are some that I would particularly like to examine. I cannot consult Mr Salt himself, of course, because I understand that he died a few years ago.'

'Yes, in 1915,' said Eleanor.

'Then, I should like to find someone else who can help me.'

'Well,' said Philip, 'Mr Salt's sons all helped him on his digs and one of them, Mr William Salt, has an antique shop in the High Street. You could consult him. He also has a large collection of the items that he and his father and brothers recovered.'

Eleanor could not resist adding, 'I think you will find that they are all properly catalogued.'

'I remember Mr William Salt telling me one day,' continued Philip, 'that his father used to send the items off to be identified and then drawn by the experts and pictures of the items were included in the scientific journals of the day, so they must have been of some significance. I believe also that Professor Boyd Dawkins from Manchester looked at some of Mr Salt's finds and verified their date.'

'Yes, although the professor is primarily a geologist, not an archaeologist and I believe he consults on engineering projects for a fee,' said Mr Ashworth, dismissively.

Philip looked across at Eleanor and, sensed that she too was feeling rather protective towards the town and the enquiring minds of its inhabitants in the face of this intrusion from academia with its rigid attitude and its condemnation of enthusiasm and natural curiosity.

'Well,' said Philip, 'Mr Redfern also has a small museum and those items are all properly catalogued as to the time and place recovered. When you go to meet Mr Redfern you should certainly visit Poole's Cavern. I can assure you, you will find it worth your time.'

'The limestone formations are quite striking,' added Eleanor, 'and it has had many famous visitors, including Mary Queen of Scots, although I have to admit that the writer, Daniel Defoe, did not think much of the cavern.'

'Even if the limestone formations don't interest you,' said Philip, 'the River Sink is very impressive. The Wye River, the one you are interested in, actually rises on Axe Edge some distance away but one part of it goes underground and doesn't reappear on the surface until much lower down-stream, on the other side of the golf course at Wye Head, where it becomes a river again. But you can see the river while it is underground if you go to Poole's Cavern. It gushes into the Cavern and then disappears again deep into the rocks. These disappearing rivers are a feature of the limestone landscape in this area.'

'Yes,' said Mr Ashworth, 'so I understand. I intend to search for springs in the area because they were very important sites for the people in whom I am interested. To the primitive mind, such things were magical and are often a location where artefacts were left as offerings.'

'I see,' said Philip, 'that's very interesting.' He stood up to indicate that the meeting was over.

Eleanor arranged to meet Mr Ashworth at Poole's Cavern on Monday morning and Philip steered him towards the door of Eleanor's office. As the archaeologist began walking down the stairs, Philip looked back at Eleanor and grimaced. She frowned back at him and shrugged. He mouthed "Sorry" and disappeared downstairs.

After Philip and Mr Ashworth had gone, Eleanor cleared her desk and put away her files. Edwin had already gone home to his family and Mr Harriman had gone to play golf. As Eleanor had not been sure how long she and Philip would be with Mr Ashworth, she had told Mrs Clayton not to wait to serve lunch. Eleanor had said she would be perfectly happy with sandwiches and when she had finished them, she took Napoleon for his walk along Broad Walk and into the Pavilion Gardens. The Season, which lasted from May to September, had only just begun but already a great many visitors had arrived. Those of more modest means who could only afford a week's stay generally arrived on a Saturday and today, every time a train arrived at one of the two stations, a fresh stream of people emerged carrying suitcases and belongings or clutching children and poured down the hill towards the town in search of their lodgings. Visitors staying at private hotels or guest houses were collected by taxi cars arranged by these establishments for their guests. Occasionally, a motor-car or a carriage pulled up in front of one of the large houses along Broad Walk bringing more affluent visitors who rented apartments there and brought their whole family to stay for a month or more.

Eleanor and Napoleon strolled through the Pavilion gardens enjoying the warm sunshine. Napoleon was always interested in what people were doing and, as they were not in a hurry, Eleanor allowed him to stop every now and again to watch the various activities taking place. The croquet lawn, the bandstand, the tennis courts, and the boating lake captured Napoleon's attention in turn so it was some time before they wound their way back through the Victorian grotto to the entrance gate on Broad Walk. As they left the gardens, Eleanor let Napoleon off his lead and he dawdled along Broad Walk prolonging his stay as long as possible.

Broad Walk was busy with visitors promenading up and down, some greeting people whom they knew from previous Seasons, others stopping to chat in groups and performing introductions to new acquaintances. The latest fashions in ladies' frocks, costumes, and hats were on display.

Eventually, Eleanor and Napoleon returned to Hall Bank and found Philip waiting for them, lounging against the wall on the opposite side of the road and enjoying the sunshine.

'Ah, there you are!' he said.

'Have you been waiting long?' asked Eleanor.

'No, only a few minutes. I guessed you would be out in the Gardens and I thought I would wait. I've disposed of Mr Ashworth and I've come back to apologise for landing you with him.'

'He is rather a bore, isn't he?'

'Totally focussed on his subject, I admit. I remembered him vaguely from the hospital, of course, but I didn't really know him, and I wasn't sure what to expect. Once you have introduced him to Mr Redfern, you needn't have any more to do with him. But, never mind him! There's something far more interesting going on in the Market Place. It's a rally of some kind, just getting started, and I adore rallies, especially the rowdy sort. Let's go and see what it's all about.'

'All right. Father's off playing golf and I didn't have anything particular in mind for the rest of the afternoon. Come on, Napoleon. You'd best be on your lead, though.'

When they reached the top of Hall Bank, they surveyed the scene. The thriving Saturday market was spread over a large part of the Market Place. Traders were offering all sorts of goods and scores of shoppers were bustling about, greeting friends, looking for the best bargains, and visiting their favourite stalls. A small crowd had formed outside the Town Hall and some people with baskets over their arms paused in their shopping to investigate the diversion being provided by the rally.

'I say, Lella,' said Philip, delightedly, 'it's a political rally. Top hole! This is even better than I had hoped.'

The current Westminster government was an unpopular Conservative-Liberal coalition which was becoming increasingly unworkable and, recently, the whole country had been disrupted by several strikes. Sensing that a General Election might have to be called soon and assessing the opportunity for change, the various political parties had begun to make speeches at rallies around the country. In front of the Town Hall, a man was standing on a sturdy wooden box and he held a large megaphone through which he was shouting at the crowd, waving his free arm energetically to emphasise each point he was making. Behind the man with the megaphone, two people were holding up a banner which read National Union of General Workers. A third man, wearing a sandwich board and a gloomy expression, was pacing slowly along the edge of the crowd. On one side of his board, the message read: End Wage Slavery! On the other side, the message was: Horace Robinson. United People's Democracy Party.

Eleanor and Philip, shadowed by Napoleon, walked along Eagle Parade, weaving their way around the market stalls in order to reach the back of the crowd which had gathered around the speaker. As they did so, Eleanor spotted Millicent Lee and her fiancé, Julian St John, at the edge of the crowd. They all greeted each other and Napoleon obediently sat down beside Eleanor to watch the passers-by while the four friends chatted.

'We were just on our way back from the golf course,' said Millicent, 'and we spotted the rally. We thought we'd stop and see what it's about.'

'Philip is addicted to gatherings of this kind,' explained Eleanor, 'so he wanted to join in as well.'

'Oh, yes! I do enjoy a political rally,' said Philip. 'All flowery language and rash generalisations. Quite diverting.

And some of the things they accuse their opponents of! Most enlightening.'

'Why are they holding it now?' objected Millicent. 'There's been no call for a General Election.'

'I know, but the present situation cannot continue,' said Eleanor, 'so it's only a matter of time before an election is called. I suppose everyone wants to get in first and have their say.'

'Absolutely,' said Julian, 'I suspect we are going to be heartily sick of these rallies by the time an election is called. We had better enjoy this one before the novelty wears off.'

'It seems that our Mr Steen is happy to join in the fun. Look over there,' said Millicent, pointing across the road from the Market Place.

A second sandwich board man, looking slightly more cheerful than the other one, was walking up and down on the opposite footpath. On the front, his board carried the message: Don't get hot under the collar! On the reverse was: Enjoy Steen's Fruit Flavoured Beverages.

Eleanor was amused. 'So that is what the mysterious Mr Steen does for a living. He clearly knows how to make the most of an opportunity.'

'What on earth has fruit flavoured beverages got to do with the golf course?' asked Millicent.

Eleanor shrugged. Turning back to the activity in the Market Place, she said: 'The other sandwich board man is advertising Horace Robinson so I assume that the speaker is the said Horace.'

'I'm sure you are right, although that megaphone is so large it's difficult to see who's actually behind it,' said Julian.

'The Hidden Face of Politics,' intoned Philip, in newspaper headline style. 'Let's move closer. I want to hear what the fellow's got to say for himself.'

The voice from the megaphone boomed: 'We should be working for a just society, a society in which industry is used for the promotion of human happiness nor for the benefit of the wealthy few.'

'Hear, hear,' called several claques in the crowd.

'Human happiness does not lie in the production and accumulation of goods, my friends,' proclaimed the speaker. 'There are better ways of living.'

'Are you sure he's not a communist?' asked Eleanor.

'Or a Protestant, perhaps, since he is opposed to worldly goods,' suggested Philip.

'All workers,' roared the speaker, indignantly, 'no matter where they are, no matter what they do, be they workers in industry or be they doctors or schoolmasters…or house-wives even…they are all producers and should be celebrated as such. They should receive an equitable share of wealth not just wages for hours worked.'

A woman in the crowd called out: 'And when has a housewife ever been paid wages, pray?' Another woman added: 'Huh, the hours I work, if I 'ad a wage for even 'alf of 'em, I wouldn't need no share o' wealth.' A third woman said loudly: 'The man's a fool!' and, as she turned away, there were murmurs of agreement from several other women. Then, at the back of the crowd, there was a burst of loud laughter from a group of men. One of them yelled at the speaker: 'Don't be absurd, man. Why would you pay a wife for doing what she's bound to do anyway?' The crowd became noisy as contrary opinions were expressed. A few more shoppers, made curious by the heckling, joined the throng. The speaker had to raise his voice so as not to be drowned out.

'We should, in fact we must, strive to change the lives of all citizens.' He waved both his arms in a gesture of embrace towards the crowd forgetting the megaphone in his right hand and it made a wide sweep, causing the man standing next to him to duck in order to avoid being knocked out. The crowd found that hilarious and jeered and clapped. Undaunted the speaker waited until the laughter subsided and then pressed on. 'John Ruskin, that great visionary and social commentator, who left us but a short twenty odd years ago, observed correctly that large fortunes are all founded either on the occupation of land, the lending of money, or the taxation of labour. The land, as a resource, should be not be bound up...'

The speaker was interrupted again. A male voice towards the front of the crowd called out loudly: 'What about this here factory idea then! That's an occupation of land. And you can take it from me, that land will be bound up and we, the citizens, will not see any benefit from it. What are you going to do about that then?'

News travelled fast in Buxton. The network of traders gossiped with their customers, and the traders' delivery people gathered information from servants who had over-heard conversations in the houses of their employers. In the evenings, when they met in the public houses, the traders exchanged rumours and speculated on them. Although Mr Steen had only arrived the previous day, his workmen had already been in the town for several days and, in the evenings, they frequented the public houses. Consequently, some people in the crowd had already heard enough rumours to know why Mr Steen was in town.

Eleanor said to Millicent: 'These people seem to know what Mr Steen is up to.'

'Yes,' said Millicent, 'that man who interjected said something about a factory. Let's ask someone, shall we?' She walked towards a group at the side of the crowd and, choosing a man who had been calling out "hear, hear" in support of the previous interjection, she tapped him on the shoulder and said: 'I say, excuse me, do you know what this Mr Steen is proposing to do?'

The man turned around and appraised Millicent. 'Aye, Miss,' he said, 'he reckons to build a factory here.'

'And where is this factory going to be? Do you know?'

'Up on the golf course. So I've heard.'

'Oh, I see. Thank you,' said Millicent. 'What sort of factory is it to be?'

'Sorry, Miss, I can't help you there,' he replied and turned back to the meeting.

Millicent returned to Eleanor and said: 'That chap says this Steen fellow is planning to build a factory on the golf course.'

'Oh, surely not,' said Eleanor. 'That would be an absurd place to put a factory.'

They turned back to the speaker. Various people called out in support of the original interjector, and others turned to each other, either nodding in agreement, or voicing opposition, or asking their neighbour what it was all about. Horace Robinson had now completely lost control of his audience. The crowd was getting noisier and was milling about, impeding the shoppers at the market stalls.

Napoleon was getting anxious and Eleanor said to Philip: 'I think we should go.'

'Yes, I've heard enough. Let's move over there near the fruit stall where there are fewer people.'

As Eleanor turned to Millicent to say that they were leaving, she saw Julian raise his hand in greeting towards someone in the crowd. Then, he turned back to Millicent and said, indignantly: 'Oh, I say!'

'What's the matter?' asked Millicent.

'I just spotted someone in the crowd I know and he cut me!' Julian was very annoyed.

'Are you sure he saw you?' asked Millicent.

'Yes, he did. Looked me straight in the eye and then cut me, the blighter.'

'Perhaps he didn't recognise you?' said Philip.

'I'm certain he did but he just turned away and then other people got in the way and I lost sight of him.'

'Perhaps it was just someone who resembles the person you know,' said Millicent.

'Possibly,' conceded Julian. 'I did only catch a quick glimpse before he disappeared into the crowd but, no, I'm sure it was the person I know, and he recognised me.'

'Who was it anyway?' asked Millicent.

'A chap from Cambridge.'

'Is he a friend of yours?' asked Millicent.

'Well, more of an acquaintance, really.' said Julian and shrugged. 'He was on my staircase but we weren't actually friends. We both enlisted at the same time but we were in different regiments. I did hear that he was wounded in France in 1916 but that was the last I heard of him.'

Before Julian could say anything further, a man approached the group and thrust a leaflet at Julian. He waved the man away and Philip took the leaflet instead.

'This leaflet,' said Philip, looking at it, 'wants me to "Support the Workers Control Party" but it's a bit ambiguous, don't you think? Do you suppose it is a party which wants to control workers or a party which wants to put workers in control?'

'If they want to control something, they should say so,' said Julian crossly, still upset at being cut.

'I do wish people would be more precise with their punctuation.' Philip shook his head and sighed.

Eleanor and Millicent laughed at the two of them and then Millicent glanced up at the Town Hall clock.

'Speaking of control, Julian,' said Millicent. 'It's time we left.' She turned to Eleanor and said: 'We're due to meet my parents at the Crescent Hotel shortly so we'll walk with you down Hall Bank.'

The four friends walked away from the meeting and down Hall Bank to Harriman & Talbot's office, where they stopped. Eleanor said to Millicent: 'At least we have some idea as to what Mr Steen is planning for the golf course.'

34

'Yes, and we are jolly well going to stop him,' said Millicent. 'I'll let you know if I find out any more.' As she left, Millicent said quietly to Eleanor: 'Ask Philip about lounge lizards.'

Philip said: 'Lella, I too must go. My father has some particularly dull but nevertheless important clients coming to dinner this evening and my mother wants me for the comedy act when the conversation flags.' He pushed back his hat to a rakish angle.

'Um, Philip, before you go…speaking of comedy acts…that favour you owe me for delivering the very dreary Mr Ashworth to Poole's Cavern…you wouldn't consider becoming a lounge lizard, would you?'

'I beg your pardon?' said Philip, taking a step backwards and giving Eleanor a look of mock horror.

'Just for one evening?'

'You jest, surely.'

'No, we need information about Mr Steen. He's staying at the Palace Hotel so Millicent thought it would be simple to go there in the evening for the dancing and spy on him.'

Eleanor described briefly the potential threat to the golf course from Mr Steen. Philip remained unmoved.

'No, Eleanor,' he said, 'I will not consider being a lounge lizard. Not even for you. Banish the thought immediately. I have my reputation to consider.' He lifted his hat, bowed towards Eleanor, and then put his hat back on, straight this time. 'I shall bid you adieu.'

'Good bye, Philip,' said Eleanor, laughing.

'I shall help in any other way I can though. Good luck with Mr Ashworth, and thank you again for agreeing to look after him for me.'

Eleanor waved to Philip and took Napoleon indoors.

Back at the Market Place, people returned to their shopping and, as the number of spectators at the political rally dwindled, the organisers gave up. For the next few days, the two sandwich board men wandered about the town vying for the attention of the crowd. Everyone learned the name, Horace Robinson, and also became aware of Steen's Fruit Flavoured Beverages. To further his cause, Horace Robinson, together with several members of his United People's Democracy Party and some of the supporters of the National Union of General Workers, frequented the public houses and loitered outside the ale houses, shaking hands and talking to anyone who would listen in the hope of inflaming their suspicion of the land-owning class and inspiring them to join the workers' opposition. Mr Steen, on the other hand, set about organising a Motor-car Rally to promote his beverages on the principle that people would much rather have entertainment than political philosophy.

~O~

On Sunday afternoons when it was fine, Eleanor, Napoleon, Cecily and Richard either visited the gardens and listened to the band or went walking. This Sunday, when Eleanor and Napoleon arrived at Oxford House, they were greeted enthusiastically by Richard.

Eleanor asked: 'Where are we going today, Richard?'

'Corbar Woods, please Aunt Lella. I should very much like to go there and I think Napoleon would like to go there too.'

'How can you tell?' asked Eleanor, keeping a straight face.

'Because he nodded his head when I mentioned the woods,' said Richard, confidently.

'Very well,' said Eleanor, smiling at him. 'That's settled then.'

Richard was now almost eight and, from an early age, had been interested in plants. On their many Sunday walks he had learnt the names of all the plants he observed. He knew that, at this time of year, Corbar Woods would be abundant with wildflowers, including bluebells. The walking party set off along Broad Walk and, after twenty minutes, arrived at the entrance to the woods. Eighty or so years ago, this part of Corbar Hill, then a bare rocky outcrop which leered bleakly at the town, had been transformed at the expense of the Devonshire estate into a wood planted with beech, horse-chestnut, larch, and other trees. Later, gravelled walks had been created on the hillside in place of an old quarry and, now, there were shaded walks edged by laurel, holly, lilac, laburnum, and other shrubs. At ground level, there was a layer of woodbine, wild briars, ivy, ferns, and an assortment of wildflowers. Eleanor and Cecily followed one of the footpaths up the hill while Richard and Napoleon meandered about examining whatever took their fancy and, in Napoleon's case, sniffing at burrows. Eleanor and Cecily strolled and chatted and occasionally paused to sit on rustic seats while they watched the two adventurers.

'Richard is growing tall,' observed Eleanor. 'He will be like his father.'

'Yes,' said Cecily. She and Richard had recently returned from a visit to Wyvern Hall, the home of Wilfred's parents. 'Last week, Wilfred's mother and I spent some time looking at family photographs, some of them taken of Wilfred at Richard's age, and we were remarking on how tall Wilfred was then.' Cecily sighed.

'Richard's very like Wilfred,' said Eleanor. 'He doesn't take after our side of the family at all.'

'No, he doesn't. Wilfred's parents asked me what I plan to do about him in September when the new term starts. Richard's the right age to go to boarding school and they want me to send him to Wilfred's old school. They're offering to pay the fees, of course, because they know that I could never afford them.'

'How do you feel about that?' asked Eleanor. Cecily did

not answer. Eleanor waited and then added: 'I don't suppose you want him to go away.'

'No, I don't,' said Cecily. Eleanor remained silent because she could sense that Cecily was fighting back tears. Cecily continued: 'I know I'm being selfish and that I should be thinking about what is best for Richard and not what I would prefer but I really do not want to have to send him away. He is the only link I have left with Wilfred.'

'I don't think you're being selfish at all. It's perfectly understandable. Although, perhaps that is just me being selfish as well. I enjoy spending time with Richard and I should miss him very much. Very much indeed.'

'It would mean sending him to Winchester and that is so far away.' They were silent for a while. 'And he really is happy here. There is a great deal for him to do and he loves the freedom of being outdoors. And he meets such interesting people, all the people who come to stay during the Season. He would miss that.'

'And he spends time with Father,' said Eleanor, 'which is important now that Wilfred is not here.'

'Yes,' agreed Cecily. 'They get on famously. Father has also offered to pay Richard's fees, although he favours sending him to Edgar's old school, which was Father's old school too, of course.'

'I don't recollect Edgar being particularly happy there.' Eleanor smiled at the memory of her younger brother. 'He had very little respect for some of the masters and at the beginning of every term, without fail, he grumbled about having to go back. He said it was beastly, if I remember correctly.'

'Yes, he did,' agreed Cecily, 'I know he didn't enjoy it very much. He was always very reluctant to get on the train to go back to school and never had his trunk packed in time. Remember what a rush it always was to get to the station before the train pulled out without him? And he used to complain that they didn't teach him anything.'

'What he probably meant was that they didn't teach him anything he wanted to learn,' said Eleanor, laughing.

'I suppose he meant architecture and the other things that he was interested in,' said Cecily, 'and not the usual things like Latin and English history. I don't think Edgar would have been easy to teach. He was such a dreamer. He might have been a good architect though.'

'Only if he had paid attention in mathematics,' laughed Eleanor, 'and if mother had not had her way. You know how much she wanted him to join the firm and work with Father.'

'Yes, but that would have been a waste. He would not have been happy and you are much better suited to it than Edgar could ever have been.' Cecily sighed. 'Oh, I know family tradition is important, especially to Wilfred's parents, and that is why they want Richard to go to Wilfred's old school, but tradition isn't everything, is it? Especially if it means one has to do things one is not suited to. Besides, the schools here have a very good reputation. I don't see why Richard shouldn't stay where he is, at least until he is a little bit older.'

'Well, anyway, you can delay the decision for a few months yet,' said Eleanor.

At this point, Richard came running up, Napoleon at his side, and asked them to come and look at a plant he had found and could not identify. He raced off again expecting them to follow.

'I hope I shall be able to recognise this plant,' said Cecily, laughing. 'I shall be in trouble otherwise. He'll be telling me their names before too long.'

'Perhaps Richard's going to be a famous botanist,' suggested Eleanor as they followed Richard to his find.

Eventually, it was time to return home and they made their way down through the woods along the footpath that came out onto Corbar Road. As they were approaching the large stone gateposts at the entrance to a long carriage drive, a well-dressed gentleman was walking along the other side of the road, coming towards them from the opposite direction. He crossed over the road just ahead of them and went through the entrance gates. By the time they were level with the gates, the gentleman was already walking along the carriage drive towards the house and Eleanor could see only his back. However, she had seen his face clearly as he had crossed over the road.

'I know that gentleman,' said Eleanor, frowning.

'He didn't seem to know you,' said Cecily. 'He didn't acknowledge you.'

'I'm certain I know him but I can't think why his face is familiar. I simply cannot place him. Bother!'

The entrance gates through which the gentleman had walked led to a large house set in extensive grounds which had once been Corbar Hill House, a private residence. Twenty years ago, it had been renamed and was now the Wye House Asylum. Eleanor had never been inside Wye House and had no connection with it at all, so she was puzzled as to why the man looked familiar. On the way back to Broad Walk, she kept trying to recollect where she had seen him before. When they reached Oxford House, they walked through the hall to the sitting room and Eleanor noticed a suitcase which had been left by a guest at the foot of the stairs for the maid to take upstairs.

'Of course!' said Eleanor, so loudly that Napoleon turned to look at her in alarm.

'What?' asked Cecily.

'That man. The one I couldn't place. He was at the Palace Hotel the other day. That's where I've seen him before. How silly of me, I don't know him at all.'

'Oh, what a relief,' said Cecily. 'It's been bothering you all the way home. Now perhaps we can have our tea in peace.'

CHAPTER THREE

When she arrived early on Monday morning, Mrs Clayton had news of Mr Walter Steen. Her brother, Alf, was one of the local undertakers and as he went about his business collecting bodies, he also collected information. As she was serving breakfast, Mrs Clayton said:

'Alf was talking to Bert after Chapel yesterday, Bert Hulley the joiner that is, he does the coffins for Alf. Well, Bert's brother-in-law is one of the clerks up at the Town Hall and he said Mr Steen's surveyor was there the other day ordering a map of the town. The surveyor told him that Mr Steen is looking for a place to build a factory so he can bottle the water and sell it.'

'That's very interesting,' said Eleanor. 'Millicent Lee saw some men on the golf course last Friday and wondered what they were doing there. Maureen Fuller said she thought one of them had a dowsing rod.'

'Well, Mr Tebbett's not going to be best pleased. He already does a tidy trade in bottled water himself and I shouldn't think he'll welcome any competition. And the grocer on Five Ways, the one who delivers here, has a spring in his cellar and Alf says he's been telling everyone that Mr Steen is free to come and bottle that water any time he wants, as long as he pays for it, of course.'

'With so many springs around us and water freely available from the spring at St Anne's Well, it does all seem a bit ridiculous, doesn't it?' Eleanor laughed.

'Yes, there's no need for a dowsing rod here. You only have to use your eyes to find water.'

'Right, I'm off to meet Mr Ashworth, the gentleman who was here on Saturday. I have to introduce him to Mr Redfern. I'll be back before the office opens.'

'Right you are, Miss Harriman. Is Napoleon going with you or is he staying with me?'

'I shan't have time to take him to the gardens for his usual walk so he can come with me now instead.'

Eleanor put on a jacket and her hat and gloves and set off with Napoleon. It was such a beautiful morning that she decided to take the long way. The two of them set out across the Market Place and down the High Street to the Five Ways. The High Street was full of activity. The shopkeepers were busily opening up and goods were being unloaded, some from newly fashionable vans and some from the traditional delivery cart pulled by a horse. Eleanor kept a steady pace, greeting the people she passed, and enjoying the bustle and the air of optimism that early morning brings, particularly at the beginning of the Season. Napoleon trotted happily along, sometimes lagging behind to investigate smells only he could identify, and then racing ahead to lead the way. Napoleon reached the Five Ways first and, having been trained to wait for permission before crossing a road, sat obediently on the footpath until Eleanor caught up. They were now opposite Smith's, the grocer's shop at which Mrs Clayton ordered the supplies for Hall Bank. The shop door was open and, as they crossed the road, Napoleon sniffed appreciatively at the smell of bacon coming from within. The delivery boy, who knew him, came out to give him a titbit. This was the shop Mrs Clayton had mentioned at breakfast. It had a spring in the cellar, an occurrence not unusual in Buxton, and Eleanor wondered why Mr Steen had chosen to investigate the golf course, given that there were so many other springs readily available. She supposed that it was because he also wanted land for a factory. She decided to put this disturbing thought out of her mind for the moment on such a beautiful morning, and she and Napoleon turned up West Street and walked towards Temple Road.

~O~

About five minutes earlier, Stephen Ashworth had donned his jacket and hat, slung the strap of his haversack over his shoulder, and left Cramond House. He too had walked along West Street and turned into Temple Road and was now a couple of hundred yards ahead of Eleanor and Napoleon. As they rounded the bend in Temple Road, Eleanor saw someone on the pavement up ahead and assumed that it was Mr Ashworth but he was too far ahead for Eleanor to catch up. She continued at her own pace until she and Napoleon reached Green Lane. Mr Ashworth was waiting for her at the turnstile entrance to Poole's Cavern and, just as they were greeting each other, Mr Redfern came out of his cottage and waved to them. He let them through the turnstile and Eleanor performed the introductions and explained to Mr Redfern the reason for Philip's absence. Mr Redfern knew Eleanor. He had been a client of her father's firm for many years and, as a child, Eleanor had often visited the Cavern with her brother and her sisters. Mr Redfern conducted them into the garden in front of the Cavern. His cottage, built in the gingerbread style popular with the early Victorians, was on the right of the garden and in front of them was a small building which provided teas and housed the museum in which artefacts and other items, mostly found in the Cavern, were displayed. The garden was scattered with flower beds and copies of Greek statues and had a small bandstand where musicians entertained visitors. Behind the museum loomed the entrance to the cavern, a huge gaping arch in the side of the rock.

Mr Ashworth thanked Mr Redfern for making himself available and explained briefly the aim of his research. Then he held out a list of items, saying: 'Mr Redfern, this is a list of items found locally over a number of years. I wonder if you can enlighten me. I believe those at the top of the list have been found in Poole's Cavern itself.'

'I shall certainly help if I can,' said Mr Redfern, taking the list. 'Now, what have we got?' Mr Redfern looked at the paper and read out loud: 'Flints and stone artefacts, late Neolithic, and early Bronze Age.' He stroked his chin. 'Hmm. Now, it's my understanding that those items, or some of them at least, were found up there on the hillside above the Cavern, beyond those trees.' He waved his arm in the direction of the hillside behind them and then returned to the list. 'Stone axes, Neolithic. Well, there have been several of those found in the area around the Cavern. At least, I understand that is what they are. To me, they just look like bits of stone, but I suppose to you they do look like something useful.'

Mr Ashworth laughed. 'Yes, I agree they are not immediately recognisable as tools. When people think of an axe they imagine a neat square blade and a smooth wooden handle, the sort of thing one finds at the ironmonger's.' He pointed to the list. 'So, these items were found in the Cavern itself as well as in the surrounding area.'

'Oh, goodness, yes,' said Mr Redfern. 'There's been quite a bit of evidence of human occupation in the Cavern over thousands of years. Animal bones, fish bones, that sort of thing, just rubbish left over from eating seemingly.'

'The list also includes metal objects and jewellery,' said Mr Ashworth, pointing to several items grouped together on the list. 'They are thought to be Roman, not earlier. Have they been properly dated?'

'Yes, these were found in the Cavern, oh, fifty odd years ago, by my father. He was just an amateur, of course, not a professional archaeologist like yourself, but the items themselves were dated by professionals. They're more recent than the time you're interested in. Sorry to disappoint you.'

Mr Ashworth nodded and said: 'I understand that on Grin Low, there was a burial site believed to be early Bronze Age. Grin Low is up there behind us, is that right?'

'That is correct. Up that path there, through the woods.' Mr Redfern pointed up the hill where, hidden behind the trees, a Victorian stone tower known locally as Solomon's Temple now marked the site. 'It's a bit over fourteen hundred feet above sea level and from there, if you go up on a clear day and look around you, you can see upwards of fifteen lows all with barrow burials and all created during the period of time you're interested in.'

Mr Ashworth frowned: 'When you say "lows" you mean the tops of the hills, is that correct?'

'Where the burial barrows are, yes,' said Mr Redfern, patiently, used to answering the question from visitors unfamiliar with the local terminology. 'Mr Salt excavated the burial chamber up there on Grin Low just before the turn of the century.'

'You see, Mr Redfern, I'm interested in the late Bronze Age and the evidence from that period is very rare, particularly in this part of the country. These people were still at the stage of hunting animals and gathering food rather than growing crops which, of course, allowed them, or should I say caused them, to move about quite freely. They weren't tied to farms the way we are so they probably didn't settle in one place for any length of time.'

'But they must have stopped sometimes, surely,' objected Eleanor.

'Yes, certainly, but they seem to have left almost no trace of such occupation. I should like to be the first to find and document it. Evidence of their existence has only been found because of the burial sites but those sites are quite isolated. On the tops of hills and exposed to bad weather. Not particularly comfortable places to live, so it is reasonable to suppose that the everyday lives of these people must have been lived somewhere else away from the burial sites.'

'I see what you mean,' said Mr Redfern, smiling. 'Especially round here.'

'If you had a choice, would you live up at Grin Low?' asked Eleanor, looking at Mr Redfern.

'Certainly not,' said Mr Redfern. 'Perishing cold in winter, and no running water. I'd be down there in the valley.' He pointed down the slope towards the river Wye, which at that point was only a small, fast-flowing stream on a rocky bed. 'You'd best look down there.'

'That's very interesting,' said Mr Ashworth. 'You see, it's my belief that these people, despite the fact that they lived so long ago, were not very different from us. Consequently, you would expect them to prefer the more hospitable areas along the valley floor. The problem is, though, it is very likely that they considered water to have magical properties, and certain places where there is water would have been sacred to them. Living one's everyday life next to a sacred river might have been considered disrespectful, offensive even. It would be the same as us eating our breakfast bacon and eggs or washing our dirty clothing in a church.'

'But surely living next to a burial mound would be just as disrespectful as us camping in a graveyard,' countered Mr Redfern.

'You have understood my dilemma precisely, Mr Redfern.'

'So where does that leave you?' asked Mr Redfern.

'It leaves me thinking that perhaps these people moved between the same, semi-permanent sites each year, in a sort of seasonal rotation. That would mean that the people who left those artefacts and bones in the Cavern and buried their relatives on Grin Low only came here for some of the time each year.'

Mr Redfern laughed. 'Aye, like all our visitors. If they had any sense, they would only come for the Season. It gets pretty cold here in the winter, even if you are wearing a bear skin. Anyway, if they did want somewhere permanent, trying to build up there on the top of the hill at Grin Low would be a stupid idea. It's solid rock underneath. Even today, with our machines, it would be nigh on impossible so how would they do it with only stone tools or bits of bone to dig with?'

'I agree,' said Mr Ashworth. 'I am thinking that the source of the river is a more likely site. That is why I am particularly interested in investigating that site down there, close to the road.' He pointed down-hill towards a group of houses on the far edge of the golf course.

'You're not the only one interested in that, then,' said Mr Redfern. 'There's someone else interested, a business man.'

'Oh, really,' said Mr Ashworth, frowning with concern. 'What is his interest, do you know?'

'Oh, I shouldn't worry. He's not a university man, like yourself. He won't steal your ideas. He's a Manchester man. He wants to make money. He's had his chaps up here surveying the land. I did hear that he has it in mind to sell the local water. Daft idea, if you ask me.'

'I see,' said Mr Ashworth. 'I jolly well hope they are not disturbing any valuable archaeological evidence.'

'So do I, because I, for one, am very curious to know who these people were who left bits and pieces of their lives in my Cavern. I shall be most interested if you do find out anything about them and I hope you will let me know.'

'I certainly shall,' said Mr Ashworth. 'Now, I do have one last question, if I may. This item here.' He pointed to the list. 'It is described as "fragments of jet possibly Bronze Age" but there is no indication as to where these fragments were found or by whom.'

'Well,' said Mr Redfern, slowly, 'I don't rightly know. What year would it have been?' He looked at Mr Ashworth's piece of paper. 'Nineteen ought three.' Mr Redfern stroked his chin. 'Now you've got me. Let's see, Mr Salt and his lads were digging up at Silverlands around about then, when Holker Road was being put through to Spring Gardens. The excavations up there caused quite a bit of interest. A bit of Roman era material was uncovered but I don't recall anyone mentioning anything older than that. Do you, Miss Harriman?'

'No,' said Eleanor. 'I wasn't very old at the time but I do remember how excited everyone was thinking that the missing Roman fort had been found. Everyone's attention was focussed on that.'

'There was a fort here?' asked Mr Ashworth, 'as well as the Roman baths?'

'Possibly,' said Eleanor. 'No-one is really sure. There certainly was a fort at Brough, which is just north east of here and it's thought that the soldiers from there came to Buxton to bathe. The remains of the old Roman road from Brough have been found but no-one knows exactly when the soldiers were here. If they only started to come in the later Roman period when life was more settled, perhaps they didn't need a fort.'

Mr Redfern had not been paying attention to the conversation. He was frowning as he concentrated his thoughts. 'No, wait a minute. Now that you mention it, I've got a vague recollection that I heard tell of something that had been found. A piece of jewellery, was it? Or a brooch? Something to do with clothing…' He paused again. 'Only it wasn't found at Silverlands.' Mr Ashworth waited expectantly while Mr Redfern stared at the ground. 'No, I can't remember. It will come to me, eventually. So, why don't I give you a tour of the Cavern and maybe it will occur to me as we go.'

Eleanor said good-bye and left the two gentlemen to their tour of the Cavern. She and Napoleon meandered their way back to Hall Bank.

~O~

Later that afternoon, when Philip returned home from Manchester, he telephoned to thank Eleanor for looking after Mr Ashworth and to tell her that he had been successful at the auction and that his client was very contented with the result. He said he would call in at Hall Bank if that was convenient because he had other news to impart. When he arrived, Eleanor, Edwin and Mr Harriman, accompanied by Napoleon, were sitting in Mr Harriman's office. At the end of the working day, they generally met for a short time to keep each other up to date with the work they were doing, and to discuss any developments in the law which might be relevant to their clients. James appeared in the doorway.

'All done, James?' said Mr Harriman.

'Yes, Mr Harriman, I'll say goodnight. Goodnight, Mr Talbot, Miss...' James was interrupted by the doorbell. '...Eleanor. I'll answer that on my way out.'

'It's only Mr Danebridge, James.' said Eleanor.

'Very good, Miss Eleanor.'

'Thank you, James,' said Mr Harriman. 'Good night.'

They all looked expectantly in the direction of the front hall and Philip Danebridge appeared. Napoleon bounded forward to greet him.

'I come with exciting news,' announced Philip, taking off his hat and patting Napoleon but not bothering with the usual greetings to anyone else. 'Or disturbing news, depending on one's attitude to this Steen fellow we keep hearing about.'

'Do tell,' said Eleanor, 'but if it is bad news, you will be banished.'

'I'll let you decide,' said Philip. He fished a leaflet out of his coat pocket. 'Mr Steen has posed this question and I quote: "What could be more refreshing at the end of a long journey than Steen's famous fruit flavoured beverages?" End of quote.'

'Why do advertising people insist on using those annoying rhetorical questions?' said Mr Harriman, dismissively.

'Was that a rhetorical question?' responded Eleanor, smiling at her father.

'What is our concern with Mr Steen and his fruit flavoured beverages?' asked Edwin. 'And, if they are famous, how is it that I have not heard of them?'

'Enough of your rhetorical questions!' said Philip, waving the leaflet about. 'In this particular case, Mr Steen actually does want an answer to his question. He is very obligingly offering both the long journey and the fruit flavoured beverages in order for us to make up our own minds. We are being invited to judge for ourselves.'

'And what form will this long journey take?' asked Mr Harriman, the note of scepticism plainly evident in his voice.

'Mr Steen is proposing a Motor-car Rally,' said Philip.

'And no doubt these beverages will be on sale,' said Mr Harriman, still unimpressed.

'On the contrary,' said Philip, referring again to the leaflet, 'each person who finishes will be offered a free bottle of Steen's fruit flavoured beverages. It says so, here in black and white.' Philip flicked the paper with his finger for effect. 'And what is more, it says that the prize for the winner of the Rally is a handsome cheque for five pounds.'

'What a stupid expression! How can a cheque be either handsome or ugly?' asked Edwin, refusing to be won over.

'Cynic,' said Philip. 'Or do I mean philistine? Either will do. Anyway, what do you all think? Shall we go?'

'Hmm,' said Eleanor, 'five pounds is quite a substantial amount of money. It sounds to me as though Mr Steen's real motive is not to advertise his products but rather to ingratiate himself with the town. I suspect him of offering bribes.'

'I'm going to ignore that remark,' said Philip, undaunted.

'The Rally is to start from the Palace Hotel...'

'That's where Mr Steen is staying,' interrupted Eleanor. 'How convenient.'

Philip glared at Eleanor and gave a theatrical sigh. He continued: '...at twelve thirty sharp on Saturday the thirteenth of May. And, again I quote: "All types of motor-cars will be eligible to compete and allowance will be made for less powerful motors." Therefore, I shall expect you all to take part.' Philip included them all in the sweep of his arm.

'And where does he intend this Rally to finish?' asked Mr Harriman.

'Castleton,' said Philip. 'The route is via Sparrowpit.'

'Good heavens!' said Mr Harriman. 'Why would he not choose the route via Hope, at least? Does this man know anything about the roads in this vicinity?'

'Apparently not,' laughed Philip.

'Absurd!' said Edwin. 'Utter madness!'

'Ten miles of indifferent roads,' said Mr Harriman. 'I don't think many motor-cars will survive that so, if he is trying to ingratiate himself as Eleanor suggests, he is going about it entirely the wrong way. I doubt many people would thank him for the repair bill for the damage after such a gruelling drive.'

'Well, at least it will make the town's motor-car repairers very happy,' said Edwin.

'Oh, I don't know,' said Philip, 'the last time I was out that way I did not find the roads in such poor condition and the weather is quite settled at the moment. I am rather inclined to join in. I'm sure the Bentley could manage it. What about it?'

'The thirteenth, you say? That's next week. It's rather short notice,' grumbled Edwin.

When Mr Steen had decided to organise the Motor-car Rally to promote his company's fruit flavoured beverages, he thought that he should allow at least three weeks in which to advertise the event, thus giving his product maximum publicity beforehand. He had consulted the calendar and favoured holding the Rally on Whit Monday, at the beginning of June. On a Bank Holiday he could expect to attract a large crowd. However, he then learned that it was usual on that day for the two railway companies to run Bank Holiday excursion trains into Buxton Spa from Manchester and Sheffield. There would be a great influx of people into the town, a captive market for his beverages, and he did not want to miss such an opportunity by being out of town in Castleton instead. He next considered bringing the Rally forward to the last Saturday in May. Then he discovered that, in Castleton, Oak Apple Day on the twenty-ninth of May, was always celebrated as Garland Day, with a parade and a ceremony. He thought that would be an ideal venue for selling his fruit flavoured beverages and he wanted to take full advantage of that event and not have it competing with the Rally. He had weighed up the advantages to be gained from these two additional marketing opportunities against the sacrifice of the short period of publicity available, and decided to bring the Rally forward to mid-May.

Eleanor could see that Philip had probably already made up his mind to join the Rally and she thought it might be rather fun. She said: 'I can see Philip is longing to take part. I'll happily go with Philip but only on condition that I can skip the fruit flavoured beverages.' Philip grinned at Eleanor and Eleanor looked from Philip to Edwin, who had recently purchased a three litre, four cylinder, side valve Riley tourer, which was both reliable and capable of speed. She looked back at Philip and smiled. 'Why don't you try it, Edwin?' she asked. 'I'm sure your motor-car would make it.' Edwin looked doubtful. Eleanor continued: 'And, if Helen will join you, Edwin, we can take a picnic and make a day of it.'

'Good egg!' said Philip. 'What do you say, Edwin?'

'I shall see what Helen thinks,' said Edwin, solemnly. 'I make no promises.'

Although Edwin did not sound very enthusiastic, Eleanor suspected that he would not be able to resist the temptation and would decide to join them.

'What about you, Mr Harriman, are you inclined to join the fun?' asked Philip.

'The nonsense, you mean. No, thank you. Fortunately, I can plead a prior engagement. I shall be in Oxford at my College's Gaudy.'

'Jolly good,' said Philip, 'but you will miss Mr Steen's fruit flavoured beverages. You won't find any of those being served in Hall.'

'No,' said Mr Harriman, gravely. 'I think I shall be able to bear the disappointment.'

Edwin stood up: 'Well, I must be off before Philip involves us in any more of his madcap schemes. Good night all.' He moved towards the front door and took his hat from the peg in the hall.

'I should go too,' said Philip. 'Don't forget we're playing golf with Catherine on Wednesday morning, Eleanor. I shall call for you at eight thirty if that suits you.'

'Yes, thank you.'

'I'll come with you,' said Mr Harriman, also reaching for his hat. 'I'm off to the club. I'll see if anyone there knows anything about this Steen fellow and his Rally. I shan't be long, Eleanor. I still have to read over that paper for the conference tomorrow.'

Napoleon stood up and looked at Eleanor, indicating that it was time for a walk. 'Come on, then,' she said, stroking his ears. 'Let's go!'

~O~

Over at the Palace Hotel, one hundred and fifteen delegates

were getting into evening dress ready to attend the welcome dinner of the National Congress of the Institute of Business Proprietors, Directors, and Investors, an annual event which, this year, was taking place in Buxton Spa. The welcome dinner was always held at eight o'clock on the first evening and the conference itself began the following day. Although the Palace Hotel was over fifty years old, it prided itself on being able to supply the very latest amenities and equipment for the organisers of conferences as well as a variety of diversions for the enjoyment of delegates. The hotel servants had been working since first light, polishing silver and glassware, arranging flowers, setting out tables and chairs, cleaning rooms, and sorting linen and, during the afternoon the delegates had started arriving and settling in to their rooms. Buxton Spa was a popular venue for conferences and attracted many of the nation's clubs and corporations. It offered a wide selection of good hotel accommodation as well as excellent entertainment facilities capable of providing welcome relief from the long days of listening which are an inevitable part of such gatherings.

Mr Walter Steen was not a member of the Institute of Business Proprietors, Directors, and Investors but its objectives, aimed at promoting capitalism, were dear to his heart and that evening he found himself chatting to some of the delegates in the bar before dinner and in the coffee room afterwards. Unfortunately for Mr Steen, the town had also attracted the attention of those at the other end of the political spectrum, including several representatives of the socialist-leaning Workers Control Party. Several of these gentlemen had arrived from Leeds in the previous week and had taken up more modest lodgings in the High Street. They had attended the political rally in the Market Place and, on the three evenings since then, had given public lectures offering an alternative view of capitalism. They had also visited various public houses in town listening to the views of local workers and sowing seeds of dissent. In the course of this activity, they had heard people discussing the water bottling scheme. Mr Steen had recently attracted their attention over the safety of his Manchester factory and his relations with his employees so when the members of the Workers Control Party sensed the general feeling of disapproval towards Mr Steen, they encouraged it.

CHAPTER FOUR

Mr Harriman had been invited to address the National Congress of the Institute of Business Proprietors, Directors, and Investors on the first day of proceedings and he had prepared a paper on the subject of the new laws relating to trademarks. The Irish Free State had been created the previous year and the southern part of Ireland, now independent, had ceased to be part of the United Kingdom. Special provisions had been introduced by the Westminster government to allow existing United Kingdom trademarks to be converted to Irish registrations. Mr Harriman had been asked to explain the effect that these new laws would have on the businesses and trademarks of the delegates at the Congress. He had read through his paper the previous evening when he returned from his club and at half past ten the following morning, had departed for the Palace Hotel ready to deliver his lecture.

At a quarter past two, Mr Harriman returned to Hall Bank. He was greeted by Napoleon and then by Mrs Clayton, who made sure that he had been given lunch at the hotel. Edwin and Eleanor were in the dining room having just finished their lunch.

'Hello, Father,' said Eleanor. 'Welcome back.'

'Well, Harriman, how was the talk?' asked Edwin.

'It went quite well,' said Mr Harriman. 'They were an attentive audience and some of the questions were pertinent. The usual grandstanders, of course, delivering a monologue in the guise of a question but, no, on the whole, I think it was worthwhile.'

'We might get some work from them, I suppose,' said Edwin, without enthusiasm.

'Perhaps,' said Mr Harriman, doubtfully. 'They are nearly all from outside the area. However, they paid me handsomely for my time. One curious thing though, and this will interest you, Eleanor. Tea was being served by the hotel servants between lectures and I was chatting to some of the delegates. I was introduced to a Mr Lester who wanted to ask me about a recent decision regarding a registered design. I knew of the case, *Alfmour Ltd.* v *Mayhew*, but, as I told Mr Lester, I had only read the headnote and not the report itself, so I was not familiar with all the details. The case involved two former partners. One of the partners had created the design for a glass bottle some time before the partnership was formed and the case turned on whether or not the design had subsequently become partnership property. The Court's decision did not alter the current position regarding assets of a partnership but Mr Lester expressed the view that he and several of his colleagues considered the result to be unsatisfactory. His sympathy was all with the partner who was unsuccessful and he could not understand why there had not been an appeal. As we discussed the merits of the decision, several other people joined in and there was quite an animated exchange of views. I even noticed one of the hotel servants stop what he was doing and listen in. He and his assistant were setting up the lantern slide projector for the next speaker. Well, to get to the point of my telling you all of this, Mr Lester told me that the person behind the litigation and in control of the plaintiff, Alfmour Ltd, was none other than your Mr Steen, Eleanor. I'm afraid Mr Lester couldn't provide any further information either about Mr Steen or his company.'

'By Jove, Harriman! That was a piece of luck!' said Edwin.

'Yes, that's marvellous. Thank you, Father. I shall read

the report of that case this afternoon,' said Eleanor. 'It might give me some idea of the sort of person Mr Steen is and it will certainly give me a lead for further investigation.'

During the afternoon, Eleanor and Edwin both read the report of *Alfmour Ltd.* v *Mayhew* and, at the end of the day, when they had tidied their desks and put away their files, they went into Mr Harriman's office to discuss the issues in the case. Napoleon settled down in his usual place beside Eleanor and snoozed happily.

'I should love to know more about the background to this case,' said Eleanor.

'Well,' said Mr Harriman, 'I may be able to help you there. I had another look at the report this afternoon. Previously, I had only read the headnote and I didn't take notice of the names of counsel appearing for the parties but, as luck would have it, senior counsel appearing for the plaintiff was Penn-Halford, K.C.'

'Your friend,' said Edwin. 'He's at Lincoln's Inn, isn't he?'

'Yes. He and I were up at Oxford together.' He turned to his daughter. 'Eleanor, you will remember my mentioning him.'

'Yes, I do remember you mentioning him but more in the context of the scrapes you both used to get into at Oxford than for anecdotes relevant to the law,' said Eleanor, dryly.

'I shall ignore that. You may also remember that on Friday I am going to Oxford for my College's Gaudy and I am expecting to see Penn-Halford there. He may be able to tell me more about your Mr Steen and his court case.'

Eleanor was delighted. 'Oh, that would be wonderful. I do hope so. I've been wondering if there was a newspaper report of the case. It is the sort of one-sided story that newspaper reporters love and they might have given personal details of the parties. The more we know about Mr Steen the better equipped the golf club will be to oppose him.'

'Why not write to our London agents and ask them to contact a press-clipping agency? You can charge it to the office account,' said Mr Harriman, as Edwin nodded in agreement. 'I suspect that it would be of benefit to us all to know a bit more about this fellow.'

'Good. I'll do that now and leave the draft for James to copy and send out first thing tomorrow morning,' said Eleanor.

~O~

Early the following morning, Philip called for Eleanor in his motor-car to take her to the golf course as arranged. They intended to play a round of golf with their friend, Catherine Balderstone, one of the local doctors, before the course got busy. At the end of the tennis season the previous year, Eleanor and Philip had decided to take up golf. They still played social tennis but as Philip's lungs, gassed during the War, were no longer strong enough for him to play tennis at tournament level, they had turned to another sport to satisfy their love of competition. Philip parked in front of the Club House and he and Eleanor got out of the motor-car. Before they could turn to go to the Club House to find Catherine, Eleanor saw one of the caddies running full tilt towards her. He was breathing hard and that made his words disjointed, but the tone of urgency in his voice was clearly apparent.

'Oh, Miss, Miss,' he called out, breathlessly. 'There's a body!' He pulled up abruptly in front of Eleanor and then half turned to wave his arm in the direction from which he had come.

Eleanor looked rather startled and frowned at him. 'A body? What sort of body, Percy?'

'I think he's dead, Miss Harriman,' said Percy, collecting his thoughts. 'He's just lying there, ever so still.'

'Where?'

'On the fourth, near where the footpath crosses the fairway. But he might not be dead though.'

'Right,' said Eleanor. 'Mr Danebridge and I will go and have a look. We're meeting Dr Balderstone this morning and I see that her motor-car is already here. You go to the Club House and find her. Ask her to come quickly in case the man is still alive.'

Eleanor and Philip headed off towards the fourth hole and by the time they reached it Catherine and Percy were not far behind. Percy was absolutely correct; there was a body. A man was lying face downwards in the rough grass at the edge of the green with his feet pointing towards the green. Catherine knelt down beside him. 'There is a pulse. Faint, but still there.'

Turning to the caddie, Eleanor said: 'Percy, you run back to the Club House and ask Mr Greenwood or Mr Saunders to call an ambulance and then get the stretcher and bring it back here quick as you can.'

'Right you are, Miss Harriman,' said Percy and disappeared at speed.

Catherine then examined the body and checked for broken limbs or wounds. As she did so, Eleanor said to Philip: 'That jacket is similar to the one that Mr Ashworth was wearing on Monday. I do hope this is not Mr Ashworth.'

Philip said: 'It is not an unusual style. It might not be him.'

'Well,' said Catherine, 'he is still alive but I need to get him to hospital as soon as possible. Ah, here's Percy. Good lad! Put the stretcher down there. Good morning, Mr Saunders.'

Percy was carrying one end of a rolled-up canvas stretcher followed by Mr Saunders the golf professional, who was carrying the other end.

'Mr Greenwood is calling the ambulance, Dr Balderstone,' said Mr Saunders, as he opened out the stretcher and positioned it next to the body.

'Excellent. Thank you. Now, Philip, you had plenty of experience at this during the War, so if you could just help me to roll him onto the stretcher...'

Eleanor said: 'Oh, dear. It is Mr Ashworth. How awful!'

'Do you know him?' asked Catherine.

'Yes,' said Philip, 'he's a visiting archaeologist.'

When the patient was safely on the stretcher, Philip took the head end and Mr Saunders took the foot end, with Percy trotting along behind. When they had almost reached the Club House, they heard the bell of the ambulance as it approached.

Catherine said: 'I'll go with the ambulance to the hospital.'

'I'll come to the hospital too. I've lost interest in golf for today,' said Eleanor.

'Good,' said Catherine, 'you can identify him. We'll both go in my motor-car. Philip, I think we should inform the police. He has a wound on the back of his head which he did not put there himself.'

'I'll go now,' said Philip, 'and I'll take Percy with me in case he can provide any further information.' As Eleanor and Catherine hurried towards the parking area, Philip turned to Percy and asked: 'What were you doing on the course this early, Percy?'

'I were weeding. We gets paid to weed the greens. The caddies do. And I need some money for the Whitsun Bank Holiday treat.'

'Oh, I see,' said Philip. 'Right, I'll just go and explain to Mr Greenwood where we're going.' He turned to Percy and said: 'It means you'll miss out on your fees for the morning but, don't worry, I'll settle up with Mr Greenwood and see that you don't go short.'

'Thank you very much, Mr Danebridge,' said Percy, as he tugged the peak of his cap. His eyes had lit up at the thought of going to the police station and at the prospect of a ride in Philip's motor-car and he now waited anxiously in case Mr Greenwood, the caddie master, refused to release him.

~O~

As there was nothing more they could do, Eleanor and Catherine left Stephen Ashworth being cared for at the Cottage Hospital and returned to Hall Bank. It was still very early and James had not yet arrived to open the office. They were greeted enthusiastically by Napoleon who bounded downstairs when he heard the front door. Mrs Clayton was in the kitchen and, as soon as she heard Eleanor's voice, she got down the tea caddy and spooned tea leaves into the tea pot. Mr Harriman was in the sitting room and had just finished reading the morning papers. He got up to greet Eleanor and Catherine and they had all just settled themselves when Mrs Clayton came in carrying a tray.

'You're back early, Miss Harriman. Good morning, Dr Balderstone. Here's tea and some biscuits.'

'Oh, thank you, Mrs Clayton,' said Eleanor. 'Just what we need.'

Mrs Clayton looked at Mr Harriman and said: 'Would you like tea, Mr Harriman.'

'Thank you, no, Mrs Clayton. What brings you two back so early? Have Mr Mycock's sheep invaded the course again?'

Eleanor laughed at this reference to a previous incident. 'No, nothing as frivolous as that, I'm afraid,' she said and explained the reason for their return.

'That's dashed unfortunate for the poor fellow. Not much of a welcome to the town. I hope things improve for him.'

Mrs Clayton expressed concern for Mr Ashworth and then, as she was about to return to the kitchen, Philip arrived and was greeted by Napoleon.

'Good morning, Mr Harriman, Mrs Clayton,' said Philip, and then eyeing the plate of home-made biscuits that Mrs Clayton was holding, said: 'Mmm, my favourites.' Mrs Clayton winked at him and went to get more tea and biscuits.

'Did James let you in, Philip?' asked Mr Harriman and when Philip nodded, added. 'Ah, I must have a word with him before he opens up the office, if you will all excuse me.'

Mr Harriman went downstairs and Philip sank into an armchair. Napoleon followed him. 'How is Mr Ashworth?' Philip asked as he scratched Napoleon behind the ears.

'Alive but still unconscious,' said Catherine. 'He is very lucky that Percy found him when he did. He seems to have sustained quite a severe blow to the back of the head. That, in itself, may have been enough to render him unconscious but it is difficult to say because hypothermia may have contributed to his loss of consciousness. Judging by the temperature of the body he had been lying there for some time, probably many hours.'

'How many hours, do you think?' asked Eleanor.

'Difficult to say but possibly all night. His clothes were damp and that would have lowered his temperature considerably. One of the nurses told me that it had rained last night.' Catherine smiled. 'When she was putting her cat out at about nine thirty, light rain was falling and he was reluctant to leave the house. I decided to get a more professional opinion as to the weather conditions than the nurse's cat, so I telephoned from the hospital to Miss Pilkington who takes the readings at the weather station on The Slopes. She told me that the overnight grass minimum was only forty-one degrees. That is quite cold enough to cause hypothermia, especially for someone with wet clothes.'

Eleanor thought for a minute and then said: 'But what would Mr Ashworth have been doing out on the golf course last night?'

'Looking for evidence of Bronze Age settlement, perhaps?' Philip speculated.

'But it would have been dark,' objected Eleanor, then she added, 'at least, I assume so. If Mr Ashworth had been attacked before it got dark, surely someone would have noticed him lying there and gone to his rescue.'

'One would certainly hope so,' said Philip. 'Perhaps there was a moon. I was indoors all evening and didn't notice. Is your Whittaker's handy? It's best to check these things and not make assumptions.'

Eleanor pointed to the bookshelf and, while Philip found and consulted the almanac, Catherine said: 'From the position of the body, I would say he stumbled when he moved from the edge of the green on to the rough, lost his footing and fell forward. If so, that would suggest that it was dark at the time.'

'Hmm,' said Philip, tracing along the line of figures with his fingertip. 'According to Mr Whittaker, it should have been almost a full moon. Moonrise was at four forty-three in the afternoon and sunset at eight forty-nine so, that means by the time it was dark, there could have been moonlight.'

'But only for a short while until it clouded over because it had begun to rain by about nine thirty, remember,' said Eleanor. 'What do you think happened, Catherine?'

'Judging by where he was found,' said Catherine, 'I have two alternative suggestions. One, he was attacked on the green and fell forward into the rough but it is hard to see why he would have been on the golf course. The other, more likely, alternative is this. The green where we found him is only a few yards from the public footpath. I suggest that he was on that footpath when he was hit from behind, that he did not lose consciousness immediately, but was dazed and staggered forward a short way. As he moved from the green to the rough, he tripped and lost his footing. Then he passed out and lay in that position long enough for hypothermia to set in. From then on, he would not have been capable of moving.'

'Which means he may have been walking up the footpath towards Green Lane or down towards Macclesfield Road,' said Eleanor.

'Very probably,' said Catherine, 'but don't ask me which.'

'Surely, if that was the case and it was still light, he would have realised that someone was behind him and been forewarned,' said Philip. 'Wouldn't he have turned towards his attacker or twisted out of the way, and so not have been hit from behind?'

'I think you may be right,' said Catherine. 'Had Mr Ashworth turned, the attacker might have been thrown slightly off balance causing the blow to lose some force. Or Mr Ashworth might have deflected the blow. The nature of the wound and the fact that he remained unconscious long enough for hypothermia to set in suggests a blow of some considerable force.'

'Would the blow have been intended to kill him, do you think?' asked Eleanor.

'That is certainly possible,' said Catherine. She paused, then asked: 'But is it probable? Is it likely even? It does seem a bit melodramatic.'

Eleanor did not respond immediately. She was thinking over Catherine's theory. Then she turned to Philip. 'We need to find out where Mr Ashworth was last evening, particularly after about eight thirty. Where was he staying, do you know?'

'Cramond House, in West Street,' said Philip.

'Hmm,' said Catherine. 'Perhaps he was on his way back there and, if so, presumably he was coming from Green Lane and heading down the footpath. It would not be the shortest way back but it might be the easiest to follow if one is new to Buxton.'

'I suppose it is possible that he had gone back to visit Mr

Redfern to discuss something with him,' suggested Eleanor. 'Mr Redfern's cottage is only a short distance from the top of the footpath. I shall ask Mr Redfern.'

Mrs Clayton came in to offer more tea and provide more biscuits and the diversion caused the trio to change the focus of their discussion.

'How did Percy get on at the police station?' asked Catherine.

'Very well indeed,' said Philip. 'Percy's a good chap. Very bright, and not lacking in self-confidence. Not at all fazed by being at the police station. He explained very clearly and precisely how he came to find Mr Ashworth and what action he had then taken. The sergeant listened carefully to what Percy had to say and noted everything down. Percy was enormously pleased by that. The sergeant asked one of the constables to accompany Percy back to the golf course so that Percy could show the constable where he found Mr Ashworth and I took the two of them back there myself. Percy was fit to burst with pride and he is extremely impressed by his new-found status as a police witness. I imagine that the other caddies will have to listen to Percy recounting his story for some days yet.'

'I suspect it won't be just the caddies either. All the club members for whom Percy caddies will be at risk as well,' said Catherine, laughing. 'Right then, I'll be off. Like you, I've gone off golf for today. I'm going back to the surgery now and I'll try and get back to the course later in the week. I'll call in at the hospital again this evening to check on Mr Ashworth and let you know how he is.'

~O~

After she had finished lunch, Eleanor walked up to Poole's Cavern to see Mr Redfern. There was quite a crowd at the turnstile and Eleanor asked the attendant if Mr Redfern was available. Before the attendant could reply, Mr Redfern spotted Eleanor. He waved to her, finished giving directions to a group of visitors getting ready to visit the Cavern, and came over to the turnstile.

'Good afternoon, Mr Redfern. Can you spare a moment, please, to answer a couple of questions?'

'Good afternoon, Miss Harriman. Certainly. Please come in.' The attendant operated the turnstile and Eleanor went in. Groups of adults and excited children were milling about and, in the small bandstand, a group of musicians was playing a lively tune.

'Come over here where it is not so crowded and we can make ourselves heard. Now then, what can I do for you?'

'Well,' said Eleanor, 'it's about the archaeologist I introduced to you, Mr Ashworth. He was found injured on the golf course this morning and has been taken to hospital. We believe that he may have been attacked somewhere near here last night.'

'Oh dear,' said Mr Redfern, frowning. 'Is he all right? What has happened?'

Eleanor had decided not to be too specific with the details at this stage, knowing from experience that the story would soon become common gossip. It was inevitable that the facts would be embellished or distorted each time the story was told to the point where potential witnesses could become confused as to what they actually saw and what they imagined they had seen.

'We're not sure yet,' she said. 'He was unconscious when he was found so no-one has been able to talk to him. He was found not far from here and we don't know why he was in this area. We wondered if, by any chance, he had come back to visit you last evening. He was very interested in what you were able to tell him.'

'Oh, I see,' said Mr Redfern. 'No, he wasn't here. I had an appointment with that gentlemen from Manchester last

evening. He wanted to know about the river in the Cavern.'
Mr Redfern paused and thought for a moment. 'I wonder,' he
continued, 'you may remember that Mr Ashworth was
interested in a find described as fragments of jet which were
thought to be from the Bronze Age.'

'Yes,' said Eleanor. 'He particularly wanted to know
where they had been found.'

'That's right, and after Mr Ashworth had left here, I
remembered that some time back, at the turn of the century
it would have been, there was a report that someone had
found what was thought to be part of a necklace. It occurred
to me that the reported find and the jet fragments on Mr
Ashworth's list might be one and the same, but I could not
for the life of me remember who had made the find. I
thought William Salt might remember because he was
working with his father then. Sometimes even the slightest
piece of information can set you in the right direction so I
telephoned to Cramond House and left a message for Mr
Ashworth to go and see William Salt.'

'That's very helpful. I'll go and see Mr Salt,' said Eleanor.
'Thank you very much for your time, Mr Redfern. I'll let
you get back to your visitors. They look as though they are
getting restless.'

Mr Redfern laughed. 'Give Mr Ashworth my best wishes
when you see him next.'

Eleanor left Mr Redfern and went back through the
turnstile. She decided to visit Mr Salt on her way back to
Hall Bank. It was only a short walk from Green Lane to his
shop on the High Street. She was pleased that Philip was not
with her because Mr Salt dealt in antiques and nothing in
the world would have deterred Philip from browsing and
then having a long conversation with Mr Salt about some
piece or another that had attracted his attention. It would
have taken some time before she was able to get Mr Salt's
attention. As it was, she was able to explain the purpose of

her visit and receive an immediate response.

'Oh, yes,' said Mr Salt, 'Mr Ashworth came to see me. I am sorry to hear that he is in hospital. He asked me about the jet fragments. Mr Redfern's recollection about pieces of a necklace being found may be perfectly correct but, unfortunately, I cannot recall such a find. I suggested to Mr Ashworth that the find might have been reported in the *Advertiser* at the time and, if so, the name of the person concerned would probably be mentioned. Mr Ashworth said he would go to the newspaper's office immediately and he asked me for directions.'

Eleanor thanked Mr Salt for his help and returned to Hall Bank. She had other work to do and did not have time to go browsing amongst old newspapers.

~O~

Edwin Talbot had been in Manchester for most of that day, first of all at a conference with counsel and then in Court. When he arrived back at Hall Bank, just before the office closed, he took off his hat and coat and went straight into Eleanor's office. Mrs Clayton, hearing Edwin come in, took two cups of tea into Eleanor's office.

'Oh, thank you, Mrs Clayton. That is most welcome. It's been a long day but an interesting one. During the luncheon adjournment, I bumped into a solicitor whom I know. We were swapping stories and he told me about a prosecution, still waiting for a hearing date apparently. It's against Mr Steen's company. There was an accident in his factory last year and a worker was badly injured. The other solicitor wasn't sure exactly what had happened but he had heard that the safety guard on some machinery had been removed to speed up production.'

'Dear me! We don't want that sort of fellow setting up a factory here,' said Mrs Clayton.

'We certainly do not,' agreed Edwin.

'It seems that Mr Steen is no stranger to litigation, then,' said Eleanor.

'There's certainly feeling against him in the town,' said Mrs Clayton. 'Those political people, the ones with something to do with workers...'

'The Workers Control Party?' suggested Eleanor.

'Yes, them, they've been talking about Mr Steen, spreading rumours about him, but perhaps they're not rumours, after what Mr Talbot has just said. Perhaps there's some truth in what they say.'

Mrs Clayton returned to the kitchen to finish preparing dinner and Eleanor and Edwin chatted about Edwin's day. Then, as Eleanor was explaining what had happened to Mr Ashworth, Philip arrived to take Eleanor to the Cottage Hospital to check on Mr Ashworth's progress.

As they drove to the hospital, Eleanor said: 'Since I last saw you, I've been thinking about what happened to Mr Ashworth. Surely, there must be some reason for his being attacked. Do you suppose it was just a simple case of robbery?'

'It's hard to think of any other motive,' said Philip. 'That's the usual reason, isn't it? Other than being involved in a fight, but from the way he was lying when we found him, he hadn't been fighting. Catherine was certain that he had been hit from behind.'

'What would he have had with him that was valuable, apart from money, say?'

Philip thought for a moment and said: 'Some of those artefacts he kept telling us about?'

'When I saw him on Monday, all he had was a list and he was still looking for the things on that.'

'What if he had found something that day?' suggested Philip.

'But he hasn't been here long enough to find anything,

surely,' said Eleanor.

'Perhaps he had been given something,' said Philip.

'Hmm. That's possible, I suppose. We could ask one of the nurses to check Mr Ashworth's things and see if anything has been stolen.'

'Yes. That is a very sensible idea.'

The nurse who had been on duty when Stephen Ashworth had been admitted was just going off duty. She was tidying her desk ready to leave. She recognised Eleanor and said that Mr Ashworth was in a stable condition but, as he was still not conscious, no visitors were allowed. Eleanor then asked what had happened to Mr Ashworth's things.

'We wondered if we could possibly check his things to make sure that nothing was stolen when he was attacked,' explained Eleanor. 'Do you think we could do that?'

'He had a haversack but it only had a few tools, sort of hammer things, and a notebook. His pockets were searched and everything of value has been noted and locked safely away. I can look at the list of valuables, if you like.' The nurse opened a folder on her desk, took out a piece of paper and read: 'Watch, fountain pen, propelling pencil, wallet containing money and a train ticket.'

'May I ask how much money?' said Philip.

'Twenty pounds in notes and eight shillings and sixpence halfpenny in coins,' said the nurse, reading from the list. She added: 'Twenty pounds is more than a year's wages for some people and certainly worth stealing, so it doesn't seem that he was robbed, does it?'

'And there was nothing else of value?' asked Eleanor.

'No,' said the nurse. 'We put this last item on the list just in case but we weren't sure what it was. It was in the top pocket of his jacket and it looked like stones, so we put "four black stones" on the list.'

'I see. Well, thank you very much for your help,' said Philip. 'We'll come back later and see how he is.'

As they left the hospital, Eleanor said: 'That seems to rule out robbery as a motive but it leaves us with a bit of a puzzle. Where did those stones come from? They might explain where Mr Ashworth was last night.'

'How so?' asked Philip.

'Well, Mr Ashworth was interested in locating some jet fragments which are supposed to be from the Bronze Age. When I went back to see Mr Redfern after lunch, he told me that he had recalled a story about part of a necklace having been found some years ago. He couldn't remember any details but he wondered if the jet fragments on Mr Ashworth's list referred to that find. He suggested that Mr Ashworth should talk to Mr Salt. I went to see Mr Salt and he confirmed that Mr Ashworth had been to see him. Mr Salt wasn't able to help Mr Ashworth but he suggested that he check the archives at the *Buxton Advertiser* office. Perhaps, Mr Ashworth went there and did find out who had the jet fragments. Perhaps they are the stones that were in his pocket.'

'That sounds plausible and, if you are right, it is also possible that the person who had the fragments lives somewhere near where Mr Ashworth was found.'

Eleanor sighed. 'We shall have to wait until he regains consciousness before we can find out.'

As he left Eleanor, Philip said: 'If you haven't been put off golf completely, shall I call for you tomorrow morning so we can play our missing round?'

'Yes, please do. I'll see if Catherine is free.'

CHAPTER FIVE

The following morning, Napoleon bounded down the stairs at Hall Bank and sat beside the front door.

'No, Napoleon, you stay here,' said Eleanor, as she reached the bottom of the stairs. 'We're off to golf.'

Napoleon gave Eleanor a reproachful look. His front paws slid forward taking his weight as he slumped down and then rested his chin on the floor. He was puzzled by this golf business. Tennis, he knew about. When Eleanor went to play tennis she was not away for long and very often he was allowed to sit on the side-lines and watch. Golf, apparently, took much longer than tennis and, worse, he was banished. When Eleanor left to play golf, he resigned himself to a lengthy wait knowing there would be hours before there was any chance of a walk. He was not happy.

'What's the matter, old chap?' said Philip. 'Not keen on golf?'

'He hasn't tried it,' said Eleanor. She paused and looked at Napoleon. 'Although I don't see why he shouldn't.'

'I've seen other dogs on the course,' said Philip. 'Not nearly as well behaved as Napoleon.' Napoleon sat up, put his head on one side, and looked at Philip. 'It should be all right, as long as he remains still during strokes, especially at the tee. I think we can trust him.'

'Come on, then,' said Eleanor, reaching for his lead. 'You'll have to stay on your lead but I'm sure you won't mind that.'

As they drove to the golf course in Philip's motor-car, Napoleon sat contentedly on the back seat, smiling at the world and enjoying the breeze through his fur. When they arrived at the Club House, they were greeted by Mr Greenwood, the caddie master.

'You're in luck, Miss Harriman, Mr Danebridge. It's not very busy at the moment. Is Dr Balderstone joining you today?'

'No, not today, unfortunately,' said Eleanor.

'Right, well, Percy'll caddy for you, Miss Harriman, if you like. Thomas is available for Mr Danebridge. There's a couple just teed off and there's no-one ahead of them.'

'Thank you, Mr Greenwood,' said Eleanor. 'Hello, Percy. How are you today?'

'Not so bad, thank you, Miss Harriman.' Percy eyed Napoleon. 'Is he coming?' Percy was very wary of large dogs and when he saw Napoleon he stood well back.

'Yes,' said Eleanor. 'This is Napoleon. He won't be any trouble, I'm sure.'

Percy had no time for the terriers and small lap dogs that some of the members brought on to the course. They were possessive of their owners and aggressive towards other dogs. They yapped shrilly and ran around pointlessly in circles making a nuisance of themselves. Percy found them very distracting and wanted them banned, as did some of the other golfers.

'Ah, here's Thomas. Good morning,' said Philip.

Thomas looked at Napoleon. 'He's big, aint he?' he said. He walked up to Napoleon confidently and held out his hand, palm down. Napoleon sniffed at it appreciatively. 'He'll do,' said Thomas. He hoisted Philip's bag of clubs onto his shoulder and set off.

At the first tee, Eleanor told Napoleon to sit and then gave his lead to Philip to hold. Napoleon sat obediently and watched with interest as Eleanor teed off. Then he watched as Philip repeated the process. Eleanor and Philip, followed by Percy and Thomas, walked forward and Napoleon trotted happily along beside Eleanor. By the time they had completed two holes, Napoleon had decided that golf was much more interesting than tennis. Instead of having to watch from the side-lines, he was part of the game. He quickly understood what was required of him: sit perfectly still at the tee or during a stroke, follow the flight of the ball, sit still at the edge of the green during putting, watch the little ball disappear into the hole, and then take a quiet stroll before repeating the process again at the next tee. His only regret was that he could not follow the tantalising scent of rabbit which he occasionally detected along the fairway.

Despite his initial reservations about Napoleon, Percy was impressed. 'He's caught on quick, Miss Harriman,' he said to Eleanor, approvingly. 'Understands the rules good and proper.' Napoleon had now conquered Percy.

By the time Eleanor and Philip arrived at the third tee, they had caught up with the couple, a lady and a gentleman, who had started well ahead of them. Those two players were now still on the fairway and Eleanor had to wait for the gentlemen to play his stroke and move to the green before she could tee off.

After watching the player ahead, Philip said to Eleanor: 'I say! That gentleman up ahead has a jolly stylish stroke. He's as good as a professional.'

Eleanor, turning to her caddie, asked: 'Percy, do you know who that gentleman is?'

'Yes, Miss. That's Mr Royston. He's the professional at Bramhall Park.'

'Ah,' said Philip. 'Then I was right.'

'Yes. He clearly is a very experienced player,' agreed Eleanor.

Thomas added, innocently enough but with a slight hint of innuendo, 'I expect he's giving the lady a lesson.'

'And who is the lady? Do you know?' asked Eleanor.

'Captain of Manchester Ladies,' said Percy.

'Mrs Steen,' added Thomas.

'Oh,' said Eleanor, nodding. She made no further comment and prepared to tee off.

They played the fourth hole, the longest of the course, which ran parallel with Green Lane. As Eleanor waited at the green for Philip to hole out, she noticed that the two players ahead were now standing at the next tee deep in conversation, a conversation which appeared to Eleanor to be rather more intimate than professional. Eleanor suspected that golf was not the subject of the conversation. Eleanor and Philip walked towards the next tee, stopped a short distance away, and waited. When the lady became aware of their arrival, she moved away from the tee and called out:

'Oh, I'm so sorry. We seem to be lagging behind dreadfully.' She gave a rather self-conscious little giggle. 'Please play through.'

'Yes, please do,' added her partner, as he moved away from the tee and waved them on.

'Thanks awfully,' said Philip. 'Very sporting of you.'

'Not at all,' said the golf professional.

Eleanor did her best not to be intimidated by having to tee off in the presence of a professional golfer and felt that she acquitted herself quite well under the circumstances. Under the pretence of watching Philip tee off, she surreptitiously assessed Mrs Steen's age (well below that of Mr Steen), her dress (an elegant tweed suit, clearly tailor-made at considerable expense), her jewellery (showy and slightly out of place on a golf course), and her demeanour (decidedly coquettish). When they were out of earshot of the couple, and Percy and Thomas had gone ahead to the next green, Eleanor said to Philip: 'What do you make of that?'

'Not a great deal of attention being given to the game,' said Philip.

'No, it did look a bit like an excuse for being together, didn't it?'

'It would be the perfect way to conduct a liaison. Still, it never hurts to take a lesson or two.'

'Except that I happen to know that Mrs Steen is the captain of the Manchester team which is playing against Millicent's team next week and is, according to Millicent, a fearsomely good golfer. So, if that is Mrs Steen from Manchester, well...'

'The need for tuition could be a little difficult to explain,' added Philip.

'There didn't seem to be too much of that going on either,' said Eleanor.

'Perhaps she just wants to familiarise herself with the course, in preparation for next week.'

'In that case, why not use our professional. Mr Saunders knows this course better than anyone from outside.' Eleanor frowned. 'Am I just being mean?'

'No. I think, as usual, your assessment of the situation is absolutely impartial and correct. I would certainly describe the lady's attitude towards her mentor as flirtatious.'

Eleanor smiled and shook her head. 'We sound like the ladies of The Park.'

They regained their concentration and finished the fifth hole. The sixth hole ran parallel with the fifth and in the opposite direction and, as Eleanor and Philip played, they could still see the other two players on the fifth. So could Napoleon. Each time that he had to sit and wait while Eleanor or Philip played a stroke he sat with his back to them and watched the other two players instead. Napoleon was always interested in people so Eleanor did not find this unusual. However, Percy and Thomas thought Napoleon's behaviour was very funny indeed. They both got the giggles and then lost concentration completely. Eleanor and Philip waited, bemused, while they recovered and then apologised. While this distraction was in progress, Eleanor had taken the opportunity to look around her. Some time in the last ten minutes or so, and certainly since they had left the fourth green, several workmen had arrived and were now standing on the golf course near the fourth green. A horse and waggon was standing in the lane. Eleanor drew Philip's attention to the workmen.

'I wonder if those are the same men that Millicent saw last week,' she said. 'They seem to be assembling some sort of equipment. Have you any idea what it could be?'

'It looks like drilling equipment of some kind, which would suggest that the rumours about Mr Steen's plans are true. Perhaps he really is looking for water.'

Eleanor turned to Percy: 'Miss Lee told me last week that she had seen workmen on the golf course. Do you know what they are doing, Percy?'

'There's been a few of 'em here on occasion but they won't say what they're 'ere for. Mr Greenwood asked 'em but he never got a straight answer. They just said they takes their orders from Mr Steen.'

Thomas added: 'They was getting in the way of the players one afternoon when Mr Saunders was giving tuition and he told 'em to clear off. One of 'em threatened to punch him.'

'Oh, that's not very sporting!' said Philip. 'I don't like the sound of that. If that's the sort of man this Mr Steen employs it doesn't reflect very well on him.'

They turned their attention back to the course and completed the round without further distraction.

~O~

The following morning, Catherine telephoned to say that Mr Ashworth had regained consciousness and was well enough to receive visitors. Eleanor and Philip arranged to go to the Cottage Hospital during visiting hours to see him and when they arrived at his ward, found him sitting in a chair next to his bed writing in his notebook.

'You have visitors, Mr Ashworth,' said the nurse, briskly, and bustled away to straighten the bed of one of the other patients.

'Hello, Ashworth, old chap,' said Philip.

'Mr Ashworth,' said Eleanor, 'please don't get up. How are you?'

'I'm recovering quite well, thank you, Miss Harriman,' said Mr Ashworth. 'I believe I have both of you to thank for rescuing me and calling the ambulance.'

'Well, no, not really,' said Philip. 'It was Percy, one of the caddies, who found you. He's a very capable lad. He had the sense to come and find us immediately and, fortunately for you, Dr Balderstone was with us.'

'Yes, she came to see me this morning,' said Mr Ashworth. 'Apparently it was lucky that I was found in time and treated so quickly. Anyway, thank you for what you did. I must go and thank Percy when I leave here.'

'We have been wondering how long you had been lying on the golf course before Percy found you and how you came to be there at all,' said Eleanor.

'When I first came to, my recollection of events was a bit confused. I think I now have a clearer picture of what happened but I must admit to being a bit puzzled.'

'Did you see who attacked you?' asked Eleanor.

'No, not at all.'

'Do you remember anything at all about the attacker?' asked Eleanor.

'No, nothing. Whoever it was took me completely by surprise. All I know is that I was hit from behind but, at the time, I didn't realise anyone was behind me and I didn't hear any footsteps either. That seems a bit odd but I suppose it's because I was on grass and not on the road. I was on the footpath which crosses the golf course, you see.'

'Can I ask why you were on that footpath? Where had you

been?' asked Philip.

'I had been visiting someone in Green Lane, a little way up from Poole's Cavern and I was going back to my lodgings. I noticed some machinery that had been left in Green Lane and that reminded me about Mr Steen. Mr Redfern had mentioned him and I'd heard rumours about his plans. I am very worried about the disturbance his men might cause to any potential archaeology. It was almost dark but I thought I'd walk a little way down the footpath to see if I could get an idea of the site that Mr Steen seems to be interested in. I stood there for a bit and someone must have come up behind me without my noticing.'

'So you were standing still when you were hit?' asked Philip. 'And facing downhill?' he added.

'Yes. Someone must have come down the footpath from Green Lane.'

'And you hadn't seen anyone in the lane before you turned off onto the footpath?' said Philip.

'No, but I might not have been paying particular attention. I was pretty elated by what I had just discovered.'

'May we know what it was that you had discovered?' asked Philip.

'Certainly, although I trust you not to mention it to anyone else. I want to check certain facts first and then make the announcement myself. You may remember, Miss Harriman, when I was talking to Mr Redfern I asked about some fragments of jet which had been found. Mr Redfern couldn't help me but he set me on a trail which eventually led me to the *Buxton Advertiser* and its office on Eagle Parade. I went there to look at the back copies. One of the clerks was very helpful and I found the report I was looking for. It mentioned the name of the man who discovered the fragments, a George Yates, who was a builder. There was a Post Office directory at the newspaper office and I looked up Yates. There were several entries under that name but no George.

However, there was a builder named Martin Yates listed at Hawthorn Cottage on Green Lane so I decided to call there on the off chance. I thought they might know of the person I wanted, even if he was not at that address.'

'And that was on the night you were attacked?' asked Eleanor.

'Yes, I went to Hawthorn Cottage and I explained who I was and what I wanted and it turned out that Mr Martin Yates is the grandson of George Yates. Unfortunately, Mr George Yates died two years ago and nobody else in the family is interested in archaeology. They had decided to give his collection to the museum but, fortunately for me, they still hadn't done anything about it. The grandson said I was welcome to have a look. He invited me in and I spent quite some time looking through the items, all of which were properly labelled and their location recorded. Eventually I found the items I was interested in and Mr Yates was very kind, and agreed to lend them to me. They certainly are fragments of a jet necklace.'

'So, they are the mysterious item described as "four black stones" on the list of your personal effects that the hospital nurse drew up,' said Eleanor.

'Yes,' laughed Mr Ashworth. 'They didn't know quite what to make of them. The really exciting thing is that the fragments were found in the area I have been concentrating on.'

Before Mr Ashworth could get carried away with descriptions of his research, Philip asked: 'And, after you left Hawthorn Cottage, you walked along Green Lane until you got to the footpath?'

'Yes, and that is the last thing I can remember.'

'We are very puzzled as to the motive for the attack,' said Eleanor. 'Of course, robbery is the most likely explanation but that only raises further questions. The things which would be the obvious targets for a thief seem to have been ignored. There was a good deal of money still in your wallet, so we assume that none of it was stolen.'

'That's right. It is all there.'

'Of course,' said Eleanor, 'the person who attacked you might have been disturbed before he found what he was looking for. He might have run away but, in that case, surely you would have been rescued by the person who disturbed the robber. Have you had any thoughts about who might have attacked you?'

'I have been wondering whether the person who attacked me was after the fragments of necklace.'

'But,' objected Philip, 'how would that person have known that you had them?'

'I've had plenty of time to think about it, lying here. The only suggestion that I can come up with is that when I was in the newspaper office, someone heard me talking to the clerk and knew where I was going that evening. There was someone in there at the time who seemed to be particularly interested in our conversation. Perhaps he followed me.'

'To Hawthorn Cottage?' asked Eleanor. Mr Ashworth nodded. 'Were you aware of anyone following you when you were going there?'

'No, not at all, but I wouldn't have been expecting to be followed so, if someone had been there, I might not have noticed.'

'But who could that person in the newspaper office have been? Someone who worked there? A customer? And why would he have followed you?' asked Eleanor.

'No, he didn't work there. I thought he was a customer but he may have been a tout. There are always people listening out for news. People will pay for information about new finds or the whereabouts of artefacts, even if they are stolen.'

'Goodness,' said Eleanor, 'I thought archaeology was a gentlemanly pursuit.'

'Oh, it is!' protested Mr Ashworth. 'But there is a lot of rivalry. People want to be the first to publish when a discovery is made. There is a lot of gossip about which sites people are working on and what progress is being made and not all the people working on the sites are gentlemen. We archaeologists have to employ labourers who, unfortunately, do sometimes try to make extra money by selling information or artefacts.'

'But you haven't seen anyone around lately who might fit one of those categories?' asked Philip, trying to bring Mr Ashworth back to reality.

'No,' said Mr Ashworth. He was about to shake his head but, sensing the pain it would cause if he did so, he remained still. 'As far as I am aware, at the moment, no-one knows of my interest in this site and there is no dig which means I haven't employed any labourers who might gossip.' He thought for a second or two and added: 'The man in the newspaper office might have been one of their reporters, I suppose, and not a customer. There are, of course, newspaper reporters who are always interested in a scoop. They are prepared to pay for information. Archaeology is in the news right now because of the excavations being funded by Lord Carnarvon in Egypt. I believe Howard Carter is constantly besieged by reporters.'

Philip was bemused by the fact that Mr Ashworth seemed to think his work was in the same newsworthy category as that of Howard Carter; however, he did not comment. He merely asked: 'So, what are your plans when they let you out of here?'

'I had only arranged to stay a week and now I shall have to get back to Liverpool but I am hoping to be able to come back fairly quickly because there is certainly material here to interest me.'

Eleanor and Philip chatted to Mr Ashworth for a while longer and then, reassured that he had suffered no permanent damage from the blow on the head, they left him to get some rest.

'Mr Ashworth's theories about the attack are plausible, I suppose,' said Eleanor, 'but I am not sure that I am convinced.'

'No,' agreed Philip. 'If the motive for the robbery was a few small stones, why didn't whoever it was take them?'

'I suppose if the stones were in the pocket of his jacket it would have been difficult to reach them,' mused Eleanor. 'Mr Ashworth was wearing a Norfolk jacket and the pockets button up so that would make the stones more difficult to get to.'

'Hmm,' said Philip, 'but if one had gone to the trouble of knocking him over the head for the purpose of robbing him, why not do a thorough search to make it worthwhile?'

'Yes, and it can't be that the attacker was disturbed and couldn't finish the job of searching because, if there had been anyone else around, Mr Ashworth would have been found earlier. But there must have been some reason for the attack. Surely it couldn't just have been random.'

'I give up,' said Philip. 'Changing the subject altogether, are you still willing to join me on the Motor-Car Rally tomorrow, even though it is organised by the wicked Mr Walter Steen?'

'Absolutely,' said Eleanor. 'Edwin and Helen are coming and Mrs Clayton is putting together a picnic hamper. Father has gone to his Gaudy so Cecily said she would have Napoleon. I just hope we get decent weather.'

'Then I shall call for you at about eleven thirty if that is acceptable.'

When Eleanor arrived back at Hall Bank, she went to find Napoleon. He was sitting at the kitchen door supervising Mrs Clayton who was rolling out pastry on the table top. Mrs Clayton paused, rolling pin in the air, and said: 'Miss Pymble and Miss Felicity called while you were out, Miss

Harriman. They're collecting for the Jumble Sale for the Girls' Friendly Society and wondered if you had anything you might like to contribute.'

The Pymble twins were the elderly cousins of the vicar who had accompanied him to Buxton many years ago. They supported themselves by taking in lodgers and, with great enthusiasm, devoted their spare time to good works. They helped organise events at the church, knew everybody in the parish, and were always interested in the welfare of other people.

'Oh dear!' said Eleanor. 'Has it come around again? I'm sure it's not twelve months since the last one. I always feel terribly guilty about not being able to contribute. We disposed of most of our things when we left Harewood and there's no point in me going to the Jumble Sale and buying something because we simply do not have room for anything else here. Do we have any jumble, Mrs Clayton?'

'I don't think so, Miss Harriman.'

'I don't like to disappoint the Misses Pymble. They work so hard to raise funds. I'll just have to make a donation as usual, I suppose, but it does seem like only half-hearted support.'

'I'm sure they will be grateful for it, nevertheless,' said Mrs Clayton. As Eleanor turned to go, Mrs Clayton added: 'Oh, there was one other thing.' Mrs Clayton put down the rolling pin and dusted her floury hands. 'Miss Pymble mentioned a friend of theirs, Mrs Flax at Woodthorpe House. She takes in lodgers and she has a young man and his wife staying with her, name of Mellor. The young man was badly injured in Mr Steen's factory in Manchester. He's lost the use of his arm and he's come to the Devonshire Hospital for hydrotherapy treatment.'

'Oh, how awful. I wonder if that is the accident Mr Talbot told us about when he came back from Manchester. He said he had heard that Mr Steen's company was being prosecuted because of a factory accident.'

'I could be, I suppose. Apparently, some of those people from the Workers Control Party have been at Mrs Flax's asking questions. They're in all the pubs at the moment so I suppose that's how they found out about him. Alf says it's hardly worth going to The Swan. You can't move for people talking politics and they're all Communists, of course, wanting your vote. Bert Hulley says it's not much better at The Bakers Arms. Alf says he's beginning to wish he couldn't vote. He says if they hadn't changed the law he could have got rid of them by telling them they were wasting their time because he didn't have the vote, although that's not strictly true because he's had it for some time, being a property owner.'

Eleanor laughed, shaking her head at this lack of logic. 'Well, if you hear any more about the man who was injured, let me know, won't you. Oh, and will you remind me about that donation for the Jumble Sale. I'll call around and see the Misses Pymble and take it myself.'

'Right you are, Miss Harriman,' said Mrs Clayton, picking up the rolling pin again and shaking flour onto the table top.

CHAPTER SIX

The office of Harriman & Talbot was generally open on Saturday mornings, but they had agreed to close on the Saturday of the Rally because Mr Harriman had gone to his reunion in Oxford and Eleanor and Edwin were taking part in the Rally. James had been given a holiday. Mrs Clayton came in to serve breakfast and finish preparing the picnic hamper and then she too would have the day free. The sky was overcast but it looked as if the clouds would clear later in the day. After breakfast, Eleanor and Napoleon took advantage of the fact that they had more time than usual for a walk and went up to Solomon's Temple and back. When they returned to Hall Bank, Mrs Clayton was in the kitchen, packing things into the picnic hamper. Napoleon flopped down in the hallway outside the kitchen door to recover from his walk and keep an eye on Mrs Clayton and the food. Eleanor went into the kitchen.

'Do you want tea, Miss Harriman?'

'Yes, please, Mrs Clayton, but don't worry, I'll do it. You keep going with the hamper.' Eleanor made the tea and then sat down at the table and poured them both a cup. 'Are you going to take your boys to see the start of the Rally?'

'I haven't been given much option,' laughed Mrs Clayton. 'They're very keen on motor-cars. They keep on asking Alf when he's going to get one. Oh, that reminds me, Alf heard from someone yesterday that some machinery belonging to Mr Steen has been damaged. He's got drilling equipment or something up on Green Lane and someone's taken to it with a sledge hammer apparently.'

'I suppose it was someone opposed to Mr Steen's project but it seems an extreme way of expressing one's opinion. Ooh, that looks delicious,' said Eleanor, as Mrs Clayton wrapped a home-made pork pie in a cloth and put it into the picnic hamper. 'I'm looking forward to the picnic, although I'm not sure that I shall enjoy Mr Steen's fruit flavoured beverages.'

'I shouldn't worry. I've put some home-made lemonade in for you. I was going to put in some of my ginger beer but then I thought all that going up and down hills wouldn't agree with it.'

Eleanor laughed at the idea of ginger beer all over Philip's motor-car. 'I think that was a very wise choice. Ginger beer would probably explode and Mr Danebridge certainly would not be happy.'

Eleanor left Mrs Clayton and went to get ready. At eleven thirty, Philip arrived at Hall Bank in the Bentley. He parked outside and was surprised to find that Richard was not looking out of the window as usual. Only Napoleon was on duty. Richard was with Eleanor and Cecily in the sitting room instead. The two sisters were occupying the sofa, together with an assortment of driving coats, gloves, scarves and hats which they were sorting through. Richard was supposed to be helping but instead he was trying things on. He was currently wearing a pair of Mr Harriman's motoring goggles and trying to get his hand into a large, leather gauntlet. He had been considered too young to go on the Rally and had expressed his disappointment at this decision. To compensate, Cecily had promised to take him to the Palace Hotel to inspect the motor-cars and watch the start. Napoleon too had been banned from taking part, although he had not yet realised this. It had been agreed that Philip would take Cecily, Richard and Napoleon over to the Palace Hotel in his motor-car and then they would walk back to Oxford House. Eventually, everyone was ready. They trooped downstairs and, after the motoring gear and the picnic hamper had been arranged to Philip's satisfaction, they were ready to start. Mrs Clayton waved them off and went back home to collect her two boys.

It was only a short drive from Hall Bank to the gates of the Palace Hotel. A wide carriage drive swept in a gentle arc from one entrance on Devonshire Road across the front of the hotel to the opposite entrance on Palace Road. As Philip turned the Bentley through the Devonshire Road entrance, one of the race stewards stepped forward in front of the motor-car, his hand raised in a stop sign. Philip stopped the motor-car obediently and the race steward moved towards the driver's side. Turning to him, Philip said: 'Good morning, steward, what's the drill?'

'Good morning, sir. Name, please, sir.'

'Danebridge.'

The steward looked at a list, said "Ah" in a knowing way and fumbled in a large canvas bag slung over his shoulder. He drew out a bundle of large circular wooden discs; each one had a hole at the top and a string threaded through the hole. The steward selected a disc on which was painted the number twenty-four and handed the disc to Philip.

'If you would be so good as to display this number on the radiator, sir, it will help the marshalling stewards. And would you park down at the far end of the line of motor-cars, please, on the far side of the Riley. It's to be a handicap race, sir, you understand.'

'Oh, absolutely,' said Philip, smiling, 'unfair advantage and all that. Mustn't be unsporting, what! Right down the far end, you say?'

'Yes, sir,' said the steward, 'if you wouldn't mind, sir. And when you hear the bell, would you be good enough to assemble with the other drivers at the hotel steps so that the stewards can explain the rules.'

'Jolly good, thank you,' said Philip, cheerfully. He handed

the wooden disc to Eleanor and said: 'Don't worry about the delayed start, old thing. We'll soon catch up.'

Eleanor smiled and said: 'Philip, I'm not in the least bit worried if we don't come first. Or second even. In fact, I shall be grateful if we finish. I'd like to get to the picnic without the bother of split tyres or an overheated engine. But, I suppose for the sake of your motor-car's reputation we shall need to make an effort.'

'We certainly shall,' said Philip, firmly. 'And it looks as though there might be some stiff competition too. Just look at all those motor-cars, Richard.'

'Wizard!' said Richard, excitedly, as they drove slowly past the competitors' motor-cars already lined up on the concourse outside the hotel, parked at an angle and facing away from the hotel ready to drive off. They were arranged in order of handicap.

'Look, Richard. Up ahead. There's Mr Talbot's car,' said Cecily.

Edwin was backing his motor-car into the angled space on the end of the line.

Richard said: 'We're next to Mr Talbot.'

'Yes,' said Eleanor, 'I wonder if there will be anyone on the other side of us.'

'Ooh,' said Richard, enthusiastically, 'I do hope so because that means they would be even faster than a Bentley or Mr Talbot's Riley.'

'I say, whatever happened to loyalty to one's friends!' teased Philip as he backed the motor-car parallel with Edwin's car.

Cecily and Eleanor got out and went to join Edwin and Helen and then Cecily came back to the Bentley together with Edwin. She said to Richard: 'Mr Talbot's going to take you to look at the motor-cars, Richard.' As Richard climbed down, she added: 'No, Napoleon, not you.'

'Come on, Richard,' said Edwin. 'Let's go and assess the

competition.'

Richard stopped in front of the motor-car which had parked in the space on the other side of Edwin's Riley. 'That's a jolly decent motor-car,' he said to Edwin, pointing to a black Crossley. He looked up in awe at the large vehicle, its chrome work gleaming in the sunlight. The driver was dressed in a leather coat and motoring goggles. He was lounging idly beside the motor-car, one arm resting on the spare wheel, and smoking a cigarette. His face was partly hidden by the goggles and Edwin did not recognise him.

'Horse power, nineteen point six,' said the driver to Richard. 'Cylinders, four. Engine, three point eight litres.'

'Golly. How fast can it go?' asked Richard.

'Sixty miles an hour.'

'Oh,' said Richard, sounding disappointed.

'Thank you,' said Edwin politely, nodding to the driver as he steered Richard away to look at the rest of the field. He knew what Richard's next comment would not have been complimentary and did not want to offend the Crossley's owner.

'It's not as fast as Mr Danebridge's motor, is it?' said Richard, as Edwin had expected.

'No, probably not,' agreed Edwin.

'But it might be faster than yours, Mr Talbot.' Richard sounded worried.

'Possibly,' said Edwin, 'but a lot depends on the skill of the driver, you know. It's not always the most powerful engine that wins.'

Richard was reassured and now examined the next motor-car in the line. Edwin recognised the driver, Rufus Wentworth-Streate, who was the son of one of the firm's clients. Two years ago, he had been ensnared by an unscrupulous motor-car salesman into a potentially ruinous purchase and Eleanor had extricated him from the contract. Edwin greeted Rufus and said: 'My friend here is assessing the competition.' He introduced Richard and added: 'Any tips?'

'I think you and Mr Danebridge are pretty strong contenders,' said Rufus, as Richard nodded vigorously in agreement. 'I'm not sure about the Crossley. I don't know the driver but he looks as though he is taking things seriously. This is father's car, of course, and a bit sedate for my taste. Nevertheless, I plan to give it a good run.'

'Well, I'm pleased that you are able to take part, at least,' said Edwin. 'Best of luck.'

Edwin and Richard continued to examine the rest of the field and paused to chat to people Edwin knew. Meanwhile, Helen had attached the numbered disc to the radiator of the Riley and Philip had attached his disc to the Bentley. He had then circled the motor-car, checking that everything was secure and ready to go and Helen and Cecily had watched in amusement at the fussing and fiddling that was deemed necessary. Eleanor and Napoleon were ignoring this activity. They were watching a scene being played out not far from them near the service entrance at the side of the hotel. A very large motor-car and two delivery vans were parked there and Mr Steen was talking to one of the delivery van drivers.

Mr Steen had arranged for two of his delivery vans to take various pieces of equipment and a supply of the fruit flavoured beverages to the finishing line at Castleton. He had also arranged with the manager of the Palace Hotel, on payment of a substantial fee, to have three of the hotel's servants on loan. They were to go with his men to Castleton and serve the beverages and they were delighted at the prospect of a day out. The three servants, one of the hall-porters, a chamber maid, and a waitress were standing in line, all in uniform, waiting for Mr Steen's orders. One of the girls, who was dark-haired, tall and very attractive, was standing close to the man, talking animatedly. The other girl, shorter and blonde, was standing a little apart, looking at the other two. Mr Steen finished giving instructions to the delivery van driver and, turning towards the hotel servants, said: 'Right, you know what to do when you get there. Two of you can go in that van and one in this one. Who's going in this one?' The man and the girl took a very slight step backwards as Mr Steen spoke, as though distancing themselves from the action and Mr Steen pointed to the blonde girl, saying: 'Right, you go in this van.' The other two hotel servants quickly climbed into the second delivery van and both vehicles drove off at speed. Mr Steen disappeared into the hotel and only the large motor-car was left. Its chauffeur, still in shirt-sleeves, was polishing one of the head-lamps.

Eleanor turned her attention back to the Rally. By now, all the competitors had arrived and there were twenty-four motor-cars along the concourse, parked at an angle, rear towards the hotel. A large crowd of hotel guests and townsfolk had gathered and was milling about inspecting the motor-cars and chatting to friends and neighbours. Edwin and Richard returned from their tour of inspection and, as it was almost time for the Rally to begin, Richard, Cecily and Napoleon took up a position on the side of the concourse from which to watch the start. A few minutes before twelve thirty, the large motor-car which had been parked beside the service entrance, an all-weather 3.6 litre Austin coupé, arrived at the front of the hotel and stopped at the foot of the steps which led up to the portico. The chauffeur, now in uniform and cap, got out and stood next to the rear door on the nearside of the motor-car. As the Cambridge chimes rang out from the clock tower of the neighbouring Devonshire Hospital, signalling the half hour, the linkman came out of the hotel entrance and rang a hand-bell. Mr Steen, now wearing a long leather motoring coat, appeared at the top of the steps of the hotel. He waited as the drivers began to congregate on the concourse below and then, stepping forward, he said:

'Welcome, everybody. It is wonderful to see so many of you here today and I am sure we shall all have a great day's motoring. The steward here will explain the rules and he will give each of you the signal to begin. I would ask you to pay careful attention and obey all his directions. I look forward to seeing you all again at the end of the Rally and, don't forget, Steen's fruit flavoured beverages will be there waiting for you. Good luck, everybody and may the best motor-car win. See you in Castleton.'

The crowd applauded. Mr Steen waved and walked down the steps. The chauffeur opened the rear door of the motor-car and Mr Steen climbed in. There was then a pause during which nothing happened. Mr Steen stared resolutely in front of him and the chauffeur resumed his position beside the rear door of the motor-car. The crowd began to murmur and wonder to itself about the delay. Then, Mrs Steen appeared at the entrance to the hotel. She posed at the top of the steps like a fashion model. A long beige coat hung casually over her left shoulder, partially hiding a calf-length skirt over which was a loose-fitting blouse top, almost as long as the skirt. The blouse had a long v-shaped collar with wide lapels which reached to the waist, a sash belt, and a frill around the bottom hem. The blouse and skirt were both made of light voile in a rose and white flowered pattern, and were entirely unsuitable for motoring. She held her right arm away from her body with her hand resting casually on a rose-coloured parasol, the tip of which was against her foot so that the parasol was angled for effect. She paused and looked around to gauge the crowd's response, then she came slowly down the steps and got into the motor-car. The chauffeur closed the door, resumed his seat, and the motor-car drove away. Mr and Mrs Steen were taking the slightly longer, but less demanding route via Hope.

One of the race stewards now came forward and

addressed the crowd: 'Ladies and gentlemen, may I have your attention, please. I hope that you have all made yourselves familiar with the route. We shall re-assemble in Castleton at the Town Ditch Field. Please make sure that your competitor number is displayed on the grille of your motor-car. As you will have realised by now, the start is to be staggered and you will leave here in numerical order. This will give all competitors a fair chance at winning. Super-intendent Johnson has particularly stressed that the Rally is not to interfere with normal traffic. Motor-cars are not to travel bunched together and must not block the roads. Also, you are reminded to go wide and give plenty of room to any horses you pass, particularly if there are several of you together in line. I expect that there will be quite a few spectators at the beginning of the route and I would ask you to take care and be aware of pedestrians, particularly along Spring Gardens. Please pay attention to the stewards and do not begin until you are authorised to do so. Thank you and good luck everybody.'

The drivers and their passengers began walking towards their motor-cars and the crowd drifted towards the starting line. Driving coats were buttoned up, goggles settled in place, gauntlets pulled on and adjusted and then, suddenly, the air was filled with noise, the smell of motor fuel and the roar of engines combined with the sound of throbbing metal. Some of the older motor-cars had to be cranked with a starting handle and as they came to life the noise increased. Excitement mounted as the stewards moved into place. A steward carrying a chequered flag stood at one end of a broad line that had been drawn on the concourse in chalk. Another steward stood close to the first of the motor-cars in the line-up. The drivers, one at a time, obeyed the scooping motion of the steward's arm and moved forward to the line, engine revving. The other steward held the driver's attention, his chequered flag poised for dramatic effect and then, after consulting his watch, he brought the flag down smartly and waved the driver off. This process was repeated for each of the motor-cars, timing their start according to the handicaps allocated. Eventually, Edwin's Riley was summoned to the starting line and Helen waved to Richard and Cecily as they passed. Only Philip's Bentley was left. Being the most powerful of the motor-cars, it had been given a considerable handicap and there was quite a long pause before it was waved to the starting line. As they pulled away, Eleanor waved to Cecily and Richard. Napoleon watched puzzled as she left without him. Then, spotting Mrs Clayton and her boys, Eleanor gave them a wave too. The noise faded into the distance, leaving the spectators to return either to the hotel or their homes for lunch. Richard, Cecily, and Napoleon headed home to Oxford House.

At the beginning of the Rally the drivers needed to accommodate other road traffic and pedestrians, so they kept their speed under fifteen miles per hour. The shoppers in Spring Gardens stopped to look at the motor-cars as they passed and waved or cheered them on. By the time the last competitors had reached the end of Spring Gardens and turned under the railway viaduct to begin the steep climb up Fairfield Road, the leading motor-cars had already passed Fairfield. A crowd of onlookers had gathered there on the green, near St Peter's church, to cheer and wave their handkerchiefs as the competitors passed. There was a large gap between Philip's motor-car and the rest of the field and, just as the Bentley was easing its way along at the end of Spring Gardens, a horse and cart pulled out into the road in front of it. Philip was forced to slow the Bentley down to accommodate the horse's pace. The horse and cart then turned left and just as the road ahead cleared, a small child escaped from his mother's grasp and ran into the road. The mother rushed after the child. Philip had seen them in time and braked. He had stopped well clear of both mother and child and there was no harm done, except to the mother's heart rate. Philip and Eleanor made sure that they were all right and then set off again. They were now even further behind the rest of the field but Philip was not concerned. He was familiar with the roads they were to take and had already calculated all the gradients, identified the difficult spots, the passing places, and the stretches of road where the Bentley would out-perform the rest of the field. He intended to keep to his plan, no matter what the competition did. He was perfectly relaxed as the Bentley cruised effortlessly up the steep incline of Fairfield Road.

From Fairfield, the road ran along a plateau through farmland to Dove Holes and, free of the built-up area, the drivers increased their speed. Also, the road had widened out, which allowed room for passing and, although many of the motor-cars kept a steady pace and remained in their starting order, the drivers of some of the more powerful motor-cars, including Edwin and the driver of the Crossley, took the opportunity to overtake and move towards the front of the line. As they reached Dove Holes, the competitors were cheered by handkerchief-waving spectators. The Bentley was now within sight of the rest of the field but, just past the far end of the village, competitor number sixteen, a two-seater Morris Oxford, had pulled over to the side of the road. A cloud of steam was coming from the front of the motor-car, watched helplessly by its driver and passenger.

'Oh, what a shame,' said Eleanor. 'To have to pull out so soon.'

'I shouldn't worry. It's probably just overheated. Once the radiator has cooled down they should be able to continue.' Philip slowed the Bentley down and, as it came alongside the Morris Oxford, he stopped and called out: 'I say, are you chaps all right?'

'Yes, thanks,' said the driver. 'As soon as this beast has settled down, we'll be on our way again.'

'Got enough water to top up the radiator?' asked Philip.

'Yes, thanks awfully,' called the passenger. 'Don't stop. We don't want to delay you.'

'Tally ho, then! See you in Castleton,' said Philip.

'We certainly shall!' they called.

The Bentley surged forward leaving the Morris Oxford driver and his passenger looking after it admiringly and, it must be said, somewhat longingly as it disappeared in pursuit of the pack. The rest of the field was well ahead but there was now a winding descent of about a mile into Barmoor Clough which the Bentley could handle at speed, closing the distance. Eleanor settled herself comfortably and prepared to enjoy herself. In such a reliable motor-car, they could indulge in the luxury of enjoying the scenery whilst those ahead were concentrating on the journey. As they passed The Bold Hector Inn at the Barmoor Clough junction, Philip said:

'That has always struck me as a rather odd name for an inn,' said Philip. 'Who was Bold Hector do you suppose? The Trojan warrior?'

'It's possible. Maybe after eating or drinking there, one goes down fighting, as Hector did,' suggested Eleanor.

'Somehow, I doubt whether the person who named that Inn had heard of Homer and his heroes.'

'You're probably right. I think there is a character in one of those medieval plays, a sort of folk hero called Bold Hector. He keeps getting killed and coming back to life. Perhaps the inn is named after him and he is named after the Trojan warrior.'

'Hmm, perhaps Bold Hector is like the guests. Despite indifferent treatment at the inn, they keep coming back for more. Anyway, we digress. We haven't got time for tom-foolery and idle chatter,' said Philip, sternly. He shook his head to regain his focus. 'We're nearly at the turn for Black-brook. Kindly bring your attention back to the matter in hand, Miss Harriman, thank you.'

'Yes, sir,' laughed Eleanor.

Philip slowed the Bentley right down so that they could make the sharp right-hand turn at Sandyway Head and onto the old turnpike road to Sheffield. They passed the old toll booth at the side of the road, long out of use, but the road itself was still in reasonable condition. After a short flat stretch, the road followed the brook and then narrowed as it entered a wooded area. The verges rose steeply on either side and with a mile-long climb to the top of the hill, the Rally began in earnest. On this early section, the gradient was one-in-eight and there was no room to pass. In the two miles since Dove Holes, all the more powerful motor-cars had passed the slower ones and pulled ahead. Now, the slower motor-cars were bunched up immediately ahead of Eleanor and Philip. Philip pulled back, biding his time.

'I'm surprised that Mr Steen chose to use this road,' said Eleanor. 'The usual route through Barmoor Clough would have been much easier. Everyone knows that this old salt route was made to accommodate pack horses not motor-cars.'

'I think that piece of local history will have passed Mr Steen by,' said Philip, drily. 'Perhaps he thought the main road would be busier and chose this one instead so that the Rally didn't interfere with normal traffic.'

'I think that's unlikely,' said Eleanor. 'He doesn't strike me as a man who cares much about inconveniencing other people, judging by what I have heard of him so far.'

'No,' said Phillip, 'you are probably right. A more likely explanation is that he just doesn't know the roads around here. This stretch of road really deserves to be descended, not climbed as we are doing. If one approaches from the opposite direction, the view from the top across the valley is magnificent. Travelling in this direction, there is no view to compensate one for the effort involved.'

'This stretch of road is pretty unrelenting,' agreed Eleanor, 'and I should think a lot of the smaller motor-cars will struggle to get to Sparrowpit.'

'Yes, and with few passing places, they certainly will slow the others down. Not ideal conditions for a race.'

'No, and a rather stupid choice if it means having a lot of motor-cars pull out so early,' said Eleanor.

'Well, I think we both know that this Rally is more about Mr Steen advertising his beverages than motorists having a pleasant day out. The Bentley will certainly have no trouble with the gradient but, for a while, there won't be much room for us to pass so we shall have to sit behind the others and bide our time.'

'What is the plan, then?'

'We won't worry too much about this stretch. After we get through Sparrowpit, there is still quite a climb. Not steep like this, but long and steady and some of the competitors will find it difficult. It will be nothing for us and that road is much wider so there will be room to pass. We should be able to leave most of the competition behind on that part of the course. Then there will only be a handful of motor-cars left ahead of us by the time we reach the most difficult stretch leading into Castleton.'

'Excellent,' said Eleanor.

When they were clear of the wood, the road was still narrow but, in places, there was a small green verge on the side which allowed the smaller motor-cars to pass each other. Philip and Eleanor watched as a few of them played leap-frog. Competitor number fourteen, veering onto the right-hand verge in order to pass motor-car number twelve, hit rough ground, bounced, and suffered a burst tyre. The driver and passenger resigned themselves to a delay while they changed the wheel. Then, further along, another motor-car had pulled over to the side of the road and the top half of the driver was hidden under one side of the open bonnet.

Philip asked Eleanor to keep a count of the motor-cars they passed. As they approached the scattering of houses that formed the hamlet of Sparrowpit, Philip slowed the Bentley down. Another motor-car, number eleven, had pulled up where the road divided and there was a choice of veering left or right. The passenger was struggling with a road map, trying to refold it so that the relevant part was visible. As Eleanor and Philip drove past, Philip called out: 'Veer to the left past the Devonshire Arms and then just keep straight on.'

'Oh, thank you!' called the passenger, gratefully.

When they had passed the motor-car, Eleanor said: 'The man with the map. Wasn't that the sandwich board man who was advertising Horace Robinson?'

'Yes, it was,' said Philip, laughing, 'and the driver was the man who handed me the pamphlet about the Workers Control Party. What can they be thinking of, joining in such a bourgeois event as this?'

'Perhaps they are gathering evidence against Mr Steen,' suggested Eleanor.

Motor-car number ten, with an overheated radiator, was parked outside the Devonshire Arms, the driver and passenger having gone inside to cool themselves down while they waited for the engine to do the same. Eleanor pointed to the abandoned vehicle. 'That makes five motor-cars we have passed so far, which leaves eighteen still ahead of us.'

'One of which, must be Edwin,' said Philip, 'because we certainly have not passed him yet.'

'We haven't passed that Crossley yet, either. Or Rufus Wentworth-Streate.'

From Sparrowpit the road broadened out as it descended as far as Perryfoot Farm and several motor-cars took the opportunity to pull out and pass their slower neighbours. When this reshuffle had been completed, Philip pulled across and passed three of these slower motor-cars which were chugging along steadily, their occupants contentedly making a day of it, instead of hurrying and paying the price for impatience. Drivers and passengers waved happily and called out encouragement as the Bentley slid past. Then the road began to climb again, another one-in-eight gradient, and Philip could see a convoy of five motor-cars up ahead, travelling quite fast. The road was now wide enough for the Bentley to pass safely and there was no oncoming traffic. Philip pulled his driving goggles down from the top of his head and adjusted them. He gripped the steering wheel and said: 'Hold on to your hat, Lella. It's time for us to join this race.' He guided the Bentley over to the right-hand side of the road and, as he did so, sounded the horn to alert those ahead. He pressed down on the accelerator and the Bentley responded immediately. It surged forward and, for over a mile, climbed effortlessly, taking the curves smoothly. It glided past the first group of five and then, further on towards the top of the hill, passed two more groups of three motor-cars, each being willed up the gruellingly long hill by their drivers. Eleanor waved in greeting as they drew parallel with each vehicle.

'I almost feel guilty,' said Eleanor, 'passing so many of them so easily.'

'Buck up, Lella,' said Philip. 'This is a contest, don't you know! There's no place for sentiment here. Please tell me how many we have passed. I've lost count.'

Eleanor turned around and looked back down the hill. 'The first group was five and that's another six, that makes nineteen altogether since the start.'

'Which leaves us four to catch, including Edwin,' said Philip, grimly.

Eleanor was amused by the change in Philip's demeanour. Until now he had been unhurried and relaxed, aimlessly enjoying a gentle country drive without thought of winning, pausing to help others with no concern for the time lost. Now he was hunched over the wheel, eyes on the road, concentrating and plotting, passing other vehicles ruthlessly, and driving as fast as he dared, determined to reach the finish line first. Towards the top of the hill another motor-car had pulled up by the side of the road. The driver was in the process of dealing with a punctured tyre, assisted by the passenger. They waved to Philip and called out "good luck" as the Bentley passed wide.

'Only three to go now,' said Eleanor.

With the road to themselves, it was safe to let the Bentley really have its head. The speedometer quickly registered sixty and Philip and the engine both purred. The road, undulating through farmland and bordered on both sides by dry stone walls, continued to climb to reach the highest point of the route. Then the road flattened out, but Philip did not ease up on the accelerator and the Bentley increased its speed. Eleanor and Philip could now see Rufus Wentworth-Streate's motor-car up ahead. They caught up with it very quickly and Rufus waved as they passed.

'That leaves Edwin and the Crossley,' said Eleanor.

They were now about three miles from their destination and had reached the point where the road divided. The old pack-horse route into Castleton veered off to the right and was not used for vehicles. It dropped very steeply and, within the space of only eight hundred yards, reached the bottom of Winnats Pass, five hundred feet below. The new road, which the motor-cars had to take, remained at the top of the pass snaking its way around the side of Mam Tor and then turning sharply back on itself before descending to valley below in a much gentler fashion than the old road. The road was narrower, the surface was uneven in places, and the recent spell of dry weather had created a considerable amount of dust. This part of the route demanded less power from the engine and more skill and concentration from the driver. However, the road was reasonably level and

Philip managed to maintain a good speed so that they soon came within sight of the last two competitors, the Crossley, being closely tailed by Edwin's Riley. Edwin was trying to pass the Crossley but it was weaving from one side of the road to the other, deliberately swerving in front of Edwin, and making it impossible for him to get past.

Eleanor said, indignantly: 'Oh, how unsporting! That's very unfair and the Crossley's making an awful lot of dust. It must be very difficult for Edwin to see the road.'

'Yes,' said Philip, sternly, 'it's rather dangerous actually, the way that driver is behaving. There's quite a steep drop on the side of the road there and not much margin for error.'

The progress of the Riley and the Crossley was slowed by the fact that they were criss-crossing the road from side to side instead of travelling in a straight line, therefore the Bentley quickly caught up. Philip was assessing the situation and considering his position and that of Edwin. They were now approaching the hairpin bend where the road turned back on itself before descending. The road was narrow and there was a steep drop on the right-hand side. Philip decided on a strategy.

'Right,' he said, speaking rapidly, 'this is what we do. After we finish with the hairpin, I expect that the Crossley will take advantage of the next, slightly easier, stretch of road. It will stop weaving about so as to gain speed and then draw ahead of Edwin. As we head round the bend, I'm going to keep as close as I can behind Edwin and then, as soon as the Crossley stops blocking Edwin, I shall pass both Edwin and the Crossley. Then I'll keep the Crossley at bay using the same tactic he has been using on Edwin and that will give Edwin chance to get past him. Can you call out to Edwin as we pass? Tell him to wait for the signal and then pass the Crossley.'

Eleanor nodded. The Crossley and the Riley now had to reduce speed considerably as they approached the hairpin bend. Philip allowed the Bentley to close the gap and then rapidly changed gear to slow down. The three competitors were bunched up together as they looped around the bend and then, coming out of the bend, Philip said: 'Here we go, Lella, give Edwin a shout.' He put his foot down and the Bentley surged forward. There was just enough room to pass safely and the Bentley swooped past both motor-cars, taking both of the other drivers by surprise. Philip concentrated on the road and Eleanor called out to Edwin: 'Wait for the signal, then pass the Crossley.'

Edwin nodded without taking his eyes off the road and Helen waved. Philip let the Bentley get a little way ahead of the Crossley and then gradually eased off the accelerator until the Crossley caught up. Then he began to weave slowly from side to side forcing the Crossley to slow down. They were now approaching a straight stretch where the road began to descend gradually, which would make it easier for the Riley to gather speed quickly.

'Is Edwin still with us?'

Eleanor turned around to check and said: 'Yes. He's dropped back a little and allowed himself room to accelerate. I think he has understood what you're doing.'

'Jolly good. I'm going to slow down to keep the Crossley at bay. After you've given Edwin the signal to pass, hang on to your hat because I'm going to pull away very smartly to give him space to shake off the Crossley. Right oh, wave him on.'

Eleanor extended her arm and signalled to Edwin to pass. The Bentley sped away leaving a large gap behind it and Philip maintained the speed for some distance.

'How is Edwin getting along?' asked Philip.

Eleanor turned to look. The swerving of the Bentley and then the sudden acceleration had caused a lot of dust but she could just see the V-shaped radiator of the Riley behind them.

'He's done it!' she cried, excitedly, 'but I can't see the Crossley. There's too much dust.'

'Now that we've shaken him off, let's enjoy what's left of the ride.' Philip slowed the Bentley slightly and settled down to finish the Rally but then, out of the corner of his eye, he detected movement on his right and he glanced sideways. 'Oh, I say!' he said, indignantly. 'That is the limit!' The Riley had drawn level with the Bentley and a grinning Edwin was challenging Philip to a race over the final distance.

'Race you to the finish,' called Edwin.

Philip shook his head in disbelief. 'Base ingratitude,' yelled Philip. 'That is the last time I do you a favour!'

The road was beginning to level out and it was wider and almost straight. In the far distance, where the road reached the edge of town, there were two stewards waiting, one with a chequered flag and the other holding a clipboard on which to note the number of each motor-car and the time at which it passed. The Bentley and the Riley were now hurtling towards them, side by side, neither driver willing to concede, and rapidly approaching the end of the road. Knowing that he would shortly have to slow down, Philip said: 'That's enough.' The Bentley pulled away and the needle on the speedometer moved swiftly past seventy. Eleanor just shook her head and said nothing. Having made his point and spotting the race steward's chequered flag up ahead, Philip slowed the Bentley and it cruised over the finishing line. The Bentley had been going so fast that the first steward only managed a cursory dip of his flag, stepping hastily aside as he did so and, by the time the Bentley had slowed to a halt, it was well past the finishing line.

Philip grinned and looked sheepish. 'Sorry, Lella, but I couldn't let this old girl be disgraced.'

'I don't know about disgrace,' said Eleanor, laughing, 'I think male pride had more to do with it. I'm surprised at Edwin. He's usually so sensible and he showed no interest in the Rally at first.'

They drove the last few hundred yards into the town at a sedate pace, the Riley meekly following, and the Bentley glided gracefully on to the Town Ditch Field. Philip followed the directions of a steward and parked the motor-car. The Riley pulled up alongside.

'Well done,' Eleanor called to Edwin and Helen.

'Oh, what a relief to reach the finish,' said Helen, sinking back into her seat. 'That was very exciting, but I was afraid I might never see my children again.'

'Where's the Crossley?' said Philip to Edwin.

'He swerved to try to block me just as I was passing him and lost control. He ran into the ditch,' said Edwin. 'That cost him a burst tyre.'

'Oh dear,' said Philip, frowning, 'he wasn't hurt?'

'No, it's all right. Helen made sure as we went past.'

Another vehicle pulled up beside them and Eleanor waved to Rufus Wentworth-Streate. She got out and went to talk to him, congratulating him on finishing. As he was on his own and knew all of them socially, Eleanor invited him to join their picnic, confident that Mrs Clayton would have packed more than enough food for them all.

CHAPTER SEVEN

The Town Ditch Field had been given a festive air for the occasion. On one side of the field, Mr Steen's men had erected a makeshift platform, protected by a red and white striped canopy and draped with a banner advertising the fruit flavoured beverages. Blue flags fluttered from each corner of the canopy. Next to the platform there was a large tent, also in red and white stripes, in which Steen's fruit flavoured beverages were being dispensed by the team from the Palace Hotel. On the other side of the field, marking the place where the motor-cars were to park, was a row of blue poles. From the top of each pole red and white streamers fluttered in the breeze.

Philip unloaded the picnic hamper and Edwin and Rufus spread rugs on the ground in front of the motor-cars. Eleanor and Helen began setting out the feast Mrs Clayton had prepared for them and, as Eleanor had anticipated, there was more than enough food for an extra person. Other motor-cars began arriving in quick succession, lining up along the side of the field in order of arrival. Their occupants got out, stretched, divested themselves of motoring gear, and began hauling their picnic hampers from the luggage racks. The hotel servants, wandered from group to group handing out bottles of drink and the competitors set about enjoying themselves and assessing the fruit flavoured beverages while they waited for the rest of the field to arrive. Competitors came straggling in, some singly, some in groups. Helen was the first to spot the Crossley when it arrived and drew attention to it. The driver had removed his goggles and driving coat when he stopped to change the burst tyre and had not bothered to put them back on again. It was now possible to see who the driver was.

As the Crossley drove past them to take its place in the line, Philip said: 'Oh, I say! That bounder in the Crossley! It's the golf professional from Bramhall Park.'

'So it is,' said Eleanor. 'I hope he's more ethical on the golf course than he is on the road.'

'Do you know the blighter?' asked Edwin. 'He'll kill someone one day, the way he drives.'

'Yes, he ought to be reported for dangerous driving,' said Philip.

'I've a good mind to report him myself actually,' said Rufus. 'He nearly had me into a ditch at one point and I'm sure it was deliberate.'

'Well, at least Philip made sure he didn't win,' said Helen, ever the peace maker. 'It served him right, getting a burst tyre.'

Philip and Eleanor then explained how they knew who the Crossley driver was and amused everyone with a description of their encounter on the golf course with him and Mrs Steen. Gradually, over the space of an hour, the remainder of the field joined the line of parked cars, except for those contestants who had abandoned the race. From time to time, Eleanor looked around for Mrs Steen and noted that she and the Crossley driver were keeping well out of each other's way. Many of the drivers knew each other and, when the picnic food had been consumed, they strolled about discussing the performance of their motor-cars and swapping stories of the difficulties and highlights of the drive to Castleton. Several motorists came over to admire the Bentley and the Riley and talk technicalities with Philip and Edwin. The last motor-car to arrive was one hired from a local garage by Mr Steen. It had followed the field to provide assistance if necessary and to ensure that no motorists were left stranded. The arrival of this hired car was the signal for Mr Steen to present the prize to the winner. Accompanied by his wife, he stepped up onto the platform. The two of them stood side-by-side facing the crowd, Mrs Steen unsmiling but adopting a pose as if she expected to be photographed. The hall-porter from the Palace Hotel handed Mr Steen a megaphone into which he bellowed: 'Ladies and gentlemen, may I have your attention, please.' As the hubbub of conversation gradually died down and people turned to look at the platform, Mr Steen continued: 'If you would all like to gather here, we shall present the winner's prize.' The competitors and their passengers got to their feet and straggled forward to stand around the platform. Mr Steen gave the megaphone back to the hall-porter and looked around him, gathering everyone's attention.

'Ladies and gentlemen,' he began, 'I should like to thank you all for taking part in the Rally today and I congratulate you on reaching the finishing line. I think it is fair to say that we have all had a jolly day's motoring and the weather could not have been more favourable. I hope you have been enjoying the fruit flavoured beverages and have taken the opportunity to sample all of the flavours.' There were murmurs from the crowd, mostly of approval. 'Now, I would like to reward you for your efforts today with a piece of news which I think will be of interest to you all and which has not been announced previously.' The crowd shuffled and exchanged looks in anticipation. 'I expect to conclude a very favourable arrangement regarding the supply of the famous Buxton Spa water to the rest of England.' Mr Steen paused. Mrs Steen remained impassive. The crowd began to murmur but before there could be any expression of dissent, Mr Steen held up his hand and resumed. 'I am also pleased to announce, and you, ladies and gentlemen, are privileged to be the first to hear this, that the water is to be supplied in a glass bottle of a very distinctive design. I have brought a sample of the bottle with me.' He held up a clear glass bottle which had a pinched in waist and looked rather like a miniature version of a wooden tailor's dummy. 'This design is unique,' he continued. 'It is owned by my company and will be used exclusively for supplying the water from the spring. You, ladies and gentlemen, are the first members of the public to see this bottle.' He paused for dramatic effect but the crowd appeared to be unimpressed and there was no applause. Mr Steen held out his hand to the hall-porter who was standing beside the platform. 'And now, ladies and gentlemen, for the prize.' The hall-porter thrust an envelope into Mr Steen's hand and then disappeared into the beverages tent. Mr Steen looked a little surprised at the abrupt way he had been given the envelope, then he turned and grinned at the crowd. 'I promised a cheque for five pounds to the winner and I always keep my promises,' he boasted. He waved the envelope in the air. 'And Mrs Steen has agreed to present the prize.' He turned to Mrs Steen and she adopted a different pose as she accepted the envelope, still unsmiling. Mr Steen concluded: 'Mr Danebridge, in motor-car number twenty-four, the Bentley, was the first across the line, despite having started at the end of the field. Come forward, please, Mr Danebridge.'

The audience applauded enthusiastically, more interested in motor-cars than glass bottles, and Philip rather reluctantly went forward and accepted his prize from Mrs Steen. Mr and Mrs Steen then left the stage and the crowd dispersed, returning to their various picnic spots. When the Hall Bank party had returned to theirs, Philip said: 'I admit I was determined to win but I hadn't considered the consequences. I'm rather embarrassed to be accepting this cheque.'

'Well, no, you won it fair and square,' said Edwin.

'Yes, but I feel such a heel. I don't need the money and I'm sure there are other competitors who would appreciate it more,' protested Philip.

'If it will make you feel any better, give the money away,' suggested Helen.

'Oh, that's an excellent idea. Thank you.'

'Yes,' said Eleanor. 'Why not cash the cheque and give the five pounds to James to put in his collection tin for the British Legion fund. He'll be delighted to accept it.'

'I'll do just that. Ah, yes, I shall feel much better about it then.'

'Good, now you can stop worrying and enjoy your fruit flavoured beverage with unclouded joy,' said Eleanor.

Philip pulled a face at Eleanor and threatened to pour the liquid over her.

'We've no intention of drinking ours,' said Helen, 'I did have a sip, just so as to be fair in my assessment. Fizzy and far too sweet, but they're just the sort of thing our boys will enjoy. I don't usually allow them to have things like this but I shall make an exception this time. I know they will be pleased. Like Richard, they were very cross at not being allowed to come today.'

'That's an idea,' said Eleanor. 'I shall give mine to Richard.'

'I'll wangle another one to go with mine, Lella,' said Philip, 'and then you can give them to Mrs Clayton. I'm sure her boys will be happy to have them.'

'No, don't bother about getting another one,' said Rufus, holding out his bottle. 'Please, have mine.'

'Oh, thank you, Rufus. That is kind,' said Eleanor.

'I'm disappointed that we didn't hear from the Workers Control Party,' said Philip. 'I was fully expecting them to interrupt Mr Steen's speech. Surely they were not just here for pleasure.'

Eleanor looked around and then said: 'I don't see their motor-car anywhere. Perhaps they didn't make it.'

'Yes, they did. I noticed them arrive. They must have left early,' said Philip.

'The frivolity and pointlessness of the gathering was probably too much for them,' said Eleanor.

'Perhaps they objected to the fruit flavoured beverages,' suggested Edwin. 'After all, they are produced in Mr Steen's factory. I'm surprised they didn't make a scene, though.'

Now that the prize-giving was over, the gathering began to break up. People started getting to their feet, shaking out rugs, clearing up their picnic things, and stowing their belongings back into their motor-cars. Before long the air was filled with the noise of engines once more. One by one the competitors drove out of the field. Some had decided to return the way they had come and they drove home in a stately convoy, enjoying the fresh air and the scenery as they had not been able to do while concentrating on the Rally drive. Others had decided to go home the long way, via Hope. Eleanor and Helen were keen to extend the day's pleasure and suggested that they should do the same. They proposed to stop in Calver for tea at the Derwentwater Arms and Rufus agreed to join them. While Philip, Edwin and Rufus were discussing the route they would take, Eleanor was watching idly as Mr Steen supervised the task of clearing up the field. The Rally stewards were taking down the tent and the stall and clearing away the platform. The empty fruit flavoured beverage bottles were scattered about the field and the two female hotel servants were occupied in collecting them and putting them into the empty crates. Mr Steen's chauffeur had been press-ganged into helping them and seemed to find the company of the blonde girl quite acceptable. The two delivery drivers were loading the crates of bottles into their vans. Eleanor could see no sign of Mrs Steen and wondered where she was. Then she noticed that the Crossley and its driver had already left.

Philip started the Bentley and led the way out of the field with Edwin and Rufus in convoy behind. Mr Steen's motor-car was parked just beside the entrance to the field and as they approached it, Philip said: 'That's odd. Mr Steen's motor-car has a list to one side. The front offside is definitely lower than the front nearside.'

Eleanor said: 'Oh, dear. You're right.' As they passed the motor-car, she added: 'One of the front tyres has been slashed. And that reminds me, Mrs Clayton told me this morning that some of Mr Steen's machinery on Green Lane has been damaged. Mr Steen clearly has enemies.'

CHAPTER EIGHT

The day following the Rally was too wet for their usual Sunday afternoon walk, so Eleanor and Cecily had agreed that they would each spend the afternoon at home reading and then meet up at Oxford House at four o'clock. Mr Harriman was due back later that afternoon and Philip had arranged to meet the train and bring him back to Oxford House. Richard was sitting in the bay window, half reading a book and half watching out for Eleanor to arrive. Richard and Napoleon greeted each other enthusiastically as usual.

When calm had been restored, Richard said to Eleanor: 'Aunt Lella, Mr Danebridge is coming to tea and he's going to meet grandfather's train at the station.' Then he added, full of importance: 'And I'm allowed to go with Mr Danebridge to the station but first he's promised to play Snakes and Ladders with me.' Richard found this game very amusing and, instead of being annoyed or disappointed when he was forced to slide down a snake, he imitated the sliding action, lying on his stomach, writhing and giggling helplessly. 'Can Napoleon come to the station too?' he asked.

'Oh, I think perhaps he had better stay here,' said Eleanor.

'Right oh!' said Richard, and went back to reading his book.

Cecily said to Eleanor: 'Father telephoned this morning. He said to tell you that Penn-Halford was at the Gaudy and he had a very interesting tale to tell. Father said you would know what that means.'

Eleanor laughed: 'It's my roundabout way of finding out

about Mr Steen. Father was giving a talk at a seminar at the Palace Hotel and, after speaking to one of the delegates there, he followed a trail which led him to his old friend Penn-Halford, KC. You remember, they were up at Oxford together. Father was hoping that he would be at the Gaudy so that he could prise some further information out of Penn-Halford about a court case that Mr Steen was involved in. I look forward very much to hearing the tale.'

Before they could discuss this further, Philip arrived. As promised, he played several games of Snakes and Ladders with Richard. When the next game ended and Richard was getting ready for another one, Cecily said: 'Richard, Mr Danebridge has been very kind but I think he deserves a rest now. Besides, grandfather's train will be arriving soon. Why don't you read some more of your book until it is time to leave for the station?'

'Right ho!' said Richard cheerfully and happily settled down again in the bay window with his book.

Cecily said: 'Please tell me about this court case that Mr Steen was involved in.'

'Yes, do tell,' said Philip, 'I'm interested in all the gossip about this man.'

Eleanor said: 'There were two parties involved. The plaintiff was Alfmour Ltd which, we discovered, is controlled by Mr Steen. The defendant was a Mr Mayhew. He and Mr Steen had been partners for several years in a business which manufactured ginger ale supplied in stone jars. Apparently, the product was called Sunnyclyme, that is, clime spelt with a Y...'

Philip pulled a face and interrupted: 'Sunnyclyme Ginger Ale. I've never heard of it, but if I had I should not be tempted to buy it. Not with a name like that.'

'It's not persuasive, is it?' agreed Eleanor. 'Anyway, during the War, they had difficulty obtaining materials. First of all, the supply of sugar was disrupted, then the price of ginger went up, and then they couldn't get the stone jars from the Potteries because many of the pottery workers were at the Front. By 1916, the business was in financial difficulty and to avert having to close the factory, Mr Mayhew suggested that they should diversify into fruit drinks but Mr Steen didn't like that idea. The partners agreed to go their separate ways and had the business valued prior to dissolving the partnership. Then, Mr Steen decided to buy out Mr Mayhew's share so that he could keep the factory and the other assets for himself. It seems that, by then, Mr Steen had come to see the wisdom of Mr Mayhew's suggestion about diversifying and he formed the company, Alfmour Ltd, and converted the old ginger ale factory into the production of...'

'Let me guess,' interrupted Philip again, 'Steen's would-be famous fruit flavoured beverages.'

'The evidence of which we declined to taste yesterday,' added Eleanor.

'Richard enjoyed it,' said Cecily.

'Well, there you are then. Say no more,' said Philip.

'Exactly!' said Eleanor.

'So, why the court case?' Philip asked.

'Now we are coming to that,' said Eleanor. 'While Mr Steen was diversifying, Mr Mayhew was setting up his own factory to produce fruit cordials to be supplied in bottles. After the first week of production at the new factory, Mr Mayhew was served with a court order and the factory had to stop work. Mr Steen's company, Alfmour Ltd, had sought an injunction restraining Mr Mayhew from supplying his products in the bottles he was using because it claimed that the design was identical to a registered design owned by it.'

'And what was Mr Mayhew's defence?' asked Philip.

'He claimed that the design for the bottle was his, that he had created it many years before he had entered into partnership with Mr Steen and was entitled to use it. I'm expecting to get some more information about the case when father arrives.'

Philip took out his watch and said: 'It's almost time for his train now. I should go to the station. Are you ready Richard?'

~O~

When Mr Harriman arrived at Oxford House, he was greeted enthusiastically by his daughters, divested of his hat and travelling coat, and plied with tea and questions.

'I have been telling Cecily and Philip about the judgment in *Alfmour Ltd* v *Mayhew*,' said Eleanor. 'Now, what is the interesting tale you promised when you telephoned to Cecily this morning?'

'Yes, Father, what was your friend Penn-Halford able to tell you?' asked Cecily.

'Well,' said Mr Harriman, 'my chat with him was quite instructive actually. I have learnt a great deal about our Mr Steen and I don't think much of him. Penn-Halford said that it was a most unsatisfactory case. He was appearing for Alfmour, of course, but he was able to tell me quite a bit about Mr Mayhew. At the beginning of the hearing, it was made clear that there was no issue as to who had actually created the disputed design.'

'So, Mr Mayhew had actually created the design?' said Philip.

'Oh, yes,' said Mr Harriman, 'and, no doubt that was why Mr Mayhew expected to be successful in defending the claim. Mr Steen accepted that Mr Mayhew was its creator but he argued that the design had become partnership property and therefore, when he bought Mr Mayhew's share of the partnership assets, he acquired the right to the design. Penn-Halford said that when he read the brief he considered that it was far from an open and shut case and he even warned Mr Steen that the decision might go against his company. Penn-Halford thrives on difficult cases, of course, and he almost sounded disappointed that success had come so easily. He said that there were some issues which should have been explored by the defence and he was expecting to have to deal with them but they weren't even raised by Mr Mayhew's counsel. He even thought there might have been sufficient evidence for Mr Mayhew to have considered a counter-claim against Mr Steen.'

'And yet Mr Mayhew lost,' said Cecily.

'Yes. It came down to his word against Mr Steen's and the judge accepted Mr Steen's version of events rather than Mr Mayhew's. Mr Mayhew's evidence was that, on several occasions, he and Mr Steen had discussed Mr Mayhew's suggestion for saving their business by changing from ginger ale in stone jars to fruit beverages supplied in bottles but Mr Steen had resisted the idea. On one of those occasions, Mr Mayhew had brought to the office a drawing for the design of a bottle, not with the intention of using the design in the business but for the purpose of illustrating what he had in mind. He said that Mr Steen had rejected his ideas completely and, shortly afterwards, had informed him that he wanted to close the factory and dissolve the partnership. Mr Steen was not prepared to negotiate and so Mr Mayhew had no alternative but to agree to the dissolution. Mr Steen gave a different version of events. In his evidence, he said that there had been several discussions about diversification and he had welcomed Mr Mayhew's ideas, not resisted them as Mr Mayhew had testified. Mr Steen said that it was he who had invited Mr Mayhew to put forward a proposal involving the use of bottles and the proposal put forward by Mr Mayhew was based on the bottle shown in the drawing. Mr Steen explained that, at the time, he had rejected the idea as being impractical and too costly to implement. He said that the parties had agreed to dissolve the partnership and close the factory and, a few days later, he had the idea of purchasing Mr Mayhew's share of the assets.

'I suppose, despite Mr Mayhew's evidence, his design might still have been regarded as partnership property, though,' said Eleanor.

'That's true,' said Mr Harriman. 'Although Mr Mayhew had said that he had not shown the design to Mr Steen with the intention that it would be used, he did agree, in cross examination by Penn-Halford, that, if Mr Steen had accepted his suggestion to diversify and his design had been used it would then have become partnership property.'

'But at least its value would have been taken into account in the negotiations and Mr Mayhew would not have used it in his own factory believing it to be his,' said Eleanor.

'Exactly,' said Mr Harriman, 'and the whole sorry dispute could have been avoided.'

'Do you suppose that Mr Steen intended all along to use the design and deliberately avoided mentioning it during the negotiations?' said Philip.

'Oh, if he did, that was very mean,' said Cecily.

'Yes,' said Mr Harriman. 'Penn-Halford was not impressed with Mr Mayhew's counsel and he said that, had he been appearing for Mr Mayhew, he would have cross-examined Mr Steen much more rigorously on that point. He would have drawn attention to the fact that almost immediately after Mr Steen had seen the design for the bottle, he rejected Mr Mayhew's idea and, from that time on, refused to discuss any further proposal for rescuing the business. Penn-Halford said that it was tempting to think that Mr Steen had deliberately rejected Mr Mayhew's proposal in order to force a dissolution of the partnership which would then enable him to set up his own factory instead. Penn-Halford had noted that Alfmour Ltd, Mr Steen's company, had been incorporated before the date on which the partnership was officially dissolved and that Mr Steen had lost no time in registering the design in the name of his company. The other disturbing aspect of the case was that there was no explanation as to how Mr Mayhew's design came to be in the possession of Mr Steen but Penn-Halford suspected Mr Steen knew something about it. Mr Mayhew said that he had intended to take the drawing of his design home with him. He thought that he had put it in the drawer of his desk after the meeting but then, when he was getting ready to leave the office that evening, the drawing was not there. He had searched for it in the office but never found it. Mr Steen's evidence was that, some time after the partnership had been dissolved, he had found the drawing amongst the office papers, although he could not remember precisely which papers.'

'Can we infer that the drawing was stolen from Mr Mayhew's office drawer?' asked Eleanor.

'Apparently Mr Mayhew never actually alleged that but the office was a small room at one end of the factory building. The partners each had a desk in there and they were the only ones with keys to that office,' said Mr Harriman.

'That does not put Mr Steen in a very good light,' said Philip.

'It certainly does not,' agreed Mr Harriman. 'I am beginning to think that this town does not need Mr Steen and his methods of doing business. Because Penn-Halford's a King's Counsel he only gets involved towards the end of preparation of the case and he had only met Mr Steen the day before the trial. He said he hadn't formed much of an opinion of him. However, Penn-Halford emphasised that he had seen no evidence that the design had been stolen and it was certainly not an issue raised by the defence. Apparently, the judge was satisfied that, because the drawing had been shown to Mr Steen and had been found amongst the papers at the factory, Mr Mayhew had intended that the design would be used by the partnership business and, accordingly, it had become partnership property. As such, it had been bought by Mr Steen along with all the other assets when the partnership was dissolved and Mr Mayhew no longer had any right to it.'

'Poor Mr Mayhew. It seems a bit unfair if it was actually his idea,' said Cecily.

'I agree,' said Eleanor. 'Of course, from a legal point of view, the decision was perfectly correct but, like you, I feel sorry for Mr Mayhew, particularly now that I know something about Mr Steen.'

'And Mr Mayhew lost everything,' continued Mr Harriman. 'It seems that, in setting up his new factory, he had used all of the money he received for the sale of his share of the partnership together with money loaned by a bank. Production at his factory had to stop because of the injunction and also because he had no other bottles available. Therefore, he had no income. Then he had to borrow funds for his legal costs' Mr Harriman turned to Philip and Cecily and explained: 'Because he was unsuccessful in court, he was liable for Alfmour's legal costs as well as his own. Of course, unlike Mr Steen, he hadn't set up a company so he was personally liable for these costs. He just couldn't find the money and was facing bankruptcy.'

'Goodness, what a terribly sad story,' said Cecily.

'It is indeed. Penn-Halford said that Mr Mayhew seemed to be overwhelmed by the court process. The evidence he gave on his own behalf was hesitant and he didn't perform well under cross-examination. Of course, it could be that Mr Mayhew's solicitor had not given him sufficient explanation as to the court process and how to give evidence but Penn-Halford said there was something very odd. It was as if Mr Mayhew was afraid to speak out. Penn-Halford said that, if he did not know better, he would say that Mr Mayhew had been intimidated by someone.'

'Was he suggesting that Mr Mayhew had been threatened in some way?' asked Eleanor, shocked at the idea.

'I couldn't be sure. Penn-Halford is a great one for making jokes. After he said that about Mr Mayhew, he laughed and said that such things only happened in criminal trials, but I am not sure whether he was being serious or not and we did not discuss it further. What he did mention though, when he was commenting on how unlucky Mr Mayhew had been, was that he had heard, some time after the hearing, that there had been a fire at Mr Mayhew's factory, just two days before the hearing. Of course, it may have been co-incidence and I don't think much damage was done, but it may have been intended as a warning and, if so, it must have been preying on Mr Mayhew's mind at the hearing. Even if he did not regard the fire as a threat, repairing the damage would have been an additional financial burden that he did not need.'

'In those circumstances, one could not blame him if he had just given up and decided not to fight,' said Eleanor.

'Can I just go back to a point you made earlier, Mr Harriman?' asked Philip. 'You said that production at Mr Mayhew's factory had to stop because of the injunction. I don't want to be too harsh on Mr Steen but is it possible that the court action was a deliberate ploy by him to eliminate the competition? Perhaps Mr Mayhew's cordials were superior to Mr Steen's fruit flavoured beverages.'

'I think that is well within the bounds of possibility, Philip,' said Mr Harriman. 'There are many things about this case that strike me as contrived. The tragic thing is that none of this would have happened if the parties had been properly represented when the partnership was dissolved. There was no written agreement. The negotiations regarding the dissolution of the partnership were conducted between the parties themselves, neither of them had a solicitor and the discussions were acrimonious. With a solicitor, Mr Mayhew may at least have received payment for his design.'

'I get the impression,' said Philip, 'that towards the end of the partnership there was some animosity between the two partners but they must have had a good relationship in the beginning and trusted each other because surely they wouldn't have gone into partnership otherwise.'

'You are perfectly correct. It's the same old story,' said Mr Harriman. 'Two friends agree to set up in business together and, because they are friends, they think they understand each other's intentions and they dismiss the notion that they need to have their agreement put into writing or they agree that it should be but never make the time to do it. Then, when something happens to challenge their friendship, they each have a different recollection of what it was they had originally agreed. They also forget what assets they each brought into the business. Over time, of course, they come to regard everything as belonging to the business, until there is a falling out and then they begin to make claims one against the other. I have seen it happen so often. It was the same in this case. They started out in an experimental way and then the business grew and I suppose they were just too busy to think about a written agreement. And, then, when the War caused production to be disrupted, the parties had nothing to guide them when they were considering the future of the business, nothing to help them resolve their difficulties.'

'It seems particularly hard on Mr Mayhew, though,' said Philip, 'given that he was the one who suggested diversifying in order to save the business and then was prevented from starting again with his own factory.'

'My impression is that Mr Mayhew may have been a little naïve,' said Mr Harriman.

'Even so, I still feel sorry for him,' said Cecily.

'I wonder what happened to Mr Mayhew,' said Philip.

'Unfortunately, Penn-Halford had no further information,' said Mr Harriman.

'Mr Steen appears to be flourishing, though,' said Eleanor.

CHAPTER NINE

During the week following the political rally which had been held in the Market Place, the sandwich board man had spent his time wandering up and down the town's main streets making sure that everyone was aware of the name Horace Robinson. Mr Robinson, himself, together with several supporters of his United People's Democracy Party had moved about the town and shaken hands with or stopped to speak to as many people as possible. The end result of this political canvassing was not quite what Horace Robinson had hoped for. His intention had been to increase support for his party and its electoral candidates but he began to suspect that all he had achieved was an increase in local opposition to Mr Steen. Therefore, he announced that he and the other political reformers would be moving on to Chesterfield to enlighten the citizens there. However, one of Mr Robinson's group decided, at the last minute, to desert him. He intended to stand as a candidate at the next election and could see an opportunity for making political capital for himself by remaining in Buxton. He had noticed the increase in feelings of animosity towards Mr Steen which had been roused by these political discussions, and the rumours of Mr Steen's disregard for his factory employees and he fancied himself in the role of people's champion.

Also, that week, the two men from the National Union of General Workers had frequented the public houses and loitered outside the ale houses, talking to anyone who would listen in the hope of inflaming their suspicion of the landowning class and inspiring them to join the workers' opposition. These activists were mostly met with in-difference from the local people unless, that is, they expressed opposition to Mr Steen and his water bottling scheme. The more the subject of water bottling was mentioned, the more the details of the scheme began to emerge and, during these discussions, like-minded people began to realise that they were not alone. People who had, until now, been mild in their opinions began to be incensed and desirous of action and, to many local people, the proposal began to look like an imposition rather than a benefit. They began considering ways of stopping the scheme.

The local Member of Parliament had been visited by some of his constituents after the rally in the Market Place and he listened sympathetically as they complained about Mr Steen. Seeing some political advantage to himself, he gave support to their request for a town meeting to express opposition to the scheme. However, when he took a sounding of the Mayor and some of the local councillors, he discovered that they, and many of their supporters, were inclined to favour the scheme. Unfortunately, they too were his constituents and, with only a narrow majority at the last election, he depended on their vote. If a meeting were to be held, the two factions would clash and it was inevitable that the Member for Parliament would be caught in the middle. With a general election constantly being threatened, he could not afford to offend anyone. He was in a quandary as to which way to turn. Eventually, to appease those who had lobbied him, he decided to promote the idea of a meeting but only on the grounds that it was his public duty to provide the opportunity for supporters of the scheme to explain it fully to the public so that the public, suitably educated, could make an in-formed choice. Hence, a meeting had been arranged and it was due to take place in two days' time. Supporters and opponents of Mr Steen had both been encouraging people to attend.

Everyone at Hall Bank was going to the meeting and, according to Mrs Clayton, so was most of the town. Over the past few days, Mrs Clayton had been picking up information either at the shops she visited or from the various delivery men who called at Hall Bank with milk, groceries, vegetables, meat, fish, and newspapers. Her brother, Alf, had also contributed snippets of gossip. On Monday morning, at breakfast, Mrs Clayton relayed to Eleanor what information she had.

'Apparently, Mr Steen thinks he has located a lost spring, somewhere up near Green Lane and he's going to build a factory on the flat land lower down on Macclesfield Road where they can bottle the water and he'll run a pipeline between the spring and the factory. Alf says that Hulley's brother-in-law, he's the one as works at the Town Hall, told him that Mr Steen has already discussed his plans with the town surveyor and with some of the councillors. Hulley says the councillors are encouraging him.'

'That would certainly interfere with the golf course.'

'Yes, and it would interfere with a lot of other things besides. I met the housekeeper from The Garth the other day, you know, the big house on the corner. We were at the draper's in the High Street, and she was telling me that the people in the houses around them are not happy with the likes of a factory being built there. And who can blame them? I mean, they're very grand houses all around there and can you imagine? What with the noise and the dirt and the nuisance of having carts collecting and delivering things at the factory, up and down the street at all hours. It just doesn't bear thinking about, a factory down there.'

'No, it doesn't, Mrs Clayton. Let us hope that sense will prevail.'

'Well, I don't know. The butcher's delivery man was here this morning – he delivers to the house of one of the councillors in The Park – and he says the housekeeper there thinks, from the talk going on in the house, it's already been decided. The meeting's just to let people know what's going to happen.'

'If that is the case, a lot of people will be very angry,' said Eleanor.

'They will, that. There's a lot of people in this town who don't agree with Mr Steen. The meeting's bound to get a bit rowdy.'

Later that morning, James came into Eleanor's office with her post. Napoleon raised his head in greeting and flopped back onto his side.

James said: 'Your post, Miss Eleanor and Miss Fuller rang to ask if it would be convenient to call on you after lunch. She asked me to tell you that she had some information which might be relevant to the golf club.'

'Thank you, James. Please tell her that I shall be free after two thirty, if that suits her. I wonder what she has to tell us. I hope it is something useful to do with this business about the water.'

James smiled. 'Miss Fuller sounded rather animated so perhaps that is a good sign. There is certainly a lot of feeling about the scheme in the town. It is quite a divisive topic, I'm afraid.'

'Where does the majority lie, do you think?'

'Definitely on the side of the opponents. At least that is my impression,' said James.

'Then we shall have to find a way of stopping Mr Steen.'

'Yes,' said James. 'I think that would be wise. I shall just telephone Miss Fuller and let her know that you can see her this afternoon.'

~O~

Promptly at two thirty, Maureen Fuller arrived at Eleanor's

office and was shown up by James. After greeting Eleanor and Napoleon, she said: 'Eleanor, I was in Brunt's this morning buying my newspaper. As I arrived, Mr McFarlane, one of the schoolmasters at the College, was just leaving. He teaches history and Mr Brunt had been showing him a document which he said he had found last week. It was behind an old cupboard. Mr McFarlane looked at the deed and said it related to land on Green Lane and he advised Mr Brunt to get legal advice because the deed might be important. When Mr McFarlane had gone, Mr Brunt said he thought the deed was no longer effective but he was puzzled as to why it had been put behind a cupboard rather than destroyed. He thought perhaps it didn't matter because the deed was so old. He said that his family has always owned land on Green Lane but the deeds for that are in his own safe. I asked him if the land they owned had anything to do with the golf course and he said if I wanted to know about the land on Green Lane, I'd be better off talking to his great uncle, Mr William Brunt. He's the family historian, apparently, and knows all about the land up there and how the family acquired the pieces of land that the Brunts own. The great-uncle is in his nineties but still active and very alert. Mr Brunt says his great uncle's memory is better than his own.'

'So, you think we should interview Mr William Brunt?' said Eleanor.

'Yes, I do and when I suggested that to Mr Brunt, he said that his great-uncle always calls in for tea in the afternoons. He said we might like to come this afternoon at about five thirty if we wanted to talk to him.'

'I see. Then we should certainly go there,' said Eleanor.

'Also, I said you might look at the old deed for him and give your opinion as to whether or not he needs to keep it. I hope you don't mind.'

'Of course not,' said Eleanor. 'Delighted to help. Right,

then I'll meet you at the shop, shall I?'

'Absolutely. See you there,' said Maureen.

~O~

Eleanor met Maureen at Mr Brunt's shop as arranged and Mr Thomas Brunt greeted them cheerily and expressed his appreciation at their coming to see him.

'I shall be glad to find out if this here deed is of any use,' he said. 'I haven't known what to do for the best.'

'I shall be very pleased to have a look at it for you, Mr Brunt,' said Eleanor. 'Miss Fuller thought it might be relevant to the golf course. I believe your family owns land there.'

'Not as such. It's not part of the golf course but it is next to it. On Green Lane. I'll get the deeds out of the safe now you're here but I'll take you upstairs first to meet Uncle William.' Mr Brunt hesitated and looked at his feet, then looked up again. 'I am sure you will understand, Miss Harriman and Miss Fuller, that Uncle William, being the age he is, is not used to dealing with ladies like yourselves when it comes to business. Times have changed since he was in business…and, well…he may not take kindly at first…to being asked questions by a lady, if you see what I mean, especially a young lady, so I hope you won't be put out if he seems a bit offhand.'

'Of course not, Mr Brunt. Please don't worry. I understand the situation perfectly. I shall not be offended,' said Eleanor.

Eleanor was used to this attitude among men generally, not just those of previous generations, like Mr Brunt, senior. Many men had little to do with women outside their own family and then only at church or chapel or on social occasions. Encountering a woman in a position of authority was extremely rare for them and Eleanor was used to experiencing surprise, doubt, suspicion, and even hostility, when she had to deal with men in her professional capacity. She was careful to present an unthreatening demeanour because she suspected that their resistance to women was largely caused by fear. Fear of interference with their plans or their opinions, fear that they would not be able to withstand opposition or criticism from their womenfolk, or might be manipulated into agreeing to something they did not want to do. Eleanor was self-confident and had devised various strategies to overcome their reluctance to be advised by a woman and was generally able to win their respect by quietly demonstrating her competence. Mr Thomas Brunt took Eleanor and Maureen upstairs to his sitting room and introduced them to his great uncle, Mr William Brunt. Then, promising to return shortly with the deeds, he disappeared downstairs to the shop.

After the obligatory conversation about the weather, Maureen said: 'Mr Brunt, I am the secretary of the Burbage Ladies' Golf Club. When I was speaking to Mr Brunt, junior, in the shop earlier today, he told me something that may be of assistance to the Club and he thought that you might be able to help us with information about the history of the land on which the golf course has been laid out. You see, we are concerned about a possible threat to the golf course by a business man from Manchester who apparently wants to develop a factory of some sort for water bottling.'

'Aye, I've heard about him,' said Mr William Brunt, ominously. 'The man's a fool, upsetting people the way he has been.'

'Oh, I agree,' said Maureen, 'but unfortunately he seems to be a fool with a great deal of money and that gives him a significant amount of power.'

'Well, anyroad, someone needs to stop him,' Mr Brunt said, abruptly.

'Exactly,' said Eleanor. 'Mr Brunt, we think you might be able to help us. We would very much like to know more about the ownership of the land along Green Lane. You will have witnessed many changes here in this town during your life time and I am sure that you know a great deal about its history.'

'You can call it history if you like, but it isn't history to me. It's my life. I were born here and I reckon on dying here.' Mr William Brunt laughed. He had experienced nine decades of the town's history and was very interested in the subject. He was willing to talk about it for as long as they, or at least he, pleased. He did not seem to be at all uncomfortable in the presence of two young ladies. On the contrary, he appeared to regard it as a novelty and was quite willing to answer their questions. 'Well now,' he began, 'as to the land on Green Lane, the Earl of Shrewsbury had the tithes of The Green in the fifteen hundreds. The old berceries were…'

'Berceries?' asked Maureen, puzzled.

'Aye. For the monks' sheep,' said Mr Brunt.

'There were monks on Green Lane farming sheep?' asked Maureen, her voice rising in surprise.

'Nay, lass,' said Mr Brunt, shaking his head at the woeful ignorance of the younger generation. 'The farmers had the sheep but the monks had the tithes. First of all, it were the Priory at Nottingham that the farmers had to give their tithes to, but that were afore King Henry with all his wives and his Reformation, of course. After that, the nobility saw to it that they got the tithes instead of the church. The Newcastles followed the Talbots and then by the seventeen hundreds it were the Devonshires.' Mr Brunt nodded decisively.

'But I understood from Mr Brunt that your family owned land there,' said Maureen.

'We're not the owners, no. That's the Duchy. But we've a right to it,' said Mr Brunt, firmly. 'That we do.'

Eleanor was used to getting information piecemeal from clients, particularly when she was drafting an affidavit or making sure she had identified all their property and their potential beneficiaries for the making of a new Will. She was patient and methodical with such clients and she adopted that method now. 'Mr Brunt,' she said, 'you have the advantage of us. Your knowledge of this town's history is bound to be much better than ours. Perhaps you would explain how your family came to have the rights over this land. When you refer to the Duchy, I assume you mean the Duchy of Lancaster.'

'Aye, lass,' said Mr Brunt, confidently, 'and you see, the Duke of Devonshire is the lord of the manor but all of this here land belongs to the Duchy of Lancaster, has done for centuries, back as far as the Conquest, well give or take a couple of hundred years. Now, along Green Lane there was the berceries, like I said, for farming sheep, and that had nothing to do with the Duke, except for the tithes. Now, when Green Lane were turnpiked they straightened up the line of the old road and some odd parcels of land got disposed of. My great-grandfather Thomas got two of 'em. They was passed down to his son but he got rid of one of 'em to the Duke. He kept t'other one, though.'

'I see,' said Eleanor, 'now I am beginning to understand. Mr Brunt, I have brought a map with me. Could you show me on the map where this land is, please?' Eleanor opened the map out onto the table in front of Mr Brunt. He hunted fruitlessly in his pockets for his spectacles and then noticed that they were on the dresser next to where he was sitting. He put them on and bent over the map, frowning and chewing his bottom lip as he concentrated. Eleanor was well aware that, despite the various Education Acts, there were still people who could not read and that many people, especially those of Mr Brunt's generation, were made anxious by paperwork.

'Here's the High Street,' she said, tracing the route on the map with her finger. 'Here's the bottom end of Green Lane, then Poole's Cavern, and opposite that is the golf course.'

'Ah,' said Mr Brunt nodding. 'That's right. Here we are.' He put his finger at a point on Green Lane across the road from Poole's Cavern and a short distance from where the public footpath crossed the golf course.

'So, that is the land you currently own?' asked Eleanor, as she pointed to a field, the boundary of which was outlined on the map.

'Aye, that's it,' said Mr Brunt, 'but not me. Thomas, my nephew, well, great nephew to be accurate, Thomas as owns this shop.'

'I see. And you said that some land had been sold. Which parcel of land would that be?'

'The one next to it, to the west.' He moved his finger to the left.

Eleanor looked at the map and said to Maureen: 'I'm not sure but I think that may be the land Mr Steen is interested in. It's where that machinery was left.'

'Oh, that is disappointing,' said Maureen. 'If he has bought that land, there may be nothing more we can do.'

'Ah now,' said Mr Brunt. 'Don't you be too sure, young lassie. I've heard tell of this Mr Steen and I know what he's up to. I've been thinking about this here scheme of his and he may not be as clever as he thinks and he may have us Brunts to deal with first.'

Eleanor and Maureen looked at Mr Brunt in anticipation. He nodded triumphantly, savouring the moment. Then, he continued: 'The feeling in town is generally against him and his water scheme, and we shall be doing our best to put a spanner in his works.'

'But, if the land is no longer yours,' said Maureen, 'I don't see how you can do that, Mr Brunt.'

'Ah, well, you see, when young Thomas brought me the deed he'd found behind the cupboard in the old parlour I saw as it mentioned Charles Brunt and I got to thinking about him and about a story my father told me. Charles were a wily old bird and not much got past him. Back then, there were a story about an old spring. No-one could be sure if it were a separate spring or if it were sommat to do with the spring lower down, the one that feeds the start of the Wye. You see, it's in line with Poole's Cavern. The river goes underground there, you understand, and comes out again further down. Now it's my belief that this Manchester man has heard about the old spring and that's what he's looking for.'

'But where was the spring?' asked Eleanor.

'Just down from Green Lane. You see, by the time they was building the turnpike along the Lane, the spring were dried up. But people still remembered it, from when it were flowing, like. Some people said it dried up because of the disturbance and they reckoned as it might start flowing again one day.'

'What sort of disturbance would that be?' asked Eleanor.

'When they started using the coaches, of course, and horses and carts. Instead of pack horses, you understand. Pack horses' feet don't cause no trouble and those horses walked the lanes for centuries without damaging them, but carts and coaches, now that's a different story.' He shook his head 'The wheels churn up the surface, especially in the wet, and of course they take up more room as well, so the road had to be widened to take 'em. The spring stopped flowing and some people said it were the road as caused it. Now, when they built the new turnpike, they took the road south of where the spring had been, just to be sure. In case it started flowing again, d'you see? That's how it came to be on the land that great-grandfather bought. His boundary took in the old spring.'

'So you think Mr Steen has heard about this old spring and is trying to find it and, if he does, he will buy the land?' said Eleanor.

'Aye,' said Mr Brunt, 'but it might not do him any good.'

Mr Brunt chuckled and sat back in his chair. He folded his arms across his chest decisively.

'But if that is the piece of land that was sold, surely there's nothing we can do,' said Maureen.

'Ah, but I just told you, everyone thought the spring were gone for good but great-grandfather Thomas, him as bought the land, he always thought the water might come back one day. Now I can't say for sure that it's true but this is what my father told me. He said that when grandfather, that's Charles Brunt, transferred the land to the Duke, he remembered what his father Thomas had said and he kept his rights to the spring, just to be on the safe side. So as to be able to use the water for the bit of land he'd kept, see. When he sold the land, it were already getting on for fifty years since the spring disappeared and, of course, it never did come back. It were a long time ago and I'd forgotten all about that spring until Thomas here mentioned he'd found that deed.'

'Ah,' said Eleanor. 'I see.'

'Could he keep the right to the water?' asked Maureen, looking at Eleanor.

'Yes, with a properly worded deed,' said Eleanor. 'He could have created an easement to give him access to the spring across the parcel of land that he had transferred. But only if the two pieces of land were adjoining. I need to check the deeds relating to the ownership of this land and its sale.'

'Well, here's the man who can help you,' laughed Mr William Brunt as Mr Thomas Brunt appeared in the doorway.

'Ah, Miss Harriman. I heard what you said about the deeds. I'm just in time. Here we are. This is the one that was behind the cupboard in the old parlour and this one labelled Green Lane has been in the safe since my father died. It belongs to the land on Green Lane that we own but I've never paid much attention to it because that land hasn't been used by us since grandfather's time.'

Eleanor unfolded the documents she had been given and spread them out on the table. The assembled company watched in silence as she studied them carefully. The first deed, from the safe, was dated 1765 and the second deed, from the parlour cupboard was dated 1785. The two Mr Brunts sat patiently contemplating the table top in front of them. Maureen looked out of the window and tried not to seem anxious. Eventually, Eleanor said: 'I am very glad that you decided to keep this, Mr Brunt. It is a very important document.'

There were grunts of satisfaction from the two Mr Brunts and Maureen sighed in relief. Mr Thomas Brunt beamed and said: 'Uncle here said so, didn't you, Uncle? You said I should get someone to look at it just in case.' Mr William Brunt nodded vigorously. 'One thing I don't understand though,' continued Mr Thomas Brunt, 'is, if it was important, why it was left behind the cupboard in the old parlour.'

'Well,' said Mr William Brunt, 'you have to admit that it were a safe place because it's been there a long time. None of us can remember it being put there and it hasn't been disturbed until now.' He laughed loudly and slapped his knee. 'P'raps whoever put it there thought there were not much chance of the spring coming back and left the deed behind the cupboard for safe keeping, just in case, and then forgot all about it. And the spring never has been back so nobody's ever thought to look for the deed.'

'I think that is very likely the explanation,' said Eleanor.

Maureen said: 'And now that the deed has been found, do you think there is something we can do about Mr Steen?'

'There certainly could be,' said Eleanor. 'The deed that was behind the cupboard relates to the parcel of land which was sold. It witnesses the transfer of the land from Charles Brunt to the Duke of Devonshire but it reserves to Charles Brunt, his heirs and assigns, the right to draw water from any spring located on the land. The sole right, that is. And it grants an easement across the land for that purpose.' Eleanor turned to Mr Thomas Brunt. 'So, you may still have the right to the water on the parcel of land which was transferred to the Duke.'

'Well, I never,' said Mr Thomas Brunt, surprised but smiling broadly. 'So, we Brunts can stop this Mr Steen and his scheme, after all.'

'Isn't that what I said afore?' said Mr William Brunt gleefully, rubbing his hands, 'I've been trying to tell you but there were no-one prepared to listen to an old man. That Manchester man has met his match, hasn't he?' With that, he thumped the table with his fist.

'I've never paid much attention to the piece of land we kept because it has been leased for grazing since my grandfather's time,' said Mr Thomas Brunt. 'Perhaps we should go and look for the spring.'

'Well, we need to check a few things before we can be absolutely certain,' said Eleanor. 'It seems an unusual thing to do, taking the land but giving someone else the right to the water from a spring. Why did the Devonshire estate not retain the right itself?'

'Happen at the time, no-one thought there were much chance of it,' said Mr William Brunt. 'If you want the land and you don't reckon much to the spring coming back, you're not giving away much, are you?'

'Yes, I see your point,' said Eleanor. 'Now, the deed provides that the right to the spring can be passed down to the heirs of Charles Brunt. Perhaps you can help me with some dates because I need to make sure that the rights to the spring have passed to you, Mr Brunt.' Eleanor looked at Mr Thomas Brunt. 'We must be able to establish an unbroken chain, you see.' Eleanor took out her note book and pen.

'Ah, Miss Harriman, as I explained to Miss Fuller, Uncle William here is the family historian. He's a great one for dates, aren't you, Uncle.'

Mr William Brunt nodded. 'That I am, I've seen a good few of them in my time. I'll be ninety-four next month. I were born in 1828, or so I've been told. I were there at the time, of course, but I were not taking any particular notice of the date.' Mr William Brunt laughed loudly at this statement, which was obviously one of his favourite jests.

Eleanor smiled politely and then said: 'Mr Brunt, it is very important that I understand the chain of ownership of this land. Can we start right from the beginning so that I can be sure that I haven't confused any of the facts? You said that your great-grandfather, Thomas Brunt, bought the two parcels of land at the time when Green Lane was turnpiked and that was in 1765, which is the date on the deed Mr Brunt had in his safe.' Eleanor picked up the first deed and pointed at the date.

'Aye,' said Mr William Brunt, nodding.

'And the Thomas Brunt referred to in this first deed is your great-grandfather?' asked Eleanor.

'Aye,' said Mr William Brunt firmly. 'Thomas, same as my father and my brother and our Thomas, here. The eldest is allus called Thomas.'

Eleanor nodded, and said: 'As there are several Thomases, I had better number them. I shall refer to the original owner of the land, your great-grandfather, as Thomas One. Now when he died, did the land pass to his eldest son?'

'Aye, allus does,' confirmed Mr Brunt.

'Do you know when that was?'

'Great-grandfather Thomas died in 1783,' said Mr Brunt, promptly.

Eleanor was impressed by the sharpness of Mr Brunt's memory. She noted the date on her note pad, then she said: 'So the next owner was his eldest son, Thomas Two.'

Mr William Brunt laughed and shook his head. 'Nay, lass. His eldest son, yes, but not Thomas.' Eleanor frowned. 'You see,' continued Mr Brunt, 'great-grandfather, Thomas, your Thomas One, him that had the land in the first place, he were a bit of a rebel. The eldest had allus been Thomas until then, but he broke with the tradition. He'd an adventurous streak, see, and as a youngster he took his horse and rode over to Macclesfield to join Bonnie Prince Charlie. Him that were on his way to London to claim the crown, he being the rightful king. That were in 1745 and it all came to nowt but great-grandfather Thomas, he were that impressed with the Prince, he vowed if he had a son, he would call him Charles, instead of Thomas. And he kept his promise. His eldest son was Charles. Born the year they changed the calendar, he were. Caused a bit of confusion, that did, I can tell you, him being in one year at first and in another year the next.'

Eleanor assumed Mr Brunt was referring to the year that the English calendar was altered to bring it into alignment with the calendar in use in Europe. As far as Eleanor was concerned it was part of history, as was the 1745 rebellion, and she was amazed to realise that she was listening to a man directly connected to these long-ago events.

'I see,' she said, and she wrote these details in her note-book. 'So your great-grandfather Thomas, that is Thomas One, acquired two parcels of land when the road was turnpiked in 1765 and when he died in 1783, both parcels of land passed to his eldest son, Charles, who was your grandfather. Now, during his life-time, Charles retained one parcel of land and transferred the other parcel to the Duke of Devonshire but, when doing so, he retained the right to the spring. That transaction is recorded in the deed that was discovered behind the cupboard downstairs.'

Mr William Brunt nodded agreement. 'The Duke had big plans for Buxton then, what with the building of the Crescent and all, and grandfather Charles could see that a lodging house was a good way to make a living so he put the money into building this house, in front of the old croft.'

'I see,' she said. 'Now, it is essential to trace the chain of ownership from your grandfather forwards. The parcel of land that your grandfather Charles kept would have passed to his eldest son when your grandfather died.' Mr William Brunt nodded. 'Which was when?'

'Battle of Waterloo,' said Mr William Brunt, promptly. 'That year.'

Eleanor wrote 1815 on her note book. 'And the eldest son of Charles, was he called Thomas?'

'Thomas, aye. Thomas Arden Brunt. Grandfather Charles were a great one for tradition, unlike his father.' Mr William Brunt laughed. 'Arden was his wife's maiden name. Mary Arden, she was.'

Eleanor nodded. She was sketching a family tree on her note pad as they spoke, trying to establish the correct sequence in the confusion of so many Thomases.

'And Thomas Arden Brunt was your father? When was he born?'

Mr William Brunt said: 'Father always used to say he were the same age as The Crescent...'

'Is that the year it was started or the year it was finished?' asked Eleanor.

'...and the revolution,' added Mr Thomas Brunt. 'I've heard that story many times.'

'The French revolution?' asked Maureen.

'Aye, the Frenchies,' nodded Mr William Brunt.

Eleanor was beginning to realise that Mr William Brunt measured his own family's history by reference to important events in the nation's history, events that Eleanor had only learnt about at school. Eleanor wrote the dates in her note book and said: 'Thomas Arden Brunt will be Thomas Two. He was your father and you are William so that means Thomas Arden Brunt had another son, your elder brother?'

Mr William Brunt nodded. 'Aye, I were the youngest of ten. Hannah were the oldest and then Mother had seven more girls while she were waiting for us two boys to come along. Our Thomas were first and then me.'

'I shall label your brother Thomas Three,' said Eleanor. 'When your father, Thomas Arden Brunt, died his son, Thomas Three, inherited the remaining parcel of land?' Mr William Brunt nodded. 'And when did your father die?'

'Same year as Prince Albert,' came the reply.

Eleanor frowned.

'That was 1861,' supplied Maureen.

Eleanor wrote down the date. It was becoming a general knowledge quiz and she was trying not to laugh. 'And your brother, Mr Brunt, Thomas Three. Is he still alive?' she asked.

'He was my grandfather,' said Mr Thomas Brunt. 'No, he died in 1891. I was fifteen at the time and I remember him well.'

Eleanor waited for the history lesson attached to the date 1891 but nothing was added. Switching generations and trying not to be confused, she continued, addressing Mr Thomas Brunt: 'So in 1891, Thomas Three, who was your grandfather and Mr William Brunt's brother, died. And your father, that is Mr William Brunt's nephew, inherited the land.' Mr Thomas Brunt nodded. 'And he was also called Thomas?' asked Eleanor, raising an eyebrow. Both of the Brunts nodded. 'I shall note him as Thomas Number Four. And is he still alive?'

Mr Thomas Brunt shook his head. 'He's gone now as well, before the War.'

'The year the old King died,' added Mr William Brunt.

'That would be 1910,' said Maureen, solemnly.

Eleanor refused to look at Maureen for fear of the giggles. She made a note of the date and continued: 'So, in 1910, the remaining parcel of land passed from your father, Thomas Number Four, to you Mr Brunt,' said Eleanor, turning to Mr Thomas Brunt. 'I shall note you as Thomas Number Five and the right to the spring should also have passed to you in 1910.' Eleanor looked at her note pad and then took a minute to complete her family tree. 'Well, the parcel of land that you own has been passed down through the Brunt family's eldest sons since it was acquired in 1765. It seems also that the right to the spring has been passed down through them since it was created in 1785. I should like to check the wording of the deeds very carefully just to be sure that the easement has been properly created. I also need to make sure that the easement has not been extinguished. I shall have to check the Wills of the various eldest sons to make sure and we can obtain copies of those if necessary. Subject to that, you Mr Thomas Brunt as the legal owner of the land, are entitled to the benefit of the spring on the land that was transferred in 1785.'

'Do you think we may be able to stop this water scheme, then?' asked Mr Thomas Brunt, speaking at the same time as Maureen, who asked: 'Can we stop, Mr Steen?'

'I think there is a very good chance of doing so, and I shall certainly do my best,' said Eleanor.

'Oh, how wonderful,' said Maureen.

Mr William Brunt sat there nodding and beaming.

'If Mr Steen buys or leases the land, or has already done so, he could use the land but that would not serve his purpose because he would not have the right to use the water,' said Eleanor. 'Unless, of course, Mr Brunt were to allow him to do so,' she added, turning to Mr Thomas Brunt.

'Not for all the tea in China,' said Mr Thomas Brunt, smiling and shaking his head.

CHAPTER TEN

As James was opening up the office on Tuesday morning, Eleanor and Napoleon returned from their walk. After greeting James, Eleanor said: 'I suppose you've heard the news about Mr Brunt's deed.'

'Yes, Miss Eleanor, I have. Mr Brunt was explaining the situation to me this morning when I was in his shop. He is very pleased.'

'The whole town will know about it by this evening's meeting, I expect.'

'Yes,' said James, smiling, 'we certainly have a very efficient news exchange in this town, don't we? Do the Brunts actually have the right to the spring?'

'I think we can establish that they do, yes, but if there were to be a dispute as to whether or not the right still exists, the necessary Court process would probably take long enough to deter Mr Steen. He seems to be the sort of person who requires things to happen quickly and would probably look elsewhere for a source of water.'

'Then, at least your golf course would be safe,' said James, smiling at Eleanor.

When James sorted the first delivery of post, there was a letter for Eleanor from their London agents providing the newspaper reports she had requested regarding the court case, *Alfmour Ltd v Mayhew*. The London agents informed Eleanor that the case had been reported in several newspapers. They wrote:

We enclose, as requested, copies of newspaper reports regarding the case of *Alfmour Ltd v Mayhew*. There are three reports, two dated 15 November 1920, which are from the more reliable newspapers, and one dated 17 November 1920 from the sensational press. The third report, which is from the evening edition of *The Daily Mirror*, does not refer directly to the court case but is included because you expressly requested any information regarding the parties involved.

The first cutting was from the legal section of *The Times*. It gave only a brief summary of the facts and the decision. The second cutting was from *The Daily Telegraph* and contained a slightly more detailed report of the case but added nothing new regarding the parties. Eleanor then turned to the third cutting from what the London agents called the sensational press.

MAN JUMPS FROM BRIDGE

LONDON, Friday. Early this morning, the London Water Police were called on to recover the body of a man who jumped to his death from Waterloo Bridge. Mr Joe Hinch, a delivery-cart driver of Brixton, told *The Daily Mirror* that, at about six o'clock this morning, he was on his way to deliver bread to the Savoy Hotel and was approaching the bridge from the Waterloo Road end, when he noticed up ahead a man walking down the middle of the road. He then saw the man walk to the left side of the bridge, climb onto the railings and jump into the water. Mr Hinch was too far away to prevent the man from jumping. He alerted the authorities immediately and the man's body was later recovered, having been washed downstream and become lodged against one of the piers of the Blackfriars' Bridge. The deceased, a Mr Albert Mayhew, was from Manchester and is believed to have been the unsuccessful defendant in proceedings recently heard in the Royal Courts of Justice.

Eleanor sat staring at the newspaper cutting contemplating the scene it conjured up and trying to imagine the level of despair that would have driven a man to take his own life in that way. Was it just the financial ruin or was it also the betrayal by his former business partner? Mr Mayhew must have felt the injustice of his position. He was the one who had suggested a way to save the business of the partnership and it was clearly a viable solution because, although Mr Steen had rejected the idea at the time, he had later adopted it for his own benefit. Then there was the method chosen by Mr Steen to bring the claim against Mr Mayhew. It was a particularly draconian tactic and it had brought Mr Mayhew to his knees. There had been alternative ways open to Mr Steen in order to bring the matter to court. He could have commenced proceedings in the usual way, giving the parties the opportunity to discuss the issue as to ownership of the design and, perhaps, reach a settlement. Instead, Mr Steen had sought a court order, effective immediately, preventing Mr Mayhew from operating his factory, paralysing his business and cutting off his means of income. Mr Steen acknowledged that he had not created the design. He must have known that his company's right to register and use the design was open to interpretation, and had never been proven. Eleanor could understand why Mr Mayhew had defended the claim and she could imagine the damaging effect that the whole experience must have had on his morale. It must have caused Mr Mayhew to doubt his own judgment, to wonder whether there was anyone he could trust, and he must have experienced a feeling of utter hopelessness. She was sure that, even if she had had no knowledge of Mr Steen, she would have felt sympathy for Mr Mayhew in this dispute and she was beginning to understand the sort of person she was dealing with in Mr Steen.

~O~

That evening, at the Town Hall, the local Member of Parliament, the Mayor, members of the Town Council, Mr Sweeting who was the Duke's agent, and several of the town's other worthies occupied the platform of the meeting room. They sat in silence, staring gloomily at the body of the hall where several hundred people had gathered. The whole spectrum of the community was represented in the audience. Everyone knew someone in the crowd and, instead of sitting patiently waiting for the meeting to begin, they had been milling about, shaking hands, and greeting each other in noisy enjoyment. Eleanor and Mr Harriman greeted, and were greeted by, many people as they arrived and Eleanor spotted Philip and his parents sitting a few rows away and waved. As the Town Hall clock was striking the hour, the ushers closed the doors and the crowd settled. Mr Steen arrived on the platform and took his allocated seat. Then, the Mayor got to his feet and came forward to the edge of the platform and the noise in the hall gradually decreased.

'Good evening, ladies and gentlemen. Thank you for coming this evening. As I am sure you all know, Mr Steen, who is with us this evening...' The Mayor turned towards Mr Steen who raised himself slightly from his chair and did a sort of half bow. '...has developed a scheme which is designed to promote our famous water. The Council has considered Mr Steen's proposal very carefully and is very favourably impressed. It has a great many advantages. The reason for the existence of this town is the presence of our unusual springs which, inexplicably, supply hot and cold water within a few feet of each other. The waters are known to provide relief for many ailments. Our livelihood has always depended on the visitors who come to take the waters and who need accommodation, treatment, and entertainment. As you will all be very much aware, many of you from personal experience, this town has been greatly affected by the international events of the last few years, events over which we have had no control. Due to the restrictions on travel and entertainment during the War years, the number of visitors to our town has declined and many of you have suffered financially as a consequence. We have been able to mitigate that loss to some extent during and immediately after the War because of the many injured soldiers who have come here for treatment, thus replacing the missing civilian visitors. When hostilities ended, we all hoped to return to our pre-War prosperity but in many ways we have been sadly disappointed. The economic crisis that this country has suffered since then, and is continuing to suffer, has affected all of us. It is also true to say that the burden of death duties and now income tax has prevented many of our wealthier visitors from returning to us during the Season and it has reduced the ability of some of our own residents to support our commerce and our charitable institutions. We, like the rest of the nation, are suffering and we must all face the fact that measures are needed to reverse the situation in which we find ourselves. Our country has been changed by the War and we need to change with it. For the sake of the future and for our children's future, I urge you not to dismiss this scheme but to give it the consideration it deserves.'

Some of the crowd clapped when the Mayor finished speaking, others remained unmoved. The Mayor then invited the Member of Parliament to speak. He talked in general terms, saying very little of substance and often repeating the same point. Clearly he had picked up the mood of the meeting and did not want to risk offending his voters by appearing to differ from them. He made no specific comments about the scheme itself and it was not clear whether he supported it or not. He concluded his speech with the formula resorted to by every politician who wishes to justify an unpopular scheme, and asked the audience to consider the additional employment opportunities which Mr Steen's scheme would undoubtedly provide for the town, although he provided no facts as to their number or origin. There was scattered applause from the audience as he finished speaking.

As the Member of Parliament resumed his seat, several members of the National Union of General Workers, and the Workers Control Party booed and hissed. They had remained in town and had occupied the seats at the rear of the hall. A man sitting amongst them stood up and called out: 'I know what sort of employment this man Steen provides. I have worked in his factory in Manchester and I could tell stories that would have the hairs on your heads standing on end. This man is not an employer, he's an exploiter and he's not interested in the welfare of this town either.'

The interjector was hurriedly bundled outside by the ushers but his interruption had loosened the tongues of the audience. The members of the National Union of General Workers and the Workers Control Party at the back of the hall began calling out questions, asking for details of how many people would be employed. As the Mayor took centre stage again, the ushers moved in and threatened these hecklers with eviction. The Mayor held up his hands for silence but it was some time before he was able to call the meeting to order.

'Now, ladies and gentlemen, I should like to introduce Mr

Walter Steen. I'd like you to listen to what he has to say about the proposal.'

Mr Steen stepped forward and addressed the meeting. 'Ladies and gentlemen, thank you for this opportunity to put before you my proposal. The whole nation is aware of the beneficial qualities of Buxton's famous water. People have been coming here to take the waters for centuries. It was known to the Romans even. It is unrivalled as a cure for rheumatism and gout and many other ailments. In addition, Buxton is a very comfortable resort and has many admirable establishments where one can take the waters. But...' He paused here for effect and looked around at the audience. 'But,' he repeated, 'unfortunately, not everyone has the luxury of coming to Buxton. Not everyone can afford the journey or the accommodation.' He paused again, letting his gaze travel around the audience, looking at some people directly, in order to make them believe that this lack of people's means was their fault. 'Now I think you will agree that it is unfair and selfish of the people of Buxton to keep this water for themselves. Why deprive your fellow countrymen of the benefits which you know are to be gained by drinking Buxton water? I appeal to your consciences and I ask you to do the right thing. Help me to share this water with a wider public. Put your own interests and financial concerns aside and think of it as a public service for which the nation will thank you and be ever grateful.'

During this speech, the audience listened in polite silence but Eleanor could sense their hackles slowing rising. They squirmed in their seats, folded and unfolded their arms across their chests, and shuffled their feet. When Mr Steen had finished speaking, those on the platform and a few people in the audience clapped. Most people sat unmoved. The Mayor again came forward, taking centre stage, and said, without enthusiasm: 'Are there any questions?' He looked down at his feet, avoiding eye contact, clearly hoping to discourage the audience.

Someone called out: 'Who owns the land where all this is supposed to happen?'

Another person called out: 'Is this going to interfere with our right to the water from the spring? It is protected by law, you know.'

The Mayor responded: 'The spring from which the water is to come is believed to be on the Duke's land.' He turned to the Duke's agent for confirmation.

Mr Sweeting stood up and said: 'I can confirm that the land in question does belong to the Devonshire estate but, at this stage, I am unable to say what the Duke's intentions are regarding either it or Mr Steen's proposed scheme.'

Someone towards the front of the hall stood up. He was the proprietor of one of the private hotels. He asked: 'I should like to put this question to Mr Steen through you, Mr Mayor. Mr Steen asks us to put aside our own interests and financial concerns to make this scheme possible but to what extent is he prepared to do the same? There seems little evidence of that to date and surely he stands to make a large profit from this scheme.'

'Good point,' said Mr Harriman to Eleanor.

Before Mr Steen could respond, a man sitting in the middle of the room stood up. In a loud, clear voice which carried right around the hall, he said: 'Yes. Mr Mayor, I'd like you to explain how giving away the very thing that attracts people to this town will be of benefit to those of us who depend for our livelihood on people coming to the town specifically to enjoy it.'

'Hear, hear,' came loudly from several directions in the crowd and then rippled through the audience. Then, the sentiment of the crowd could no longer be contained and everyone began to talk at once. Those who saw the sense of the scheme shouted at those who did not. The Mayor and the worthies saw no point in prolonging the discussion. They had said all they wanted to say, the Mayor hastily declared the meeting closed, and the officials and Mr Steen retreated from the platform. The ushers now had the difficult job of moving the audience out of the hall. As people stood up and began shuffling to the door, their progress was impeded by groups of people forming and either arguing or agreeing with each other, and friends and neighbours who stopped to greet each other and exchange their opinions.

'Mr Steen appears to have made a few enemies,' observed Mr Harriman to Eleanor.

'He certainly does,' agreed Eleanor, 'in addition to the members of the golf club. According to Mrs Clayton there are also many householders who are not happy at the prospect of a factory outside their door. I am very glad that Lady Carleton-West is not in Buxton at the moment. I believe she has gone to London for the whole of the London Season this year because one of her nieces is being presented at Court. Lady C is always anxious to distance herself from any hint of her origins connected with trade but she is, nevertheless, part of the capitalist class rather than the landed class and I doubt whether she would ever be able to pass up an opportunity for investment. She would certainly have appreciated the commercial advantages of Mr Steen's scheme and would be likely to support it.'

'Yes,' agreed Mr Harriman, 'I don't think she would give him her overt support but she would be unlikely to oppose the scheme, and others in her circle would be bound to follow her lead.'

'Precisely,' said Eleanor. 'Had she been here, she would have summoned the ladies of The Park and formed a committee on the subject. I am very relieved that there is no chance of my being summoned to give her advice.'

Mr Harriman looked around at the groups of people, still talking animatedly. 'I fear that the meeting has achieved little in the way of informing people, and it certainly seems to

152

have had the effect of dividing the town even further,' he said, gloomily.

~O~

On Saturday afternoon, Millicent Lee and her team from the Burbage Ladies' Golf Club were due to play their match against the team from Manchester, captained by Mrs Audrey Steen. Philip had gone to Chesterfield because a client wanted an opinion on some antique furniture being offered for sale so Eleanor went to the golf course alone. She had arrived at the Club House early to chat with the Burbage team and then, just before the match was due to begin, she wished them luck and went to join the group of spectators at the first tee. A large crowd of onlookers and sporting enthusiasts had assembled, including other members of the golf club, and supporters of both the local and the visiting players. As it was Saturday, the usual group of the town's idlers had also joined the crowd, mainly for the sport of heckling. There was a great deal of chatter as people milled about the Club House waiting for the match to begin. Many of the members were experienced players and the spectators anticipated a well-played game. The fact that ladies played golf was no longer a novelty. The Burbage Ladies' Golf Club had been founded twenty-three years ago and, for the twelve years prior to that, the ladies had played at the Buxton and High Peak Golf Club at Fairfield. That club, founded in 1887, had accepted ladies at first but, after ten years, the committee had voted itself the power to withdraw the ladies' playing rights and refuse them membership. It was this action which had prompted the creation of the Burbage Ladies' Golf Club. The ladies had not retaliated and did allow some gentlemen to become members of their club.

Today, there were two foursomes. The Burbage players were the first to appear from the Club House: Miss Millicent

Lee, Miss Maureen Fuller, playing in the first team and Miss Dorothy Shipton, and Mrs Hilda Tristram playing in the second team. They were joined at the first tee by their caddies. Then the four Manchester players appeared and walked across to the first tee. 'Ah,' thought Eleanor, 'Percy was right.' The captain of the Manchester team was the golfer whom she and Philip had seen on the course with the golf professional from Bramhall Park. Eleanor noted that Percy, as the most experienced caddie, had been assigned to Mrs Steen and Thomas was caddying for Mrs Steen's partner. Sensing that the match was about to begin, the crowd now surged forward behind the first tee. Order of play had been decided and Manchester had the honour at the first tee. The crowd had its favourites and was both enthusiastic and partisan. There was a great deal of noise and movement when Audrey Steen teed off but Millicent Lee was a favourite with the crowd and they were much quieter and more respectful as she teed off. As the match progressed through the first two holes, the crowd of followers cheered, yelled encouragement or criticism, or loudly condemned a poor stroke. The ladies were quite used to this disruptive behaviour and did not allow it to affect their concentration.

The third hole, known as Westward Ho! was par three. After the players had teed off, the crowd surged up the incline following the players towards the green. Millicent's last stroke had taken the ball very close to the hole and it was Manchester's turn to putt. The Manchester player's stroke sent the ball across the green and it now lay between Millicent's ball and the hole. There was uproar from the Burbage supporters and cries of 'She's stymied!' 'That was deliberate!' 'Oh, bad show!' One of the Manchester supporters called out loudly: 'Perfectly legal!' A Burbage supporter countered, just as loudly, with 'But not very sporting!'

It was now Maureen's turn to putt. She moved on to the

green and considered the situation carefully. The two balls were not quite in line but blocking a direct putt and an ill-considered stroke would send the opponent's ball straight into the hole, giving the hole to Manchester. The Burbage supporters now began to argue about the dilemma, calling out conflicting advice. 'A chip shot, definitely. That's the best option.' 'No, slice round it!' The Manchester supporters called out: 'Get on with it, girlie!' and 'Just play it and give us the point!'

Maureen ignored the crowd and its advice. She had been a keen croquet player and, with two brothers who were experienced billiards players, she understood perfectly how to place the ball so that it would send her opponent's ball off at an angle rather than shunt it into the hole. She crouched down in order to assess the line of the two balls and then gauged the distance between them. She took her club from her caddie and as she moved towards the ball, the crowd became silent with anticipation. Her stroke sent the ball in a very gentle curve across the green to drop neatly into the hole. It brushed against the opponent's ball as it passed sending the other ball off at an angle. The Burbage crowd roared their approval and even some of the Manchester supporters applauded. Eleanor had been holding her breath and now let it out with a loud sigh. Mrs Audrey Steen chose to play the ball where it now lay and with one stroke holed out.

The players had now reached the Green Lane edge of the course and from here the holes zig- zagged back and forth almost parallel with each other. Through the next four holes, the players gradually worked their way back down the slope towards Macclesfield Road and the play was uneventful. After the fifth hole, some of the crowd drifted back to the third hole to watch the second foursome who were now on their way to the third green. At the end of the seventh hole, Audrey Steen and her partner were one down. If they won the next hole, there was still the chance of victory. If they lost the next hole, the match would be over. The eighth hole, known as The Mere was one of the shorter holes, being only one hundred and twelve yards, but it was tricky because there was a downhill slope towards the green and the green itself sloped slightly.

The crowd followed the players, stroke for stroke, and by the time they reached the green of the eighth hole, the crowd could see the determination on the faces of the players and sense the tension in the air. The Burbage team had holed and it was Mrs Steen's turn to putt. This was the stroke for a birdie which would win the hole. The ball was some distance from the hole and a too energetic stroke would cause the ball to overshoot the hole and roll to the far side of the green. Audrey Steen took the putter from Percy and moved forward to address the ball. She looked down at the ball and then across to the hole, judging the distance, but then instead of playing the stroke, she stepped back from the ball and looked around at the crowd. As she did so, a group of four people at the back of the crowd began heckling. Turning to Percy and raising her voice she said: 'Go and tell those people over there to make less noise.' She waved her club in the direction of the hecklers and the eyes of the crowd naturally followed the line of her club to see who had offended her. Then the crowd looked at Percy to see what action he would take and watched as he walked to the other side of the green towards the people making the noise. While no-one was paying attention to her, Audrey Steen gingerly shifted her weight from her left foot to her right and, as she did so, slid her left foot forward slightly. It connected with the ball, sending it closer to the hole.

Not everyone was watching Percy or the crowd on the opposite side of the green. Maureen nudged Millicent. 'Did you see that?' she whispered.

'I certainly did. Whatever happened to "honesty, integrity

and courtesy" at all times?' hissed Millicent, through gritted teeth.

'What should we do? Ought we to say something?' asked Maureen.

Millicent considered the position for a moment. 'No,' she said. 'We don't want any unpleasantness. Let's just hope she misses the next shot.'

The attention of the crowd moved back to Mrs Steen but Millicent's hopes were not realised. Mrs Steen sent the ball cleanly into the hole. Mrs Steen's putt had saved Manchester and the teams were now even. When Audrey Steen had complained of the noise from the crowd, Eleanor too had looked across to the people on the opposite side of the green and she had noticed the golf professional from Bramhall Park standing right at the back of the group which was making the noise. She was surprised to see that he too was contributing to the noise. Eleanor had looked back at Mrs Steen, wondering if she had noticed that the golf profess-ional was in the crowd and she had seen Mrs Steen move the ball.

As she walked the short distance to the next tee, Eleanor pondered on the scene she had just witnessed and wondered if anyone else had noticed what had happened. She had the impression that the heckling from the far side of the green had only started after Mrs Steen had complained about it, as though her complaint was the cue for it to begin. It crossed Eleanor's mind that the noise might have been deliberately manufactured by the golf professional in order to distract attention from Mrs Steen's foot. Eleanor was disturbed by the idea that someone would cheat in this way. She consoled herself with the thought that often, on the tennis court, a player who has taken the benefit of a doubtful call, loses the next point and fair play prevails. Eleanor hoped that, in this case, the same thing would happen and Manchester would lose the last hole.

The final hole, prosaically called Home, was one hundred and thirty yards. 'Another par three, Mrs Steen,' said Percy at the tee, as he handed Mrs Steen her club. After the players had teed off, the crowd straggled forward and then paused to watch the second stroke. When the players and the crowd began walking again, Percy veered slightly off the fairway towards Eleanor so that he could talk to her.

'Miss Harriman,' he said, quietly, as he walked alongside Eleanor, 'did you see what happened at the eighth hole?'

Eleanor looked at the worried expression on Percy's face. She knew Percy well enough to trust him and decided not to pretend that she did not know what he was talking about. 'Yes, Percy,' she said, 'I did see what happened.'

'Thomas said Mrs Steen moved the ball with her foot.'

'Thomas is right. It's troubling, isn't it?'

'I thought for a minute 'e were mistaken, or that 'e were 'aving me on.'

'No, he was not mistaken,' said Eleanor, shaking her head.

'Ah,' said Percy, nodding decisively, 'that settles it, then.'

He veered back onto the fairway leaving Eleanor to wonder what he thought was settled. Then she saw him, up ahead, speaking to Thomas as they walked towards the green. The players reached the last green. Millicent's ball had landed towards the far edge of the green but her putting was very reliable and she knew the course well. She judged the distance, took into account the slight rise of the green, and the ball sped straight into the hole. Mrs Steen's ball lay on the other side of the green and was closer to the hole than Millicent's had been. Thomas noted the position of Mrs Steen's ball, nodded at Percy, and went to stand on the far edge of the green exactly in line with the ball and opposite Mrs Steen.

Percy, tight-lipped and frowning, silently handed Mrs Steen her putter. Mrs Steen then asked Percy to attend and he went to stand beside the pin. The crowd fell silent. Mrs

Steen took her time, lining up the hole carefully, and just as she raised her club to begin the swing, Thomas moved sideways, and dropped the bag of clubs he was holding. He was in Mrs Steen's direct line of sight and the movement distracted her, causing her to hit the ball harder than she had intended. The ball jerked forward, missed the hole, and then, because of the slope of the green, rolled a considerable distance away from it. There was an intake of breath and a loud 'Oh!' from the Manchester supporters. Mrs Steen glared at Thomas. Visibly angry, she walked around to the other side of the green and putted again, although the match was already lost. She picked up the ball and conceded the round.

The crowd then lost interest in the first foursome and, turning its attention to the other team of players, went to join the spectators around the seventh green. Eleanor hoped that Dorothy Shipton and Hilda Tristram were having better luck with the integrity of their Manchester opponents and she was beginning to have some appreciation of the difficulty that the Golf Club was facing in opposing the water bottling scheme. She thought about Mr Steen and wondered if his ethics and sense of fair play were any better than those of his wife. In the Club House, tea was served as the first four players waited for the second team to finish. The atmosphere was decidedly frosty. Maureen silently handed Mrs Steen and her partner a cup of tea without her usual concern for the welfare of her guests and did not offer them any cake. Millicent gave her full attention to her cup of tea and ignored her guests completely.

The match was eventually won by Burbage but without the usual feeling of satisfaction. After all the players had left, Percy and Thomas were sitting on the steps of the Club House cleaning golf clubs and discussing the afternoon's play.

Percy said to Thomas: 'Shame I forgot to remind Mrs

Steen about the slope on that last green.' He grinned and shrugged.

Thomas grinned back and said: 'Shame I'm so clumsy with a bag of clubs.'

CHAPTER ELEVEN

Once a month on Sunday afternoons during the Season, instead of walking with Cecily and Richard, Eleanor and Napoleon joined three friends and went for a long walk in the countryside surrounding Buxton. Today, however, two of the group had other commitments and only Eleanor and Dr Catherine Balderstone were free. They planned to walk to Wormhill, a small village to the north east, and then cut across the fields to Miller's Dale, an easy seven miles mostly through farmland. At Miller's Dale, they would stop for refreshments and then take the train back to Buxton. Eleanor and Napoleon had agreed to meet Catherine at Hardwick Mount and when they arrived there at two o'clock she was waiting for them. They set off downhill, walking in single file, until they reached Spring Gardens, then turned right towards Fairfield Road and the railway viaduct. They were now able to walk side-by-side and were out of earshot of other people.

Catherine said: 'I have some news which will surprise you.'

'Oh, what sort of news?' said Eleanor.

'I was at the Palace Hotel earlier today. Mr Steen was found dead this morning.'

Eleanor stopped walking and looked at Catherine. 'Good heavens!' she said, frowning, 'but that is so sudden. I admit that I have wished some awful things on him over the last few days but not that. What happened?'

Catherine said: 'I'm not sure. It's difficult to say.' They began walking again. 'Mr Steen was found by his valet this morning at about eight o'clock.'

'And you were called out?'

'Yes. The hotel manager telephoned to the surgery soon after Mr Steen was found and the call came through to me because Dr McKenzie is off fishing today. I went in his stead and I've only been back about an hour. I had to wait for the police to finish.'

'The police?'

'Yes. I had to call them in.'

'But how did Mr Steen die? What did he die of?'

'He appears to have died in his sleep. That is all that can be said for certain at the moment. I could find no obvious cause. There was absolutely no evidence on which to base a conclusion. Because I couldn't identify the cause of death, obviously I couldn't issue a death certificate.'

'So, there'll have to be a post mortem?'

'Mmm,' said Catherine, nodding, 'then I should have a better idea as to cause of death.'

'This is all so unexpected. I'm finding it difficult to comprehend. So much of our time and attention has been taken up lately with Mr Steen and his water bottling and now, it all seems rather irrelevant. Have you no inkling at all as to the possible cause of death.'

'No, it's very puzzling. I could see no sign of anything untoward, no sign of distress or pain. I did consider the possibility of heart attack but there was no evidence on which to base such a conclusion. I questioned the valet as to Mr Steen's general health and whether or not he had complained of any pain or discomfort the previous evening or in the preceding days. The valet assured me that Mr Steen was never ill and prided himself on that fact. Apparently, Mr Steen was in the habit of boasting that he was as fit as a man half his age. The valet said that in the eight years he had been with Mr Steen he had never known him to have even half of a day's illness. He also told me that Mr Steen had recently

162

had a medical examination for an insurance policy and he had been pronounced fit in every way. So, in the circumstances, I couldn't possibly issue a death certificate.'

'No, quite. But why the police?'

'Partly as a precaution and partly because there were some items that had to be removed from the room for testing. I had to get those items formally labelled and taken into evidence.'

Eleanor nodded. 'I suppose there will now be several days of uncertainty until the death certificate is issued. I wonder what will happen to the water bottling project.'

'I imagine that, at the moment, there is a question mark over that too,' said Catherine. 'Just as there is with the cause of death.'

Eleanor frowned. 'I am still trying to take in the news. Did Alf do the collection?'

'Yes, he's taken Mr Steen to the mortuary for the moment. No doubt Mrs Clayton will have more news for you tomorrow. Shall we go along the old road?'

They had now reached Fairfield Road and they began walking up the hill which followed the original road into Buxton. Near the top of the hill they stopped and looked back towards Buxton. The air was warm and the sun was highlighting the decorative stone work of the town's many elegant buildings.

'This is a lovely view,' said Eleanor. 'I always enjoy it.' She paused. 'I'm sure I shall regain my composure as we walk, but your news has completely taken me by surprise.'

They continued up the hill at a leisurely pace, crossing Queen's Road and arriving at The Green where they sat on a bench to enjoy the sunshine, each absorbed in thoughts of Mr Steen. Napoleon watched the passers-by with interest: families out for a Sunday stroll, and people carrying flowers to lay on the graves of their relatives in the churchyard. At this point, Fairfield Road divided into three and, when they were ready to set off again, Eleanor and Catherine crossed the road and veered to the right along Waterswallows Road. They were now passing the golf links belonging to the men's Club. Eleanor noticed that there were four players on the course, risking a letter to the Club from one of the local ministers of religion objecting to sport being played on a Sunday. They walked past the golf links in silence and then Eleanor asked: 'So what happens now?'

'Dr McKenzie will be back tomorrow. Then, after the post mortem, we shall have a better idea as to the cause of death. There's nothing more to be done today so let's forget about Mr Steen for the moment and enjoy our walk, shall we?'

'Good idea,' said Eleanor firmly. As they had now reached the beginning of farmland, Eleanor said: 'Sorry, Leon, you'd better be on your lead. I don't want you chasing sheep.'

~O~

On Monday morning, Mrs Clayton was in the kitchen preparing breakfast and Eleanor went in and said good morning to her.

'Good morning, Miss Harriman. I suppose you've heard the news.'

'About Mr Steen, you mean? Yes, I have. I was out walking with Dr Balderstone yesterday. She was called out to the hotel. I gather Alf was called out as well.'

'Yes. Spoilt his Sunday morning, it did. There's plenty of people had it in for Mr Steen and I know some of them have been talking about stopping him, by force even, but it seems they've been deprived of the opportunity.'

'And, fortunately for them, they also have been relieved of the responsibility,' said Eleanor, smiling. 'I know there has been a lot of wild talk but you don't really think any of the opponents of his scheme would have resorted to violence, do you?'

'Like as not, no,' said Mrs Clayton, shaking her head, 'although anything's possible, I suppose.'

'Buxton's just not that sort of town though, is it?'

'No, thank goodness,' agreed Mrs Clayton, as she turned back to preparing breakfast.

Eleanor went into the dining room and greeted her father. The previous evening when Eleanor returned from her walk they had discussed the news of Mr Steen's death and speculated on the likelihood of an inquest and of Mr Harriman being appointed coroner. This morning, therefore, they discussed the news items in *The Times* instead of Mr Steen.

At lunchtime, Philip left the antiques showroom and made his way to the Pavilion Gardens where he knew Eleanor and Napoleon would be taking their after-lunch stroll. He caught up with them at the boating lake. After Philip had greeted Eleanor and Napoleon, Eleanor said: 'You've heard about Mr Steen, I suppose.'

'Yes, I have. One of my clients told me. That is partly why I came to find you, in case you hadn't heard. The client didn't have any details though. Do you know anything?'

'Apparently, Mr Steen died in his sleep. Catherine and I were walking yesterday. She was the one who was called out when Mr Steen was found yesterday morning. She said it looked like natural causes but she couldn't say for certain. She'll know more after the post mortem today.'

'I suppose Mr Steen's death will put the water bottling scheme in doubt.'

'I should think so. In any event, that scheme was already in doubt. As a result of my conversation with members of the Brunt family, I think they may be able to stop the scheme permanently.'

'So the golf course is safe?'

'For the moment, yes.'

'That is good news,' said Philip. 'I just came to make sure

you had heard about Mr Steen, so I won't hold you up but there is one other thing. Mr Ashworth telephoned this morning.'

'Is he back in Buxton?'

'Yes, apparently he's been given another week's leave. He wants to get on with his digging as soon as possible because he thinks someone has heard about his ideas. Yesterday, he spotted two people down near the source of the river and one of them was the person he had seen in the office of the *Advertiser* when he was trying to find out about the jet necklace.'

'Is he suggesting that the person he saw in the office was his attacker?'

'He didn't go that far, but I had the impression that he was thinking along those lines. But Mr Ashworth didn't telephone me to talk about the attack. He wondered if we would join him at Collinsons on Thursday afternoon for tea. He wanted to thank us for rescuing him. Are you free?'

'That's very kind of him. Yes, I shall be free.'

'Good oh! I'll let him know.' Philip looked at his watch. 'I'd better be getting back.' Philip gave Napoleon a pat and then turned to go. Then he turned back, fished an envelope out of his pocket and said: 'Oh, I nearly forgot. I cashed Mr Steen's cheque for the Motor-car Rally. Will you give this to James, please, and ask him to put it in his British Legion tin.'

'With pleasure. He will be very happy to receive it.'

~O~

At four thirty that afternoon, James came upstairs to Eleanor's office and said: 'Miss Eleanor, Dr Balderstone is downstairs. She doesn't have time to stop properly but she wonders if she could have a quick word with you.'

'Certainly, James. I'll come down.'

Napoleon got up and went bounding down the stairs ahead of Eleanor.

'Ah, Eleanor,' said Catherine, making a fuss of Napoleon, 'sorry to disturb you. The post mortem has finished but I really am puzzled by this case and I would value your opinion. Could we make a time to meet?'

'Yes, of course. Come to supper this evening, if you like, after you finish at the surgery. Father will be at his club so we can please ourselves as to the time. Mrs Clayton is always happy to feed an extra person.'

'Thank you, I'd enjoy that and Mrs Clayton's cooking is far superior to my homely efforts.' Catherine glanced at the clock on the wall in James office. 'Look, I must dash. I'm due at the Cottage Hospital in five minutes. Good bye, James.'

Eleanor went upstairs to tell Mrs Clayton that Catherine was coming for supper and then returned to her office. Putting Mr Steen firmly out of her mind, she settled down to work.

CHAPTER TWELVE

Eleanor was in the sitting room reading a book while she waited for Dr Balderstone to arrive for supper. The office was closed. Edwin had gone home to his family and Mr Harriman had gone to his club. Mrs Clayton was in the kitchen preparing supper for the two ladies. Napoleon was looking forward to a quiet night in. He was lying on his side in the hall outside the kitchen door, ostensibly resting after his walk, but actually supervising Mrs Clayton.

When the front door bell rang, Eleanor called out: 'I'll go, Mrs Clayton. That will be Catherine.'

'Perfect timing. Supper's ready,' said Mrs Clayton.

Eleanor and Catherine came back upstairs and Eleanor said: 'Don't worry about staying to serve supper, Mrs Clayton. We'll look after ourselves, thank you. You get on home to your boys.'

'Well, if you're sure, Miss Harriman, I won't say no.' Eleanor nodded. 'Thank you, then I'll say goodnight. Goodnight, Dr Balderstone.'

Mrs Clayton tidied up the kitchen and then left. Eleanor and Catherine sat down at the dining room table and helped themselves to the food Mrs Clayton had prepared. Catherine looked at it with approval and anticipation because Mrs Clayton was an excellent cook.

When they were served, Eleanor said: 'Now, what's troubling you about Mr Steen?'

'It is not uncommon for someone to die in his sleep without there being any obvious cause but Dr McKenzie said I was right not to issue a death certificate. If the valet is to be believed, Mr Steen was very healthy and in good spirits on the night he died. And that view has been supported by the post mortem. There was no evidence of any disease which would explain Mr Steen's death and no post mortem changes which would suggest an unnatural cause. His death is unexplained.'

'But you are not happy leaving it at that?' said Eleanor.

'No, I am not. I need an explanation. For my own sake, if for no-one else's. It is very frustrating. There is something about this case that makes me uneasy, something I can't put my finger on, and yet, when I examine the evidence, there is nothing at all that should make me suspicious.'

'Apart from the fact that Mr Steen, an apparently hale and hearty man, is inexplicably and very unexpectedly dead,' said Eleanor.

'Yes. When you put it like that, it all sounds perfectly clear and simple,' said Catherine.

'I know that there has been a lot of animosity towards him but I suspect it is mostly talk. However, it is sensible to explore every avenue, just in case.'

'Exactly,' said Catherine. 'One has to be extremely cautious because there may be a perfectly innocent, unknown cause which, so far, I have been unable to detect. And yet, if all the normal explanations for the death have been eliminated, surely one is justified in considering the abnormal.'

'Just in case?'

'Yes,' said Catherine. 'Just in case.'

'Such as…?' asked Eleanor.

'Given the absence of any unusual physical cause, the first abnormal factor to consider is whether the death was caused by some form of poison having been ingested, either deliberately or accidentally but it is unwise to request a post mortem unless there is some evidence which justifies it. One is always reluctant to request a post mortem because it is distressing for the relatives.'

'Quite,' said Eleanor. 'No doctor is going to risk asking for one without having some foundation for the request. If the result of the post mortem is inconclusive, one's reputation could so easily be ruined.'

'It is not a tempting prospect, I agree. Over-caution on the part of the doctor in a case of poisoning is understandable and I suspect that, in the past, many a poisoner may have walked away free. Nevertheless, if there are grounds for suspicion, it is quite unpardonable not to order a post mortem. The other important factor, of course, is the difficulty of detecting the poison if, in fact, the ingestion of poison is the cause. One could form an opinion and find that, even after a post mortem, there is no evidence to support the allegation.'

'I can see why you need to think about this very carefully. Particularly if there is not enough evidence to even justify a suspicion of foul play.' Eleanor paused and looked at Catherine. 'Or is there some evidence?'

'Well, no. That is my difficulty. Not evidence as such, but the means of poison were definitely at hand...'

'Ah,' said Eleanor, 'so this is more than mere idle speculation!'

'...and some of the hotel servants were aware of the poison. In fact, some of them appear to have started a rumour that Mr Steen's death was not due to natural causes. At the moment, they are not going as far as to suggest that he was poisoned but there are rumblings and speculation because his death was so very unexpected. That is not good for the hotel. Mr Hewlett, the manager, telephoned Dr McKenzie and asked him, almost pleaded with him, to issue the death certificate immediately because he was afraid of false stories getting into the newspapers.'

'I suppose it is understandable for the hotel servants to speculate. People like to have answers and, in the absence of any, they make them up, especially if someone is known to have opponents, as Mr Steen was. There is fertile ground there.'

'Nevertheless, if the question of poison is not followed up, it may look like negligence on the part of the doctors involved.'

'Meaning you. And you feel that you need to pursue this, just in case?'

'Not because of anything that might appear in the newspapers. That's not what is making me uneasy. It is the very absence of evidence that is troubling me. I am afraid that you are going to find this irresistible, Eleanor.'

Eleanor laughed. 'I already am, so stop teasing me and get on with the story, please.'

'Well, I have thought about this very carefully and either we are dealing with a natural but unexplained death or a very clever murder.'

Eleanor stopped smiling and looked at Catherine with surprise. 'You're serious, aren't you? Gracious! Do tell.'

'Yes, I thought that would make you sit up. We may be looking at the perfect crime...'

'How thrilling.'

'...or I may be making a perfect fool of myself.'

The two friends looked at each other, assessing the situation.

'I doubt that, Catherine. You are always very sensible and very practical. You do not worry for no reason. But if there is something that troubles you, we need to confront whatever it is and deal with it.'

'I shall be very grateful to have your analytical mind to unravel things, Eleanor, and give me a second opinion.'

'Right,' said Eleanor, as she nodded her head firmly. 'All the facts, please, from the beginning. No holding back. What sort of poison are you considering?'

'Barbitone. After I had examined Mr Steen, I looked

around the room, not for anything in particular, just to get a general impression of the circumstances and I noticed on the bedside table a box of *Veronal.*'

Eleanor frowned. 'Sleeping tablets?'

'Yes,' said Catherine.

'Who'd have thought Mr Steen would be the sort to take sleeping tablets?' said Eleanor.

'I asked Mr Steen's valet about them and he said that, for some months now, Mr Steen had had trouble sleeping...'

'Guilty conscience,' interrupted Eleanor.

'... to the extent that his doctor had prescribed medication. The valet showed me the box of tablets and, from their brand name, I know that they contain barbitone. So, naturally, I had to consider that substance as a possible cause of death, or at least a contributory factor.'

'Careless or deliberate?' asked Eleanor. 'If it was sleeping tablets, I mean.'

'Does Mr Steen strike you as a man who would be careless? With medication or with anything else?' asked Catherine.

'No,' said Eleanor. 'On the contrary, he strikes me as a man who likes always to be completely in control of everything.'

'Does he strike you as a person likely to commit suicide?'

'No,' said Eleanor, shaking her head, 'definitely not. And certainly not just now when everything regarding his project seemed to be going his way.'

'Although there was the issue of the Brunt deed,' said Catherine.

'I'm not sure how much he knew about that. Besides, surely, if he had known about it, he would not have regarded it as an obstacle, just a minor hindrance. Mr Steen struck me as a very optimistic, self-confident person, used to getting his own way, in fact, used to making other people let him have his own way. I'm sure he would have expected to be able to negotiate an arrangement with the Brunts so that he could do as he wanted. Although I have to confess that, if he had actually met the Brunts, he might not have been so confident. I am sure they would have stood up to him.'

'Hmm. That's interesting. I have never met him, of course. I only saw him briefly at the town meeting, so I'm not really in a position to consider whether suicide was an issue.'

'Oh, I have never actually met him either. I have only observed him and I was just giving my impression of the man.'

'I see. Naturally, I wanted more information about the *Veronal*, particularly about his nocturnal habits, and I asked to speak to Mrs Steen but she wasn't available. In any event, she may not have been much use. I was told that Mr and Mrs Steen have adjoining suites in the hotel and, in those circumstances, I realised that the valet was probably better informed. He said the separate suites were necessary because Mr Steen normally retires quite early and Mrs Steen prefers to stay up late. However, last night Mr Steen went to bed much later than usual. He had been entertaining guests in the hotel. Then I asked the valet for details of the usual routine. Mr Steen had been prescribed one tablet per night.'

'Is that the usual dose?'

'For the relief of insomnia, yes. One tablet, that is, five grains. However, according to the valet, more recently Mr Steen had been taking a second tablet.'

'I told you, he had a guilty conscience.'

'Well, the trouble with this drug is that prolonged use makes it ineffective and, over time, the dosage has to be increased but two tablets are not sufficient to cause death.'

'So, how many tablets would it be dangerous to take?'

'Thirty grains is considered to be a dangerous level, that is, a minimum of six tablets, although the lethal dose varies depending on the person's tolerance. As I said, the more you take, the more you need. Also, it depends on how the drug is taken.'

'So, are you saying that, to have died of barbitone poisoning, Mr Steen must have taken at least six tablets?'

'May have. But, yes, if an excessive amount of barbitone is the cause of death. Six tablets could be fatal.'

'May? Could? You doctors are always so cautious,' teased Eleanor.

'Now, coming from a lawyer, that is definitely the kettle talking to the pot,' said Catherine, laughing. 'I won't burden you with the clinical details but the first reason for caution is alcohol. That has an accelerating effect and has to be taken into account in determining the level of barbitone which can be fatal. When Mr Steen was dining on Saturday evening, he drank alcohol. Quite a lot, apparently. The maître d'hôtel confirmed that for me. He said that Mr Steen and his guests appeared to be celebrating something and had ordered quite a quantity of wine.'

'Well, a celebration surely argues against suicide,' interjected Eleanor.

Catherine nodded. 'I agree. Particularly as the valet said that Mr Steen had been hoping that two of the guests would agree to provide the finance for Mr Steen's water project. Presumably the celebration meant that they had agreed. Anyway, coupled with alcohol, a lower dose could be fatal. The second reason for caution is that a person who takes an excessive dose of barbitone lapses into a coma. If the person is found in time, the effect of the drug can sometimes be counteracted, even if the amount taken is normally lethal. In Mr Steen's case, if he had not been alone, if he and Mrs Steen had not had separate rooms, his condition might have been discovered early enough, and a high dose may not have been fatal.'

'You mean, he may have survived even if he had taken a large number of tablets?'

'It is possible. Unlikely, but possible.'

'So it may have been an accident? A mistake made by a man desperate for sleep?'

'No, one of the advantages of this drug is that the level of the therapeutic dose is well below the toxic dose and therefore accidental death is unlikely. When medication is in liquid form, it is sometimes easy to take too large a dose by mistake but not when it is in pill form. If one tablet is the prescribed dose, one does not swallow six or seven tablets by mistake. I am sure Mr Steen's doctor would have warned him of the dangers of taking too many tablets so a mistake is highly unlikely.'

'Even if he had spent the evening in the unbridled consumption of alcohol?'

'Even if his faculties were affected by alcohol. And even if, as you suggest, he was desperate for sleep and had taken double the prescribed dose, he would very probably still be alive. There is no getting away from it. The fatal dose has to be a minimum of six tablets and more likely seven or eight. So, to sum up, the difficulty is that there is no evidence that he did take more than his usual two tablets.'

'Therefore, if we have ruled out suicide and accident, any overdose would have to be due to the deliberate act of a third party,' said Eleanor.

'Yes. The trouble is, though, the facts themselves are at odds with a deliberate act.'

'What facts?' asked Eleanor, sensing an anomaly of the kind she enjoyed.

'The tablets are supplied in a small box containing twenty tablets. The valet showed me the box. He said that it was his responsibility to see that Mr Steen always had a supply of his tablets. Now, pay attention. In the normal course, at one tablet per night, a box of twenty tablets would be sufficient for twenty days. However, based on what the valet told me, if Mr Steen had been taking two tablets per night, one box would only last for ten days. The valet said he opened a new box on the Monday before Mr Steen died. He had ordered the box on the previous Friday and it was delivered the next day. The first two tablets from that box were taken on the Monday night and Mr Steen died on the following Saturday so that makes six nights on which he took two tablets from that box.'

'And at two tablets per night, that is twelve tablets which have been consumed,' said Eleanor.

'Correct. Twelve from twenty is eight. So, in the normal course of things, on Sunday morning, when Mr Steen was found, there should have been eight tablets left in the box.'

'But if he had died of an overdose,' said Eleanor, 'he would have needed to take some of those eight for the dose to be fatal.'

'Yes. Say, he took five tablets on top of his usual two, making a fatal dose of seven tablets. There would have been only one tablet left in the box,' said Catherine.

'Why do I feel as though I am watching one of those magician's tricks with cups where things disappear and reappear?' asked Eleanor.

'Because, you are. It is one of those tricks. The tablets magically reappeared. The valet showed me the box of *Veronal* and it contained all eight tablets. Just as it should have.'

'Let me see,' said Eleanor. 'Point one. Eight tablets left in the box is consistent with the correct dose having been taken on the Saturday night. Point two. If the correct dose had been taken, Mr Steen would still be alive. Point three. He is not alive. Ergo? He was poisoned with extra tablets from some source other than the box of tablets which the valet showed you.'

'Or, he died of natural causes and my suspicion as to the cause of death is totally wrong.'

'Or the valet is lying.'

'Or the valet is lying. That is possible, I grant you,' said Catherine, 'but why would he lie?'

'Because he was responsible for the overdose.'

'Oh, I see what you mean,' said Catherine. 'I suppose we should consider that. After all, he is in a better position than anyone else to tamper with the tablets.'

'He also would have known how many tablets Mr Steen usually took and, therefore, he could be certain as to how many extra ones were needed for a fatal dose. He could easily have accumulated the tablets, removing one at a time, over a few weeks.'

'But what motive would he have had?'

'I shall have to think about that. I suppose Mr Steen could have hidden extra tablets at some earlier time in anticipation of taking an overdose,' said Eleanor.

'He could have, but why would he? One would need to do that only if one was being handed one or two tablets per night and needed to store them up. He had access to the whole box and could have taken as many as twenty tablets in one gulp if he was so minded.'

'I've just thought of something,' said Eleanor. 'In the days before the new box of tablets was delivered, the number of tablets left in the current box would be quite low, so it would be obvious if some tablets were missing. In fact, in the two days immediately before the new box arrived, there would not have been five or six tablets left to steal and, stealing five or six tablets three days before, would have left the box empty. If that had happened, surely the valet would have noticed and reported the theft.'

'So that's another black mark against the valet.'

'We need to speak to the valet,' said Eleanor.

'So, if some of Mr Steen's tablets were stolen, let's see. They would have to have been removed some time after a new box was opened and before there were too few tablets to make the theft obvious. The new box was opened on the

Monday before Mr Steen died, that is the fifteenth and it had been ordered on the Friday before that and delivered on the Saturday, the thirteenth.'

'That was the day of the Motor-car Rally,' said Eleanor. 'Are the boxes sealed when they are new?'

'Definitely, they have to be because they contain a substance classified as poison.'

'So,' said Eleanor, 'one could not safely steal any tablets until the new box had been opened, that is after the Monday night. But for the next few days it would be safe because there would still be enough tablets in the box for the theft not to have been noticed.' They sat thinking for a moment or two. Eleanor continued: 'If this was a deliberate act on the part of a third party, we are dealing with someone very cunning. Leaving the correct number of tablets in the box was a very clever thing to do. It draws suspicion away from the sleeping tablets. If there are no tablets missing, one might not suspect an overdose, at least not immediately.'

'Absolutely. It does suggest a degree of planning, doesn't it? It is not a crime committed on the spur of the moment.'

'Definitely not. It also suggests someone who knew how many tablets to leave in the box in order to avoid suspicion and that suggests someone who knew how many tablets Mr Steen usually took. We seem to be back at the valet again,' said Eleanor. They pondered that problem and then Eleanor said: 'Setting aside for the moment the problem of the sleeping tablets, it does seem unlikely that Mr Steen deliberately took an overdose. If the maître d'hôtel is right and Mr Steen was celebrating with his dinner guests, he would have been in a reasonably optimistic state of mind.'

'Agreed. On the other hand, something was troubling him and preventing him from sleeping...to the extent that the prescribed dose of one tablet per night was proving inadequate.'

'Perhaps he was worried about Mrs Steen,' suggested

Eleanor. 'The need for separate hotel rooms shows that their lifestyles were not particularly compatible. She is a great deal younger than he is. Philip and I saw Mrs Steen on the golf course with a golf professional from Bramhall Park and it was clear that they were on friendly terms. Very friendly.'

'Perhaps she was intending to leave Mr Steen,' suggested Catherine.

'Mr Steen did not strike me as a man who would be too concerned about personal relationships. I suspect the water project was more important in his scheme of things than his wife.'

Catherine laughed: 'Surely, that would be precisely why Mrs Steen would be likely to desert him.'

Eleanor said: 'So, that leaves us with a deliberate act by a third party. Any ideas?'

'If, as the valet stated, the box was regularly left on the bedside table, anyone could have removed some tablets. And, as you have suggested, if the tablets were taken from a nearly full box, it is unlikely that Mr Steen or the valet would have noticed their loss at the time.'

'Something has just occurred to me and it is not helpful,' said Eleanor. 'We know that no tablets were taken from the box which was opened on the Monday before Mr Steen died. When would there previously have been a full box from which to take tablets unnoticed?'

'Ten days before that Monday. That Monday was the fifteenth, so that takes us back to the tenth and counting backwards from Monday,' said Catherine using her fingers, 'the tenth was a Friday.'

While Catherine had been counting, Eleanor had been thinking. 'I saw Mr Steen the day he arrived at the hotel, and that was Friday the tenth, therefore, if tablets were stolen from that new box they must have been stolen in the first few days after Mr Steen arrived. Does that give anyone in the hotel time to find out that they were there and how many tablets were needed?'

'Or a reason to want Mr Steen dead?' added Catherine. 'That takes us back to the valet again, doesn't it?'

'Or Mrs Steen. We are not getting on very well, are we?' sighed Eleanor. They sat in gloomy silence, each thinking over the possibilities. Eventually, Eleanor asked: 'Did Mrs Steen have any useful information?'

'I didn't actually speak to her. All our attention was on Mr Steen at first and then I was told that Mrs Steen was not available. The manager sent one of the chamber maids to knock on the door of her suite but there was no response. He checked the public parts of the hotel and couldn't find her there either. They assumed that she had had a late night and was still asleep and did not want to be disturbed. Mr Hewlett didn't think opening the door with the master key was warranted and I saw no need to press the point.'

'Did you speak to her maid?'

'She didn't have a maid with her.'

'And there was nothing more you could do?'

'No, apart from have the police record the state of the room and take away the water carafe from the bedside table for testing.'

'That sounds like a very sensible thing to do. What does Dr McKenzie think?'

'He is as puzzled as I am. However, he is inclined to wait for the inquest.'

'What additional evidence would there be available then?'

'That is another problem. Samples were taken at the post mortem and they have been sent to the Home Office pathologist but it will take some time before the results are available and, even when we do receive them, they may be inconclusive. It is always difficult to determine whether or not someone has been poisoned even when the type of poison is suspected or known. Chemical analysis is possible, of course, and reliable tests have been developed for traditional poisons, such as arsenic and strychnine, but barbitone is a relatively new drug and not easily detected. The tests currently available may not be sufficient. There is nothing more I can do for the moment, or possibly, at all. So, there it is.'

'Well, I think you are right to be cautious because, if you do not find an explanation you will feel dissatisfied every time you think about this case.'

'I certainly shall. In my view, if we do not know the cause, it is not safe to say that his death was natural.'

'Neither is it good enough to simply say "there is no obvious cause of death" and leave it at that. People do not die without there being a cause. The fact is, Mr Steen died unexpectedly. Therefore, something must have caused his death. If it is even remotely possible that his death was caused deliberately, there raises a doubt, and that doubt needs to be resolved.'

'Thank you, Eleanor. You are right. I feel much better having talked it over with you and, as usual, your ability to think logically has clarified the issues. I was afraid that I was being irrational. We must take this further, even if there doesn't seem to be a way forward just now.'

'Well, let's just go over the facts again in case there is something you have overlooked, something that you thought or noticed at the time but that you are not now aware of. There may be something there in the background of your brain, and that may be what is making you uneasy about this case. Describe to me what you saw and what you did when you arrived at the hotel.'

'Mr Steen was lying in bed and the valet was sitting on a chair beside the bed, watching, as is the custom when someone dies. When I saw him, Mr Steen gave every appearance of being dead. I checked for a pulse and, of course, there was nothing. I then sent the valet out of the room and carried out all the usual examinations.'

'I don't need to know about those, thank you,' said Eleanor, pulling a face, 'but I imagine that you estimated a time of death?'

'Yes, Mr Steen had been dead for about three hours, four at the very most, which would put the time of death somewhere between about five and six in the morning. When I had finished my examination, I had the valet brought back and I asked him to tell me how he found Mr Steen. He said that he had come into the room to open the curtains and wake him as usual.'

'Was the door locked?'

'Yes, the valet has a key. He said he thought that Mr Steen was still asleep, which was unusual but he wasn't concerned because Mr Steen had been to bed later than usual the night before.'

'And the curtains were drawn?'

'Yes.'

'So, if the curtains were still drawn, the valet probably didn't see Mr Steen very clearly. What time was that?'

'Seven thirty,' said Catherine, 'which apparently was the usual time that Mr Steen awoke. According to the valet, Mr Steen was a man of very regular habits and liked a firm routine.'

'So Mr Steen was probably already dead then,' said Eleanor.

'Certainly, yes. The valet went back again at eight because he knew Mr Steen had an appointment and would want to be woken in plenty of time. So, when he went back, he drew the curtains and then, being able to see Mr Steen, realised that there was something wrong. He tried to rouse him and then he called the manager and asked for a doctor.'

'And did anything in the room seem to have been disturbed?'

'No, there was no sign of any disturbance. Mr Steen was lying on his back. His clothing and the bed clothes had not been disturbed. I asked the valet to look around and tell me if there was anything out of place and he said he could not see anything. I asked him to look again really carefully and the only thing he commented on was that the carafe of water beside the bed had more water in it than he would have expected. Apparently, the level of water was generally lower. Oh, and that one of Mr Steen's slippers was missing. One of them was on the floor beside the bed and when the valet looked, he found the other one under the bed a little way in. The valet wondered if Mr Steen had got up in the night.'

'No clues there, then,' said Eleanor, 'so really all you can do is wait for the Home Office pathologist?'

'Yes, and until then or even then, we may not know the truth because the results might be inconclusive. I feel as though we have gone around in circles without achieving anything very much.'

'No, on the contrary, I think we have achieved something,' said Eleanor. 'There's lots to be clarified but, at least, we now know what questions to ask.'

'I suppose that is something,' said Catherine. 'However, shall we forget about this case for the moment and take Napoleon for his walk?'

'Yes, if you will answer one last question. It has just occurred to me. You pointed out that it is not possible to take six or more tablets by accident. Similarly, it would not be easy for a third party to persuade someone to take that number of tablets voluntarily, particularly if that someone had been warned not to exceed the prescribed dose. So, how could that happen?'

'I have thought about that and I have no idea. There was no sign of force having been used, no bruising, etc. That is another reason why it is possible that I am suffering from a severe case of over-imagination or have become overly suspicious of even the most ordinary facts,' said Catherine. 'Probably as a result of my association with you,' she added.

She stood up. 'Come on, Napoleon, let's go for that walk before Eleanor thinks of another question.'

Napoleon and Catherine went out of the sitting room door and Napoleon was already half-way down the stairs when Eleanor said: 'No, wait. Perhaps you should check at the chemist shop and verify that the valet did order the new box and have it delivered on the Friday and not later.'

'Napoleon and I have ceased to listen,' called Catherine as she followed Napoleon down the stairs.

CHAPTER THIRTEEN

The following morning, as Eleanor came into the dining room for breakfast, Mrs Clayton said good morning and then added: 'Alf said when he went to collect Mr Steen there was a right "to do" at the hotel. The manager trying to hush up the death and the hotel servants wanting to talk about nothing else.'

'Well, it's not good for business is it, having a death in a hotel.'

'No, it is not. Puts people off. And it's in the papers this morning because apparently someone told the newspapers that Mr Steen was done away with.'

'Oh?' said Eleanor, with interest, thinking of last night's conversation with Catherine. 'Why would they think that?'

'Well, as Alf said, a sudden death and no death certificate. There's bound to be talk, isn't there? A newspaper reporter interviewed one of the hotel servants, it didn't say who, and whoever it was had found out that the police had taken away something from Mr Steen's room for examination so, according to the newspapers, that could only mean one thing.'

Eleanor assumed that the hotel servants were referring to the items Catherine had asked to be kept safe. 'I see,' she said, smiling, 'for the newspapers, one small fact plus a large helping of speculation is enough to build a whole story.'

Mrs Clayton laughed. 'I don't suppose the hotel manager will be very happy that some of the hotel servants have been talking to the newspaper reporters about Mr Steen.'

Mr Harriman took *The Times* which had not mentioned

Mr Steen's death, so Eleanor had not seen any reports. Mrs Clayton favoured the tabloids, and one in particular which was dedicated to speculation and providing its readers with the more interesting background information about people in the news. Eleanor asked: 'What else are the newspapers saying about Mr Steen? I'm curious to know.'

Mrs Clayton poured Eleanor's tea and stood, teapot in hand: 'Well, someone they interviewed at the hotel said that Mr Steen was fit as a flea the night before and they can't understand why he died so suddenly. Dining with some people from London, he was, money men who were going to invest in his scheme, apparently. Ordering lots of food and drink and splashing his money around. Now, that didn't come from the hotel servants. Two of the lady guests at the hotel took particular notice and they were interviewed by the papers.' Eleanor briefly thought of her conversation with Millicent about the ladies who dance with lounge lizards. Mrs Clayton continued: 'And the next morning, he's found dead, so the newspapers are saying it must have been foul play.'

'And who, according to the newspapers, is to be suspected? Someone who wanted to stop the factory plan, perhaps?' asked Eleanor.

'That's been suggested but one of the papers has got hold of a story about Mrs Steen and that makes much more interesting reading than some dull old factory. According to the papers, Mr Steen was a very wealthy man. Self-made, of course. He came from Nottingham but went to London. Made a lot of money there, not always honestly apparently. At least, that's what was being hinted at and then he went to Manchester and set up a ginger ale factory. He only got married four years ago and he'd not been married before. Too busy making money, I suppose. Mrs Steen was an actress, at least, that's what the papers say but, I've never heard of her. They say she gave up her career to marry Mr

Steen. She's a good bit younger than him.'

'How old is she?' asked Eleanor.

'Twenty-six. He was forty-five. With that sort of age difference, well, there's bound to be trouble, isn't there?'

'Did the newspaper report suggest that there was trouble?'

'Not in so many words,' said Mrs Clayton, 'but they're calling her the merry widow. And it said in the paper that they had separate suites at the hotel. It was made pretty clear that she had reason to want him dead.'

'Oh, I see. Then, the implication is that she killed him?'

'Well, her or her fancy man. He plays golf apparently but he's disappeared, according to the papers. The hotel staff told the papers that there had been rumours about them.'

'It's an amusing thought,' said Eleanor, 'Mr Danebridge and I saw Mrs Steen with the golf professional on the golf course last week and we remarked that they seemed to be very well acquainted. Nevertheless, I think it is rather irresponsible of the newspapers to make such a suggestion before any of the facts are known.'

'And the papers said she cheated at golf as well.'

'Well, that statement is certainly true. I can vouch for that. I wonder how they got that information.'

'Anyroad, she'll be able to please herself now, won't she, there not being any children. I suppose he's left her some of his money, so perhaps she will be a merry widow, like they say.'

Mr Harriman arrived in the dining room and said good morning to Eleanor and Mrs Clayton.

'Good morning, Mr Harriman,' said Mrs Clayton. 'I'll just make some fresh tea. Here's your newspaper.' She handed Mr Harriman his *Times* and retreated to the kitchen.

~O~

After lunch, when Eleanor and Napoleon returned from their

walk in the Gardens, James allowed Eleanor time to go upstairs, take off her hat and coat, and tidy her hair and then went up to her office and stood in the doorway.

'Miss Eleanor,' he said, his tone deliberately neutral, 'while you were out, Mrs Steen telephoned.' He paused. Eleanor looked at James, open mouthed in astonishment. 'She requested an appointment with you.'

'Mrs Steen?' Eleanor frowned.

'Yes,' said James, imperturbable as usual. 'She would like to consult you as soon as possible about Mr Steen's death. I enquired whether or not it was to do with his Will and she said that it was not but she would not specify further. I told her that I would enquire and telephone her back. Shall I make an appointment for her?' James raised one eyebrow and waited for Eleanor's response.

'Yes, I suppose so, thank you, James,' said Eleanor. 'Goodness! Whatever can it be?'

'She particularly asked to see you today. Shall I say three thirty?'

'Please do. But definitely no later. I can't possibly stand the suspense for a moment longer than that.'

James smiled and retreated.

Shortly before three thirty, Napoleon was banished and Eleanor tidied her desk ready for the arrival of Mrs Steen. Mrs Steen, however, was used to keeping people waiting. She believed that it reinforced her importance in the minds of others. It was another fifteen minutes before she arrived at Hall Bank and was shown upstairs to Eleanor's office.

'Mrs Steen, Miss Harriman,' said James, his face an impassive mask.

'Thank you, James. Good afternoon, Mrs Steen,' said Eleanor, coming forward ready to shake hands. Mrs Steen did not return Eleanor's greeting. As Eleanor was closing the office door, Mrs Steen looked around her, assessing the quality of her surroundings. 'Won't you sit down?' said

Eleanor as she offered Mrs Steen a chair and then went and sat down at her desk. She looked at Mrs Steen. Previously, she had only seen her at a distance and had noted the bright red lipstick and blonde hair. Now, Eleanor could see that the blonde hair was bleached and Mrs Steen wore a great deal of make-up as well as lipstick, far more than would have been acceptable to the matrons of The Park. Eleanor could imagine their disapproval. She could also imagine their opinion of Mrs Steen herself but she was determined not to follow their example. Eleanor tried not to be judgmental, although it was difficult considering Mrs Steen's appearance and demeanour.

Mrs Steen was dressed in a peacock blue suit of silk taffeta: a loose fitting, three quarter length coat in the latest style with a belted dropped waist, wide sleeves and rolled collar in a deep V-shape, an ankle length matching skirt, a blouse in white silk charmeuse with elaborate pleating, a wide-brimmed hat, also in peacock blue, trimmed with a frothy feather in fawn, and fawn kid gloves and shoes. Mrs Steen sat down in the visitor's chair, and adopted a pose, slightly angled so that she could use her head and eyes expressively as she looked at Eleanor. She raised one gloved hand negligently as though to push back a strand of hair that had escaped from under her hat but the gesture was simply designed to draw attention to her wrist and the large gold bracelet set with several diamonds, worn over the glove so as to be visible. Whether she had been on the stage or not, Mrs Steen clearly knew how to act a part and it certainly was not the role of newly bereaved widow. Eleanor sensed that the usual expressions of condolence would not be welcome so she waited for Mrs Steen to speak.

'I'm being hounded,' said Mrs Steen, abruptly and loudly, 'and I want you to do something about it.' Her accent was east of London, overlaid with a stage imitation of Belgravia.

'May I ask who is hounding you, Mrs Steen?' asked

Eleanor calmly.

'Those newspaper reporters, of course, and the press photographers. I was an actress before I married Walter and they know I make a good story. News about me sells their rotten newspapers for them. That's why they won't leave me alone.'

'And what is it, exactly, that you would like me to do, Mrs Steen?'

'Stop them accusing me,' she said, angrily.

'Of what are you being accused?'

'Of getting rid of my husband. Don't you read the newspapers?'

Eleanor thought to herself: 'Not the kind you read, obviously.' She was reminded of her conversation with Mrs Clayton that morning and the information Mrs Clayton had relayed. Instead of replying to Mrs Steen's question, she asked, keeping her tone completely neutral: 'I assume by "getting rid of" you mean killing.'

'Of course,' said Mrs Steen, impatiently.

'Mrs Steen, the cause of death has not yet been officially established, so there is no suggestion that anyone killed your husband. Why would someone accuse you of doing so?'

Mrs Steen did not reply. She looked down at her left sleeve and brushed away an imaginary speck. Then she said: 'Official or not, that doesn't worry the reporters. It doesn't stop them from making up stories. Look, the rubbish they're writing about me and Walter, it's just not true. I did not kill him. I am not a merry widow.'

Eleanor could not detect in Mrs Steen any emotion at the loss of her husband and wondered whether Mrs Steen realised how much she was playing into the hands of the newspaper reporters. She thought that if Mrs Steen had previously been an actress, she could easily play the part of the grieving widow no matter what her true feelings were. That would surely have helped to allay suspicion. Wearing the traditional black instead of peacock blue would have helped her image. As it was, Eleanor could see why the reporters thought they had a story worth running.

'I'm sorry, Mrs Steen, I am not sure exactly what action you have in mind. Do you want to sue for defamation?' asked Eleanor.

'No,' said Mrs Steen, impatiently, 'I want you to find out how Walter died. Somebody told me you were good at that sort of thing. You find murderers. Well, I want you to find this one. That will prove that I didn't do it. And then I might think about defamation.'

Eleanor hesitated before responding. She was not sure that she wanted to be labelled as someone who found murderers. Although Eleanor had successfully resolved two cases in the past, she had had some personal connection with those involved and it was for that reason that she had carried out an investigation. She was not available for hire in the way that Mrs Steen implied. Recalling her conversation with Catherine the previous evening, she thought that, even in the absence of evidence, Catherine need have no fear of offending Mr Steen's relatives by suggesting that his death was not due to natural causes. His wife was, very conveniently, making the allegation herself.

Seeing Eleanor's reluctance to reply, Mrs Steen continued: 'I can pay, if that's what you're worried about.' The Belgravia accent slipped slightly.

Eleanor shook her head: 'Mrs Steen, the sort of enquiry that you are suggesting would be difficult and very time consuming. It could involve you in a great deal of expense. If there is anything suspicious about the way Mr Steen died, the police will investigate. Wouldn't it be better to leave the enquiry to them?'

'No, that's not good enough,' said Mrs Steen, forcefully. 'If someone did away with Walter, I want that person found because until then, I will always be under suspicion. I can't have that. I want you to prove that I am innocent and I need it done now.'

Eleanor was not sure that Mrs Steen was thinking very rationally. She asked: 'Just supposing that someone did take Mr Steen's life, do you have any ideas yourself as to who that person might be?'

'No, none at all. Except for the loony who's been sending him threatening letters.'

Eleanor was amused by the slang and assumed that Mrs Steen was copying American motion pictures and perhaps had ambitions to be a film star herself. She asked: 'What sort of threatening letters did he receive, Mrs Steen?'

'I've no idea. I didn't take much notice. He got very angry and ripped them up.'

'When did he receive them?'

'At breakfast.'

'I meant when did the letters start and how often did he receive them? Do you have any idea what…'

'Look, I didn't read them. I don't know anything about them. I just saw him deal with one, at breakfast, a couple of days ago when I happened to be up early and he said it wasn't the first. That's all I know.'

'What gave you the impression that they contained threats?'

'Because Walter said: "They can threaten all they like, it won't make a bit of difference" and then he tore it up.'

'I see,' said Eleanor.

'Anyway, this is not about Walter. This is about me. I want you to stop people pointing a finger at me.'

Eleanor considered the situation. It was clear that Mrs Steen was used to getting her own way and she was prepared to pay to prove her innocence. Eleanor did not consider that this course of action was in Mrs Steen's best interests. However, she thought that if Mrs Steen was as innocent as she claimed, the task of establishing her whereabouts at the relevant time and eliminating her from suspicion would be fairly straightforward and would not involve a great deal of expense. Since her conversation with Catherine, Eleanor had been curious about Mr Steen's death and she wanted to help Catherine. Accepting instructions from Mrs Steen provided a perfect opportunity to do so because she would be able to approach people and ask questions legitimately.

'Well, can I suggest this?' said Eleanor. 'I shall carry out a few enquiries and make an assessment of the situation. Then I'll provide you with a preliminary report and you can decide what you would like to do from there. My time will be charged on an hourly basis which Mr Wildgoose, my clerk, will arrange with you. Is that acceptable?'

'I suppose so, if that's the best you can do,' said Mrs Steen, ungraciously. 'But I need action right away. I know how you lawyers like to delay things and that's no good to me.'

Eleanor was beginning to feel quite cross with Mrs Steen but she did not let it show. She could see one very simple way of dealing with this troublesome client. Eleanor decided that it was time for the truth.

'Very well, Mrs Steen,' said Eleanor, pulling her note pad towards her and taking up a pen. 'In order to prove that you had nothing to do with the death of Mr Steen, I need to know where you were on the day that he died and, more particularly, that night.'

There was silence in the room. Eleanor waited, pen poised. Mrs Steen glared at Eleanor, eyes narrowed. Then she opened her handbag and produced a gold cigarette case. She flipped it open and took out a cigarette. She looked up at Eleanor, who was watching her impassively, looked down again at the cigarette, returned it to the case, snapped the case shut and put it back in her bag. She looked down at her glove and fiddled with the small safety chain on her bracelet. The silence continued and Eleanor waited, looking directly at Mrs Steen, pen poised, like a headmistress waiting for an explanation from a pupil accused of breaking the rules. Eventually, Mrs Steen looked up at Eleanor.

'Look,' she said, defensively, 'is this really necessary?' It was the tone of someone used to bargaining.

'I'm afraid so,' said Eleanor, 'but I can assure you that anything you tell me will be treated as confidential unless, of course, you have committed a crime. If, as you say, you are innocent, whatever you tell me need never be revealed unless you want it to be.' Eleanor put down her pen and pushed away her note pad, making it clear that she would not be writing anything down. She paused and then said, quietly and reassuringly: 'Now, when did you last see Mr Steen alive?'

'On the day before they found him. I had breakfast with him at the hotel.'

'What time did you finish breakfast?'

'About nine thirty. Walter said he was going to meetings during the day and then entertaining clients for dinner. I had a golf match that afternoon, with the Burbage Ladies. I sat in the lounge during the morning and read magazines while I waited for the others to arrive. Then we had lunch and went to my suite and got changed and went on the course.'

'When you said the others, did you mean your team members?'

'Yes, and some friends. They were coming from Manchester.'

Eleanor decided to feign ignorance in order to get Mrs Steen's version of the facts. She asked: 'Can I just clarify? Did you and Mr Steen have separate suites at the hotel?'

'Yes, Walter had trouble sleeping and didn't like to be disturbed. I like to stay up late so it was easier that way.' This was said with a note of defiance.

'And are the suites interconnected?'

'No.'

'So, you went to the golf course and played the match.'
Eleanor decided not to mention that she had been there at
the match and seen Mrs Steen cheat. 'And after the match?'

'Tea in the Club House, very dreary.'

Eleanor thought that, given the events of that day,
Millicent and Maureen would have been struggling even to
be polite, let alone entertaining. It was generous of them to
have provided tea at all. 'And after that?' prompted Eleanor.

'We couldn't leave town soon enough. We decided to go
for a drive so we went to Cheshire. Somebody had membership of a golf club there and we had a few drinks at the Club
House. Then we went to a hotel and had dinner because it
was late and we knew we wouldn't be back at the Palace in
time for dinner. In any event, I didn't want to come back
because of Walter's clients. I knew I would have to join them
and the whole evening would be taken up by them and there
would be no dancing. His clients are always tedious people.
You cannot imagine how dull and dreary that is!'

'When you say "we" had dinner at a hotel. How many
people were with you?'

'Oh, all of us were there.' Mrs Steen counted silently
using her fingers. 'Eight, no ten of us altogether.'

'So, that is at least nine people who knew where you
were. At what time did you finish dinner?'

'About nine thirty. Perhaps a little later.'

'So, nine other people were with you until nine thirty. And
the rest of the evening you were where?'

'On the dance floor. Gilbert is a superb dancer. Walter is
not interested in dancing.'

'And Gilbert's surname is…?'

'Royston.'

'And Mr Royston is…?

'My golf coach…' said Mrs Steen, '…and he's a friend,'
she added. Mrs Steen looked directly at Eleanor as though
challenging her to disapprove.

When she arrived at the office Mrs Steen had shown no sign of recognising Eleanor. She obviously had not realised that Eleanor and Philip had seen her with the golf professional on the golf course. Eleanor assumed that Mrs Steen was the sort of person who did not take particular notice of anyone else, unless perhaps they were of use to her.

Eleanor asked: 'And what time did you and Mr Royston leave the dance floor?'

'Midnight. The dancing stops then. It was Saturday.'

Eleanor thought for a minute, picturing the activities of that day. Then, she asked: 'Had you taken evening clothes with you?'

There was a long pause and eventually Mrs Steen said: 'It wasn't that kind of hotel?'

'What is the name of the hotel?'

'What do you want to know that for?'

'It is relevant, I assure you.'

'The Swinford, it's just near Wilmslow.'

'And the other members of the party. When did they leave the hotel?'

'After dinner.'

'So, you were with Mr Royston at the hotel until midnight. You then drove back to the Palace and went to your own suite without seeing Mr Steen.' Eleanor deliberately phrased this as a statement rather than a question so as not to antagonise Mrs Steen further.

Mrs Steen remained silent. Until now she had looked at Eleanor as she spoke, but now she was looking at her hands and began toying again with the bracelet, twisting it round and round her wrist. Eleanor recalled the facts which Catherine had given her. Catherine had said that she had been unable to speak to Mrs Steen on the morning when Mr Steen was found dead. Mrs Steen was thought to be in her room asleep. Mrs Steen still had not contradicted Eleanor's previous statement so, keeping her tone deliberately neutral,

Eleanor said: 'In fact, you didn't return to the Palace at all that evening.' Mrs Steen shook her head, holding her lips tightly together. Then she turned her head and looked out of the window, still refusing to meet Eleanor's gaze. 'What time did you return to the Palace Hotel?'

'About six thirty in the morning,' said Mrs Steen.

'And then you fell asleep and were not aware that Mr Steen had been found by his valet.' Mrs Steen continued to stare out of the window. 'Did Mr Royston return to the hotel with you?'

'Yes, but he's gone. He'd left before Walter was found.'

'Mrs Steen, I am beginning to understand why you cannot take steps to prove your innocence and why, therefore, you want me to conduct this investigation. Disclosing the facts regarding your whereabouts would probably expose you to criticism...'

Mrs Steen now turned and looked at Eleanor. 'Gilbert would lose his job,' she said, barely above a whisper.

'...and the truth would not assist you. In my opinion, a mutual alibi of this kind would not improve your current position significantly; in fact, it could make your position even more difficult.' Eleanor paused. 'I do sympathise with you but I am not sure that there is anything I can do to help you. If you feel that you cannot explain where you were when Mr Steen died, it will be necessary to establish the facts surrounding his death. As I said before, that could take quite some time and, in the meantime, you would still be the subject of speculation. Wouldn't it be better to wait for the police to act or, at least, wait until there is an inquest?'

'No!' said Mrs Steen, loudly and impatiently. 'The damage is being done to me now. I can't afford to wait. I need immediate action. You've got to help me.'

'Very well. I can make whatever enquiries it is possible to make and then report to you. That is really all I can do at this stage. Would that be acceptable?'

Mrs Steen nodded. Now that she was getting what she wanted, she became even more brusque. 'Start immediately. Send the bill to me at the Palace.' With that she stood up and turned towards the door. Eleanor opened the door and followed Mrs Steen downstairs.

'I'll say good afternoon, Mrs Steen. Mr Wildgoose will discuss our fees and expenses with you.'

Mrs Steen glanced at James and said: 'No need. Just send the bill.' She dismissed him with a wave of her hand and turned towards the front door. James skilfully manoeuvred past her and opened the door for her. She sailed out without a backward look. After James had closed the door, Eleanor and James looked at each other, eyebrows raised. James slowly shook his head and returned to his desk.

'I know you never fail to take proper details from clients, James, so I am sure you have an address for Mrs Steen, other than the hotel I mean, to which to send the bill?'

'Yes, Miss Eleanor. I took the precaution of ascertaining those details from Mrs Steen before showing her up to your office. She didn't strike me as being the reliable sort.'

'Thank you, James. Very wise. I think your judgment was absolutely correct. I'll go and rescue Napoleon and then I need to consult Mr Talbot.'

~O~

'Edwin, I'm sorry to interrupt you but I need your advice. Would now be a convenient time, or would you rather I come back later?' Eleanor was at the door of Edwin's office.

'Come in, come in. I'm not doing anything that can't wait. I am expecting a client in half an hour though.'

Eleanor, followed by Napoleon, went in and sat down.

'What's troubling you?' asked Edwin.

'Mrs Steen.'

'Oh?'

'She's been in to see me.' Edwin's eyebrows went up. 'While you were out of the office. She has only just left.'

'Ah,' said Edwin, 'when I came back in, I saw that your door was shut and Napoleon had been banished. James wasn't about and I wondered who you had with you. I would never have guessed that it was Mrs Steen. It was about Mr Steen's death, I suppose.'

'Indirectly, yes, but it was more about her really. You see she is being hounded by newspaper reporters and press photographers. She seems to think they are interested in her because she was once an actress but I suspect they are only interested in her because they can make her the basis of a story which will sell newspapers. Mrs Clayton told me the things they are writing about her. The implication is that Mrs Steen wanted her husband out of the way so that she could play the merry widow with her golf professional friend.'

'My goodness, is that what is being said? And what does Mrs Steen want you to do about these reporters and their speculations? Defamation?'

'No, she doesn't want me to take action against the reporters. She wants me to prove that the things they are saying about her are not true. She wants me to prove that she didn't kill Mr Steen.'

'As simple as that, eh?' Edwin smiled.

'Well, it would be simple if she would just tell the truth about where she was on the night Mr Steen died but that would implicate her in a different sort of scandal and not necessarily solve the problem. It would probably guarantee an increase in the number of press photographers and reporters at the hotel and might also cost someone else his job. That is quite definitely not the result she wants.'

'I see, so she is between the devil and the deep blue sea, as it were.'

'Yes. Literally as well as figuratively. She came here wearing an outfit in deep blue when, if she really wanted to avoid notice, the traditional black would have been more sensible. I explained to her that, if she was unwilling to reveal the facts which would establish that she could not have killed her husband, the only way to establish her innocence would be to discover who did kill him if, in fact, he was killed.'

'And she instructed you to do just that?'

'Yes.'

'And what is troubling you about those very clear and perfectly straightforward instructions,' asked Edwin, laughing at Eleanor's frown.

Eleanor rolled her eyes. 'The instructions may be clear but the way forward certainly is not. It could be difficult and expensive and I did try to dissuade her.'

'But she wants to proceed nevertheless and you are reluctant to do so?'

'Yes. Two things are troubling me. First of all, I need advice. I know that you are very busy at the moment but I cannot discuss any of this with Father because there will be an inquest and he is bound to be appointed coroner. He may have to take evidence from Mrs Steen. The second thing is this. Mrs Steen said that she was not at the Palace Hotel on the night Mr Steen was killed. That is essentially her alibi. However, I am not sure whether to believe her or not.'

'Hmm. That is difficult. What makes you doubt her?'

'I witnessed her cheating on the golf course. I know that is not the same thing as disposing of one's husband but, if she is prepared to cheat in order to win a match, how can I be sure of her honesty in other matters? And that's not all. Her alibi is Mr Gilbert Royston, the golf professional from Bramhall Park. He was at the Rally.'

'What, that cad in the Crossley?'

'Yes, and, do you remember, Philip and I described seeing him and Mrs Steen on the golf course. It was definitely not a professional arrangement and it appears to have gone beyond friendship.'

'Oh dear! And you are afraid that this Mr Royston would be prepared to lie for her.'

'Yes. And also because of him, she may have viewed her marriage as an inconvenience. She has a lot to gain by her husband's death, and apparently that is what the newspapers are hinting at. According to Mrs Clayton, Mr Steen was a very rich man and presumably will have made some provision for Mrs Steen and she is considerably younger than he was.'

'I understand your dilemma, Eleanor. I think I would probably feel the same way in your position.'

'So, what would you advise? Should I act for her, given that I have these doubts?'

'Well, she may have behaved unwisely, even immorally perhaps, but, as long as you have no reason to believe that she has done anything illegal, I think it is safe to continue. The first rule is that one must not judge the morals or beliefs of one's client even if one does not share them. The second is that one accepts what he or she has to say, initially at least and unless there is evidence to the contrary. The third is to carry out their instructions to the best of our ability unless, of course, those instructions involve something illegal. Assuming that she is telling the truth, did you have any thoughts about where you would begin?'

'I did actually. She told me that on the night Mr Steen died she was at a hotel in Cheshire with the golf professional. I don't really fancy interrogating him and according to Mrs Steen he has left Buxton. In any event, I'm not sure I could trust him to tell the truth but I thought that I could get someone independent to check Mrs Steen's story. To satisfy myself more than anything, I suppose. And if her story proves to be true, I should feel confident that I could act for her.'

'Yes, that would be the sensible thing to do and it should

be relatively easy to have her story verified.'

'But could I reasonably expect her to pay for that, given that it is mainly for my own reassurance?'

'Hmm, I see what you mean,' said Edwin. 'Perhaps if we were to engage the services of an enquiry agent to provide a report and meet the cost ourselves, initially at least, and then, depending on what use we make of the report, we can ask Mrs Steen to reimburse us if it seems appropriate. If, for example, she needs to produce the report in evidence.'

'That would be ideal.'

'Did she tell you the name of the hotel?'

'Yes, it's called The Swinford Hotel, near Wilmslow. Do you know it?'

'No, I don't think so. There is a very reliable and efficient enquiry agent in Manchester whose services I have used previously. James has his name and address. It would be helpful to have a photograph. Has Mrs Steen's photograph been in the newspapers at all?'

'Yes, and that is another thing that made me wonder about how truthful she was being. She complained about being hounded by press photographers and yet it seemed to me that, despite what she said, she was actually enjoying the attention. She could easily have moved to a different hotel and they would not know where to find her but instead she has chosen to remain at the Palace. She claims to have been an actress before she married Mr Steen so perhaps she is thinking of resuming that career and wants the publicity.'

'Dear me, she seems to be a rather difficult client,' said Edwin.

'It is not easy to warm to her,' said Eleanor. 'I suspect James has her measure though.'

'I am sure he has. Nothing gets past James. Well, we must do our best,' said Edwin.

'Thank you, Edwin.' Eleanor looked at her watch. 'Your client will be here shortly but there is more to tell. I shall draft instructions to the enquiry agent immediately and then set about sorting out the facts so that I can discuss them with you later if you have time.'

'Yes, of course. All right, ask James to charge the cost of the enquiry agent to the office account for the moment and then we can discuss the matter in more detail. Will tomorrow do for our conversation, because I shall no doubt be engaged with this client until closing time.'

'Yes, that will be perfect.'

Eleanor drafted the letter to the enquiry agent and took it down to James. Then she went back to her desk and, as she put away her files, she considered the death of Mr Steen. Previously she had been interested in the case from Catherine's point of view and had been concerned only to establish whether or not a crime had been committed. However, from Mrs Steen's point of view, a crime had been committed and it was now her task to identify the killer so as to establish Mrs Steen's innocence. Eleanor sighed and looked at Napoleon. He returned her gaze with his gentle, brown eyes, probably more in the hope of a walk than in sympathy with her situation. However, she reached for her hat and his lead. Walking with him always helped her to clear her thoughts.

CHAPTER FOURTEEN

The following day, Eleanor and Mr Harriman were due to meet some clients for lunch at the Palace Hotel. When the Harrimans had lived in The Park, Mr and Mrs Denfield had been their neighbours for many years and had known Eleanor as a schoolgirl. They had recently sold their house and were moving to Bournemouth. Being now homeless, they were staying at the Palace Hotel until their departure from Buxton. Theirs had been a complicated conveyance and they were very pleased at the way Eleanor had conducted the matter. In order to thank her, they wanted to offer her their hospitality in the usual way but, no longer having a dining room of their own, they had invited her and Mr Harriman to lunch at the hotel.

Mr Harriman and Eleanor went in Mr Harriman's motor-car and as soon as they turned on to the concourse in front of the hotel they were besieged by newspaper reporters and press photographers.

'Goodness!' said Eleanor, 'Mrs Clayton was right.'

'Just ignore them,' said Mr Harriman.

When it became apparent that Mr Harriman and Eleanor had no connection with Mr Steen, the group dispersed and then swarmed around another motor-car which was just turning into the concourse. On the steps of the hotel, the linkman greeted them and summoned a minion to park Mr Harriman's car. Mr and Mrs Denfield were waiting in the front hall to welcome Eleanor and Mr Harriman. After they had exchanged greetings, Mrs Denfield said:

'Did you have to run the gauntlet of those dreadful newspaper reporters? They have been following people about in a quite disgraceful manner, hurling questions at them and thrusting their cameras into people's faces. Their behaviour really is horrid.'

'Very disrespectful. Intimidating, in fact,' said Mr Denfield. 'I complained to the manager about it. Shall we go straight to the dining room?'

The dining room was a large and well-proportioned corner room with a twenty-foot high ceiling, and fifteen-feet high windows on two sides. In keeping with the Second Empire style of the exterior, the ceiling was decorated with moulded plasterwork and below the cornices was a plasterwork frieze in a delicate pattern, painted pale blue and embossed at intervals with plaster escutcheons. The long windows, hung with velvet curtains, were separated by panels edged in white plaster and painted a deep blue. The internal walls were hung with large, oblong mirrors also separated by panels in deep blue. Although the style of the décor was an imitation of the grand hotels of Europe, the room avoided their heavy opulence. It was light and airy and had an elegant simplicity. The tables in the dining room were round, with starched white tablecloths, sparkling glassware and silverware, and there was an abundance of flowers and potted palms.

The maître d'hôtel, Monsieur Maurice, was also in keeping with the Second Empire style and affected a French accent, although he was actually plain Mr Fletcher born in Bermondsey and like the Prioress in Chaucer's *The Canterbury Tales* "French in the Paris style he did not know." Monsieur Maurice greeted Mr Denfield deferentially and conducted his party to their table, which was towards the centre of the room. When they were seated, he bowed, wished them bon appetit, and clicked his fingers to summon a waiter forward. The waiter bowed to Mr Denfield. Mr Denfield had chosen the à la carte menu instead of the table d'hôte and the waiter handed unpriced menus to the guests and gave Mr Denfield the menu which showed the prices of each dish. He then provided advice as to the day's selection.

As Mr Denfield was dealing with the business of ascertaining preferences and giving the waiter their order, Eleanor looked around her. Another waiter, assisted by a waitress, was serving at a nearby table. Eleanor recognised the waitress as one of the hotel servants who had been at the Motor-car Rally, a tall, dark-haired girl whom Eleanor had seen talking animatedly with the hall-porter before the start. Eleanor was struck by how very different she looked today. At the Rally she had been immaculately turned out and her appearance was very attractive. Today she seemed tired, rather lifeless, and ill at ease. Her appearance was untidy as well. Her hair had been pinned up carelessly and her apron was creased. Eleanor thought that, somehow, this was not the same person but, before she had time to consider a possible reason for this change, she was distracted by activity at the next table. Monsieur Maurice had conducted a party of six guests to the table and was seating them, with a great deal of deferential fussing, interspersed with French phrases, and much bowing. This was particularly so in relation to one of the female guests, a middle-aged lady very elegantly and expensively dressed, who seemed to accept the attention as her due. Monsieur Maurice addressed her as m'lady. Mrs Denfield raised her eyebrows and smiled at Eleanor, conspiratorially and while Mr Harriman and Mr Denfield were engaged in conversation, the two ladies surreptitiously watched this scene with amused interest.

During lunch, conversation at the table flowed easily because they had many topics of common interest to talk about. In addition, Mr Denfield was a Justice of the Peace and he frequently discussed legal matters with Mr Harriman when the two of them were dining at their club. They progressed amicably through the soup and the entrée to the main course and Mrs Denfield, having expressed her regret at leaving Buxton, listed the things that she knew they would miss.

Mr Denfield said: 'Well, my dear, I am sure that we shall be able to come back to see our old friends here and perhaps some of them can be persuaded to come and visit us in Bournemouth.'

'Oh, but it will be many months before we are settled enough to think of inviting guests,' said Mrs Denfield. Then she sighed. 'And besides, this town may be very different by the time we are at liberty to return. Things change so quickly these days and if that horrid water bottling scheme goes ahead who knows what changes there might be.'

'Very true, my dear,' said Mr Denfield. 'It would mean quite a significant change, I fear, but surely it is unlikely that the scheme will go ahead. What do you think, Harriman?'

'It does seem unlikely, I agree. Now Mr Steen has died,' said Mr Harriman.

'Do you think so?' said Mrs Denfield. 'Oh, that is a relief. The damage to the town would have been irreparable. I know one should not speak ill of the dead but really that Mr Steen was too much. It is difficult to be sorry he is gone, despite the suddenness of his passing.'

'You have to admit, Harriman, it was rather fortuitous, wasn't it?' said Mr Denfield. 'What have the police being doing? Have you heard anything?'

'Only that no death certificate has been issued. I understand that the cause of death is yet to be determined,' said Mr Harriman.

'I suppose you will be appointed coroner,' said Mr Denfield.

'Yes, I have been appointed. I heard this morning. I expect that, after the usual formalities, I shall be asked to adjourn pending further police investigation.'

Mrs Denfield said: 'Of course, his death has been a topic

of speculation amongst the guests here at the hotel although nothing has been said by the management. The newspaper report I read said that Mr Steen had been in perfect health the night before, celebrating here in the hotel, and then was found dead the next morning. It did seem rather sudden.'

'I gather that there has been a lot of idle talk,' said Mr Harriman. 'It seems that the absence of a death certificate has led people to speculate. An unexplained death always attracts attention and, of course, Mr Steen was newsworthy to begin with.'

'So, it is possible that his death was not from natural causes?' said Mr Denfield.

'It is too early yet to form a view,' said Mr Harriman, cautiously, 'but Superintendent Johnson informed me that enquiries are certainly underway. This is not a straight-forward case.'

'It may seem callous to say so but, if his death was deliberate, whoever that person was, he did the town a service,' said Mrs Denfield. She paused, then added: 'I said he, but it might have been a she, mightn't it? Rather than a he, I mean.' She added, mischievously. 'The ladies at the golf club had a lot to lose.'

'On the contrary,' said Eleanor, laughing and shaking her head at Mrs Denfield, 'we had found a much more effective way of stopping him and all completely legal thanks to the Brunt family.'

'I overheard someone talking in the breakfast room this morning,' said Mrs Denfield. 'Her room is near Mr Steen's suite apparently. She was saying that the police had been in and out of Mr Steen's room the day before, presumably looking for clues.'

'Fingerprints, probably,' said Mr Denfield, confidently.

'Of course, living in a hotel,' continued Mrs Denfield, 'even an excellent one such as this, one is always vulnerable. Such a lot of people have access to one's room, chamber maids and porters, for example. I suppose the police will want to interview them because it would be perfectly possible for someone to come in and...'

The last part of this sentence was lost in the commotion that followed. The waiter who was attending to the six guests on the neighbouring table was in the process of serving the main course assisted by the waitress Eleanor had recognised. The waitress had been standing in the space between the two tables, and holding a silver tray on which were balanced several large sauce boats. Suddenly, without warning, the waitress had collapsed. Her legs buckled under her, the tray slid sideways, and its contents fell to the floor accompanied by the sound of breaking china and clattering silverware. Conversation in the dining room stopped immediately and, in that moment of complete silence in which all of the diners turned to look in the direction of the noise, a high, shrill voice pierced the air. 'Oh! You stupid, clumsy girl!' The waiter had momentarily frozen and looked aghast but then his training took over and he assessed the situation quickly. He stepped over the fallen waitress as if she did not exist, took the clean table napkin which he had over his arm and offered it to the m'lady whose silk dress was now ruined by gravy and sauce. Monsieur Maurice, hearing the noise, reacted immediately. Without appearing to hurry, he glided swiftly over to the table armed with additional table napkins and began making profuse apologies, mainly addressed to the affronted lady whose name it appeared was Lady Aycliffe. The rest of the diners returned to their food and the hum of conversation resumed. No-one paid any attention to the waitress lying crumpled on the floor just to the right of Mrs Denfield's chair.

Mrs Denfield, who was closest to the collapsed waitress, had stood up saying: 'It's all right. I was a VAD during the War.' She bent down and began to examine the waitress and Eleanor joined her.

'Did you see what happened?' Mrs Denfield asked Eleanor, as they both knelt beside the waitress.

'Yes,' answered Eleanor. 'She fainted. She seems to be unconscious. Perhaps she bumped her head on the way down.'

The waitress was not unconscious but she was so appalled by what had happened she remained where she fell, lying perfectly still, her face pressed into the carpet.

'We should roll her on to her side, just to be on the safe side,' said Mrs Denfield. As she did so, the waitress began to sob and mutter to herself.

'Let's get her out of the dining room,' said Eleanor.

'Yes,' agreed Mrs Denfield. 'No-one else seems to be at all concerned about her.' Mrs Denfield said to the waitress: 'Can you try to stand up, my dear?'

The waitress looked at Mrs Denfield, eyes blank, the depth of her misery evident on her face. Mrs Denfield and Eleanor helped the waitress to stand up and stood either side of her ready to walk her to the door of the dining room. She winced as Mrs Denfield touched her arm where the hot gravy had burned her wrist. Her appearance was even more dishevelled now than previously. Monsieur Maurice, having placated Lady Aycliffe and ministered to her party at the next table, and having satisfied himself that the calm atmosphere of the dining room had been restored, now turned his attention to the waitress. His eyes narrowed and he gave her a callous stare. 'Disgraceful,' he muttered. He made a small bow, first to Mrs Denfield and then to Eleanor, and, in obsequious tones, said: 'Merci, ladeez. I am grateful for your assistance.' He put the emphasis on the last syllable of the last word. He jerked his thumb at the waitress, motioning her to leave the dining room. Eleanor and Mrs Denfield reluctantly let go of her and she moved slowly away. Monsieur Maurice pulled out Mrs Denfield's chair for her to sit down. Eleanor seated herself, preferring independence to help from the maître d'hôtel. Then, addressing the whole table, he added: 'I do most sincerely regret this unfortunate incident and I apologise for interrupting your luncheon.' Turning to Mr Denfield, he bowed and added: 'Naturallement, there will be an adjustment in the tariff of today as a small compensation.' Before Mr Denfield could speak, the maître d'hôtel glided off, no doubt intending to deal with the clumsy waitress.

Eleanor said: 'I hope the waitress gets away with just a dressing down but I am afraid the maître d'hôtel was very cross, despite his unctuous exterior.'

'Poor girl,' said Mrs Denfield. 'I wonder what caused her to faint. It is rather warm in here.'

'I noticed her when we came in. She was serving at a different table then and she didn't look at all well,' said Eleanor.

'She was muttering something but I couldn't catch what it was. Did you understand her?' asked Mrs Denfield.

Eleanor replied: 'I'm not altogether sure. I think she said: "He shouldn't have" or something like that and then "It's wrong" but I don't know what was wrong.'

'Dropping the tray, perhaps?' asked Mr Harriman.

'Possibly,' said Eleanor.

'Well, dropping the tray like that was certainly the wrong thing to do if she wants to keep her job,' said Mr Denfield.

'Yes, whatever she meant, I should think she will find herself scrubbing dirty pots from now on, poor girl,' said Mrs Denfield.

~O~

After lunch, Mr Harriman had taken Eleanor back to Hall Bank and then gone on to Fairfield to play golf at the course belonging to the Buxton and High Peak Golf Club of which he was a member. Edwin had finished his lunch and was back at his desk. Eleanor went into his office and said: 'I'm sorry to take up your time with the Steen matter again, but have you got time now for that chat?'

Edwin waved her in, saying: 'Of course. How is it progressing?'

'I didn't have time yesterday to tell you all the details, nor did I confess that I have an ulterior motive in accepting instructions from Mrs Steen. You see, it is very likely that Mrs Steen is innocent but the newspapers may be correct in suggesting that Mr Steen's death was not due to natural causes.'

'Oh dear,' said Edwin, frowning. 'Is there any credible evidence of that?'

'Well, the other evening, Catherine and I had a long talk about Mr Steen's death. There is something about this case that is making Catherine uneasy and I think, with good reason. It may sound irrational given that the post mortem did not reveal anything sinister but we both think that Mr Steen's death merits further investigation. Catherine suspects that this was not a natural or an accidental death but she cannot justify that opinion with anything concrete. All of our theories so far lead to dead ends. I have been assembling all the information we have at present to see if I can make any sense out of it.'

'His death certainly was very sudden and unexpected. I agree that it is tempting to consider it as a suspicious death,' said Edwin. 'However, we do need to be cautious, don't you think?'

'Absolutely. That is exactly what Catherine said. Can I explain to you what we have discovered so far? I want to be sure that I've got things in perspective.'

Edwin nodded and Eleanor set out the facts and explained the theory that she and Catherine had put together. 'What we really need now,' concluded Eleanor, 'is to find a motive because then that would give us some idea as to who, if anyone, might have poisoned Mr Steen. I have been considering all the possible suspects.'

Edwin smiled. 'Very well, then. Let us assume, for the moment, that there has been foul play. It's time to draw up the old "means, opportunity, motive" table, don't you think?' Edwin pulled a note pad towards him and picked up a pencil.

Eleanor laughed. 'Yes. That is one of the first things you taught me and it has been very useful.'

Edwin drew up a grid with three columns on his note pad. He headed the columns respectively: means, opportunity, and motive.

'I predict that you won't be able to put this matter out of your mind until you are satisfied that there is no-one who could be regarded as a suspect. We shall consider everyone even remotely connected and that will give you a better idea as to whether your suspicions are fanciful or whether there is something further which should be pursued. So, let us begin with means.'

'Well, if this was an unnatural death,' said Eleanor, 'the only cause we can identify is an overdose of barbitone.' Eleanor outlined to Edwin the discussion that she and Catherine had had regarding Mr Steen's sleeping tablets and the fact that the correct number of tablets remained in the box on the morning of Mr Steen's death.

'Hmm,' said Edwin. 'That is a poser. 'I suppose that, for the average person, sleeping tablets would be the only form in which they would have access to a substance such as barbitone and those pills are prescribed by a doctor, so to some extent that limits the sort of people who might have had access to their own supply. How many tablets would be required to cause death?'

'Catherine says a minimum of six but it is more likely that seven or eight would be required. As Catherine pointed out, it is not possible to take seven or eight tablets by accident and it would be even more difficult to persuade someone to take them voluntarily.'

'This really is a puzzle, isn't it?' said Edwin, slowly. 'But is it certain that the cause of death was an overdose of barbitone.'

'No. It is only a suspicion at this stage. It could only be described as a possible cause, no higher than that. All natural causes have been eliminated by the post mortem and the barbitone seems to be the only possible unnatural cause.'

'I see. Then, let's accept that, for the moment, as the means of causing death and move on to opportunity.'

'Mr Steen died in his bed at the hotel,' said Eleanor. 'Unobserved access to his room would have been relatively easy to manage both for someone from within the hotel and an outsider. Once the tablets had been obtained, of course.'

'Right, the motive will become obvious as we consider each suspect. Who shall we put at the top of the list? Mrs Steen or Mrs Steen's alibi, the golf professional?'

'Well, Mrs Steen with a question mark and only until we get the report from the enquiry agent. Gilbert Royston, the golf professional, is certainly Mrs Clayton's first choice.'

Edwin laughed. 'He's certainly a bit of a bounder.'

'Yes, and apparently Mr Royston has now left the hotel. That is not a point in his favour. He's left Mrs Steen to weather the storm of publicity, as it were. It does not show much concern for her.'

'And his behaviour at the Motor-car Rally was less than honourable. He engaged in some very underhand tactics. Unsporting and lacking in courtesy. And there is the fact that he has been paying too much attention to another man's wife...but it does not make him a murderer, does it?'

'No.'

'If he is genuinely interested in Mrs Steen, he certainly had a motive for killing Mr Steen but, even if he is desperately in love with her, murdering her husband does not seem to be the best way to secure her affection.'

'As far as I can see, he and Mrs Steen went about pretty much as they liked while Mr Steen was alive, so there was no reason for them to want him dead. Anyway, I am not sure how Mr Royston would have obtained barbitone.'

'Didn't you say that he was staying at the hotel? He would have had the opportunity to enter Mr Steen's room,' suggested Edwin.

'But, if Mrs Steen is telling the truth, he was not at the hotel on the night Mr Steen died. He may well be cleared by the enquiry agent. Best put question marks for him for means and opportunity, I think.'

'You are very persuasive, Miss Harriman,' said Edwin, smiling as he applied his pencil to the chart. 'All right, I shall put a tick in the box labelled motive and a question mark in the other two boxes.'

'The person who had the greatest access to Mr Steen and his tablets is the valet. So far, Catherine and I have based our theories on his evidence and accepted everything he has said as the truth. That may be unwise, of course. He could have been lying about the number of tablets in the box but Catherine thought that he was being open and direct when she spoke to him. However, there certainly are a few unanswered questions in relation to him.'

'Well, he will have to have a tick in the means and opportunity boxes. What about motive?'

'I can't think of one, at the moment,' said Eleanor.

'So, a question mark for motive. What is his name?'

'Mellor,' said Eleanor.

'Who's next?'

'I did briefly consider Mr Ashworth, the archaeologist, because he was afraid that Mr Steen's proposed factory would disturb the evidence of Bronze Age settlement that he is looking for. He left Buxton after he was attacked but I heard from Philip that he had returned the day before Mr Steen died.'

'It does seem a little extreme, doesn't it?' said Edwin. 'I shall add his name to the list for the sake of completeness but with three question marks. What about the person who attacked Mr Ashworth?'

'The reason for that attack may be linked to archaeology rather than Mr Steen's project. According to Mr Ashworth, there have been people snooping around who may be interested in stealing a march on him, so it may have nothing to do with Mr Steen's death.'

'I shall label him "A's attacker" and give him three question marks,' said Edwin.

'There are a lot of people in town who do not support Mr Steen's project. Mrs Steen told me that, since arriving in Buxton, Mr Steen had received anonymous notes from someone threatening to kill him. Apparently, they were delivered to the hotel but she was not able to give me any details about them. I suppose we do need to consider the likelihood that whoever sent those threats meant them.'

'Did Mr Steen keep any of these threatening letters, do we know?' asked Edwin.

'Not according to Mrs Steen,' said Eleanor. 'Perhaps his papers should be searched.'

'I suppose the letters were the usual kind, anonymous and designed to intimidate,' said Edwin.

'Yes, and according to Mrs Steen, he just dismissed them. He said he could deal with them. As well as the threatening letters, there was that slashed tyre on his motor-car after the Rally. Oh, and some of the drilling equipment his men were using was damaged one night. Given the attack on Mr Ashworth, there is clearly someone among us prepared to use violence.'

'Then, for the moment, let us label that person or persons "opponent of project" although it seems a bit far-fetched,' said Edwin. 'Threats are easy to make but killing someone to put a stop to a business venture seems rather unlikely.

Until we know the identity of this opponent we cannot say whether he had either the means or the opportunity.'

While Edwin made the appropriate notes, Eleanor added: 'I suppose we should include those strangers who were in town. Some of them were at the meeting at the Town Hall and one of them, in particular, was very angry with Mr Steen. He seemed to have some association with Mr Steen's factory.'

'So there might be a motive there because remember there is outstanding litigation against Mr Steen's company,' said Edwin. 'I suppose the current term for such people is "activist" so I shall use that.'

'But query means and opportunity. If Mr Steen was killed by one of them, perhaps they did not know about Mr Brunt's deed and his ability to stop the project. Do you suppose I should have advised the Brunts to make a public statement about it?'

'No,' said Edwin, laughing, 'I find that hard to believe because I gather Mr Brunt has been telling anyone who will listen. It was pretty much public knowledge straight away. Now, who else can we suspect?'

'In relation to dangerous conditions in Mr Steen's factory. Mrs Clayton told me that there is a man staying in Buxton who was severely injured there. He is receiving treatment at the Devonshire Hospital.'

'Hmm, a motive of revenge? But would he have the means and the opportunity?'

'I suppose if he is receiving treatment he might have access to barbitone.'

'True. So, a tick for means and motive but a question mark for opportunity. Perhaps he needs to be investigated further,' said Edwin. 'What is his name?'

Eleanor thought for a moment. 'I'm not sure if Mrs Clayton mentioned his name. I shall find out.'

'So is there anyone else we should consider?' asked

Edwin.

'Well, there is always X, the person about whom we currently know absolutely nothing, who may exist and may have a motive. The hotel is very big and always full of people. It is relatively easy to gain access to the rooms. We still have the problem as to how the tablets were administered though and it is possible that X is two people not one, so we may be looking for X and Y. X who had access to the poison from some other source and Y who could gain access to Mr Steen's room. The motive is not obvious but whoever X or Y is, there must be some connection between him and Mr Steen.'

'Then I shall add person X/Y to the list.' Edwin considered his list. 'Perhaps that is where you need to concentrate your efforts because the rest of the names on the list are not very compelling.' Edwin looked at Eleanor and saw that she was frowning. 'What is it? Have you remembered something?'

'No, there was a thread, a half-thought going through my brain, an association of facts triggered by something one of us just said.' Eleanor shook her head. 'No, it's gone. I can't think what it was.'

'You said "him" when you were referring to X and I suppose we can assume that we are looking for a man, although poison is supposed to be a woman's weapon, isn't it? So, that brings us back to Mrs Steen.'

Eleanor said: 'Yes, and there will be a tick in all three boxes for her. She definitely had the means, the motive and the opportunity.' She watched as Edwin filled in the chart. 'Mrs Steen is the only one on the list with three ticks,' she said. 'Ironic isn't it. The most likely suspect is the one who has retained me to prove her innocence.'

'Well, we shall just have to get to the truth. What are you proposing to do next?'

Before Eleanor could answer, Mrs Clayton appeared with

a cup of tea for Edwin.

'Thank you, Mrs Clayton,' said Edwin.

'Are you having your tea here, Miss Harriman, or shall I put yours on your desk.'

'On my desk, thank you Mrs Clayton. We've nearly finished here. Have you heard any fresh news from the Palace Hotel?'

'Only that Mrs Steen has left. According to the newspapers she's gone to London. They said to "resume her acting career" whatever that means. No-one I've spoken to has ever heard of her. You'd think she would at least stay for the funeral. It's not decent to just run off like that.'

'Well, you can't believe everything you read in the papers, Mrs Clayton,' said Edwin. 'I suppose the funeral will be in Manchester. Perhaps she has gone there to make arrangements and not to London.'

'Perhaps. Alf is still waiting on instructions and there's no death certificate as yet. Anyway, the newspaper reporters have gone from the Palace but Alf said one of them had been interviewing that archaeologist chap, Ashworth, is it? He reckons he's found a spring up on Green Lane although I don't see why that would be of interest to the papers. I suppose that's the one Mr Steen was looking for. The town's had a lucky escape, by all accounts. I'll just put your tea on your desk Miss Harriman and then I'll take James his.'

'Before you go, Mrs Clayton, you told me about a worker from Mr Steen's factory who is staying in Buxton for treatment at the hospital. The Misses Pymble mentioned him to you. Do you happen to know his name?'

Mrs Clayton thought for a minute and then said: 'Mellor. Yes, that was it.'

'Oh,' said Eleanor. 'You're certain?' Mrs Clayton paused and then nodded. She left to finish her tea round and Eleanor and Edwin looked at each other. Eleanor said: 'The valet and the injured worker. They both have the same surname. Are they related, I wonder?'

'If they are, it might give the valet a motive. Revenge for the damage to his relative.'

'I definitely shall look into that a bit further.'

'I shall just amend the table,' said Edwin. 'The valet gets a tick in all three boxes. Well, now you have a list to consider but I am not sure that it takes us much further.'

'Oh, it does. I think it is a very good start. Thank you, Edwin. I should interview the valet first of all. There are several things I want to know and I assume that he is still at the hotel. I shall go to interview him tomorrow.'

'Very well, but do bear in mind that we may be dealing with someone very clever who has a great deal at stake.'

'Yes, I think you are right about that,' said Eleanor.

'Also, it is possible that the valet is no longer at the hotel. Now that he is not in Mr Steen's service he may have had to find somewhere else to lodge. I know that some of the strict rules of the last century are frowned upon and considered outmoded, so please don't get cross and protest your independence, but it is still not considered proper for an unaccompanied and unmarried lady to pay a call at the house of a gentleman and calling alone on a manservant would be bound to cause the same level of comment. Whilst your father might understand the necessity of your interviewing the valet, your mother would certainly not have approved, so rather than risk your reputation it would be sensible not to go alone. I am sure Philip will not mind.'

'I know what you mean, Edwin, although I don't agree with the rules, of course. Philip and I have arranged to meet Mr Ashworth this afternoon so I shall ask Philip then.'

~O~

Philip and Eleanor were meeting Mr Ashworth for tea at Collinson's in Spring Gardens at five o'clock and Philip arrived at Hall Bank at a quarter to five. As they walked to the tea rooms, Eleanor asked: 'When did Mr Ashworth come back?'

'I'm not entirely sure. Last Saturday, I think.'

'Has he heard anything from the police? Have they discovered anything about his attacker?'

'I asked him about that and he said that so far they have had no success, but you know, Lella, I've had an idea. Our first thought was robbery but then we discovered that nothing had been taken. We haven't had any other ideas since but it struck me this morning that it might have been a case of mistaken identity.'

'How so?'

'Well, a few days before Mr Steen died, I was down in Spring Gardens and I saw someone walking along the pavement a little distance ahead of me and I thought it was Mr Ashworth. It was after he had left Buxton and I thought he must have returned without letting me know, although there was no reason why he should have done so, of course. Anyway, I put on a bit of pace in order to catch him up but when I was almost behind him, I realised that it was not Mr Ashworth at all. It occurred to me that whoever hit Mr Ashworth might have made the same mistake that I had made, only the other way around.'

'How do you mean? The other way around?'

'Intended to rob someone else and mistaken Mr Ashworth for whoever that person was. Although perhaps not rob him but kill him, considering who it was that I had mistaken for Mr Ashworth and what has happened since. You see, the person I had mistaken for Mr Ashworth was actually Mr Steen.'

'Oh!' said Eleanor, puzzled. She frowned as she thought about the implications of what Philip had just said.

'It was only when I realised my own mistake,' continued Philip, 'that I thought about the similarities. You see, Mr

Steen was wearing a Norfolk jacket and knee breeches of the same design as Mr Ashworth's, and a similar hat, and they are about the same height. Also, Mr Steen was carrying a small haversack like the one Mr Ashworth has for his tools. There I was following the wrong person in broad daylight, and it wasn't until I was almost upon Mr Steen that I realised who it was that I was following. So, in the twilight that evening when Mr Ashworth was attacked, it would have been even easier for the assailant to be confused and to have mistaken his target, particularly from the back. Mr Ashworth was hit from behind, remember.'

'Hmm,' said Eleanor, frowning in concentration. 'So, you're suggesting that someone intended to kill Mr Steen and attacked Mr Ashworth by mistake. That is certainly not something we considered at the time but I see what you mean. It is a very plausible explanation, isn't it?'

'Catherine did say Mr Ashworth was lucky to be alive, remember. He had received a very severe blow.'

Eleanor nodded slowly, thinking over the facts, and then added: 'So, if someone intended to kill Mr Steen on that earlier occasion and, having failed...'

'Perhaps he tried again by a different method and this time succeeded,' concluded Philip. 'Although, as it seems Mr Steen died peacefully in his bed, I admit that it is a wild idea.'

'No, Philip, it is not a wild idea. It is a brilliant suggestion. You see, Mr Steen probably did not die peacefully of natural causes. I know that I can trust you not to disclose this information to anyone but Catherine is worried that Mr Steen was actually poisoned.'

Philip stopped walking and looked at Eleanor. 'Phew!' he said, 'and I thought I was being too fanciful.'

'No, your idea makes complete sense. A flash of genius, in fact. Let's think this through.' Eleanor sat down on one of the seats at the foot of The Slopes and Philip joined her.

'We assumed that the attack on Mr Ashworth was related to archaeology and the only motive we could suggest was robbery. We discovered that, before he was attacked, Mr Ashworth had been to Hawthorn Cottage on Green Lane and we thought perhaps the attacker was after the pieces of jet necklace he was given there.'

'Yes, although we were puzzled as to how the attacker could have known that Mr Ashworth had them, given that he had only just received them.'

'It seems that, in following the "theft of pieces of jet" theory, we provided ourselves with a red herring which stopped us from thinking beyond it.'

'But, if I am right and it was a case of mistaken identity, it means that his attacker must have been somewhere in that vicinity already and was there for a reason completely unconnected with Mr Ashworth,' said Philip.

'And, also, if the attacker thought he was following Mr Steen, it suggests that the attacker expected to see Mr Steen in that vicinity.'

'Although, the attack might not have been pre-meditated. The attacker might not have known Mr Steen was going to be in that vicinity.'

'True. He might have been there for some other reason and seen a person, that is, Mr Ashworth, and mistaken him for Mr Steen and taken the opportunity to follow him and attack him. That sounds a bit feeble, doesn't it?'

'Well, either way,' said Philip, 'planned or on the spur of the moment, it doesn't matter. What we need to know is whether Mr Steen was anywhere near Green Lane that night and, if so, who might have known that.'

'It seems unlikely, doesn't it?' said Eleanor. 'What reason could Mr Steen possibly have had for being there? He was in Buxton because of the water bottling scheme and when Mr Ashworth was attacked, Mr Steen had only just arrived. He hadn't really had enough time to make enemies. And if he wanted to look at the golf course, surely he would have gone there in the day time. There is only Poole's Cavern up there and that would have been closed.'

'So we can rule out sightseeing, then,' said Philip, dryly.

'Let's think about the timing of the attack. You introduced Mr Ashworth to me on the Saturday, which was the day after he arrived. I think Mr Steen arrived in Buxton at about the same time as Mr Ashworth.'

'Then, on the Monday you very kindly stood in for me and introduced Mr Ashworth to Mr Redfern and then, first thing on Wednesday morning, Mr Ashworth was found on the golf course having been attacked the previous night. We need to know where Mr Steen was on the Tuesday evening.'

Eleanor sat thinking, reviewing in her mind the questions she had asked at the time, and then suddenly she said: 'That's it! To meet Mr Redfern. I've just remembered. After Mr Ashworth had been attacked and we were trying to work out why Mr Ashworth was near Green Lane, I went to speak to Mr Redfern. I thought Mr Ashworth might have gone back that evening to see him but he hadn't. But Mr Redfern did say that he had an appointment with the man from Manchester. That must have been Mr Steen. Don't you see? When Mr Ashworth was attacked, Mr Steen was in the vicinity of Green Lane. Oh! How stupid of me not to have thought of that before.'

'So the attack on Mr Ashworth could have been a mistake,' said Philip, 'and that would account for the fact that he was not robbed, because the attacker intended to kill not rob, and he intended to kill Mr Steen not Mr Ashworth.'

'It certainly does put a different complexion on events, doesn't it?' said Eleanor. 'And it also is a simpler explanation without all the question marks that we had previously.' Eleanor briefly considered the implications of this new theory and then, said: 'Philip, I think your theory may well be correct. Thank you for telling me.'

'Don't mention it, old thing. Always glad to be of service,' Philip looked at his watch and stood up. 'Anyway, we had better go and meet Mr Ashworth.'

Mr Ashworth was already at the café waiting to greet them. He had ordered a splendid afternoon tea and, as they sat enjoying it, he thanked them for their kindness to him. He also explained what he had been doing over the past few days.

'When I heard that Mr Steen was looking for a spring, I decided to investigate the areas that he was interested in. You see, springs were very important to these early inhabitants because they were places where one could gain access to the spirit world. Valuable items were offered as gifts and placed at the entrance to the spring. I reasoned that if there was an ancient spring near to where the river magically reappeared, the people I am studying would have found it a very attractive site. Then I heard about the spring being owned by the Brunts and I went to see old Mr Brunt. He told me exactly where the spring used to be. He also told me that the current road follows the pack horse route and that route is believed to follow an old prehistoric trackway. Trackways are the old paths that criss-crossed the country-side thousands of years ago when people only moved about on foot. Bronze Age people certainly knew of the existence of the cavern so they must have used the trackway. That means that the spring would have been close to the trackway and easily accessible. I have begun searching the areas where Mr Steen's men have been investigating in the hope of finding some evidence of occupation. Mr Steen's men seem to have stopped now and that has made access much easier for me.'

'That must be very satisfying for you,' said Philip, 'and it proves the old adage that someone's bad luck is always someone else's gain. You seem to have recovered fully from the attack.'

'I must confess to a small amount of trepidation when I returned to Buxton, not knowing why I had been attacked and fearing that it might be some unknown rival who was still in the vicinity and likely to strike again. However, as Mr Steen is no longer interested in that area I am not in danger from interference from his men and it is safe for me to continue my research. I am hopeful of finding evidence of early human presence in that area.'

Eleanor was struck by the completely disinterested and academic way that Mr Ashworth regarded Mr Steen's death. It was simply a fact to be examined, assessed, and put into its proper place during a discussion.

'It might be wise to continue being cautious though,' said Philip. 'When we spoke to you in hospital, you recalled that when you were in the *Advertiser* office looking through the archives, someone there showed interest in what you were doing.'

'Ah, yes! But I have spoken to him. He tracked me down at Cramond House. He is, in fact, a member of the Derbyshire Archaeological Society and when he realised that I am an archaeologist with an interest in Buxton he thought there might be something to report in the Society's journal. I have promised him an article if I do find the evidence I am looking for.'

'Oh, I see. That's very gratifying,' said Philip.

'Yes. And you will have seen the reporters outside the Palace hotel, they too have expressed interest in what I am doing. With archaeology being so much in the news, I suppose, and there is not much to report on Mr Steen's death at the moment.'

When they had finished their tea, they left the café and Eleanor and Philip thanked Mr Ashworth and wished him luck with his digging.

CHAPTER FIFTEEN

The following morning at nine o'clock, Philip arrived at Hall Bank in the Bentley to take Eleanor to the Palace Hotel to interview Mr Steen's valet and, while he waited for Eleanor, he went in to say good morning to Mr Harriman who was reading the morning's paper.

Mr Harriman said, gloomily: 'You are likely to be hounded by newspaper reporters when you arrive at the hotel, I'm afraid. Eleanor and I were there on Wednesday and the reporters were everywhere, making a nuisance of themselves. I gather that they are printing a lot of nonsense about Mr Steen having been killed.'

'Yes,' said Philip, 'someone told me yesterday that Mrs Steen is cast in the role of first murderer, with the golf professional as second murderer. I can't quite see them in that role myself, even though I suspect that the relationship between them is not platonic. I assume that these ideas are a complete invention by the press.'

'It is a lot of nonsense,' said Eleanor, joining them as she put on her hat. 'In any event, the cause of death has not yet been established. It may not have been a suspicious death at all.'

'It is irresponsible speculation,' said Mr Harriman. 'They should wait for the inquest.'

'Well,' said Philip, 'even if somebody didn't dislike Mr Steen enough to damage his person, they certainly disliked him enough to damage his property. There was the drilling equipment that was deliberately damaged and don't forget the slashed tyre on his motor-car after the Rally. That was no accident and there was no mistaking whose motor-car it was. We had all seen Mr Steen drive off in it before the Rally began.'

'I do agree that the damaged machinery and the slashed tyre suggests that someone was angry with Mr Steen, but the damage might just have been intended as a warning. There is a big gap between slashing a tyre and killing someone,' said Mr Harriman. 'And, as yet, there is no suggestion as to how he was killed, if he was killed, that is.'

'But someone may have had a motive connected with the water bottling scheme,' said Philip.

'Possibly but Eleanor tells me that there was a simpler method of stopping the scheme. Mr Steen may not have been able to use the water from the spring, even assuming that he was able to find it, because the Brunt family probably has the sole right to use that water.'

Yes,' said Eleanor, 'and their claim was quickly made public. According to James, Mr Brunt lost no time in telling everyone who came into his shop the morning after Maureen and I had been to see Mr William Brunt.'

'So, if Mr Steen was killed to stop the water scheme, whoever it was has put his neck in the noose for nothing,' said Philip.

'Probably,' said Mr Harriman. He looked at his watch and added: 'You'd better be off. Thank you for accompanying Eleanor, Philip. I appreciate it. When I decided to give up the house in The Park and move here I took Eleanor away from her rightful social sphere and she ran the risk of being ostracised and I made things even worse by allowing her to work in this practice. That has exposed her to criticism, I know, and I sometimes wonder what my wife would have said. It is important for Eleanor to observe the proprieties expected of young ladies as much as is consistent with her doing her job but an unaccompanied female interviewing a male servant is bound to cause comment.'

'You know that I wouldn't have it any other way, Father, I do not miss the life I led when we lived in The Park and I enjoy the work I do. But it is kind of Philip to help me keep up appearances.'

Leaving Napoleon with Mr Harriman, they went outside to Philip's motor-car.

~O~

Mr Harriman's predictions were not fulfilled. The reporters and press photographers seemed to have deserted the hotel. Most people who arrived by motor-car, drove up to the front door and tipped the linkman who arranged for the motor-car to be removed and then brought back when they were leaving. Philip, however, never allowed anyone to drive his motor-car and, although other people thought it undignified, he always insisted on parking it himself. Eleanor was quite used to his eccentricity and was not at all surprised when Philip drove past the entrance, then steered the motor-car off the concourse and parked at the side of the hotel. They were near the service entrance and Eleanor got out of the motor-car intending to walk around to the front door. As she did so, she glanced over to her right towards the edge of the hotel grounds and saw someone sitting on a seat under a tree. It was a woman dressed in black and wearing a white apron and cap. 'Certainly not a guest,' thought Eleanor. 'So, what is a hotel servant doing sitting idly in the grounds at this time of day?' Then she realised that it was the waitress who had fainted and dropped the tray during lunch. Eleanor then recalled that the waitress had been saying something while she was lying on the floor. Eleanor was sure that she had said "It's wrong" but what was wrong? And what had caused the waitress to faint? Something was amiss in the hotel and Eleanor needed to know what. She realised that she was being presented with the perfect opportunity to find out.

Eleanor then entered into a debate with herself. The waitress would be an ideal source of information about what was going on in the hotel. The seat on which the waitress was sitting was secluded and out of sight so Eleanor could interview her unobserved. She could approach the waitress with the excuse of asking if she had recovered. Because she had come to the aid of the waitress when she had dropped the tray, that counted as an introduction and it would be easy to gain her confidence. On the other hand, Eleanor said to herself sternly, the fact that the girl is sitting out here instead of getting on with her work suggests that she is in trouble. If that is the case, she is likely to be very vulnerable at the moment and probably needs protection not cross-examination. Eleanor considered the morality of taking advantage of the waitress and measured that against the likely benefit of the information the waitress could provide. Like many people since Machiavelli, she found that she could justify her dubious actions by contemplating the ultimate benefit to be gained. She could hear her father saying "Eleanor" slowly and with the emphasis on the last syllable of her name and she mentally promised him to be respectful of the girl's position.

'Philip, do you mind waiting a moment. I just want to go and talk to the waitress who is sitting under the tree there. I shall only be a minute or two.'

Philip squinted at Eleanor and said: 'We are here to see the valet remember? You are wearing that look which says you are about to interrogate someone. If you are going to poke your nose into other people's business, I shall just sit quietly in the motor-car and keep right out of your way.'

Eleanor smiled, gave him an innocent look, and walked away.

'Good morning,' said Eleanor to the waitress. 'I'm Miss Harriman. You may not remember me. I was in the hotel dining room on the day you fainted.'

The girl looked up at Eleanor and frowned defensively. She lifted the corner of her apron and wiped at the tears on her cheeks. 'Are you the lady who helped me up?'

'One of them, yes,' said Eleanor. 'May I sit down?' The girl nodded. 'Are you all right? Have you recovered?'

'Yes, miss. Thank you, miss,' she said, very quietly.

'Oh, your arm is bandaged. Were you scalded?' asked Eleanor. The girl nodded. 'What is your name?

'Annie, miss. Annie Baird.'

'But there is something wrong, Annie, otherwise you would not be sitting out here instead of getting on with your work. Is there anything I can do to help?'

In response to sympathy, Annie began crying again. Eleanor waited patiently. She was concerned at the girl's appearance. She looked even more pale and drawn than on the last occasion. The sobs subsided enough for Annie to say, barely above a whisper: 'I've lost my place.'

'Because you dropped the tray at lunch?' asked Eleanor. 'Is that why you are sitting out here instead of serving in the dining room?'

There was a silence and then Annie said: 'I were given a warning for that and then I muddled up an order at breakfast yesterday and Monsieur Maurice complained about me again and then they said I spoke to the newspaper men but I didn't.' She looked at Eleanor and shook her head. 'I didn't! And then they said I were a liar. But I'm not! Mr Hewlett said that I must leave today. He said forthwith and without a character.' This was all said in a rush and then she began sobbing, quietly but deeply, her pent-up emotion suddenly released by Eleanor's concern. Her face was hidden by her apron. Eleanor was troubled by how upset Annie was. She waited for the sobs to subside a little.

'When I helped you up in the dining room after you fainted you were trying to say something. I think you said that something was wrong. Are you in some sort of trouble?'

Annie shook her head. The sobbing began again and Annie muttered, barely audibly: 'I didn't do anything. It weren't me.'

It occurred to Eleanor that, if Annie had been dismissed, she might now be homeless and, as she had been refused a character reference, she would not find another situation very easily. She seemed quite young, Eleanor guessed probably only sixteen or seventeen. Compassion and concern for Annie prevented Eleanor from pursuing her goal of questioning her about the hotel. Instead, Eleanor asked: 'Do you live in Buxton or do you live here at the hotel?'

The sobs subsided enough for Annie to reply: 'Here.'

'Where does your family live?'

'Holmfirth.'

'Would you like me to lend you some money for a train fare so that you can go home?'

Annie shook her head violently. 'No. I daren't tell my father I've lost my place. He'd be that ashamed if he knew I'd been accused of lying. He's a lay preacher.' This brought on a further bout of crying and Annie was now trembling. 'But I'm not a liar. It's not true what they said. I didn't talk to anyone.'

Annie was now working herself up into quite a state and Eleanor could see that, if she had been wrongly accused and punished, she was quite helpless to defend herself. Eleanor remembered the scene at lunch with the Denfields, the way the other waiter had stepped over Annie as if she did not exist and the cavalier manner in which Monsieur Maurice had bundled her out of the dining room. If Annie was innocent it meant that she was being bullied and needed protection. She probably also needed to clear her name and get a proper reference. Eleanor felt reluctant to abandon her when she seemed so vulnerable.

'Do you have anywhere you can go, at least for today?'

Annie shook her head. Eleanor thought of the Misses

Pymble. They were kind-hearted and always willing to provide shelter for people in need. Being a pair of elderly spinsters, they were a category of person commonly supposed to be naïve and ignorant of the ways of the world. Their style of dress and their manners belonged to the previous century but they were by no means harmless little old ladies who could easily be taken advantage of or whose eccentricities needed to be humoured. They were very worldly-wise, very observant, mentally alert, and excellent judges of character. Eleanor was confident that they would be able to seek out the truth about Annie and the reasons for her dismissal. She said: 'I know some very kind people with whom you could probably stay, at least for tonight, just to give yourself time to decide what to do next. They run a lodging house on Bath Road, and the Season has only just begun so they may have room for you.' Eleanor gave Annie time to think about this offer, then she said: 'Would you like me to telephone them and see if they can take you?'

Annie lifted up a tear-stained face, full of relief and surprise at the kindness being shown to her: 'Oh, yes, please, miss.'

'All right, Annie. I shall telephone from the hotel. You wait here.' Eleanor pointed to Philip, absorbed in his own world and not paying any attention to them. 'That is Mr Danebridge in the motor-car over there. He is a friend of mine.'

Eleanor walked back to Philip. He put down the auction catalogue he had been studying and listened as Eleanor explained what was happening. He nodded in understanding when she asked him to keep an eye on Annie while she was away. After some time, Eleanor returned. As always, the Misses Pymble were willing to help someone in distress. Eleanor went back to tell Annie.

'The Misses Pymble can take you,' she said. 'You'll like them, I'm sure. They have lived in Buxton a long time. They are quite elderly but still very active and very generous with their time and resources when it comes to a good cause. I've arranged to take you there. I shall wait here for you so that you can pack up your things. Have you been paid your wages?' Annie shook her head. 'All right. I shall sort that out for you. Now, don't hurry. Just make sure that you have packed everything.'

'Thank you ever so much, miss,' said Annie, smiling wanly but still in danger of crying again. She hesitated and then hurried back into the hotel.

Eleanor returned to Philip and said: 'After I had telephoned to the Misses Pymble, I asked at reception about the valet. He is no longer living at the hotel because Mr Steen is not there to pay the bill. The concierge said he had gone to stay with his cousin but he didn't know the address. I think the Misses Pymble might know where that is. I shall ask them when we deliver Annie.'

While they waited for Annie, Eleanor described for Philip the events at the hotel during her lunch with the Denfields. Philip remembered seeing Annie at the Rally and agreed that she seemed changed. While they waited, Eleanor and Philip reflected on the sudden changes in fortune that some of the people involved in the Rally had experienced in the last few days. After a quarter of an hour, when Annie hadn't returned, Eleanor began to be anxious in case Annie had been prevented from leaving. She was just considering going to look for her when Annie appeared. She had changed out of her hotel uniform into a dress and carried a coat and a small suitcase which contained the rest of her belongings. Eleanor helped her to put the suitcase in the motor-car and they drove away from the hotel without a backward look.

Annie was welcomed kindly and taken in by the Pymble twins. Eleanor gave Annie her card and said: 'I shall sort out the matter of your wages, Annie, in the next few days. In the meantime, if you need anything, you can telephone me at

Hall Bank.' After the Misses Pymble had enquired as to the health and well-being of everyone at Hall Bank and of Cecily and Richard as well, Eleanor asked for directions to Woodthorpe House where she thought the valet would be staying and Miss Pymble gave her the address. Eleanor thanked the Misses Pymble once again for their kindness and she and Philip left a rather overwhelmed Annie, and drove away.

Eleanor looked at her watch and said: 'Thank you for rescuing Annie, Philip. She really was in a state and I couldn't just leave her. We won't have time to interview the valet now. I'm sure you need to get to the showroom.'

'I do rather, old thing. I've got someone coming in at ten thirty for a valuation and tomorrow I'm in Derby for an auction. Do you want to go on Saturday, or is that too late?'

'That would be marvellous. You are generous, Philip.'

'Well, I did owe you a favour remember because you looked after Mr Ashworth for me and I refused to be a lounge lizard.'

~O~

Eleanor needed to tell Catherine about the threatening letters which Mr Steen had received but she couldn't give her that information over the telephone. Conversations could be overheard at the telephone exchange and one could never be sure who might be listening in. So, instead, she telephoned to Catherine and invited her to come to Hall Bank for lunch. Mr Harriman and Edwin were both out and they had the dining room to themselves.

'Now,' said Catherine, when Mrs Clayton had served them and returned to the kitchen, 'what did you want to tell me?'

'Did you know that Mr Steen had been receiving threatening letters?'

'No, no-one mentioned that.'

'I can't tell you how I know, because that is information I received from a client, but it is reliable information. It is possible that the valet may have seen the letters and may be able to provide more information but I thought it was something you should know in case it proves to be relevant.'

'I see,' said Catherine. 'I don't suppose he kept them?'

'Apparently not.'

'Well, I shall keep them in mind. Oh, that reminds me. I did check on the tablets supplied to Mr Steen. Mr Pugh on Cavendish Circus was the chemist who supplied the *Veronal* and he confirmed that a new box was delivered to the Palace Hotel on the Friday in the week before Mr Steen died. That was the second box he had supplied.'

'So, now we can be certain how many tablets there were. That is a good starting point,' said Eleanor.

'I've been thinking about the things we discussed before and trying to make sense of this case. There is something about it that troubles me but, at the moment, I cannot say what.'

'How often do people just die in their sleep without a cause being discovered?'

'It's not an uncommon thing, dying in one's sleep, but doctors are generally able to state a cause, especially if the deceased was a patient they had been treating, although I have to admit that sometimes, if there is no post mortem, they may get it completely wrong. As to statistics, it would probably be very difficult to provide accurate figures.' Catherine paused. 'I think what is troubling me most is the fact that there is a very obvious possible cause, that is, the sleeping tablets, and yet there seems no justification for suspecting barbitone poisoning.'

'Because there were no tablets missing?' asked Eleanor.

'Yes, and somehow, because of that fact, I sense that we are being presented with a very clever puzzle, the perfect crime, and we are being challenged, defied even, to detect it. Does that sound melodramatic?'

'Not at all. I think sometimes, although one cannot immediately put one's finger on the reason, one does get a vague feeling that something is not quite right. An insignificant detail that does not match, a pattern that has been slightly disrupted. It is important to pursue the issue and not just ignore it. I know that from experience.' said Eleanor. 'One has to keep asking questions, especially in relation to facts which do not seem to fit.'

'Thank you, Eleanor, you have reassured me. I was beginning to think that I was getting things out of proportion. After all, murder is not a common cause of death but the truth is, I am worried. I don't want to make too much of an issue of the sleeping tablets in case it was just a natural death. It would be easier just to accept things as they are and think no more about it. On the other hand, if it was not a natural death, I would not be doing my job properly with respect to Mr Steen. I would be letting him down. I should hate to think that someone might escape detection because I am not conscientious, or determined, enough to carry out a thorough investigation.'

'Catherine, you are a very good doctor and you have an excellent reputation. You think about things rather than just accept what you are told. You find ways to help patients even when there seem to be no answers. You have a very loyal following in this town and your judgment is highly prized. If we are dealing with murder, the person responsible may well be relying on the fact that, as you yourself pointed out, a doctor would not want to make a fuss and would prefer to accept things at face value rather than risk his or her reputation. You must not doubt your ability and, if you sense that something is not right, we must investigate things further and find the answer. Now, there is only one way to deal with this.' Eleanor stopped and looked at Catherine in surprise. 'What is the matter? Why are you laughing?'

'I knew I could rely on you. You won't let this rest until you find a solution, will you? I do appreciate this, Eleanor, even though I know you are doing this for your own satisfaction as well as mine.'

'Well, of course I want to get to the bottom of this. I did not particularly like the man but the fact is Mr Steen died suddenly and with no obvious explanation. That is a very good reason to be asking questions and we must keep that in mind if we begin to doubt what we are doing. Now, to be able to sort this out, we must proceed on the basis that a crime has been committed. The easiest way to approach this is to assume that Mr Steen died from an overdose of barbitone and try to prove ourselves wrong. If we cannot work out how an overdose was administered, perhaps we must accept a verdict of death by natural causes. But, if we can work out how it could have been done, we shall know that it was possible and, if we conclude that it was possible, we can start thinking about who might have committed such a crime. Agreed?'

'Agreed. You make it all sound very straightforward and simple.'

'Right, so to summarise. We have ruled out accident and deliberate act by Mr Steen himself. That leaves deliberate act by a third party. How could a third party have persuaded Mr Steen to take five extra tablets, because it is impossible to believe that he would have done so voluntarily.'

'No, he certainly would not,' said Catherine. 'That is the main stumbling block, isn't it? I've been considering that question since yesterday. I tried to put myself in the shoes of a killer and imagine what I would do. I think I know how it could be done but it still presents a bit of a puzzle.'

'All right, how could you do it?'

'The only way I can think of is to dissolve the tablets in liquid that you know the victim will drink. These tablets are readily soluble and, once dissolved, would not be detected by the naked eye or by taste.'

'Well, if Mr Steen was in the habit of taking two tablets at bedtime, presumably he took them with water,' said Eleanor. 'Most people do.'

'Yes, but that poses another problem,' said Catherine. 'One would need to know in advance how many tablets Mr Steen was going to take that night and, therefore, how many extra tablets to dissolve in order to ensure that he took a lethal dose. If one relied on the instructions on the box of *Veronal*, and based the calculation on one tablet being taken, the dose dissolved would not be sufficient to kill.'

'But someone who knew that Mr Steen usually exceeded the prescribed dose would base the calculation on two tablets,' said Eleanor.

'The second problem is that, for the dose to be fatal, Mr Steen would have to drink all of the water in which the tablets were dissolved, not just some of it.'

'Hmm,' said Eleanor, 'so someone would need to know how much water he usually drank. Let's put that aside for the moment. How easy is it to dissolve enough tablets so that one would not notice them?'

'Well,' said Catherine, 'I have considered that as well. Once dissolved they are practically tasteless. In any event, when one takes water to help swallow tablets, the taste of the tablet is often still discernible, so if the water containing the dissolved tablets did have any residual taste, it probably would be attributed to the two tablets that were being swallowed and not to the water itself.'

'So, assuming that five or six tablets were dissolved, how much water would one need?'

'Last evening I made a few enquiries of a friend who is a chemist. She estimated that thirty grains, that is six tablets, could be dissolved in about eight fluid ounces of water, in other words, one cup. And it seems that if one uses hot or boiling water rather than cold, a much smaller volume of water is required.'

'Which suggests a degree of premeditation,' mused Eleanor, 'because one would not normally have boiling water to hand in a hotel room.'

'That is true, nor would one have chemical knowledge readily to hand. I then imagined myself arranging to dissolve the tablets in some other place. When the solution was ready, I would put it into something unremarkable that one would normally find in a hotel room.'

'Such as?'

'Well, the hotel very obligingly provides a carafe of water which is refreshed twice during the day and then again in the evening. A carafe containing adulterated water would look much the same as one containing unadulterated water but, as you so rightly observed, premeditation is required. There was a carafe of water on the bedside table in Mr Steen's room. However, there is one difficulty with my theory.'

'I think I know what you are going to say. For that method to be effective, one would have to ensure that the entire contents of the carafe would be consumed.'

'Exactly, because the carafes contain much more water than Mr Steen would have needed to take his usual two tablets. My preferred method would be to dissolve as many tablets as possible in the minimum amount of water, less than a cupful, and put only that amount of water in the bedside carafe. One could ensure that all of the water would be consumed.'

'Well, there is one factor that favours that theory,' said Eleanor. 'You said that Mr Steen had consumed a significant quantity of alcohol as well as food that evening and he may have been unusually thirsty when he retired for the night or become thirsty during the night and consumed all the water in the carafe.'

'That's possible but, of course, one could not anticipate that,' said Catherine.

'No. Now, as well as access to boiling water one would need access to the carafes. Does that rule out a guest at the hotel?'

'Well, guests have a carafe in their hotel room,' said Catherine, 'but query access to boiling water. Of course, it could be someone from outside the hotel, but access to the room would be difficult, which leads me to conclude that we are looking for someone at the hotel with somewhere private to do the dissolving, access to the carafes, and access to the room.'

'A chef or one of the servants in the kitchen? One of the chamber maids? The servants who do the cleaning?' suggested Eleanor.

'But who amongst them would have a motive? Who at the hotel might have wanted Mr Steen dead? He had only been there a short while and I don't suppose most of them even knew him, let alone would have been affected by his factory scheme,' objected Catherine. 'You are going to have to find a motive, Eleanor, if we want this theory to go any further.'

'Before we explore that, let me think this through.' Eleanor was silent for a minute. 'If I leave only a small amount of water in the carafe to be sure that Mr Steen consumes all of it would Mr Steen have had enough water to take his usual two tablets?'

'Yes, so he would be unlikely to ask the valet for more water or for a fresh carafe,' said Catherine.

'How do I get the carafe into Mr Steen's room? One would not want to risk putting the adulterated water in during the day because the tampering might be discovered,' objected Eleanor. 'Or the water might be thrown out and the carafe refilled during the day. Or the wrong person might drink it.'

'Well, as to that, the chamber maids go in each evening to

turn down the beds and put fresh water in each room so any tampering would have to be done after that. In order to clarify this point, I went back to the hotel and asked to speak to the chamber maid who looked after Mr Steen's room. Her name is Beryl. Between about eight and eight thirty in the evening, while the guests are in the dining room, she goes in to turn down the beds and, at the same time, puts a fresh carafe of water in each room. The carafes are not just re-filled in the rooms. Clean carafes are filled in the kitchen and taken upstairs on a trolley which the chamber maid leaves in the corridor. She puts the fresh carafe in the room and puts the used carafe on the trolley. She was on duty the night Mr Steen died and she does not remember anything unusual about the room or about her task.'

'So, in theory,' said Eleanor, 'someone could have dissolved the tablets in water in the kitchen and then substituted the adulterated water for the clean water in one of the carafes on the trolley. But that seems unlikely, doesn't it? How could one be certain that the carafe which had been tampered with would end up in Mr Steen's room?'

'One couldn't. That is the difficulty. So, if that is how the deed was done, the carafes would have to have been exchanged in the room itself after the chamber maid had serviced the room,' said Catherine.

'Yes,' agreed Eleanor, 'and Beryl, the chamber maid, would seem to be the obvious suspect. How did the chamber maid seem? Was she nervous at being questioned?'

'No, not at all. She explained very clearly what her work entailed. She didn't seem surprised or curious as to why I was interested in the carafes. She is quite young, sixteen or seventeen perhaps, nicely spoken, very polite. A very down-to-earth young woman, one of those practical, reliable sorts without much imagination. I don't think it occurred to her that she might be suspected of tampering with the carafe.'

'In any event, it is difficult to imagine her having the

knowledge required to calculate the number of tablets and the minimum amount of water needed to dissolve them,' said Eleanor. 'Is it safe to eliminate her?'

'I think so, unless she was being used, unwittingly or not, by a second person who did have the right knowledge,' said Catherine.

'Oh dear, this is getting complicated. We shouldn't just stop at Beryl though. We probably need to know who else could have had access to Mr Steen's room.'

'The housekeeper, perhaps, or a workman if something about the room needed to be attended to or repaired,' said Catherine, 'but access to the room is only one factor. I think we are also looking for someone who knew about Mr Steen's habits and about his sleeping tablets. I am sure that the servants at the hotel notice the comings and goings of the guests, probably more than the guests realise. They probably sum up the guests fairly accurately. They go behind the scenes, as it were, and see the actors when they are not on stage. They get glimpses of people's private lives that fellow guests do not see and I am sure that they talk amongst themselves about what they see and hear. The chamber maids particularly are in a unique position. And, there is the valet, Mellor, of course. It seems that some of the hotel servants knew that Mr Steen took sleeping tablets although they may not have known how many he took.'

They were silent for a while thinking about their theory. Then, Eleanor said: 'If you are right about the method used to introduce the barbitone into Mr Steen's system, it would seem that the murder weapon was a carafe of water. How very odd.'

'Yes, that is unusual but certainly possible. However, as I said, I know how this crime could have been committed but I don't know how it was committed. You see, there was some water left in the carafe in Mr Steen's room.'

'So Mr Steen might not have ingested the full dose of

tablets?'

'And, more importantly, I had the carafe removed and the water tested. Unfortunately, we do not have a test which will allow us to detect the presence of barbitone in the water. All we can do is test for its absence. The water left in the carafe was found to contain no impurities at all.'

'Oh,' said Eleanor, deflated. She frowned with disappointment. 'So, that means all of this detail that we have been discussing is pure speculation and completely irrelevant?'

'No, I don't think so. What we now have to explain is why the water found in the carafe in the morning was not contaminated because that clearly was not the water he drank.'

'In that case, we have only two impossible things to do,' said Eleanor, still frowning. 'First to all, find where the tablets came from, and secondly, where the water came from?'

'Yes,' said Catherine, cheerfully.

'Our suggestions as to the solution to this problem are getting more and more complex. Are you sure we are not just completely off track and wasting our time?'

'No,' said Catherine, 'I am sure that for someone with your formidable talent for solving problems it should not be too difficult.'

'Thank you very much!' said Eleanor. 'Come on, Leon. This conversation is getting tedious. It's time for your walk.'

During lunch, Napoleon had been lying in the hallway chewing on his favourite old tennis shoe. As Eleanor looked at him, something from her previous conversation with Catherine flashed through her mind.

'Napoleon has just reminded me of something you told me earlier. You asked the valet if anything was different in the room and he said that one of Mr Steen's slippers was beside the bed and the other one had been pushed under the bed and he found that unusual because Mr Steen was particular about them being side by side. The valet thought perhaps Mr Steen had got up in the night and left the slippers the way they were found but, if Mr Steen had taken six or seven tablets, would he have been capable of getting up?'

'Now that you mention it, no. It did not occur to me before but, no, unless he got up very soon after he had taken the tablets. If he had tried to get up later on he would have been dizzy at first and then, later on, unstable and probably would have stumbled and fallen. He would most likely have been found out of bed, lying somewhere in the room.'

'If a pair of slippers is placed tidily beside a bed and someone accidently bumps them, one slipper can easily end up under the bed. Now, that result can be brought about by the occupier of the bed or by another person who approaches the bed. Which side of the bed were the slippers?' asked Eleanor.

'I don't recall,' said Catherine, 'Why?'

'I need to know,' said Eleanor.

'You are impossible,' said Catherine. She laughed as she accompanied Eleanor and Napoleon down the stairs and they headed for their lunchtime stroll through the gardens.

Chapter Sixteen

When Philip was next free, he called at Hall Bank to collect Eleanor and they drove to Woodthorpe House so that Eleanor could interview Mr Steen's valet. Philip parked the motor-car in London Road and said: 'Do you want me to come in or shall I stay here?'

'Do you mind waiting outside?'

'Not at all. It will probably be easier for you. After all, this is more for appearances than anything else, isn't it?'

'Yes,' laughed Eleanor. 'I don't think it is a question of my safety although Edwin did caution me. I'll try not to be too long.'

'Take as long as you like,' said Philip, 'just make sure you come out alive.'

Eleanor walked up to the front door and pressed the bell. She had to wait quite a while before a rather flustered woman opened the door, and stood wiping her wet hands on her apron as she said: 'Yes?'

'Good morning,' said Eleanor. 'Mrs Flax?'

'Yes.'

'I'm Miss Harriman. Mrs Flax, I'm sorry to call so early but I need to speak to someone who, I believe, is staying here. Mr Mellor…'

'Which one did you want?' interrupted Mrs Flax.

'The Mr Mellor who, until recently, was staying at the Palace Hotel and was the valet of Mr Steen.'

'You want Mr Arthur, then.' Mrs Flax looked intently at Eleanor. 'You're not with the newspapers?' Or the communists?'

No,' said Eleanor, smiling, 'here is my card.'

Mrs Flax glanced at the card. 'You'd best come in. He's in the front parlour reading the paper. The other one's at the hospital.'

Eleanor followed Mrs Flax into the hall and was shown into a room at the front of the house. Mr Mellor was sitting in an armchair and stood up as Eleanor entered the room.

'You've got company, Mr Mellor,' said Mrs Flax, and she left to return to the kitchen.

'Good morning, Mr Mellor. I'm Miss Harriman,' said Eleanor, as she handed a card to Mr Mellor.

Mr Mellor looked at it and frowned. 'What is this about?' he asked, cautiously.

'It is about Mr Steen. Mrs Steen is my client and I should like to ask you a few questions if I may.'

'Please sit down then,' said Mr Mellor, indicating an armchair opposite his. He sat down and looked intently at Eleanor. 'Are you a legal person, then?'

'Yes,' said Eleanor. 'I'm with Harriman & Talbot. Their details are on my card.' Eleanor pointed to the card she had just given Mr Mellor. She waited for him to say how unusual it was for a woman to be involved with the law, as this was generally the reaction she got, but he did not comment. 'I don't want to take up your time unnecessarily Mr Mellor so I will come straight to the point, if I may.' Mr Mellor nodded. 'You will no doubt have heard that a death certificate has not yet been issued for Mr Steen, and Mrs Steen is anxious to know the cause of Mr Steen's death. To establish that, there are several issues that I need to consider. First of all, about the sleeping tablets Mr Steen was taking.' Mr Mellor frowned and drew back slightly in his chair as he looked intently at Eleanor. 'I believe he took two tablets every evening and that, on the morning you found him, that is the Sunday morning, there were eight tablets remaining in the box.' Mr Mellor nodded. 'You had ordered that box from Mr

Pugh, the chemist, on the previous Friday and it was delivered on the Saturday but it wasn't opened until the Monday. The first two tablets from that new box were taken by Mr Steen on the Monday night.' Mr Mellor looked at the ceiling as he thought about this and then nodded. 'That means that on the night before, that is on the Sunday, Mr Steen must have taken the last two remaining tablets from the previous box.' Another nod of agreement from Mr Mellor. 'Now, according to my calculation, at two tablets every night, that previous box would have been opened ten days earlier, that is, on Friday. That was the day you and Mr Steen arrived at the hotel, which was the eighth of May.'

Mr Mellor looked at the floor and concentrated. He pursed his lips and then shook his head. He looked at Eleanor. 'No, it wasn't that day. No, that's not right,' he said, slowly. Eleanor waited, allowing Mr Mellor time to cast his mind back to the day they had arrived at the hotel. 'Is it important?' he asked.

Eleanor said: 'Yes, Mr Mellor, it could be very important so, if you don't mind, I'd like you to try to remember exactly when you opened that box.'

'Let me see now,' said Mr Mellor. 'When we arrived at the hotel, I asked the linkman where the nearest chemist shop was. First thing the next morning I went across the road to Mr Pugh's and he supplied a new box. I had to go myself instead of having them delivered because the next day was Sunday and there were only a couple of tablets left and I didn't want to run out.'

'So the new box would have been opened on the Sunday after you arrived and the first two tablets taken on that night. Let me just count the days.' Eleanor paused and then said: 'Are you sure, Mr Mellor, because that does not seem right.' Eleanor was beginning to suspect that some tablets were unaccounted for but, if so, they were missing from the previous box of tablets and not the one that was being used when Mr Steen died. She was still not sure about Mr Mellor and she decided to tread very carefully. She counted the days in her head again and when she was sure that she was right, she said: 'Mr Mellor, I am sorry to keep worrying you with these questions about the tablets but I do need to get this right. According to my calculation, that first box of tablets that you got from Mr Pugh was finished by Saturday but it should have lasted until the following Tuesday. Can you help me out here? Have I miscalculated?'

Mr Mellor did not respond and Eleanor waited patiently, sensing that he was considering his position. 'No, you are perfectly correct,' he said, at last. 'You see, some tablets were lost.'

'I see,' said Eleanor, trying to stay calm and not look too interested. 'Could you describe for me, please, how that happened?'

Mr Mellor did not respond. Eleanor tried a different approach.

'Perhaps you could explain to me your usual routine with regard to the tablets,' said Eleanor. 'For example, did you leave the box on the bedside table for Mr Steen or did you put out just two tablets each night?'

'Oh, I always left the box out so Mr Steen could take what he wanted. After the chamber maid had been in to turn down the bed, I would put the box on the bedside table. It was kept in the drawer of the table during the day time.'

'And in the mornings, did you put the box away or did the chamber maid?'

'I generally put the box in the drawer, first thing, out of harm's way.'

'So that it didn't get mislaid, for example?' asked Eleanor.

'Yes,' said Mr Mellor.

'Or…to make sure no-one took one by mistake, perhaps?'

'Yes, and because of the chamber maids,' said the valet.

Eleanor was sure that there was more information to be

obtained but she could not immediately think of the right question to ask. She reflected on what Mr Mellor had said and then she asked: 'You said that you generally put the box in the drawer. Was there an occasion when you did not do so?'

Mr Mellor was silent and looked slightly uncomfortable. He moved about in his chair. Then he said: 'I might as well own up but it does me no credit. I was careless but fortunately Mr Steen didn't seem to notice. One morning, I must have overlooked putting the box back in the drawer where it should have been. I don't recall doing so, because it was important and I was always very careful, but I must have forgotten because there's no other explanation for what happened. When I came back after the chamber maids had been in to see to the room I found the box on the carpet and the tablets all spilled out on the floor. I supposed that one of the chamber maids had been clumsy and knocked the box off.'

'And did you mention it to anyone? The chamber maid or the manager?'

'Well, no, I didn't like to because I couldn't be sure that I had put the box away. I knew the tablets were poison and I was always very careful to see that they were out of sight. As I said, I don't recall leaving the box out. If I had left the box out, I shouldn't have and it was my fault that some were lost.'

'I understand that the drawer was not locked.'

'No, it wasn't.'

'Is it possible, Mr Mellor, that you did put the tablets away in the drawer and that someone later deliberately removed them?'

'I suppose someone could have moved them.' Mr Mellor paused. 'I did think it odd that the tablets were on the floor. If it had been the chamber maid that knocked the box over, I'm sure she would not have left them lying about. She would have put them back so as not to get into trouble. I'd not thought about it before but it does seem unusual, doesn't it?'

Eleanor said: 'Yes,' and then remained silent leaving Mr Mellor to think things through.

'I suppose I should have thought about it a bit more but, at the time, I was just anxious not to let Mr Steen know that I had been careless. It doesn't really matter now though, does it?'

Eleanor asked: 'So, when you found the tablets on the floor, what did you do?'

'I picked them up and put them back in the box. They were sort of scattered about and I couldn't be sure whether I had got them all. I looked very carefully and I thought I had but after a few days I did think the box was emptying quicker than it should have done and I wondered if I had missed some.'

'And do you have any idea how many were missing?'

'No, not really. Although, there were a good few in the box. I only really noticed how many tablets there were when the box was getting low. It was easy to see when there were only a few left, so I didn't need to count them to know that I needed to order a new box.'

'And you ordered that second box a few days earlier than expected?'

'Yes. So there must have been some missing, mustn't there? At least, four, I suppose.' He paused, then added: 'Perhaps even more.'

'Thank you for being so honest with me, Mr Mellor. I appreciate your help very much. Now, I think when Dr Balderstone came on the Sunday morning to examine Mr Steen, she asked you to look around the room and tell her if anything was out of place. The first thing you mentioned was the carafe of water. You said that it had more water in it than usual. What did you mean by that?'

'Only that Mr Steen usually drank a glass of water about half an hour before retiring. He considered this beneficial to a healthy body and then he drank some more when he took his sleeping tablets.' Mr Mellor paused. 'Mr Steen was a man of regular habits. He believed that was the secret of his success in business. If I remember correctly, the carafe was about two thirds full that morning, which was unusual. It was more like one third, generally. Sometimes less.'

'You also noticed that one of Mr Steen's slippers had been pushed under the bed. Is that correct?'

'Yes.'

'Which side of the bed were they?'

'The same side as the bedside table.'

'When the chamber maid turned down the bed at night, did she always turn down the same side?'

Mr Mellor reflected on this subject, picturing the room. 'Yes,' he said, 'always on the side next to the bedside table. It stands to reason, doesn't it?'

Eleanor smiled. 'Yes, I suppose it does. That is the side where you would be standing before getting into bed. And you would have expected the slippers to be tidy.'

'Oh yes, almost every night I had to straighten them before Mr Steen retired. The chamber maids always seemed to be in a hurry when they turned down the beds and one or other of the slippers would be crooked. That made Mr Steen cross the first time it happened and, as a consequence, I always made sure they were straight. And I know I straightened them up that night after the chamber maid had been. That is what made me think that perhaps Mr Steen had got up in the night.' Mr Mellor sighed and looked at the carpet. 'Mr Steen was a very tidy man and, as I said before, liked everything regular. Things always had to be straight and not left higgledy-piggledy. And he couldn't abide crooked pictures. Meals had to be on time as well. Mrs Steen was very different. She was that untidy, it used to make Mr

Steen cross and, I wouldn't say this to just anybody, but it was one of the reasons they had separate suites. It saved unpleasantness, instead of him having to remind her all the time.'

Eleanor had the impression that Mr Mellor had enjoyed his time with Mr Steen despite his odd habits and that he was sorry that Mr Steen was gone. She realised that Mr Mellor must have had several years of service with him before the arrival of Mrs Steen. Perhaps that made him a little proprietorial as far as Mr Steen was concerned, and he saw himself as Mr Steen's ally.

'Mr Steen seems to have been a very successful business man and I suppose he was the sort of person who likes to be in control. Was he an easy person to work for?'

Mr Mellor smiled. 'Being a valet is not an easy job, Miss Harriman, but if you find a situation that suits you it can be tolerable. Mr Steen liked everything just so and it made him anxious if things weren't right. As you say, he liked to be in control and he could be a bit demanding at times, I'll grant you, but as long as things were in order the way he liked them, well…once I worked that out, we had a good enough relationship. Fortunately for me, I'm a creature of habit so it wasn't difficult to stick to routine, although we had our moments. Some people would not have been able to put up with it, I suppose.'

Eleanor thought about the chart she and Edwin had drawn up. Mr Mellor had two ticks against his name for means and opportunity but Eleanor was beginning to think that he was not the sort of person likely to take that opportunity. All that remained now was the question of motive. Eleanor said: 'Mr Mellor, you have been very patient and I won't take up much more of your time with my questions. I believe that someone with the same surname as yours was employed in Mr Steen's factory. I have been told that he is a lodger here.'

Mr Mellor nodded and said: 'Yes, Harry. He's my cousin.'

'And he was badly injured. I believe.'

'Yes, he's here in Buxton for treatment. Mr Steen is paying for it, or at least, his company is. His company is in trouble over it but it wasn't really Mr Steen's fault. The foreman was showing someone over the factory and demonstrating some machinery. He turned off a safety switch and forgot to turn it back on again. The machinery started when it shouldn't have and Harry's arm got caught. It was the foreman's fault, not Mr Steen's. Mr Steen's been very good to Harry, getting him back on his feet and that.'

'I see. Well, I hope that he will benefit from the treatment he is receiving here. He will be well looked after, I'm sure. I had heard that a worker in Mr Steen's factory was injured because a safety guard had been removed in order to speed up production. That must have been someone else, not your cousin.'

'That certainly wasn't Harry but I did hear that there is another court case against Mr Steen's company, something to do with safety so it might be to do with that. I do know that there has been trouble in his factory and some of the workers are against him but, as far as Harry is concerned, he couldn't have been fairer.'

'I see. Well, thank you very much for your time, Mr Mellor. You have been a great help. Please don't get up, I'll see myself out. Goodbye, Mr Mellor.'

Mr Mellor stood up as Eleanor rose to go and said goodbye as she left the room. Mrs Flax was nowhere in sight so Eleanor let herself out of the front door and returned to Philip. He was happily immersed in a book on Georgian cabinet making. He looked up and said: 'All done, old thing? Nothing for Edwin to get in a flap about?'

'Absolutely not. No, Mr Mellor was very helpful and what he told me made sense. I am inclined to believe that he was telling the truth.'

'Back to Hall Bank, then?'

'Yes, please.'

'Are you still free for golf tomorrow?'

'Rather, Millicent said she would pick me up so I'll see you at the Club House.'

'Right ho!' said Philip as he started Bentley.

~O~

When Eleanor arrived back at Hall Bank, James had sorted the first post of the morning and he handed Eleanor the report from the Manchester enquiry agent, providing answers to the questions Eleanor had asked. The agent had been to the Swinford Hotel and spoken to the manager. He had confirmed that two guests had stayed at the hotel on Saturday the twentieth and he recognised Mrs Steen from the newspaper photograph that the enquiry agent had shown him. He said that the two guests had been in the hotel with their friends during the whole of the evening and then on the dance floor until the dancing finished. They had settled their bill that night and had left the hotel the following morning at about a quarter to six. The manager was sure that they had been in the hotel all night. The enquiry agent reported that there was space for parking motor-cars in the grounds of the hotel and that the grounds were surrounded by a high wall which had only one gate onto the street. The manager confirmed that Mr Royston's motor-car and those of the other people in the party had been parked in the grounds on the Saturday evening and, by midnight, only Mr Royston's motor-car remained. On Sunday morning, the manager had unlocked the gate earlier than usual in order to allow Mr Royston to drive his motor-car out. When asked, the manager was certain that Mr Royston's motor-car could not have left the grounds during the night. The gate was always locked at midnight and unlocked again at seven in the morning. He, the manager, was the only person who had access to the key for the gate.

Eleanor put the report away, satisfied that Mrs Steen had been telling the truth. She took out the chart of suspects that she and Edwin had compiled and drew a line through Mrs Steen and Mr Royston. She couldn't decide what to do about Mr Mellor, the valet. He appeared to have nothing to hide and to be telling the truth and the motive that she thought he might have had now seemed unlikely. Undecided, she left that line untouched. She thought about the missing tablets that the valet had confessed to. The chamber maid who normally looked after Mr Steen's room was the most likely person to have knocked the box of tablets off the bedside table. Did that mean that she had stolen some? She tried to picture the scene, imagining the chamber maid in a hurry, accidentally swiping the box with a duster, the box flying off the table, bursting open and scattering tablets on to the floor. What would the chamber maid's reaction have been? Eleanor was almost certain that she would have retrieved the scattered tablets, returned them to the box, put the box back on the table where it had been, and hoped that no-one would notice. But the tablets were left scattered on the floor. The more she thought about the incident, the more puzzled she became. She wondered if the box would actually have popped open if it fell. If not, the tablets would not have been scattered. She decided to think about that later.

Eleanor looked at her chart of suspects and on the line labelled chamber maid put a tick in the box for opportunity. Apart from the valet, the chamber maid had the best opportunity of all the suspects. But would she have known what to do with the tablets if she had stolen them? And what motive could she possibly have had? Was there some connection between her and Mr Steen? Eleanor thought back to the incidents involving Mr Steen and could think of nothing to link the two people. Eleanor gave the chamber maid a tick for means and a question mark for motive.

Eleanor sighed. This was proving much more difficult than she had anticipated. She thought how much simpler it would be if Mrs Steen would just explain where she had been on the night Mr Steen died, especially now that the evidence supported her version of events. However, there was still Catherine to consider. She too needed answers. She put the Steen file to one side, resolving to work solidly on other files until lunchtime.

Eleanor had just started work on the new file when Edwin came up the stairs two at a time, hat in hand. He greeted Napoleon as he came into Eleanor's office, pulled up a chair and sat down abruptly, saying: 'Well, here's another puzzle for you, Eleanor. I've just seen Superintendent Johnson in the street and he stopped to chat. He has given me some very interesting information about the Steen case. This really is a most extraordinary case. First of all, there are no missing tablets, then the water in the carafe is found to be unadulterated, and now? What do you think? There are no fingerprints on the carafe that was in Mr Steen's room. What should we make of that, pray?'

Eleanor thought for a minute and then said: 'But, surely that is entirely understandable because a guilty person would not want to leave their fingerprints...' Then she frowned as she saw Edwin shaking his head. 'Oh, you mean there were no fingerprints at all?' Edwin nodded. 'But there should have been fingerprints on the carafe. Mr Steen's prints should have been there.'

'Precisely,' said Edwin.

'Somebody deliberately wiped clean the carafe after Mr Steen had touched it. That is the first sign we have had that a third party was involved.'

'It certainly suggests that someone handled that carafe who shouldn't have,' said Edwin.

'And wanted to hide the fact,' said Eleanor.

'Yes,' said Edwin. 'I was beginning to think that we had

the perfect crime on our hands but perhaps this absence of fingerprints may prove to be the killer's undoing.'

'This could be the most important piece of information we have,' said Eleanor. 'We need to think this through, don't we? Who would have left fingerprints on the carafe? Possibly someone in the hotel's scullery where the carafe had been washed. Certainly the chamber maid who delivered the carafe to the hotel room. Probably the valet who might have moved the carafe in the course of tidying the room. Mr Steen, certainly.'

'And those fingerprints would be layered in a sequence which reflected the order in which the people handled the carafe. Mr Steen should have been the last person to touch the carafe,' said Edwin.

'But if someone had tampered with the water in the carafe, his or her fingerprints would be on the carafe and, therefore, it would need to be wiped clean,' said Eleanor.

'Let's consider the alternatives,' said Edwin. He picked up a pencil holder and placed it in the centre of Eleanor's desk. 'Here is the carafe, previously delivered by the chamber maid as usual. Her fingerprints are on it. I empty the original contents and in so doing leave my fingerprints on the carafe overlapping those of the chamber maid or I wear gloves and the chamber maid's fingerprints are smudged. I refill the carafe with the water containing the barbitone, which I have brought with me. Mr Steen drinks the water and now his fingerprints are on the carafe superimposed on both the chamber maid's fingerprints and my smudges. After Mr Steen is dead, I repeat the process by emptying out any remaining contaminated water and I refill the carafe with fresh water. My smudges would now be both underneath and on top of Mr Steen's fingerprints.'

'Yes, in changing the water twice it would be difficult to handle the carafe without smudging the existing fingerprints,' said Eleanor. 'Also, using only one carafe would be risky because, even with a change of water, traces of barbitone might remain. I think it would be safer to work with two carafes.' They looked at each other, considering this suggestion and Edwin nodded in agreement. 'So, the first carafe is delivered by the chamber maid as usual,' continued Eleanor, pointing to the pencil holder. 'That carafe is emptied and refilled with the adulterated water, which leaves smudges overlapping the chamber maid's finger-prints. Then, after Mr Steen is dead, the first carafe is removed and a second "innocent" carafe filled with clean water is put in its place.' Eleanor put a paper weight beside the pencil holder and then removed the pencil holder. 'There would be no fingerprints on the second carafe because I would have worn gloves.'

'My objection to that theory,' said Edwin, 'is that the chamber maid's and Mr Steen's fingerprints are missing. In order to commit the perfect crime, I have to leave, on the bedside table, an "innocent" carafe with clean water but with the fingerprints of the chamber maid, possibly the valet, and certainly Mr Steen in the correct layers. Let's try this.' Edwin picked up the pencil holder and the paperweight. 'The chamber maid delivers the first carafe.' Edwin put the pencil holder on the desk. 'I remove that carafe, carefully and without smudging the existing fingerprints. I substitute the "guilty" carafe in its place.' Edwin replaced the pencil holder with the paperweight. 'I take the original carafe away with me and I tip out the amount of water that I think Mr Steen would have drunk. Early in the morning, I take the original carafe back to the room and remove the "guilty" carafe.' Edwin replaced the paperweight with the pencil holder. Edwin looked at Eleanor and then shook his head.

'No,' agreed Eleanor, 'because you have removed the first carafe before Mr Steen has used it. It would have the chamber maid's fingerprints but not Mr Steen's.' Eleanor picked up the pencil holder and the paperweight. 'Just to complicate the picture, there are three carafes: the original carafe is supplied by the chamber maid as usual when the beds are turned down.' Eleanor put the pencil holder back in the centre of the desk. 'At some time before Mr Steen retired for the night, I remove the first carafe and exchange it for the "guilty" carafe, which contains barbitone but no fingerprints.' Eleanor removed the pencil holder and put the paperweight in its place. 'At some time after Mr Steen has consumed the contaminated water, I remove the second carafe and exchange it for a third carafe "innocent" of any barbitone, which is the carafe that was found in the morning.' Eleanor removed the paperweight and put her desk calendar in the centre of her desk. She looked at it and then said: 'And there would be no fingerprints on the third carafe.'

'The chamber maid's fingerprints would not be on the third carafe and that would have caused questions to be asked,' said Edwin. 'Perhaps it was less risky to wipe all the fingerprints than leave only some and not others.'

'Fingerprints would also have provided evidence of the sequence of events, which again would have caused questions to be asked. Without fingerprints, there is no record of that sequence.'

Edwin thought for a minute. 'Why touch the carafe at all? If the killer handled the carafe carefully enough, the existing fingerprints would not be disturbed. Why not just drop the tablets into the water and leave them to dissolve. That way, the fingerprints would be in the proper sequence with Mr Steen's on top.'

'No, that wouldn't work. The concentration of barbitone in the water would not be sufficient. The tablets have to be dissolved in boiling water first to ensure the maximum amount of barbitone in the smallest amount of water. There needs to be at least two carafes, the original carafe which is replaced with a second one, the "guilty" one. But then if the second one is rinsed out and clean water put back in it would take too much time and some residue might be left so there would be the risk of discovery. That second carafe needs to be removed. So a third carafe already filled with clean water is substituted.'

'Hmm,' said Edwin, 'so three carafes but then the killer is presented with a problem. The third carafe will be free of fingerprints. It is the only anomaly in this whole plot. The method chosen to kill Mr Steen suggests both a degree of preparation and an above average knowledge of the properties of barbitone.'

'Yes, it seems to have been very carefully planned and executed.'

'Except,' said Edwin, 'for the absence of fingerprints. If, as we surmise, we are dealing with someone reasonably well-educated and intelligent, why commit such a basic error.'

'It is rather ironic, isn't it? It is generally the presence of fingerprints that gives away the criminal. In this case, the very absence of fingerprints may be the key,' said Eleanor.

'But the absence of fingerprints, in itself, suggests knowledge and careful calculation,' said Edwin. 'The killer must have realised that whatever carafe remained in the room would be tested for residue and fingerprints. It is safer to substitute a third carafe which is clean of fingerprints than leave a carafe with residue.'

'The absence of fingerprints only poses a problem for the killer if he wanted the death to look like accident or suicide, because then it would be essential for Mr Steen's finger-prints to be on the carafe,' added Eleanor.

'Yes,' agreed Edwin, 'if the killer had wanted the death to look like accident or suicide, he would also have removed sufficient tablets from the box to give the impression that the tablets had been taken. But, in the case of a deliberate act by a third party, the police would not be surprised to find that fingerprints had been erased.'

'And,' said Eleanor, 'a carafe which has been wiped clean of fingerprints is suspicious but it tells us very little.'

'I see your point,' said Edwin. 'The absence of fingerprints merely confirms our suspicion that the death was brought about by the act of a third party.'

'Yes. The killer is not increasing the risk of being identified. Whereas a sequence of fingerprints would provide some evidence as to the order of events and that information might help with a conviction.'

'In wiping the fingerprints it was, no doubt, a question of choosing the lesser of two evils,' said Edwin.

'Even so, there is something untidy about this,' said Eleanor.

Edwin watched as Eleanor returned the pencil holder, paperweight and desk calendar to their rightful places on her desk and then he sat staring at the vacant space in the centre of her desk, seeking inspiration. Eleanor watched the steady rise and fall of Napoleon's chest as he lay on the floor beside her desk, snoozing and oblivious to the anxieties that beset the human world. Eventually, Eleanor said: 'If the killer had been able to retain the carafe from the previous day or even an earlier day, he could have used that instead of the third carafe.' Edwin looked at Eleanor in surprise. She continued: 'He could have replaced it on the bedside table when he removed the "guilty" carafe. It would have had all of the appropriate fingerprints in the correct sequence and it would have contained an appropriate level of water. Nobody would have been any the wiser.'

'Hmm. That is an ingenious and very cunning idea,' said Edwin.

'It would have been the perfect solution. The perfect crime, in fact. Perhaps our criminal is not as clever as we thought.'

'Certainly not as clever as you. In fact, your father and I

have agreed on several occasions that it is a blessing that you are on the right side of the law because, given your ability to imagine clever ways of committing crime, the general public would not be safe otherwise.'

'I shall ignore that comment,' said Eleanor, laughing. 'Perhaps the killer thought of my solution but concluded that it was too risky. The timing would be very, very tight. He would have to wait until Mr Steen had gone down to breakfast and the valet had finished tidying up and left the room and then remove the carafe before Mr Steen came back from the dining room and before the chamber maid arrived. He couldn't afford to be seen walking around with it so he would need to hide it somewhere handy. Somewhere near Mr Steen's room.'

'Not an easy task, I agree. Perhaps a carafe without fingerprints seemed an easier option. So where has all this taken us?' said Edwin.

'Not very far. There must be something we have missed,' said Eleanor, giving him a piercing look.

Edwin laughed. 'When you are determined to find an answer to a problem, I am reminded of a beagle or a foxhound following a scent. I know there will be no rest until we find the answer.'

'All right, let us put ourselves in the shoes of the killer and imagine the steps necessary and match those against the information we do have.'

'Very well,' said Edwin, with a sigh. 'I am the killer. I have acquired the necessary knowledge regarding the properties of barbitone. I need some barbitone.'

'You remove some tablets from Mr Steen's box of tablets and to hide the theft you spill the remainder of the tablets on the floor of his room to make it look like the chamber maid has been clumsy and to account for any lost tablets.'

'I dissolve the tablets in water and put the water into a carafe. I can't just put the carafe with the others on the trolley waiting to go into the rooms because I cannot be sure that the right carafe would end up in Mr Steen's room. So, I am going to have to put the carafe in the room myself and risk being seen. And I am going to have to go back to Mr Steen's room in the morning to exchange the "guilty" carafe for the "innocent" one. That is doubly risky.'

'Yes,' said Eleanor, 'however, I think that there might be evidence that someone was in the room during the night, probably after Mr Steen had died. When Catherine asked the valet if anything had been disturbed, he noticed that one of Mr Steen's slippers was under the bed and not beside its pair. The valet was very particular about straightening the slippers. They were on the side of the bed next to the bedside table and could easily have been knocked out of line by a person intent on swapping carafes and not watching where his or her feet were. Particularly if that person was in a hurry.'

'And concentrating on swapping the carafes,' said Edwin.

'Catherine also told me that when she asked the valet to look around the room and see if anything struck him as different or unusual, he said that the carafe contained more water than usual. I asked Mr Mellor about that and he confirmed that the carafe was two thirds full.'

Edwin looked at Eleanor intently. 'The killer probably would not have known how much water Mr Steen usually drank from the carafe during the night. Perhaps in planting the "innocent" carafe the killer forgot to adjust the level of water appropriately. That may have been a fatal mistake.'

'On the other hand,' said Eleanor, 'perhaps that was deliberate. If the third carafe, the "innocent" one had been left with only a small amount of water in it, one would conclude that Mr Steen had drunk the water and that would draw attention to the source of the poison. Making it look as though he had not drunk much water would have the opposite effect. It probably would not have occurred to anyone that Mr Steen had been poisoned by water in the carafe.'

'Hmmm,' said Edwin, 'I see what you mean. It was very clever of Catherine to think of the possibility of dissolving the tablets as a method of killing.'

'Yes. Another doctor might not have thought of it and then Mr Steen's death would have remained unexplained.'

'As you said, a carafe is an unusual murder weapon. But all of this switching of carafes that we have been imagining, it does suggest someone connected with the hotel, doesn't it?' said Edwin. 'Someone who can come and go easily without being noticed.'

'Yes, I think so, which means we can start eliminating some of my suspects and narrowing our original field. I've already taken Mrs Steen and the golf professional off.'

'And talking of suspects, that reminds me of something else Superintendent Johnson told me this morning,' said Edwin. 'Two men have been arrested in connection with the damage to Mr Steen's machinery. They turned out to be members of the Workers Control Party. So, I think you can take them off your list. They were probably only interested in damaging Mr Steen's property and not in murdering him.'

'I think it might be safe to remove the valet from the list also, but not the chamber maid,' said Eleanor. 'She certainly is the person with the greatest opportunity to substitute the carafes. No-one would have remarked on seeing her go in and out of Mr Steen's room and she certainly had the opportunity to spill the box of tablets and remove some of them.'

'Are we making any progress, do you think?' asked Edwin.

'Yes, I think so.'

By the time Eleanor and Edwin had reached this point in their analysis, James had begun closing up the office. It was Saturday and James was mentally planning the tasks he intended to do in his garden that afternoon. When the telephone rang, he was surprised and mildly annoyed. He answered it and was relieved to find that it was not an emergency or a client with a last-minute request. He went up to Eleanor's office.

'Miss Pymble has just telephoned, Miss Eleanor. She wondered if you could spare the time to visit Waverton House, either this afternoon or tomorrow afternoon at whatever time is convenient for you. She asked me to say that she thinks you will want to hear what Miss Annie Baird has to say about her time at the hotel.'

'Oh, that is interesting. Yes, I shall certainly go. I'm free this afternoon. Would you telephone Miss Pymble, please, and say that I shall come at two thirty.'

'Very good, Miss Eleanor. Miss Pymble asked me to say that Napoleon would be most welcome and that she and Miss Felicity always enjoy seeing him.'

Eleanor laughed. 'They spoil him terribly although he is always disappointed when he cannot find their cats. I shall combine the visit with his walk.'

James departed and Eleanor and Edwin cleared their desks and put their files away, agreeing to discuss the file again on Monday morning.

CHAPTER SEVENTEEN

Shortly before two thirty on Saturday afternoon, Eleanor and Napoleon walked along Broad Walk towards Bath Street, Napoleon, head up eagerly watching the passing parade of groups and families taking their afternoon stroll, and Eleanor, head down pondering the problem of Mr Steen and oblivious to passers-by. When they reached Waverton House, the parlour maid opened the door and greeted them.

'Miss Pymble says will you wait here, please.'

Although Napoleon had never seen them, he was certain that cats lived in this house and he never gave up hope of finding them. He stood at the foot of the stairs gazing up and sniffing the air. Miss Pymble bustled into the hall from the sitting room, greeted Eleanor and then made a fuss of Napoleon.

'The cats are safely upstairs, Napoleon, so you are out of luck again today, I'm afraid,' she said and then, turning to Eleanor, continued: 'Miss Harriman, thank you so much for coming and for waiting here. I hope we haven't inconvenienced you. It is, after all, your free afternoon. We couldn't get a word out of Annie at first she was so upset and then, this morning, the whole story came flooding out and that's when I telephoned to your office. I wanted to talk to you first before I took you through to the sitting room.' Miss Pymble put her finger to her lips and then said, barely above a whisper: 'Oh, Miss Harriman, she's been taken advantage of. Dreadfully. The poor girl. She's in such a state and I really don't know what's to be done. I'm so pleased you could come.'

'Who has taken advantage of her, Miss Pymble?' asked Eleanor, calmly.

'Why, one of the men at the hotel. Such a wicked, wicked thing to do.'

'Which man is that, Miss Pymble?' asked Eleanor.

'Jack. His name is Jack Apparently, he's very tall, dark, and handsome. Oh, and well spoken, too. According to Annie he looks and sounds just like a film idol.' Miss Pymble tutted. 'Girls these days are so easily influenced by appearances, aren't they? They like to think that good looks guarantee a good character. Sadly, that is not always the case.' Miss Pymble sighed. Before Eleanor could comment, she added: 'Very rarely, in fact,' and sighed again. Eleanor wondered if perhaps there had been a good looking, badly behaved man somewhere in Miss Pymble's youth. Someone who was responsible for her having remained single. 'Handsome is as handsome does,' Miss Pymble continued, pronouncing the words with conviction. 'That is a very good motto.'

'Oh, I thoroughly agree, Miss Pymble,' said Eleanor. 'Perhaps Annie has seen too many films at The Picture House.'

'Oh, yes. The modern taste for romance is quite shocking to someone of my generation and the things these young girls talk about...well! It surprises me sometimes during the discussion times we have for the girls at the Girls Friendly Society. Only the other day...'

The Misses Pymble were notorious for straying from the subject, disappearing down a rabbit hole and taking the conversation with them. Eleanor had felt as puzzled and helpless as Alice on many occasions. To bring the conversation back to the subject in hand, she said: 'And someone called Jack has taken advantage of Annie. What has happened?'

When someone stated that a girl had been taken advantage

of by an unscrupulous male, the evidence generally manifested itself fairly quickly and the proof arrived nine months later. This was the explanation Eleanor was anticipating. She recalled Annie's fainting fit at the hotel and was preparing herself for the usual sad story.

'Annie thinks she knows something relevant to what happened to Mr Steen,' said Miss Pymble. 'She's got it on her conscience and it is making her ill.' This was not at all what Eleanor was expecting to hear. She stood still for a moment, her mind racing. Miss Pymble continued: 'It is best if you hear the story from her, I think.' She opened the door into the sitting room to allow Eleanor and Napoleon to enter the room.

The sitting room was furnished in a style fashionable when Queen Victoria was the reigning monarch and was crammed with chairs, potted palms, little side tables containing photographs and ornaments, all protected by crocheted d'oyles and anti-macassars. It always amazed Eleanor that Napoleon managed to find a clear space and settle down without upsetting something. She had great difficulty doing so herself. Annie was sitting on a sofa with Miss Felicity next to her. She stood up as soon as she saw Eleanor. Miss Felicity got up too and greeted Eleanor and then went to stand beside her twin sister. Eleanor greeted Annie and when Eleanor was settled in a large armchair, with Napoleon at her feet, Miss Pymble said: 'Now, Annie, I want you to tell Miss Harriman exactly what you told us this morning. We'll leave you to it, Miss Harriman and when you have finished, just ring and we shall have tea and freshly made cake. Annie helped us make it this morning. Come along, Felicity.'

The Misses Pymble departed and closed the door of the sitting room. Annie looked troubled. Eleanor noticed that Annie's arm was still bandaged.

'It's all right, Annie,' said Eleanor, trying to sound

reassuring. 'Miss Pymble says you have something on your conscience about Mr Steen. If you haven't done anything wrong, you will feel better for talking about it and being reassured. And if you have done something wrong, no matter what, the sooner I know about it, the sooner I can help you.'

Annie looked at Eleanor doubtfully and remained silent.

'Miss Pymble tells me you are friends with someone called Jack. Has he been at the hotel very long?'

'About a year, I think.'

'And is he a friend of yours?'

Annie hesitated. 'I didn't have much to do with him at first. It were only a couple of weeks ago, he started paying attention to me. He took me to the pictures, gave me some chocolates even. I thought he were interested in me, wanted to be friends, like, but I see now, he were just using me.'

'What made you think that, Annie?' asked Eleanor.

'Well, he wanted to know about Beryl and then he started paying attention to her instead of me.'

'Who is Beryl?' interrupted Eleanor, recalling the name mentioned by Catherine.

'One of the chamber maids.'

'And what do you think this Jack was using you for? To get to be friends with Beryl?'

Annie nodded. 'He kept asking questions about Beryl, about her job, what she did, what time she went to the rooms, what time she went to bed. I thought that were a bit funny and I tried to pretend it didn't matter. When I asked him why he wanted to know, he said it helped him do his job better. But I didn't know the answers to his questions and then he started asking Beryl to go for walks with him, instead of me. I didn't speak to Beryl after that. She weren't playing fair. She knew Jack were interested in me first.'

'And you liked him?'

'Yes, very much. He were different. You could tell that from the way he spoke and the way he knew things, lots of things. And he hadn't always worked in hotels. He said his family had lost money, because of the War or something, I think.'

'So Jack started paying attention to Beryl instead of you and, naturally, you were upset by that,' said Eleanor.

'Yes,' said Annie.

'And did you mention it to Beryl?' Annie was silent and Eleanor waited, suddenly aware of a large clock on the chimney piece whose ticking was slightly ahead of that of a smaller competitor on a side table beside her.

'Oh, Miss Harriman. I'm so ashamed,' said Annie, her voice barely audible. 'When he were paying more attention to Beryl than to me, I were right jealous. And I know it were wrong but.... And Beryl didn't come back to our room until late one night and I thought she were with Jack and that upset me. I followed Jack. I spied on him. It were such a silly, childish thing to do but I were so unhappy. That's how I know he did sommat. And Beryl, she weren't even interested in him so it were all for nothing. Oh, I've been such a fool.'

Eleanor sifted quickly through all of these strands and asked: 'And what do you think Jack did that was wrong, Annie?'

'I saw him come out of Mr Steen's room and he had no business to be there and then he said I were not to tell and then Mr Steen died.'

'And when did you see him do that?' asked Eleanor, her thoughts racing ahead.

'On the night before Mr Steen died.'

'On the Saturday night?'

'Yes.'

Eleanor paused before continuing. She said, calmly: 'This is very important, Annie. I want you to describe exactly what happened that night. I need to know where you were and what you saw. Right from the beginning, please. Let's start when you finished work. Were you on duty serving at dinner that night?' Annie nodded. 'And Mr Steen was dining with friends.' Annie nodded again. 'When you had finished serving at dinner what happened then?'

'The guests went into the lounge to have their coffee.'

'And do you serve coffee?'

'No, the waiters do that. We, that is the waitresses, start on tidying the dining room and getting it ready for breakfast the next morning.'

'So, the night that you saw Jack, what did you do after you had finished in the dining room?'

'I went back down to the kitchen. There's a break then and we can have something to eat. Then we go back upstairs to the lounge and clear up the coffee things and see that everything goes back down to the scullery to be washed up. Then when the guests have left the lounge we make sure that all the coffee things get put back there proper. Ready for next time.'

'So during the break you had something to eat and then…'

'No,' said Annie, shaking her head. 'I didn't stop to eat. I went straight upstairs to our room, Beryl and me shared a room.'

'That must have been awkward,' said Eleanor, 'if you had fallen out.'

'Yes, it were a bit, but Beryl weren't there. She hadn't been there much, not since the Rally. She should've been though. We never have permission to leave the hotel at night.'

'And you thought she might have been with Jack?' asked Eleanor.

Annie took a deep breath. 'Yes, he weren't on duty and he weren't downstairs in the servants' hall where he should've been so I went looking for them. I couldn't see them anywhere. One of the other chamber maids were upstairs and I asked her if she'd seen Beryl but she hadn't and she said perhaps Beryl had been sent back to her floor.'

'And which floor was that?'

'The floor she looked after. Sometimes the guests ask for extra towels or soap or if something is wrong with the room that needs sorting out the chamber maids have to see to it. So I went down to Beryl's floor to see and someone came out of Mr Steen's room and went round the corner.'

Eleanor was surprised at this statement and ideas began whirling around in her head. She said: 'Can I just stop you there, I want to get this clear in my mind. You were on the floor where Mr Steen's room was?' Annie nodded. 'And that was the floor that Beryl worked on?' Another nod. 'And you saw someone come out of Mr Steen's room and go around the corner. Can you just describe for me where Mr Steen's room was?'

'At the front of the hotel, facing out to the garden. The last room before the pavilion suite.'

'And you were in the corridor that runs parallel with the front of the hotel but at the opposite end of the corridor from where Mr Steen's room was.' Annie nodded. 'And you were walking along that corridor towards Mr Steen's room when you saw someone come out of his room.' Annie nodded again. 'And just past Mr Steen's door, there is the pavilion suite on the corner of the building and there the corridor turns and runs at right angles to the front of the hotel. The person you saw came out of Mr Steen's room and disappeared out of sight down that other corridor which leads towards the back of the hotel. Right, I think I have a clear picture now. And you saw Jack come out of Mr Steen's room?'

'Oh, yes.'

'Are you sure it wasn't Mr Mellor, Mr Steen's valet?'

'No, no, it were Jack,' said Annie, shaking her head.

'You're certain of that?'

'Oh, yes.'

'And what happened then?'

'I didn't want Jack to know as I'd been spying on him. I knew he would guess because I had no business to be in that corridor so I turned round to go back the way I'd come but he must've turned back too because I were nearly to the end of the corridor away from Mr Steen's room and Jack caught me up and he said "What are you doing up here?" very rough like, and I didn't know what to say. I didn't answer him. I just ran up the service stairs and back up to my room.'

'And was Beryl in your room then?'

'No. Then I thought about Jack being there and I wondered if maybe Mr Steen had wanted something and they couldn't find Beryl and Jack had gone instead but later on, the next morning, when they found Mr Steen, I thought about it again and I knew that weren't right.'

'How did you know that?' asked Eleanor.

'Because Mr Steen weren't in his room when I saw Jack. Mr Steen had wanted supper served for his guests and, as a special favour, the manager had agreed and the kitchen had to be kept open later than usual. Mr Steen must've been downstairs at supper when I saw Jack, so he wouldn't have been asking for something to be brought to him in his room, would he? So, Jack had no reason to be there.'

'And it was earlier than eleven thirty when you saw Jack coming out of Mr Steen's room?'

'Yes, much earlier.'

'And you are sure it wasn't the valet that you saw?'

'No, I'd been in the servants' hall and Mr Mellor were there playing cards with some of the other valets. Their gentlemen hadn't left the lounge yet so they was not needed and Jack sometimes played cards with them but he weren't there.'

'So, when you saw Jack coming out of Mr Steen's room, his valet was downstairs playing cards and Mr Steen was still in the lounge with his guests.' Annie nodded. Eleanor thought for a moment and said: 'Once the guests have gone down to dinner, is it likely that anyone would be about in the corridors upstairs? Would Jack have expected the corridors to be empty?'

'Yes, because the chamber maids go in to turn down the beds and tidy the rooms straight after the guests go down. And then the guests generally go into the lounge after dinner or go on to the dancing in the ball room. They mostly don't start going back upstairs until after about ten o'clock.'

'And you didn't see Jack again that night?' Annie shook her head. 'And you went back on duty as usual and made sure that the coffee things went back upstairs to the lounge, and then you went back to your room. Was Beryl there by then?'

'No, and I fell asleep and she weren't there when I woke up the next morning either.'

Eleanor made a mental note to pursue this issue in due course because the chamber maid was near the top of her list of suspects. 'And did you find out where she was?'

'Oh, yes. There were quite a fuss about it too when it all came out. She got locked out that night.'

'That is the night Mr Steen died?'

'Yes. Next morning we found out she'd been sneaking out of the hotel to meet Tom Rawley. That night they got back late and the servants' door were locked and she couldn't get in. She daren't rouse the caretaker because he would have given her away so Tom hid her in one of the garages for the night and she walked in at six o'clock next morning as if nothing had happened. Quite brazen she were. Nobody has dared let on. And here were me thinking she were interested in Jack. I were a right little fool, weren't I?'

Eleanor mentally crossed the chamber maid off her list of suspects. 'And who is Tom Rawley?' she asked.

'Oh, he's Mr Steen's chauffeur. And nobody knew about them, but it doesn't matter now, does it, because Mr Steen is not here to object. Anyway, Beryl's given notice.'

Eleanor briefly wondered if the chauffeur should be on the list of suspects. 'And all this happened before Mr Steen was found?' she asked.

'Yes. But I didn't know about him at first because I were in the dining room serving breakfast. And then, everyone were talking about it down in the servants' hall, how could it have happened and how might he have died and no-one knew. And then Jack came and found me and said what did I think I were doing last night in the corridor. I'd no reason to be on that floor at all, you see, and he knew I'd get into trouble if anyone found out. I said I'd been looking for him and he asked why and I wouldn't tell him. And then he said that if anyone asked, I were not to say that he were there and if I did, they would know that I were there and he would say that he saw me coming out of Mr Steen's room and that I had sommat to do with why Mr Steen died.'

'And that must have made you very worried.'

'I were really frightened then and afterwards, when I were waiting at table, I heard someone talking about Mr Steen dying and the lady said it must have been someone who could get into Mr Steen's room and then I didn't know what to think. I got such a shock. I thought maybe the newspapers were right about Mr Steen dying and they would blame me.' Annie ran out of breath as she came to the end of this explanation and was on the verge of tears.

'So is that what caused you to faint in the dining room. Hearing Mrs Denfield taking about getting into Mr Steen's room?'

'Yes, I expect so. But I never had anything to do with Mr Steen, Miss Harriman, I swear.'

'Annie, do you have any idea who talked to the newspapers?'

At this question, Annie's face crumpled and she burst into tears. Napoleon sat up and looked concerned. Eleanor stroked his head while she waited for Annie's tears to subside.

'It weren't me,' said Annie.

'Who said that it was?' asked Eleanor.

'Jack,' said Annie, barely above a whisper.

'Take your time, Annie, and when you are ready, I'd like you to tell me about that.' Eleanor waited and Napoleon lay down again, reassured.

'We all talked about it, of course, and we thought there were summat not right. One of the waiters serving at supper said Mr Steen had been celebrating that night and he were in very good spirits. Mr Mellor couldn't understand it because he said Mr Steen were always healthy. We all talked about what it could have been. When Jack came in and heard what were being said he got cross and he said they was talking nonsense because it were obvious Mr Steen had just died in his sleep.'

'And I suppose someone repeated the gossip to one of the reporters.'

'Jack told Mr Hewlett that it were me talking to the newspaper men and Mr Hewlett believed him. But, it weren't me, Miss Harriman.'

'Mr Hewlett, the manager?' Eleanor assumed that this was the reason why Annie had been dismissed.

'Yes. Miss Pymble says it were probably to pay me back for having seen Jack in the corridor.'

Eleanor said confidently: 'I don't think you need worry. I think Miss Pymble is probably right. No-one is going to blame you, Annie, despite what Jack says. Did Jack know that Mr Steen took sleeping tablets?'

'Yes, I told him.'

'And how did you know about them?'

'Beryl told me. One day when we was talking she said they was in the top drawer beside the bed with no lock. She thought that were careless.'

'And you mentioned the tablets to Jack?'

'Yes, one day when he were asking me questions about Mr Steen and it were only because I wanted him to like me and I thought he'd be pleased with me if I knew the answers.'

Eleanor sat thinking things over and then she said: 'What happened after you fainted that day in the dining room?'

'Well, Monsieur Maurice. He give me such a dressing down and he said he wouldn't have that sort of behaviour in his dining room and I were on a warning because Lady Aycliffe, it were her frock that I spoilt, she had already made a complaint about something else. And he told me to go and get changed because I had gravy and sauce all down my apron and uniform. And Jack must have heard about what happened because when I came back down from getting changed, he grabbed me and twisted my arm. This one that got burnt and he asked me what I thought I were doing making an exhibition of myself and attracting everyone's notice. He said I were a fool and he wished he'd never laid eyes on me. He said he'd get rid of me.'

Annie looked forlorn. Eleanor sat watching Annie and listening to the clocks ticking. Annie was staring at the carpet and Eleanor imagined that she was thinking of happier times when she believed Jack was interested in her before she realised that she was just being used as a source of information about Mr Steen. Napoleon noticing that the conversation had stopped, lifted his head to check if Eleanor was about to leave. There was no sign of activity so he flopped back down again and closed his eyes. Eleanor wondered what she could say to lighten her mood and make Annie a bit more cheerful, then she remembered Lady Aycliffe at lunch and said, laughing: 'Well, you certainly made a good job of spoiling Lady Aycliffe's frock. She seemed to me to be a rather demanding client. What had she complained about previously?'

'Oh, it were funny really. Alice, she's a chamber maid, were getting some clean sheets out of the linen cupboard. They was on the top shelf and she were in a hurry. She pulled out the things she wanted, all in a heap like, and a carafe fell out of the cupboard and spilled water all over her. She got such a fright, she screamed. She weren't hurt, just surprised really because there never should have been a carafe there. Lady Aycliffe heard Alice scream and she complained to Mr Hewlett. She said the scream had startled her awake. She wanted Mr Hewlett to give Alice warning.' Annie shrugged. 'I don't see what she had to complain about. It were ten o'clock in the morning when decent, God-fearing people are already up and about.'

Eleanor was thinking rapidly, fitting this new piece of information into her theory of the carafes and trying not to look too eager with her next question to Annie. She took a deep breath in order to focus her mind and asked: 'Annie, do you remember what day it was when this happened?'

'Oh, yes. Lady Aycliffe only arrived the day before. She made such a fuss and wanted a different room and Mr Hewlett gave her the other pavilion suite.'

'Where was her room originally?'

'Oh, on the same floor as Mr Steen. She had the pavilion suite on the corner, next to Mr Steen's room. The linen cupboard is in the corridor opposite where Lady Aycliffe were.'

'And what day was it?'

'Oh, didn't I say. The Saturday. The day before Mr Steen died.'

'You are sure of that?'

'Yes. Poor Alice had all the trouble of making up another room and traipsing up and down the corridor moving all of Lady Aycliffe's things over, as well as doing all her usual work and she was complaining about it downstairs because it were her half day and she were going to visit her mother and she were late getting away and missed her train.'

'I don't suppose you know what happened to the carafe?' Annie slowly shook her head, looking puzzled. 'Annie, I need to ask you about one last thing and then we can have tea. When I found you on the seat in the grounds of the hotel, you were very upset because you said that you had been accused of lying. What were you accused of lying about?'

'About the newspaper men. But I didn't talk to them.'

'And who said you had?'

'Jack. He told Mr Hewlett he'd seen me talking to one of them the day after Mr Steen were found but I didn't. I didn't know anything about Mr Steen. Mr Hewlett didn't believe me when I said I hadn't told anyone anything and, because I were already on a warning, he gave me notice. I couldn't understand why Jack said those things. When I told Miss Pymble she said it were probably deliberate. She said he would know how angry Mr Hewlett would be about the newspapers and he wanted to get me into trouble so he could get rid of me.'

'And Mr Hewlett believed Jack and not you?'

'Yes. And it were a horrid thing to do. Why would he do that?'

'Annie, I think Miss Pymble may very well be right. What job does Jack normally do?'

'He's one of the hall-porters.'

'What is his surname?'

'Carruthers. Jack Carruthers.'

'Was he at the Motor-car Rally?'

'Yes,' said Annie.

'Annie, you have been a very great help today, thank you. Is there anything else you want to tell me?' Annie shook her head. 'Or anything you want to ask me?'

'No, thank you, Miss Harriman.'

'Now, I don't want you to get too hopeful, but I think that I may be able to prove that Jack was lying and that means we

280

can clear your name…'

'Oh!' cried Annie.

'…and if so, would you like to go back to work at the hotel or would you prefer to find somewhere else?'

'Oh, I could never go back! I shouldn't like that.'

'Then I shall ask for a character reference for you so that you can apply for another situation.'

'Oh, thank you, Miss Harriman.'

'Now, would you mind ringing to let Miss Pymble know that we are ready for tea.'

Facts were whirling around in Eleanor's head and she desperately wanted time to think. She needed to get away as quickly as possible and be alone. However, etiquette demanded that she stay for the tea that the Pymble sisters had prepared specially and, for the next half-hour, Eleanor was a model of social decorum. She sat sipping tea, complimented the Pymble sisters and Annie on the delicious homemade cake, made small talk, exchanged gossip, and enquired about preparations for the jumble sale, and all the while her brain was linking up pieces of information about Mr Steen and exploring possible motives for his murder. As soon as it was polite, Eleanor thanked the Misses Pymble for tea and their care of Annie and got ready to leave. Annie was now calm and plainly comfortable in the company of the Misses Pymble. Eleanor was confident that it would be safe to leave her with them.

Miss Pymble accompanied Eleanor and Napoleon to the front door. 'Thank you for coming to see Annie,' she said. 'She seems much happier now. She's a lovely girl. You can tell that she comes from a good home.'

Eleanor said: 'Yes, indeed and it is very kind of you and Miss Felicity to take her in. I am very grateful to you, Miss Pymble.'

'Oh, think nothing of it, Miss Harriman. We are only too pleased to help,'

'You were right about Annie having some important information and she should give it to the police. I will arrange for her to do that but, in the meantime, I am concerned for her safety. Will you keep a close eye on her? And if anyone from the hotel comes to visit her, he or she should be refused entry. Particularly, Jack.'

'Oh, don't make yourself uneasy, Miss Harriman. We'll look after her very carefully and there is no question of that Jack fellow crossing our threshold.'

Eleanor smiled at the formidable lady and said goodbye. Miss Pymble stroked Napoleon and said: 'It's always a pleasure to see you, Napoleon. I'm sorry there were no cats for you today. Better luck next time, eh?'

Instead of returning to Hall Bank, Eleanor decided to walk. She wanted to unravel all of the strands of thought that were tumbling around in her head. Napoleon, of course, made no objection. He trotted along happily as they went down Bath Street and followed Macclesfield Road to Burbage. At Burbage, they turned back along Green Lane towards their starting point. Their route had taken them along the boundaries of the golf course which was busy with Saturday afternoon players. However, there seemed to be no sign of machinery or any activity related to Mr Steen's project. Eleanor had spent the whole of her walk thinking about Mr Steen's death and Napoleon had been left to meander and dawdle as he pleased. By the time they had reached the end of Broad Walk, Eleanor had assembled her thoughts sufficiently to come to a decision as to what action to take next. As they were about to pass Oxford House, Cecily and Richard were just coming out of their front door.

Cecily said: 'What perfect timing! We are just going to call on Father. Richard and I have been to the market and I've got some of the honey he particularly likes.'

'Look. Aunt Lella,' said Richard, holding up the jar that he was carrying. 'It's got the bee's comb in it, but I don't quite see what the bees need a comb for. Will you carry this for me, please? I should like to run with Napoleon.'

Eleanor took the jar from Richard and he and Napoleon raced ahead. Cecily, looking closely at Eleanor, said: 'You look a bit strained. Are you all right?'

'Yes, thank you, I'm quite well. I've just been thinking something through.'

'One of your horrible cases, I suppose. Are you involved in this Steen business?' asked Cecily.

'I'm afraid so, yes,' said Eleanor.

'And, let me guess, you've sorted out what happened and you are now wondering how to deal with the consequences?'

'Something like that. At least, I think I have understood what happened but I am still not sure why it happened. I need to talk to Catherine tomorrow.'

'I heard that Mrs Steen has caused quite a stir by not wearing black, but I believe she has left Buxton now.'

'So Mrs Clayton tells me. She has been relaying to me the gossip in the newspapers about the Steen affair. Father's newspapers haven't mentioned it of course. I suppose there was no need for Mrs Steen to stay. The death certificate hasn't been issued yet and no funeral arrangements can be made.'

'What is causing the delay?'

'The test results from the Home Office pathologist haven't arrived yet so the cause of death hasn't been confirmed.'

'Oh, I see. I know I won't get any sense out of you until you have solved whatever problem it is that is bothering you so I'm going to change the subject altogether and talk about the weather instead. It is really lovely today, although I don't suppose you have noticed, and I do hope it will be like this for Millicent and Julian's wedding.'

Eleanor looked at her sister and laughed. Cecily could always bring her back to reality. 'Yes, let us hope so. Is your new frock ready yet?'

'Not quite. I have an appointment on Monday at Madame Veronique's for the final fitting. I was thinking the other day that this will be the first proper wedding I've been to in years. The weddings of our friends during the War were rather pared down, almost informal, and since then no friends or relatives have been married.'

'No, although we did have the proxy enjoyment of Princess Mary's wedding, thanks to Mrs Clayton. She is still talking about it, and that was at least two months ago. Goodness only knows how long she will be talking about Millicent's. She's very keen on all the old customs being observed and she threw up her hands in horror when she heard that Millicent hadn't planned "something blue" to wear. She scolded Millicent for being too modern and then sewed the most beautiful blue garter for her. She's a great one for tradition is our Mrs Clayton and it really is a lovely piece of needlework.'

'Yes, she makes the most beautiful things for the church bazaar and they always sell quickly. Mrs Clayton can turn her hand to almost anything.'

'I know. She keeps us all fed and up to the mark. I don't know what we would do without her.'

'The present arrangement seems to suit her very well and I don't suppose there is much chance of her finding a new husband and having a place of her own, not with the current shortage of men. Millicent is very lucky to have found Julian. We are jolly well going to enjoy this wedding. There probably won't be another one for a while.'

Cecily and Richard spent an enjoyable evening at Hall Bank together with Eleanor and Mr Harriman and Eleanor was able to forget about Mr Steen, temporarily, although something had been niggling at the back of her brain since Cecily had mentioned Julian St John.

CHAPTER EIGHTEEN

The following afternoon Eleanor called on Catherine Balderstone and provided her with all the information she had gathered from Annie and they discussed at length the method chosen to administer the barbitone to Mr Steen. They were then both satisfied that they had understood how Mr Steen died. Eleanor also told Catherine about Philip's suggestion that the attack on Mr Ashworth was a case of mistaken identity which had pushed the attacker to make a second attempt to kill Mr Steen. Eleanor left Catherine in a much more settled frame of mind. She had all of the facts neatly sorted in her head and was confident that she now knew how Mr Steen had been killed and by whom. However, she still did not know why he had been killed. When the office opened on Monday morning, Eleanor sought out Edwin and asked if he had time to talk.

'Certainly,' said Edwin. 'I have a client coming in at ten-thirty but I am free now. I'll come in to your office.'

When they were settled, Edwin said: 'How did you get on with Annie on Saturday?'

'I learnt a great deal from her about the comings and goings in the hotel and about what has been happening there. After I left the Misses Pymble, I went for a walk to think and to sort out my ideas. Yesterday I had a long discussion with Catherine and we are fairly confident that we now know how Mr Steen was killed. You remember that, when we last talked, we had concluded that it must have been someone who can enter or leave the hotel without anyone noticing. I am sure we were right.'

'We had the chamber maid at the top of our list of suspects, didn't we?'

'Yes, Beryl certainly had the means and the opportunity. It was just the motive that was lacking but, if Annie's information is correct, we can rule her out. I discovered via Annie that Beryl has been motivated in a very different direction lately which led to her not being in the hotel on the night Mr Steen died. Apparently, she recently formed a liaison with Mr Steen's chauffeur and, strictly against the rules, has been staying out late with him. On the night Mr Steen died, Beryl was not in the room she shared with Annie. She was out with the chauffeur and didn't get back to the hotel in time for curfew. She found herself locked out and the chauffeur smuggled her into one of the garages. That is where she spent the night and why she was not in her room the following morning. I'm not sure whether it was with or without the chauffeur. I haven't spoken to Beryl and verified this story and I am not sure that Beryl would own up anyway but I have no reason to doubt Annie.'

'Goodness, Beryl would certainly be dismissed if that story got out.'

'Yes, but apparently she has given notice instead.'

'Probably very wise. So, who do you favour now?'

'The hall-porter. He certainly can come and go unremarked in any part of the hotel. His name is Jack Carruthers. However, I'm still not sure of a motive. This is what Annie told me and I must say I am inclined to believe her, despite the fact that she was dismissed for being a liar.' Eleanor then gave Edwin a summary of Annie's evidence.

'And you think Annie is telling the truth?'

'Yes, I do. She was quite honest about her feelings towards him and clearly ashamed of her jealousy. I don't see why she would have confessed to those if she had been lying. She could have invented a story more flattering to herself. Also, there are several facts to be taken into account in relation to the hall-porter which fit with Annie's story and which I did not realise the significance of at the time. The first thing is this. I was at the Palace Hotel with my friends, Millicent and Maureen, on the day that Mr Steen arrived in Buxton. Carruthers, the hall-porter, was standing in the front hall. The clerk at the desk called him forward and told him to fetch Mr Steen's luggage and I remember distinctly the startled look on Carruthers' face when that happened. He sort of froze and I think that it was when he heard the name Steen, as though the name meant something to him.'

'So that might be at least a hint of a link between the two men. It's a start.'

'Yes, now this is a bit of a digression. You will recall that there was an attack on Mr Ashworth the archaeologist. That took place shortly after Mr Steen arrived. The other day, Philip told me of an incident he experienced and he suggested a possible explanation for the attack on Mr Ashworth. Philip actually mistook Mr Steen for Mr Ashworth one morning in Spring Gardens. From the back, both men are similar. They both wore Norfolk jackets and knee breeches and the same sort of hat and they are of similar height and build. Philip suggested that the attack on Mr Ashworth could have been a case of mistaken identity. The person who attacked Mr Ashworth might have intended to attack Mr Steen.'

'I see,' said Edwin, slowly, 'and you are suggesting that, when the attacker realised his mistake in having hit the wrong man, he resorted to the sleeping tablets instead and the barbitone poisoning was, in fact, the second attempt.'

'That's right,' said Eleanor, 'and if Mr Steen's death at the hotel was the second attempt to kill him, I think it rules out Mrs Steen as the killer. Mrs Steen might have known that Mr Steen was going to see Mr Redfern that evening but I find it difficult to imagine her going about in the evening stalking someone, even a superfluous husband. I think it would be quite out of character.'

'Besides,' said Edwin, 'from what you have told me about that incident, I doubt that someone of Mrs Steen's build would have had the strength to inflict such an injury.'

'I agree. Now, there is a further link between Carruthers and Mr Steen. Carruthers appears to have used Annie and other hotel servants to glean information about Mr Steen. Apparently, Mellor, Mr Steen's valet was in the habit of playing cards with some of the other hotel servants when he was off duty and Carruthers played cards with the valet. Servants talk about their employers so Carruthers may have obtained information from Mellor. Also, Jack Carruthers also ingratiated himself with Annie, and then transferred his attention to Beryl, the chamber maid, apparently to get the information about Mr Steen that he wanted. He certainly knew that Mr Steen took sleeping tablets and that Mr and Mrs Steen had separate suites. Annie, Beryl, and Carruthers were all at the Motor-car Rally and I remember seeing Carruthers before the start. He was being very chummy with Annie and ignoring the other girl, Beryl. I went back over the events of that day and I recalled the slashed tyre on Mr Steen's car. Philip and I blamed the political activists because a couple of them were at the Rally but I wonder if that damage was done by Carruthers.'

'I see, yes. At the time, we couldn't understand why anyone would want to do such a thing.'

'Yes, slashing a tyre is a deliberately violent act, isn't it?' said Eleanor.

'If it was the hall-porter, presumably there was something that Mr Steen had done that afternoon that had provoked him. Surely it must have been something significant to make him angry enough to act in that way but I don't recall anything untoward happening, do you?'

'No, I don't. The final thing is this, and this is the most damning piece of evidence I think. You remember when we

288

were speculating about the switching of carafes and the lack of fingerprints? We concluded that this whole sequence of events had been carefully and cleverly planned and we wondered why the killer had not thought to keep back the carafe from a previous day and substitute it for the "guilty" carafe so that all of the correct fingerprints would be in place and the appropriate amount of water would be left in the carafe. Annie unwittingly provided the answer to that little mystery. I think our killer did remove a carafe in readiness and concealed it in a linen cupboard close to Mr Steen's room. On the morning before Mr Steen died, the carafe fell out when one of the chamber maids went to get clean linen. I suspect that it had been removed from Mr Steen's room on some earlier morning. It would have displayed all the correct fingerprints in the correct order and contained the usual amount of water. That would have been the third carafe, the "innocent" one. The incident with the chamber maid happened on the Saturday morning, the day before Mr Steen died, Annie was quite sure of that. The chamber maid would have put her fingerprints on the carafe and spoilt the plan and there would not have been time to obtain another used carafe so the only alternative was to leave a carafe without fingerprints in Mr Steen's room.'

Edwin looked at Eleanor, slowly nodding his head as he considered what she had told him. 'A very clever piece of planning. Rather frightening, really. We are clearly dealing with someone very intelligent. It really would have been the perfect crime.'

'Oh, I agree,' said Eleanor. She frowned: 'But why was it committed?'

'Why indeed.'

'If Philip's theory about Mr Ashworth is correct, it does suggest that the killer was driven by some very strong motive, doesn't it? To have been so determined the second time, I mean, having failed once already.'

Before Edwin could reply, James appeared in the doorway of Eleanor's office.

'Mr Talbot's client has arrived.'

'Thank you, James, bring him up, please. This won't take long, Eleanor. It's just to go over some documents and witness signatures.'

Edwin and James left Eleanor's office, closing the door so that Napoleon could not go out to greet the client. Eleanor doodled on her desk blotter while she thought about the motive for wanting Mr Steen dead. Apart from the day Mr Steen arrived, the only time Eleanor had seen Carruthers was at the Motor-car Rally. She recalled him paying attention to Annie in the morning before the Rally and then she tried to summon up the details of that afternoon in the field at Castleton. Mr and Mrs Steen had been mingling with the competitors most of the time. Eleanor supposed that Carruthers was helping to distribute the fruit drinks to the participants but she could not recall seeing him. The first time she could remember noticing him was when Mr Steen was announcing the winner. Eleanor stopped doodling and stared blankly out of the window as she tried to visualise the scene on the platform. Carruthers had handed the megaphone to Mr Steen, who then made a speech and announced the winner. Carruthers then handed the envelope with the cheque in it to Mr Steen. Mrs Steen presented Philip with the prize. Where was the hall-porter then? Eleanor could not remember seeing Carruthers still at the platform when Philip was collecting his prize and she could not recall seeing him at any time after that either. Very soon after the prize giving, the party had started to break up and then she and Philip had noticed the slashed tyre. Eleanor wondered if there was something significant in Mr Steen's speech that had motivated the slashed tyre.

Resting her elbows on her desk, Eleanor sat with her head in her hands and her eyes closed as she concentrated on conjuring up a picture of Mr Steen making his speech that afternoon. Mr Steen had spoken about his water bottling scheme and had announced that it would go ahead. Then a picture of Mr Steen holding up a glass bottle came into Eleanor's mind and she remembered that he had told the crowd that it was a unique design and it was to be used for bottling the water. 'Yes!' said Eleanor, so suddenly that Napoleon raised himself up onto his haunches and looked at her with concern. Eleanor got up from her desk, reassured Napoleon and, leaving him shut in her office, went downstairs to Mr Harriman's office where the law reports were kept. Mr Harriman was out at a meeting. Eleanor ran her finger along the shelves looking for the volume with the report of *Alfmour Ltd* v *Mayhew*. She took the book down from the shelf and flicked through the pages hurriedly until she found the passage she was looking for. She read the passage, slowly and carefully, and then, taking the book with her, returned upstairs to her office. She pulled out a note pad and began scribbling down her thoughts, trying to get them into a coherent sequence. She had just finished and was looking over her notes when Edwin came back into her office, having seen his client out.

Eleanor looked up and said: 'Edwin, I think I have got it!'

'Got what?'

'Please sit down and let me explain.'

'Right-ho! You look as though you'd lost a penny and found a pound.'

'I think I have. While you were away I was thinking about the Rally and the slashed tyre and trying to recall whether there was anything that might have made the hall-porter angry enough to do such a thing. Then I remembered Mr Steen's speech before the prize-giving. He told us that the water bottling scheme was going ahead and then he held up a glass bottle, do you remember?'

'Yes, I do. He said that was the bottle that was going to be used for the water.'

'Exactly, and it occurred to me that it might also be the bottle Mr Mayhew designed, the design that Alfmour had registered as its own. I went back to the law report and found the description of the disputed design. Here it is,' Eleanor handed the law report to Edwin. 'Page 303 beginning at line 21. What do you think?' Eleanor sat back and waited.

Edwin said: 'I'm trying to visualise the bottle Mr Steen held up to the crowd. It was unusual. It was sort of squeezed in at the middle.' Edwin frowned in concentration as he read the description of the design and then he said, slowly: 'You know, I think you might be right.'

'I think he was intending to use Mr Mayhew's design. I know that the court decision means that he was perfectly entitled to do so but it does seem a bit unfair. I recollect that Father said there was an animated discussion about the decision at the conference he spoke at.'

'Yes, that was where he first heard the story behind the dispute and he did say that there seemed to be quite a bit of sympathy for Mr Mayhew.'

'If I had been Mr Mayhew and seen the way Mr Steen was gloating about using my design, I too would have considered slashing the tyres of his motor-car,' said Eleanor.

'But Mr Mayhew was not at the Rally. He has died.'

'Yes, but I wondered whether or not he had any children.'

'I think I know where this is leading,' said Edwin. 'I know that revenge can be a very powerful motive but you are going to need quite a bit of evidence to convince me that we are looking at the murder of Mr Steen by a relative of Mr Mayhew. It seems a little extreme.'

Eleanor nodded and said: 'I know, but there is a son. The early part of the law report sets out the evidence Mr Mayhew gave as to when the disputed design was created and he refers there to his son, who was twelve years old at the time. Based on the evidence regarding the length of the partnership, I did a rough calculation as to the likely age of this son now.'

'The hall-porter and the son would be of a similar age?'

'Yes,' said Eleanor. 'Mr Mayhew killed himself after the decision went against him. He lost a great deal of money defending the claim against him and, at the same time, his factory would have had to either acquire a different kind of bottle or cease operations. It seems Mr Mayhew may also have received threats because his factory was damaged by fire. If your father's financial ruin and then his death had been brought about by Mr Steen's actions and the consequent financial loss had blighted your own future and then discovered that Mr Steen, far from showing remorse, was gloating about using your father's design for his own profit, could you imagine hating Mr Steen enough to want him dead? I'm not sure that I could, but I think I can understand why someone else might feel that way.'

'The desire for revenge certainly does create powerful emotion, and sometimes it is sustained enough to cause the person to take action. I can well understand that desire in the son, but turning the desire into reality is quite a different thing for most decent minded people. I concede that, in this case, there is a very strong possible motive, but the hall-porter's name is not Mayhew, is it?'

'No, his name is Jack Carruthers, but it is easy to change one's name,' said Eleanor.

'Well, if Jack Carruthers is actually Mr Mayhew's son, the motive for killing Mr Steen would seem all too clear,' said Edwin. 'Can we be sure that this Carruthers knew anything about Mr Steen's intention to use the new bottle design?'

'Possibly. When the winner was announced at the Rally, I was paying attention because I knew Philip had won. I do recall that Carruthers was standing beside the platform where Mr Steen was making his speech and he handed the envelope with the cheque in it to Mr Steen. So he must have heard Mr Steen's announcement about the bottle.'

'I recall Mrs Steen handing out the prize immediately after Mr Steen had mentioned the bottle design but I don't recall much else,' said Edwin.

'I've just remembered something else Father said about the discussion that took place at the conference. He said that it was quite animated and that even some of the hotel servants had joined in. I think he said that they were getting the lantern slides ready for the next speaker. I wonder if Jack Carruthers was one of those people helping with the equipment.'

'Right, let's go back over the facts and see how your theory about Carruthers fits,' said Edwin.

They spent some time meticulously examining all the facts and discussing each one.

'Well, despite my scepticism regarding the strength of the motive, I have to agree, Eleanor, all the facts do fit with your theory. Do we know anything about this hall-porter other than the information you got from Annie?'

'No, if he is Mr Mayhew's son and there are no brothers or sisters, he is the only one likely to seek revenge. I suppose his mother isn't involved in any way?'

'Do we know where she is?' asked Edwin.

'No. She must have been very badly affected by the suicide of Mr Mayhew.'

'And by the decision of the court as well, knowing that her husband had actually created that design. She must have experienced a certain degree of resentment towards Mr Steen,' said Edwin.

'It would only be human,' said Eleanor. 'And the family was ruined financially…Oh! I've just remembered something else Annie said. She mentioned that Carruthers was well spoken and that he hadn't always worked in hotels. He said that his family had lost their money…'

Eleanor broke off as James came up the stairs and said: 'Mr Talbot, Mr Harriman telephoned. He's at a meeting at Chillingham & Baynard's Bank. He wonders if you could provide some figures for him. The papers are in his office.'

'Yes, of course. I'll come down.'

Eleanor picked up her pencil in order to jot down all of the facts she knew about the hall-porter. She began with the arrival of Mr Steen at the hotel and then she was about to move on to the Motor-car Rally when she remembered an earlier occasion on which she had seen him: the Sunday afternoon when she was coming back from Corbar Woods with Cecily and Richard. Eleanor looked at Napoleon, flopped on the floor asleep, as she recalled that day. They had been returning from the woods when a man passed in front of them and went up the carriage drive to Wye House. Eleanor had not been able to place the man at first but later on she realised that it was the hall-porter from the Palace Hotel. Annie's Jack. Eleanor said to Napoleon: 'It was a Sunday afternoon, so it is unlikely that he had something to deliver there and, anyway, that is not a hall-porter's job. But people visit their family on Sunday afternoons, and that may well have been what he was doing. Visiting his family, someone who is a patient there. Perhaps he was visiting his mother.' Eleanor put down her pencil and stood up. 'I think I know where Mrs Mayhew is and there is only one way to find out.' Eleanor went downstairs, closing the door of her office so that Napoleon could not follow her.

'James, I'm just going up to Wye House. I'll take Father's motor-car.'

'I shall have it brought round from the garage for you.'

'Yes, thank you.'

Eleanor went back upstairs. Napoleon watched with anticipation as she put on her hat and coat expecting a walk. 'No, Leon, you stay here.' Napoleon subsided, rested his chin on his front paws, and gave Eleanor a reproachful look.

Eleanor ignored him and went back downstairs again.

'I shan't be long, James. I've left Napoleon in my office; he'll be all right there.'

'Very good, Miss Eleanor. The motor-car is outside.'

Eleanor drove up to Corbar Road thinking about Wye House as she did so. The original Wye House Asylum had been established fifty years ago in a very much larger building, constructed according to a design by Henry Currey, on an extensive site on the lower side of Corbar Road opposite the current asylum. Nestled into the hillside and surrounded by parkland, it had extensive grounds and an uninterrupted view across the town to the other side of the valley. During those fifty years, it had been privately run by three members of the Dickson family. It advertised itself as "an establishment for the care and treatment of the insane of the higher and middle classes" and it was a place where wealthy families could send inconvenient relatives whom they wanted to have hidden discretely away. At the time that Wye House Asylum was established, illnesses which affected the mind or conditions such as epilepsy and Downs syndrome were not properly understood and were not spoken about openly. Families were ashamed of such relatives and the affected person was shut away from public view. This practice even extended to one of the King's sons who suffered from epilepsy. The families of these patients could afford to pay the considerable fees involved and this allowed Wye House to be run, as far as was possible for such a facility, not as an institution but as a country gentleman's family residence. It offered amusements which reflected the social status of its patients: music, drawing, croquet, tennis, billiards, theatricals, excursions, and a library stocked with books, newspapers and periodicals. It was a very different, far more enlightened establishment from the publicly run "mad houses" where patients were often treated like animals or displayed to visitors as freaks. However, twenty years ago, the original Wye House had been turned into a school for girls and the remaining patients had been transferred to Corbar Hill House, a much smaller building across the road. It had been a private house and was renamed Wye House and now provided a much more restricted version of the original facility. Some of the patients were there because, on too many occasions, they had over-indulged in alcohol and they had been sent there by despairing families in the hope of a cure.

As Eleanor turned the motor-car onto the long carriage drive and then parked outside Wye House, she was contemplating what she was going to say and how she was going to explain her reason for wanting to visit Mrs Mayhew. She walked up the steps and rang the bell. She asked to see the Matron and handed her card to the porter. He showed her in and asked her to wait in the hall. Eleanor had never had occasion to visit Wye House before. As she looked around her at the tiled entrance hall, the potted plants in brass containers, and the elegant furniture, she did indeed have the impression that she was visiting a rather grand house and not an institution. This impression was reinforced when, after a few minutes, the Matron appeared. Eleanor had expected a brisk, no nonsense woman in a stiffly starched uniform and veil but the person who greeted her could have been mistaken for the middle-aged, well-dressed mistress of a family home.

'Good afternoon, Miss Harriman,' said the Matron. 'I'm Miss Horton. How can I help?'

'Good afternoon, Miss Horton. Thank you for seeing me. I wondered if it would be possible to see Mrs Mayhew.'

'Ah,' said Miss Horton, 'I'm afraid that will not be possible. Could I ask you to come into my office for a moment and I shall explain.'

Eleanor followed the Matron across the hall, congratulating herself on the fact that her guess had been correct.

She had now been able to establish that Mrs Mayhew was a patient here. The matron led Eleanor into a small room off the hall, furnished with a desk, shelves, and chairs. The Matron asked her to sit down.

'I see from your card that you are with Harriman & Talbot. Your firm has a good reputation and I know that the families of some of our residents have had occasion to use the services of your firm on behalf of their relatives. May I ask whether your interest in Mrs Mayhew is professional or personal?'

Eleanor paused before she replied. 'Professional. On behalf of a client. I am conducting an investigation into an unexpected death and I need to confirm someone's identity and whether or not something which I suspect is, in fact, true. I wanted to ask Mrs Mayhew about an incident relating to her husband's business affairs. More particularly about some litigation that her husband was involved in.'

'I see. Thank you for being so open with me. What do you know about the litigation which you mentioned?'

Eleanor gave the Matron a brief summary of the case. Then she added: 'I should like to know if Mrs Mayhew became a patient here after the litigation, and more particularly, whether her need to come here was caused in any way by that event.'

The Matron nodded. 'I see.' She paused as she considered how much she could say. 'It is true that Mrs Mayhew is one of our residents, we prefer not to call them patients, but I am afraid that I cannot give you permission to visit her. She sees no-one, apart from her son, unless the doctor authorises it.' Eleanor gave herself another mental tick now that she had confirmed the existence of a son. 'However, I can confirm that she is the person you suppose her to be. The court case you mentioned has had a very detrimental effect on the family. As you may already know, shortly after the case concluded, Mr Mayhew took his own life. The family was ruined financially and Mrs Mayhew's health deteriorated. Ultimately, she suffered a nervous collapse. She was referred here by her doctor and, due to the generosity of her brother, has been a resident ever since. I believe that asking her to speak about these past events would have a very profound effect on her. It would be detrimental to her recovery.'

'I understand but thank you for the information you have provided. That is very helpful and I am grateful to you. And her son. You mentioned that Mrs Mayhew sees him. Does he live here in Buxton?'

'I believe so.'

'Is he her only child?'

'Yes.'

'Do you know if he is employed in the town?'

'I'm sorry, I know very little about him, although Mrs Mayhew did mention that he had been at Cambridge.'

'Could you tell me his name?'

'John. John Mayhew.'

Miss Horton stood up to indicate that the interview was over and Eleanor also stood up. As they walked across the hall towards the front door, Eleanor said: 'Thank you very much for seeing me, Miss Horton. I do appreciate it and your information has been most helpful. May I ask one last question?' The Matron nodded. 'Do the residents have facilities in their own rooms for heating water?'

The Matron looked surprised: 'What an odd question. No, such an arrangement would not be safe for residents such as ours. If they wish to have tea, they can send for it.'

Eleanor smiled. 'Thank you again, Miss Horton. Good-bye.'

'Good-bye, Miss Harriman.' The Matron watched as the porter opened the front door for Eleanor. She remained until the door closed behind Eleanor and then turned away.

As Eleanor drove back to Hall Bank, she reviewed her theory and the evidence which supported it. She delivered the motor-car back to the garage on the Market Place and walked the short distance back to Hall Bank. Edwin was now back in his own office, having found the information Mr Harriman had requested. Eleanor described to him the results of her visit to Wye House. He tried not to show his astonishment at Eleanor's capacity to make connections between isolated facts and the initiative she showed in obtaining the proof she needed.

'I heard you go out but had no idea what you were up to.'

'I have revised the list of suspects we drew up. I have crossed off Mrs Steen, Mr Royston her golf professional, Beryl the chamber maid, Mellor the valet and Mellor the injured factory worker, the political activists and people opposed to Mr Steen's water bottling scheme. I have left in Mr Ashworth's attacker, of course, and ticked all the boxes for him because I believe he is one and the same with the main suspect. There is nothing more I can do for the moment. I suppose we just have to wait for the Home Office to complete its analysis and provide a report. In the meantime, there is plenty of work to be done on other files, so I shall leave you in peace.'

'I think you have put together a very convincing explanation of this case, Eleanor, and I congratulate you. I should like time to consider the facts and decide what action we can or should now take. Can we talk again in the morning?'

'Of course, and thank you for your help and support, Edwin.'

~O~

That evening, in anticipation of Millicent and Julian's wedding, now only days away, Millicent's parents had invited Eleanor, Philip, Cecily, Catherine, Maureen and Maureen's two brothers to dinner at their house in The Park.

Maureen was to be bridesmaid and her two brothers, together with Philip were to be ushers at the church. Richard had been considered for the role of pageboy but when the subject was raised with him he had looked very solemn and said in his politest manner: 'Thank you very much for asking, but I don't think that would suit me at all.' Cecily and Millicent had had difficulty keeping a straight face.

Philip had arranged to call at Hall Bank and take Eleanor and Cecily to Millicent's parents' house in The Park. Mr Harriman had agreed to look after Napoleon and Richard and he had promised to read Richard's latest book with him. As she was deciding which evening frock to wear, Eleanor was still musing on the day's theories and discoveries. When she was ready there was still plenty of time so she went back to her office to have another look at her notes. She was still sitting at her desk when Cecily and Richard arrived. Richard raced on upstairs to find Mr Harriman and Cecily came in to talk to Eleanor. She moved one of the visitors' chairs forward intending to sit down and winced as she did so.

'What's wrong?' asked Eleanor.

'Oh, it's nothing. I just knocked my finger against the back of the chair. I was clumsy this afternoon and cut my finger while I was cutting up rhubarb to make jam.'

Eleanor looked at Cecily with a startled expression. 'Oh! Of course!' she said. 'How stupid of me!'

'Whatever is the matter?' asked Cecily. 'It's just a small cut and I'm the one who was stupid.'

'No, no,' said Eleanor, 'it's not that.' Eleanor continued to look at Cecily and then she looked at her watch. 'I must telephone. I need some information.'

Cecily was used to Eleanor's sometimes unaccountable behaviour, and she smiled at her sister and shook her head. 'I'll go up and see Father,' she said.

Eleanor went to the telephone but before she could pick up the receiver Richard came racing down the stairs to let

Philip in, calling: 'It's time to go, Aunt Lella.' Cecily followed him down the stairs at a more sedate pace, carrying Eleanor's cloak and evening bag. Philip, immaculate in evening dress, appeared on the threshold and then stepped into the front hall. In a pincer movement, Cecily and Philip shooed Eleanor out of the house, leaving her no alternative but to give in to the enjoyment of the evening.

The party of friends was welcomed by Mr and Mrs Lee and they were all assembled in the drawing room chatting happily. The maid was making her way around with a tray of drinks. Eleanor waited until it was convenient to speak to Julian and then said: 'Julian, do you recollect that day Philip and I met you and Millicent in the Market Place? We stopped to listen to the political rally.' Julian nodded. 'You thought you saw someone in the crowd whom you had known at Cambridge?'

'I certainly do remember,' said Julian. 'The fellow cut me.'

'Yes. That person. Who was he?'

'John Mayhew.' Julian frowned, thinking back to his Cambridge days. 'John Albert Carruthers Mayhew to be precise. Quite a mouthful, isn't it? I'm sure it was he.'

'What did he read at Cambridge, do you know?'

'Oh, chemistry. That's how I knew him. We had the same tutor.'

'That's it then,' said Eleanor.

'What is?' asked Julian, frowning.

When he had arrived at Hall Bank, Philip had noticed how preoccupied Eleanor was and how silent she had been during their drive to The Park. He now listened, with interest, to the exchange between Eleanor and Julian regarding John Mayhew. He said to Julian, rolling his eyes, 'It's best to just ignore her.' Then he smiled at Eleanor and said: 'Are you happy now? Is your puzzle solved?'

'Yes, I think so,' she said confidently.

'Then, could Miss Harriman, solicitor, please go away and can we have my friend Eleanor back so we, and she, can enjoy the evening?'

Eleanor smiled back at Philip and then nodded contritely. 'Sorry,' she said and they both burst out laughing.

CHAPTER NINETEEN

The following morning, when Edwin arrived at Hall Bank he checked his diary for the day and then went into Eleanor's office. 'Well, Eleanor,' he said, 'I have given this problem quite a bit of consideration since we last spoke and I think we are now confident that we know who killed Mr Steen and how it was done. And you have identified a motive which appears to be strengthened by the fact that Mrs Mayhew has also clearly suffered because of Mr Steen's actions.'

'Yes. When I agreed to accept instructions from Mrs Steen, I didn't realise where the enquiry would end. Now, thanks to her and her concern for her reputation, I have burdened us with the knowledge of a crime committed against her husband.'

'The question now is, what do we do with this knowledge?' said Edwin. 'The evidence we have against Mayhew/Carruthers is circumstantial at best. Is it enough for a conviction? Where do we go from here?'

'I think we should confront Mayhew with the facts that we have and get his reaction. I have a suggestion as to how we might get him to a meeting without arousing his suspicions,' said Eleanor. 'I propose that we go to the Palace Hotel to see the manager on the pretext of speaking to him about Annie. She doesn't want to return to the hotel and I have said that I will arrange to get her a proper character reference and also make sure her wages are paid, so that is a perfectly legitimate reason for us being there.'

'Right,' said Edwin. 'Let me make an appointment to see

the manager and I shall check whether any of Superintendent Johnson's men are still up there. I think he said they would be taking statements from the hotel servants this morning.'

When all the necessary arrangements had been made, Edwin and Eleanor walked over to the hotel and handed their cards to the clerk on the reception desk. He disappeared through an unmarked door behind the reception desk and, while he was gone, Edwin went across to the other side of the front hall to a small office which had been put at the disposal of the police. He said a few words to the policeman sitting behind the desk there and then returned to Eleanor and nodded. The manager's office had two doors, one behind the reception desk and another door which led into the hallway at the side of the reception desk. The manager came out of the hallway door and walked around into the front hall. He was holding the two calling cards. 'Miss Harriman, Mr Talbot, how do you do. My name is Hewlett. I am the manager of this hotel. Please come this way.'

Eleanor and Edwin followed him into the hallway and through the door into his office. When they were settled, Edwin began: 'Mr Hewlett, thank you for seeing us at such short notice. We should like to discuss a few matters with you, if we may. First of all, you had a waitress employed here. Her name is Annie Baird.'

'Is she in more trouble?' asked Mr Hewlett, abruptly. 'I'm not surprised.'

'No, Mr Hewlett she is not,' said Edwin, patiently, 'but we should like to talk to you about the reasons for her being dismissed.'

'Annie was dismissed for talking to the newspapers about hotel guests, spreading rumours, and then denying that she had done so. Put plainly and simply, she was a liar,' said Mr Hewlett, firmly. 'I can't tolerate that sort of behaviour amongst my employees.'

'No, absolutely not,' said Edwin. 'However, we have

reason to believe that Miss Baird was falsely accused.'

'Well, that doesn't matter. She was already on a warning,' said Mr Hewlett. 'She was clumsy during lunch service and spilt hot gravy all over Lady Aycliffe. Lady Aycliffe is one of our most valued clients and she demanded that I dismiss Annie immediately. The only reason I didn't do so was that I don't take kindly to being told what to do by my clients, even important ones like Lady Aycliffe. I prefer to make my own decisions.' Mr Hewlett crossed his arms across his chest and leaned back in his chair. Eleanor thought that Mr Hewlett was starting to sound rather defensive.

'Of course,' said Edwin, calmly. 'That is quite understandable. Would you be good enough to confirm some facts for me? We understand that the accusation against Miss Baird, which I believe she denied, was that she had spoken out of turn to some newspaper reporters about the death of Mr Steen. The accusation against Miss Baird was made by the hall-porter, Jack Carruthers.'

'That's correct.'

'After we have demonstrated to you that Miss Baird is innocent,' said Edwin, 'I should like you to provide her with a character reference so that she can obtain another suitable position. Miss Baird does not wish to return to this hotel.'

Mr Hewlett puffed out his cheeks and frowned. 'Are you saying she didn't speak to the newspapers. How do you know that?' he asked abruptly.

'Because we know that the accusation by your hall-porter was false. It was designed to persuade you that Miss Baird could not be trusted, the intention being to get her dismissed. It is true that Miss Baird knew something about the death of Mr Steen but she did not speak to the newspaper reporters nor did she disclose the information to anyone here. Carruthers wanted to protect his own position.'

'Well, of all the...' spluttered Mr Hewlett. 'If Carruthers...Can you prove any of this?'

'Yes,' said Edwin. 'Mr Hewlett, how long has Carruthers been employed here? What do know of him?'

'Just over a year, I should think. I would need to check.' Mr Hewlett frowned in concentration and then added: 'I don't know very much about him, now you mention it?'

'Did he come with references?' asked Edwin.

'No, he just turned up. The hotel was full at the time and I was short of a hall-porter. I assumed he'd got word of that and thought he'd try his luck. He was well-spoken, polite, neatly turned out, the sort of thing the guests like. I thought I'd give him a try. I've never had any trouble with him.'

'And you have no idea as to his background or his family.'

'No, he gets on and does his job. I've never had occasion to ask him where he came from. It's difficult to place him, as to his origins, I mean. He's got an educated sounding voice, posh like, but...I've never really thought about it before. How does someone like him come to be in service?' Mr Hewlett paused. 'Family lost its fortune, I suppose. There's a lot of that about, what with the War and taxes and everything.' Mr Hewlett shrugged, satisfied with the answer to his own question.

Edwin glanced at Eleanor and nodded slightly in confirmation of her theory as to the identity of Jack Carruthers. Then, Edwin said: 'Perhaps you would allow us to speak to him so that we can clear up this business of Miss Baird's dismissal.'

'Why should I believe you and not Carruthers? Why would he want Annie dismissed?'

'If you will allow us to ask Carruthers some questions, we may be able to establish that.'

Mr Hewlett considered the situation for a moment and, given his recently expressed objection to being told by others what to do with his employees, Eleanor was afraid he would refuse but then he said, firmly: 'All right.' He unhooked the telephone receiver which connected him to the reception desk and, speaking into the mouthpiece, said: 'Tell Carruthers to come to my office immediately.'

Eleanor and Edwin waited in silence until the hall-porter arrived. He stood just inside the door, to one side of Mr Hewlett's desk and, although there was a spare chair next to where he was standing, he was not asked to sit down.

Mr Hewlett said: 'Carruthers, this is Mr Talbot and Miss Harriman. Mr Talbot wants to ask you some questions.'

Carruthers looked at Edwin. Edwin looked at Eleanor and nodded.

'Mr Carruthers,' said Eleanor. Carruthers swivelled his head abruptly to look at Eleanor, surprised that a woman would speak in such circumstances. 'I believe that I am correct in thinking that Carruthers is not your surname?' The hall-porter flinched but did not reply. Eleanor continued. 'I believe your surname is actually Mayhew. You are John Albert Carruthers Mayhew, the son of Albert Mayhew, late of Manchester.'

'What?' interrupted Mr Hewlett. 'Here, is this true? Are you Carruthers or not?'

Carruthers had looked away from Eleanor as she spoke and was now staring fixedly at the wall opposite.

'Answer the lady,' barked Mr Hewlett.

Carruthers continued to stare silently at the wall.

'Are you Carruthers or Mayhew?' bellowed Mr Hewlett.

Carruthers still did not respond. Mr Hewlett glared at him.

'Mr Hewlett,' said Edwin, speaking in his most placatory tone and using words chosen to defuse the situation, 'I seem to have put you in a difficult position and I am sorry.' Mr Hewlett transferred his angry gaze to Edwin. 'Of course, you are perfectly entitled to know the truth about your employees.' Mr Hewlett, while still keeping his eyes on Edwin, reached for a pencil from the tray on his desk and began tapping it slowly on the blotting pad. 'However,' continued Edwin, 'in the circumstances, I wonder if we might perhaps be permitted to interview Mr Carruthers in your absence. It is possible that the information we have is completely wrong and, if so, we would not want to embarrass Mr Carruthers with our questions. It would assist us greatly with our enquiries if we were able to speak to him to establish the accuracy of the facts we have and clarify the situation.' Edwin looked at Mr Hewlett and spread his hands in a gesture which he hoped conveyed the impression that Mr Hewlett remained firmly in control and that the power of choice lay entirely with him.

Mr Hewlett looked at Edwin, his eyes narrowed, the pencil slowly tapping, and then said: 'Very well.' He put down the pencil and stood up. 'But I expect a full explanation when you have finished with him.'

'Naturally,' Edwin assured him, giving a bow with his head.

Mr Hewlett moved from behind his desk to the door, forcing the hall-porter to step backwards out of the way. When Mr Hewlett had gone, Edwin looked at Eleanor raising one eyebrow. Eleanor nodded her head slightly to confirm that she was ready and Edwin addressed the hall-porter.

'Mr Carruthers, please listen to what Miss Harriman has to say. And, please sit down if you wish.'

Carruthers did not move. He stood with his arms by his side, completely expressionless and impassive, staring straight ahead at the opposite wall, like a soldier being upbraided by an angry sergeant-major. Speaking very quietly and calmly, Eleanor began: 'Your father, Mr Albert Mayhew, was once a partner of Mr Walter Steen, the man who has just died in this hotel. Mr Steen caused your father to be deprived of his business interests and a large part of his fortune and he was responsible for your being reduced to earning your living in this way. Very probably he was the reason your father took his own life and I suspect that he was also responsible for your mother's nervous collapse, which is why she required medical treatment.' Eleanor noticed that Carruthers had now clenched his fists. She continued: 'Your mother is currently a patient at Wye House. I imagine that you came to Buxton in order to be near her and, by chance, you found employment at this hotel which enabled you to support yourself. I should mention that I saw you visiting Wye House a little while ago and I have also been to Wye House and confirmed that your mother is there.'

Carruthers turned and glared menacingly at Eleanor. 'You leave my mother out of this,' he said, angrily.

Confident now that her suspicions had been well-founded, Eleanor continued: 'Mr Carruthers, I was in the hotel lobby on the day Mr Steen arrived. You were asked to take his luggage up to his room and I saw the way you looked at him when you heard his name. It was clear that his name meant something to you.' Carruthers had now resumed staring at the wall, dissociating himself from Eleanor's speculations. 'I assume that you encountered him purely by chance that day and it was not a meeting that you had sought out. Had it not been for your mother needing treatment at Wye House, you would probably never have come to Buxton and your path and that of Mr Steen would never have crossed.' The hall-porter maintained his stubborn silence, but he was clenching and unclenching his fists. 'Given what I have learnt recently about the court case in which your father was involved, I can well imagine how much you must have hated Mr Steen for the wrong he did and the hurt he caused you and your mother. You knew that your father designed the bottle Mr Steen had claimed as his own. It seems that Mr Steen's current prosperity was gained at the expense of your own family's wealth and happiness. It must have been galling watching Mr Steen flaunting his money in the hotel and using it to buy influence in the town, and probably also you even had to accept tips from him. The fact that Mr Steen was staying at the hotel gave you an unlooked-for opportunity for revenge, an opportunity which must have seemed to you more than co-incidence. I imagine that you persuaded yourself that it was meant to be. That you were only redressing the balance.'

Eleanor stopped speaking in order to collect her thoughts. The silence in the room was oppressive. Eleanor began again: 'Mr Carruthers, I believe that, almost immediately after Mr Steen arrived here, you tried to kill him with a blow to the head. I suspect that you were acting under strong emotion generated by the sudden and unexpected meeting with the author of all your misfortunes. You mistook Mr Ashworth, an archaeologist, for Mr Steen and attacked the wrong person. Fortunately for you, that gentleman has survived and you will only be charged with one murder, not two, although you will probably also be charged with assault occasioning grievous bodily harm. Having failed at that attempt, you ingratiated yourself with Annie, one of the waitresses here, and then with Beryl, one of the chamber maids so as to gather the information which allowed you to make a second attempt to kill Mr Steen. That action was very carefully planned. Perhaps you had doubts about what you were doing, you had had more time to think about the consequences of your action and that is why you didn't act immediately. Perhaps you even had second thoughts. But then, at the end of the Motor-car Rally, Mr Steen announced that he was going to use his new design for the bottled water. Your father's design. In your anger, you slashed one of the front tyres of his motor-car. And then, you went about meticulously preparing a way of killing Mr Steen, no doubt as a way of paying him back for your father's death and your mother's collapse.'

The hall-porter now looked directly at Eleanor as though trying to gauge the strength of his opponent. Eleanor returned his gaze unflinchingly. 'Mr Carruthers,' she said, steadily, 'I can well understand your anger and your motive but, nevertheless, the action you took was wrong, very wrong. It appears that Mr Steen died from an overdose of barbitone, the substance which was in the sleeping tablets that he was in the habit of taking. I have reason to believe that you removed some of those tablets from Mr Steen's room and used them to poison him. Before the War, you were reading chemistry at Cambridge which is where you acquired the knowledge you needed to bring about Mr Steen's death. It was a very cleverly concealed crime but, unfortunately for you, your guilt has been uncovered.'

Eleanor noticed that a tiny muscle on the side of the hall-porter's face had begun to twitch. She thought that he was probably surprised at her knowledge of his personal history. He was obviously considering the strength of his position, wondering just how much of his crime had been uncovered and how much evidence there was against him. He could not afford to ask questions. He feigned ignorance and in-difference and returned to stare at the wall opposite him. Eleanor watched him closely. He probably hoped that it was only Annie's evidence that could implicate him and it would be Annie's word against his. She had been branded a liar and it was still possible that she might not be believed.

'I shall leave you now, Mr Carruthers,' said Eleanor, 'but I want you to know that your crime has been discovered and that there is evidence to prove your guilt. Your fingerprints will help to convict you.' Carruthers was certain that he had left no fingerprints but he was too clever to be trapped by this statement. He realised that challenging Eleanor's assertion would only betray his guilt so he held his tongue. Edwin stood up and moved to the door of the manager's office to prevent Carruthers from leaving. Eleanor con-tinued: 'There is a police sergeant outside this door and Mr Talbot is going to ask him to escort you to the police station.' Eleanor turned towards Edwin and as she did so, Carruthers slumped down on to the empty chair next to the manager's desk and put his head in his hands. Edwin opened the door and beckoned to the police sergeant. No-one spoke as he entered the room and led Carruthers away.

Edwin looked at Eleanor and, concerned by the expression on her face, said: 'Rest assured, Eleanor, we have done the right thing. Your reasoning was perfectly accurate. I am certain of that.'

'Yes,' she said, nodding in agreement. 'When I read the newspaper report of Mr Mayhew's death I began to understand the effect that Mr Steen had had on his life and I felt some sympathy for Mr Mayhew. Now I wonder what is going to happen to Mrs Mayhew. How will she deal with this second blow?'

'Three lives ruined,' said Edwin, sadly. 'Mr Steen had a lot to answer for.' He paused and then said: 'Now, what about Annie? Do you have the strength to deal with her problem?'

'I certainly do. At least she will have a happy ending. When I called around to give the Misses Pymble our donation to the Girls Friendly Society jumble sale, I learnt that they have found her accommodation in the house of one of their parishioners who has a daughter of a similar age and there is a position for her in the tea rooms at Poole's Cavern if she can provide a suitable character reference.'

Mr Hewlett had been hovering about in the front hall and when he saw Carruthers being led away, he accosted the police sergeant and demanded an explanation. Receiving nothing more than an 'Out of the way, please, sir' he stormed into the hallway and opened the door of his office, saying abruptly: 'What on earth is going on! Why is Carruthers being taken away?'

Edwin said: 'Mr Carruthers is being taken to the police station to answer some questions in relation to the death of Mr Steen.'

Mr Hewlett was looking astonished. 'Are you saying that Carruthers had something to do with the death of Mr Steen?' he asked.

'That is possible,' said Edwin, 'but I can assure you that he had reason to lie in relation to the allegations made against Miss Baird and we would like to deal with that matter now please.'

Mr Hewlett asserted his authority by resuming his place behind his desk but he could only babble, talking to himself. 'I can't believe it. To think that one of my employees is mixed up in this affair. We must keep this quiet. What are the guests going to think? And what are the newspapers going to make of this? It was bad enough before. Having someone die in the hotel attracts all the wrong kind of publicity but this could be far worse! Far worse! And what are the directors going to think? How am I going to explain it to them? I shall be lucky if I don't lose my job.' As he spoke, he looked in despair from Edwin to Eleanor and back and added: 'I want you to know that I knew nothing at all about any of this.'

Eleanor said: 'Which brings us back to the first point we discussed, Mr Hewlett. Miss Baird was falsely accused of being a liar and of talking to the newspaper reporters. Carruthers engineered that story for his own ends. At this stage of the investigation I cannot disclose to you the details of what happened but I can assure you that the claims made against Miss Baird were entirely false. I should be grateful, therefore, if you would reconsider your position in relation to her. She does not wish to be re-employed but she does require a proper reference so that she can obtain another suitable position. Would you have it delivered to our office at your earliest convenience, please. I believe also that some wages remain unpaid and I should appreciate it if you would remedy that as well. Good morning, Mr Hewlett.' Eleanor stood up, ready to leave.

'Good day, Mr Hewlett,' said Edwin, 'and thank you for your assistance.'

Edwin and Eleanor left Mr Hewlett's office and, in silence, walked across the front hall and down the steps of the hotel. When they were out of earshot of the linkman, Edwin said: 'Right. I think we should call on Superintendent Johnson now, don't you?'

'Definitely. He needs to have all of the information we have before he confronts Carruthers.'

~O~

The following day, Eleanor and Edwin were in the dining room and Mrs Clayton was serving lunch. The inquest into the death of Mr Steen had been opened that morning by Mr Harriman, the appointed Coroner, and he had just returned to Hall Bank.

'Well, Harriman, do we have a verdict?' asked Edwin, as Mr Harriman came into the dining room.

'No, I've adjourned. I was able to take evidence as to identity and Catherine's evidence as to the fact of the death …Ah, thank you, that looks delicious.' He turned to speak to Mrs Clayton as she served him with a bowl of soup. 'Superintendent Johnson requested an adjournment in order to continue his enquiries. There was nothing more I could do for the moment. I understand from Superintendent Johnson that suicide or accidental death are unlikely and that one of the hall-porters from the Palace Hotel has been arrested. Superintendent Johnson is investigating the theory that this is a case of poisoning although Dr McKenzie has advised that the poison in question is difficult to detect. I gather that although he and Dr Balderstone suspect foul play, they are not hopeful that the report from the Home Office Pathologist will be conclusive. Superintendent Johnson informs me that, as things stand, the evidence is likely to be largely circumstantial but when he has finished interviewing all of the potential witnesses, he believes he will have enough to secure a conviction. He tells me he is even hopeful of a confession.' Mr Harriman looked at Eleanor and raised an eyebrow. 'I don't suppose you had anything to do with finding those witnesses, did you?'

'I did find one or two,' said Eleanor, nonchalantly. 'Purely in my capacity of acting for Mrs Steen, of course.'

'Of course,' said Mr Harriman, poker faced. He turned his attention to his soup but not before Edwin had noticed the look of pride he gave his daughter.

~O~

Millicent was popular with the caddies at the Burbage Ladies' Golf Club and in the week before her wedding they had clubbed together to buy her three new St Mungo Colonel brand golf balls as a wedding present. The golf balls, carefully wrapped in tissue paper and placed in a box, were presented to Millicent at the Club House by Percy on behalf of the caddies as she was getting ready to leave at the end of her last day before the wedding. The caddies, always very professional in their dealings with Club members, were lined up outside the Club House for the presentation. Millicent was fond of the boys and genuinely touched by their gesture. Golf balls were very expensive items even for wealthy golfers and this brand of golf ball was the best quality sold at the Club House. She knew how limited the boys' means were and felt sure that they had sacrificed pocket money in order to get the necessary funds together. Mr Greenwood, the caddie master, and Mr Saunders, the golf professional, had noticed how many of the caddies had offered to do weeding in the previous two weeks in order to top up their earnings and the greens had never looked better. Millicent expressed her delight and appreciation, shaking hands with each of the caddies in turn. Fortunately for Millicent, she went away blissfully unaware of the banter on the subject of three balls and a honeymoon which had been exchanged between Mr Saunders and Mr Greenwood when the caddies were deciding on their gift.

On the Thursday before the Whitsun Bank Holiday weekend, Millicent and Julian were married in St John's church. Completed in 1812, it had been built in the Georgian basilica style then fashionable, and was a much simpler and more elegant building than the later gothic revival style of church favoured by the Victorians. The organist was playing a Bach prelude and the congregation was arriving. Mrs Clayton, in her best hat, had claimed an aisle seat towards the rear of the church on the bride's side. Philip, immaculate in striped "sponge bag" trousers, grey waistcoat, morning coat, and grey kid gloves bowed elaborately to Eleanor in his role as usher, as he welcomed her. 'You look charming as ever, Miss Harriman,' he said.

Eleanor, with mock formality, inclined her head, smiled, and replied: 'Thank you, Mr Danebridge. I look forward to speaking to you after the service.' Philip led her to one of the front pews where Cecily was sitting with Catherine and other members of the golf club.

Eleanor contemplated the elaborate stained-glass window behind the altar as she sat listening to the organ and waiting for Millicent to arrive. She was reflecting on the fact that she and Alistair would have been married in this church if he had not been killed in the War and she imagined him and Philip standing where Julian and his best man were now standing, waiting at the altar rails with their backs to the congregation. Although she experienced sadness and regret at this image, she realised that she was beginning to find fulfilment in a different kind of life from the one she had imagined six years ago. Alistair was becoming part of her past life and the pain of loss no longer clouded her future.

ACKNOWLEDGEMENTS

Alan Doig, former Chairman of the Cavendish Golf Club, Buxton, for information regarding the game of golf and its history, and for his advice and suggestions regarding the rounds of golf, and the competition match played by the characters in this book.

Richard Allerton, The Golf Historian of the Cavendish Golf Club, Buxton, past Club Captain and Vice-President of the Club, and secretary of the Alister Mackenzie Society of Great Britain & Ireland, for the history of the Burbage Ladies' Golf Club, which existed between 1899 and 1924. See also, *The Spirit of Cavendish Golf Club*, Malcolm Mortimer, Grant Books, Worcestershire, 2000.